* * * * * * *

When Joshua reached the top of the ridge, he stopped suddenly. What he saw made his heart race and his breath catch. Laid out before him were two dozen or more tepees scattered along the west bank of a wide, but rather shallow river at the bottom of a long valley.

When the initial shock of seeing so many tepees and so many Indians began to wear off, he realized his cart was out in the open for all to see. He quickly pushed his cart down off the top of the ridge so it could not be seen from the river valley. He then sat on the ground next to his cart as he tried to gather his thoughts and catch his breath.

So far, in his travels across the prairie, he had only seen two or three Indians. They had been off in the distance, and he had managed to avoid contact with them. Now there were at least thirty to forty Indians, maybe more, right in front of him.

* * * * * * *

Other titles by J.E. Terrall

Western Short Stories
  The Old West
  The Frontier
  Untamed Land
  Tales From The Territory

Western Novels
  Conflict in Elkhorn Valley
  Lazy A Ranch
  (A Modern Western)

Romance Novels
  Balboa Rendezvous
  Sing for Me
  Return to Me
  Forever Your

Mystery/Suspense/Thriller
  I Can See Clearly
  The Return Home
  The Inheritance

Nick McCord Mysteries
  Vol – 1 Murder at Gill's Point
  Vol – 2 Death of a Flower
  Vol – 3 A Dead Man's Treasure
  Vol – 4 Blackjack, A Game to Die For
  Vol – 5 Death on the Lakes
  Vol – 6 Secrets Can Get You Killed

Peter Blackstone Mysteries
  Murder in the Foothills
  Murder on the Crystal Blue
  Murder of My Love

Frank Tidsdale Mysteries
  Death by Design

THE STORY OF JOSHUA HIGGINS

THE MAKING OF A
SOUTH DAKOTA CATTLEMAN

by

J.E. Terrall

Printed in the United States of America
First Printing / 2014 – www.createspace

Cover: Both front and back cover photos were taken by the author J.E. Terrall

Book Layout /
Formatting: J.E. Terrall
              Custer, South Dakota

THE STORY OF JOSHUA HIGGINS

THE MAKING OF A SOUTH DAKOTA CATTLEMAN

To my long time friends,
Gerald Shaw and his wife, Mary

FORWARD

The Story of Joshua Higgins is the story of a young man who seeks to build a life for himself in a new land. Although it is told as the story of one man and what he encountered over the years in the land that became known as the Dakota Territory, and later South Dakota, it is really a collection of stories of many men and their conflicts with nature and the other dangers they faced on the Frontier. Each chapter is almost a story in and of itself of the conflicts those men faced in their quest for a future in the Frontier.

Although this story is fiction, it shows what it took for those men of adventure to make their way in the wilderness. In the early days, most of these men were frontiersmen, some of them eventually became ranchers and farmers who settled down and made homes for their families. It is also the story of some of the things that helped shape the men of the Frontier and helped our country grow into the great country it is today.

PROLOGUE

Joshua Higgins had read many books about the great blue-gray mountains and the life of the frontiersmen while growing up on his father's farm in the county of Yorkshire, England. It was the stories of the Indians, frontiersmen, and the mountains in the western part of a large territory that belonged to United States of America that captured his imagination.

He would dream about the life of a frontiersman most of the time. Even while milking the cows, he would think about the adventures of the mountain men. When he would go out to the woods, he would find himself thinking about the Indians he had read about that lived on the land he wanted so much to see. He knew one day he would go to America and see the mountains and the Indians that were located in a part of the United States referred to as the Frontier.

Joshua was a tall, slim young man who had just turned eighteen years of age when he left his native land of England. He had broad shoulders and a narrow waist. His hair was dark brown and hung down almost to his shoulders. Joshua's eyes were a dark brown and sparkled in the bright sunlight. He was a strong man as a result of working hard on his father's farm. Joshua was a good-looking man who was about to set out on the adventure of a lifetime.

The day finally arrived when Joshua knew it was time to pack up his meager belongings, leave his home and family, and sail to the United States. Joshua said his goodbyes, then set out for the Port of Liverpool, England. There, he bought passage and sailed to the United States of America.

CHAPTER ONE

The Adventure Begins

Joshua arrived in the United States in late May of 1852. He bought the things he was sure he would need for his journey into the Frontier. Since he had little money left after paying for his passage and getting a few supplies, he found that he didn't have enough money to purchase a couple of horses or to build the type of cart he wanted so he could start west. In fact, he didn't even have enough money to get a room for the night. Joshua did not let it discourage him, however. He was determined to seek his dream, so he began looking for work.

With all his belongings in a pack on his back, he began walking down the street from the Mercantile Store. He had not gone very far when he came upon a freight hauler who didn't seem to be very happy. The man was working hard loading his wagon, and cussing at the same time. From what Joshua could hear, the man's helper had apparently quit earlier in the day without giving notice. Joshua saw it as an opportunity and approached the freight hauler.

"Excuse me, sir," Joshua said looking up at the man in the wagon.

The man stopped what he was doing and looked down at Joshua. He looked over the tall young man as he wondered what he wanted.

"What is it?" he asked rather sharply, not really in the mood to have a conversation.

"I am in need of work. I'm strong, and I'm not afraid of hard work. Do you have work for me?"

The man looked at him for a moment, then began to smile.

"Are you free to travel?" the man asked.

"Yes, sir. My name is Joshua Higgins."

"Well, Joshua Higgins, I'm looking for a helper. I haul freight into the mountains. We will be gone for several weeks at a time. Do you have a problem with that?"

"No, sir."

"I'm Franklin Waters. The work is hard and the hours are long, but I pay well."

"That will be fine."

"When can you start?"

"How about right now?" Joshua asked.

"Good," Mr. Waters said with a big grin. "Toss your pack in the front of the wagon, then help me finish loading these supplies."

Joshua put his things in the wagon and began helping Mr. Waters load the wagon. It wasn't long before they had the wagon loaded and were on their way. Joshua had no idea where they were going, but it really didn't matter. He had found work with a freight hauler who hauled freight to several of the small towns in the Allegheny Mountains. He knew they were not the mountains he wanted to see, but the work did pay well.

Even though his lack of money delayed him, Joshua never gave up on his dream to see the Frontier and the great blue-gray mountains in the west. He worked hard hauling freight into the Allegheny Mountains, and returning with freight to be shipped out to other countries.

After working for more than a year and saving up his money, he finally got his chance. Joshua was offered work to join another freight hauler who was taking supplies to a trading post on the Missouri River. The trading post was located at Lone Tree Crossing on the east bank of the Missouri River. The small settlement of Omaha was located just across the river. Since it would put him closer to a place where he could start his journey into the Frontier, he jumped at the chance.

The trip to Lone Tree Crossing was a long and tiring trip. There were long hours of walking alongside the teams of oxen that pulled the large and very heavy freight wagons. It took several months to get to Lone Tree Crossing.

Once Joshua arrived at Lone Tree Crossing, he helped unload all the supplies they had brought to the trading post. As soon as he had finished his work for the freight hauler, he quit and collected his pay. He walked down to the river and got on the ferry that took him across the Missouri River to Omaha.

Once he arrived in Omaha, he started looking around. There were a lot of people who were looking for the things they would need to head west into the Frontier. He quickly discovered that mules, oxen and even horses were going at outrageously high prices. Wagons of almost any size were very expensive, too. He quickly found he didn't have enough money to buy horses, or a wagon, or much of anything else. Even a room at one of the boarding houses cost so much that to stay very long would soon deplete his funds.

Discouraged, but not ready to give up, he sat down on a bench in front of the boarding house and looked around. Joshua had no idea how he was going to be able to make his dream come true, that was until his eyes fell on a livery stable just down the street. The man running the place seemed to be very busy. The one thing Joshua knew how to do was care for animals. He decided to talk to the man and ask him for work.

Joshua got up and went to the livery stable. He stood at the door of the stable and waited for the owner to notice him.

"Is there something I can do for you?" the man asked.

"My name is Joshua Higgins. I'm looking for work. I know a lot about caring for animals, especially horses, mules and oxen. It looks to me like you could use some help."

The man just looked as Joshua for a minute. There was no doubt that he could use help. Eric McMillan, the owner of the stable, didn't think he could afford to hire anyone right now.

"I'm sorry, young man, but as much as I could use the help, I can't afford to hire anyone."

Joshua looked at him for a minute, then turned and looked at the stable. Sleeping in the stable would be preferable to sleeping in the street, he thought.

"I'll work for lodging, meals and for the materials I would need to build a hand cart. As for the lodging part, I could sleep in the stable."

Mr. McMillan thought about it for a moment or two. It wouldn't cost him very much to feed the young man. He could eat with him and his wife. As for sleeping in the stable, that wouldn't cost him anything at all.

"Okay. You have a deal. You will eat with my wife and me. You can sleep in the stable for now. If you work out, I will provide a place to sleep in my house when the weather gets cold."

"Thank you. I can start right now."

"Good. I'm Eric McMillan."

"I'm Joshua Higgins," he said with a smile as they shook hands.

Joshua worked hard cleaning stalls and taking care of the horses and other animals at the stable. He was given a place to sleep in a small room in the stable. He ate his meals in the kitchen with Mr. McMillan and his wife. Mrs. McMillian grew close to Joshua and made sure he had clean clothes to wear.

During his time off, Joshua began the task of making the two-wheel cart he would use to carry his supplies on his way west. The cart was typical of those used for many centuries by the peasants in his native country.

It was close to Christmas when he finally finished the cart. Rather than start out and have to spend the winter on the open prairie, he continued to work at the stable.

At Christmas, the McMillans gave Joshua a good winter coat and a new pair of boots. He grew to like the McMillans and looked at them as his second family.

During the winter, he spent a lot of time talking to those in Omaha about the best way to get to where he wanted to go. Most of them told him that he should get a wagon and join a wagon train, but he didn't have the money for a wagon and the animals it would take to pull it. Nor did he have the money to join a wagon train.

One afternoon, he met an old man who was sitting in a café drinking coffee. They began to talk. The old man claimed to have been to the great mountains. They spent hours talking about the Frontier and drinking coffee. The old man suggested that when spring came Joshua should follow the Missouri River north. When he got to the trading post at Fort Pierre, he should leave the river and head straight west. The old man emphasized "straight west". The old man said it would be wide open country, but he shouldn't have much trouble if he avoided the Indians.

When spring finally came, Joshua quit his work at the stable, packed up his cart and said his goodbyes to the McMillans. He waved to them as he began his journey by heading north out of Omaha.

Joshua was sure that Mr. McMillan thought he was crazy to be walking and pulling a cart, but it was all he had to carry his supplies. He could not afford one horse, let alone a team of horses and a wagon. Joshua left the town of Omaha behind as he began his journey along the west bank of the Missouri River. He was convinced that he was finally headed into the Frontier.

He had heard the tales about the tall mountains west of the Missouri River, and that those mountains were rich with beaver and other fur bearing animals just for the taking.

Joshua was not only a dreamer at heart, he was also a realistic young man. He knew nothing came without a price. It would take a lot of hard work, but he was used to working hard on his father's farm, and at the different work he had done in getting to where he was now. He also knew that there would be times when it would seem as if he had taken on more than he could handle, and times when he would feel lonely.

He had also heard of the many dangers he would face if he wasn't careful, especially since he was traveling alone. But Joshua was convinced that the price he would be called upon to pay for the riches that he hoped to find would be well worth it. Little did he know what really lay west of the Missouri River.

It took Joshua several weeks to get to Fort Pierre. He turned west and headed across the prairie. He had been pulling his cart across the land for a little over a month and a half, but didn't seem to be getting anywhere. He had no idea how far away the blue-gray mountains were, but he had been told it would take a very long time to reach them, especially walking.

There was no doubt in his mind it was a hard life he had chosen, and nothing would come easy. His travels had already proven that. Joshua had no idea what would be in store for him in his quest just to get to the mountains.

It was late August when Joshua Higgins found himself slowly plodding across the vast open prairie west of the Missouri River. The weather was hot and dry with a warm breeze blowing in from the southwest. The buffalo grass covering the prairie was brown and dry. It crunched under Joshua's feet as he pulled his two-wheel cart slowly across the land. It had been weeks since he had seen any rain, and it didn't look like he was going to see any today. The only good thing about the ground being so dry was the wheels of his cart did not sink into the ground.

Sweat rolled down Joshua's face as he continued moving west making only about ten to twelve miles a day, on a good day. The cart had been built with fairly large wheels so it would roll over the ruts and rocks with ease. He had also made the wheels slightly wider than those on the carts in his homeland to help it move across soft ground easier. The cart was well balanced allowing for only a minimum amount of weight for Joshua to bear.

CHAPTER TWO

First Encounter On The Prairie

On a hot mid-September afternoon, Joshua was working up a sweat as he pulled his cart up a long gently sloping hill toward the top of what appeared to be a long ridge. The ridge seemed to run for miles in generally a north-south direction.

When Joshua reached the top of the ridge, he stopped suddenly. What he saw made his heart race and his breath catch. Laid out before him were two dozen or more tepees scattered along the west bank of a wide, but rather shallow river at the bottom of a long valley.

When the initial shock of seeing so many tepees and so many Indians began to wear off, he realized his cart was out in the open for all to see. He quickly pushed his cart down off the top of the ridge so it could not be seen from the river valley. He then sat on the ground next to his cart as he tried to gather his thoughts and catch his breath.

So far, in his travels across the prairie, he had only seen two or three Indians. They had been off in the distance, and he had managed to avoid contact with them. Now there were at least thirty to forty Indians, maybe more, right in front of him.

When he had finally caught his breath and thought he was ready, he took his field glasses from the cart and crawled up to the top of the ridge. Lying on his stomach in the short buffalo grass, he looked over the valley below him. He first scanned the entire area looking for roaming bands of Indians who might discover him. Once he felt it was safe, he turned his attention to the encampment.

The Indian village was located on the far side of the river. Just to the north of the cluster of tepees, he could see a herd of horses grazing peacefully on the green grass that covered the valley floor close to the river. He could see several older boys were keeping watch over the horses.

A little further along the river there were several women washing clothes on the large rocks along the bank. He could see them scrubbing the clothes and rinsing them in the clear water. When he looked toward the encampment, he could see other women were cooking over the fires in front of several of the tepees.

Joshua could see some of the men of the tribe were gathered in a group around a large fire pit. They appeared to be talking. The fire pit was located close to the center of the camp and appeared to be the gathering place for talks, and for meetings of the leaders. He also noticed a couple of men that looked like they were drawing on some kind of hide.

Some of the younger children were playing games and running around between the tepees. He could see several of the women had babies they carried around on their backs in what looked like cradleboards. Joshua remembered that a child small enough to be carried in a cradleboard was called a papoose.

As he continued to watch and mull over in his mind his options, he saw half a dozen young braves on what looked like sturdy mounts come over the hill behind the encampment. They had several deer slung over their horses. It was a hunting party returning from what was obviously a successful hunt.

The approach of the hunters seemed to get the attention of everyone in the village. Women and children alike ran to greet them. There was a lot of excitement at the return of the hunting party.

Joshua watched as the women took the deer and began skinning and dressing them out. The young braves sat down with the elders around a campfire to tell the story of their hunt. The children gathered around behind the elders to listen. There seemed to be much joy in the camp.

The scene being played out before Joshua didn't seem to be much different from the family gatherings he had attended back in his homeland of England. Joshua had grown up on a small farm on the English countryside. He could remember as a small boy listening to the stories his father and his uncles would tell when they returned from a morning of hunting in the fields near his home. There, too, the women took the animals the hunters had taken that morning and began fixing dinner for all who had gathered while the men sat around talking about the hunt. It was a time of storytelling and laughter.

It suddenly occurred to Joshua that he was feeling a bit homesick. It was the first time on his journey he had felt that way. But homesick or not, there were decisions to be made, and he needed to make them now.

Joshua continued to watch the activities in the Indian camp while he tried to decide what he should do next. Should he go on downstream to find a place to cross the river where they could not see him, or should he walk down to the Indians' encampment in an effort to find out if they were friendly? What if they weren't friendly? Would they accept him as no threat to them and let him continue on his way without bothering him, or would they capture him and torture him before they killed him?

So many of the stories Joshua had heard about the Plains Indians were not ones that would make him feel very secure about walking into their village. They were stories of how the Indians had tortured and even skinned the white man for no apparent reason other than for their own amusement. Joshua did not believe all the stories he had heard, but he could not see any reason to take any unnecessary chances, either. The best and safest thing for him to do would be to avoid contact with them whenever possible by going around their encampment.

With the decision made to avoid contact with the Indians, Joshua began by scanning the river, both upstream and downstream, using his field glasses. He was looking for a place where he could cross the river without being seen. It would have to be a place where the water would not be too deep, a place where he could get his cart across safely and quickly. The real question was should he go upstream, or would it be better to go downstream in order to avoid contact with the Indians?

After several minutes of searching the valley through his field glasses, he noticed a bend in the river over a mile downstream. If he followed the ridge downstream, it would put him around the bend and out of sight of the Indian encampment. He decided that going downstream to cross the river would be his best option. It looked like it might provide the best place to get across the river where he would not be seen.

Joshua crawled down off the top of the ridge and returned to his cart. After securing his field glasses on the cart, he began to pull his cart southward staying off the top of the ridge. In that way he could not be seen by anyone near the river, from the Indian encampment, or from the ridge on the other side of the river.

After traveling about two miles, he stopped. Leaving his cart, he took his field glasses and went to the top of the ridge again. Joshua immediately scanned the surrounding area looking for anything that might cause him harm or for anyone who might be able to see him. He had gone far enough to be around the bend. He could no longer see the village. It looked like he would be able to get across the river without being seen.

Joshua didn't see any other signs of life in the area except for a fairly large group of antelope on the hill on the other side of the river. He was sure the antelope would not be grazing so peacefully if there was anyone around.

He also saw a small grove of cottonwood trees along the bank on the far side of the river. It looked like it might be a good place to spend the night. He had to admit it also looked rather inviting. He was tired as a result of it having been a long hot day of pulling his cart. He was sure that the tension caused by seeing so many Indians had a lot to do with it, too.

A look up at the sky told Joshua it was getting late in the day. He knew that it was getting on toward time when he should find a safe place to spend the night. He thought about the grove of trees on the other side of the river. It would provide him with some cover for the night, and protection should he be attacked. If he got up early, he could be over the hill and well on his way before he would be discovered.

Joshua carefully scanned the valley one more time for as far as he could see in all directions using his field glasses. He saw nothing moving except the antelope on the other side of the river. He decided he would take his cart down to the river and see if he could find a place to cross, hopefully not too far from the grove of trees.

He returned to his cart and began to slowly move it over the ridge. Keeping a watchful eye out for any danger, he moved down the hill toward the river. When he got to the river, he found it was like many small prairie rivers during the late summer and early fall, very shallow. It was hardly more than ankle deep. He stepped into the river and pulled his cart across.

Once he was on the other side, he pulled his cart in among the large old cottonwood trees that grew close to the river. The large trees would help hide the cart. The grass around the base of the trees was thick and looked like it would make a comfortable place to lie down. He decided it would be a good place to spend the night before he continued on west over the hill.

Joshua knew he would have to be very careful about building a fire. It could not have much smoke because it could be seen for miles from the tops of the hills on both sides of the river. He searched around for dry wood for his fire to keep the smoke to a minimum. He found a lot of small branches that would make a good fire, one hot enough to cook his dinner. He gathered up the branches and put them near his cart.

Staying close to his cart, he cleared an area just large enough to build a small fire. Once he had his fire, he began cooking his evening meal and making himself a cup of coffee. He kept his eyes moving and his "Kentucky" long rifle close at hand. He kept his pistol tucked in his belt where it would be handy in case he should need it in a hurry.

As darkness started to fill the valley, he let his fire burn down to coals. He knew the glow of a fire could be seen for miles out on the wide-open plains at night. By the time it was dark, his fire had burned down to just a few small glowing embers among the ashes.

He got his bedroll from the cart and laid it out on the ground. Joshua put his rifle and his English made single shot pistol in the cart under the tarp to keep the morning dew off them. They would be of no use to him if the powder was damp.

Joshua then sat down and leaned back against the wheel of his cart. He took a few minutes to listen to the sounds of the night. He had learned quickly how important it could be. He wanted to get used to the sounds of the breeze in the trees, the sounds of the water in the river as it flowed over the rocks and the sounds of the animals as they were all a part of the night. That way, if he heard a strange sound he would know something was not right.

It wasn't long before Joshua knew what to listen for. He laid down on his bedroll next to his cart and looked up at the sky. It was filled with stars too numerous to count. Even after sleeping under the stars for many weeks, he still couldn't get over how big the sky looked on a clear night. After watching the stars for a little while, Joshua closed his eyes and drifted off to sleep.

* * * *

Joshua woke as the sun was coming up over the ridge on the east side of the river. It had been his intention to be over the ridge to the west and well on his way before the sun was up. It had been so peaceful and quiet next to the river that he slept much later than he had planned. The soft grass in among the large cottonwood trees, the gentle cool breeze, and the soft sounds of the water flowing over the rocks had given him a very peaceful and restful night's sleep. It was the first time in many nights that it had been cool enough to get a good night's rest. Up until now, the nights had been almost as hot as the days.

Still lying on his bedroll, he stretched to loosen the stiffness in his muscles before sitting up. As he sat up, Joshua rubbed the sleep from his eyes then began to look around. He stopped suddenly, freezing in place at the sight of eight young Indian braves sitting on their horses and looking at him. He had slept so soundly that he had not heard their approach. They were only about fifteen feet away from him in sort of a half circle just looking at him. The braves didn't seem to be afraid of Joshua, but then why should they. There were eight of them.

The Indians didn't know what to make of the strange looking man lying on a blanket. They were rather curious about the white man. In their experience, all white men seemed to have horses, mules or oxen to pull their big heavy wagons. They had never seen a white man with a two-wheeled cart that he pulled himself.

Joshua was curious about them, too. He was also rather nervous. All of the braves were dark skinned and appeared to be very strong. They wore nothing but a loincloth and moccasins. Each of them had a single eagle feather in their hair. There was also a single eagle feather in the mane of each of their horses. They all had a bow hung over a shoulder and a quiver full of arrows. They carried knives in their belts. One of the braves also carried a long sharp lance held firmly in one hand. The lance had several small clumps of hair attached to it. Joshua was not sure if it was human hair. The one with the lance seemed to be their leader.

None of the young warriors were wearing war paint on their faces, which was a bit of relief to Joshua. However, the expressions on their faces gave Joshua no hint of how they felt about seeing him on their hunting grounds. He had no idea what they were intending to do, although several unpleasant thoughts came to mind.

Joshua's first thought was to grab his rifle from the cart to defend himself, but his rifle was under the tarp and would not be easy to retrieve. There was also the fact that it would be easy for them to kill him before he could get it. Even if he did get one of them, they could easily kill him before he could reload.

The one thing that seemed to ease Joshua's feelings about them was the young braves didn't seem to be threatening him, nor were they showing any signs they wanted to do him harm. Joshua decided to take a chance and stand up. He slowly stood up and faced them.

Joshua tried not to show he was afraid, even if it was the way he was feeling. Not sure what he should do, he decided to raise his hand in a gesture of friendship. He could only hope they took the gesture in the manner it was meant. He raised his hand, but the braves simply looked at him as if they didn't know what it meant.

Since his gesture had not drawn a response, he decided to try something else. He put his fingers together and raised his hand to his mouth in the hope he was asking them if they wanted something to eat. The braves looked at each other, then turned and looked at him, but didn't say anything.

After a moment or so, one of the braves nodded slightly. He seemed to be the one the others looked up to even though Joshua didn't think he was a chief. At least he didn't look like any of the Indian chiefs he had seen pictures of in the books about the American Indians he had read. He wasn't wearing a big feathered headdress like in the books. Joshua wasn't sure what his status was in the tribe or with the small group of braves, but he seemed to be the leader.

Joshua motioned for them to get down off their horses and sit down around the place where he had had his fire. Again they looked at each other as if they were not sure if getting down off their horses was a good idea. Finally, the brave who had nodded at Joshua swung his leg over his horse's neck and gracefully slid off the back of the horse. He stood on the ground next to his horse for a moment or two before walking toward Joshua.

Again Joshua gestured for him to sit down near the fire. The young brave then turned and motioned for the rest of the braves to join him. The rest of the braves got off their horses, but none of them sat down.

After the leader sat down, Joshua turned his back to him and reached into the cart. It was only after he had turned his back to them that he remembered the advice he had gotten from an old man he had met in Omaha. The old man had told Joshua that he should never turn his back on an Indian. Joshua didn't really have a choice if he wanted to feed them. All the food Joshua had was in his cart which was behind him when he was facing the Indians.

Joshua took a deep breath, then reached under the tarp. He only hoped they would not think he was going for a weapon. Joshua pulled out a slab of salt pork wrapped in a cloth. Without turning back around, he unwrapped the salt port, took his knife from his belt and cut several thick slices from the slab. He placed the salt pork in a fry-pan.

Leaving the pan on the back of the cart, Joshua turned around. He was going to restart his fire, but was surprised to see the young brave was starting the fire for him. The young brave seemed to understand enough to know that Joshua was offering them something to eat and a fire would be needed to cook it.

Joshua smiled at the young brave, nodded his approval of what the brave was doing and then reached under the tarp for his coffee pot. He motioned for the others to join the young brave at the fire. Reluctantly, the others walked over to the fire and sat down.

As soon as the Indians were sitting around the fire, Joshua took another big risk. He took his coffee pot down to the river and filled it with water. He could feel their eyes on him every step of the way. He had turned his back on them again. It made him very nervous, but by being polite and offering them a sign of friendship it might keep them from killing him.

After filling the coffee pot with water, he returned to the fire. Again they watched him walk back to the fire. They never seemed to take their eyes off him.

Joshua put coffee in the pot and put it on the fire. While it was brewing, he retrieved the fry-pan from the cart, put it over the fire and began cooking the salt pork.

Everything seemed to be going along pretty well. The Indians seemed to understand what he was doing. It wasn't until Joshua reached for his knife to turn the salt pork over in the fry-pan that there was a problem. When he reached for his knife, every one of the Indians reached for their knives. Joshua froze as he looked at them. He knew he had made a gesture they did not understand, one they might have thought was threatening. Joshua didn't move for a moment or two while looking at them.

After several tense moments, Joshua slowly removed his knife from his belt. Very carefully, and very slowly, he leaned toward the fry-pan. He stuck the point of his knife into a piece of salt pork and slowly turned it over. When the braves saw what he was doing, they took their hands away from their knives and seemed to relax a bit. Joshua let out a sigh of relief and smiled at the braves. The braves continued to watch his every move as Joshua finished preparing breakfast.

Once the coffee was ready and the meat was done, Joshua cut up the meat into small pieces. He then stuck a piece of salt pork with the point of his knife, put it to his mouth and blew on it. When he thought it was cool enough, he put it into his mouth. Joshua smiled then motioned for them to do the same.

As soon as they started to eat, Joshua got up and went to his cart again. He got the only two cups he had, a bag of hardtack and a little sugar. He returned to the fire and poured coffee in one of the cups, added a little sugar and passed it to the brave next to him. He then filled the second cup with coffee, added a little sugar then took a sip from it.

The other braves didn't know what to think until he handed the second cup to the brave on the other side of him. He motioned for them to take a sip then pass it onto the next. He then passed the hardtack around. They sat around the fire and shared the salt pork, hardtack and coffee in silence.

When the food and coffee were gone, Joshua sat looking at them. He wasn't sure what to do next. The leader said something in his native tongue to Joshua, but he didn't understand it. From the look on the leader's face, Joshua was almost sure he was thanking him for the food and his hospitality. The leader stood and the others did the same. When Joshua stood, the leader handed Joshua the empty cups, nodded slightly and smiled.

The young Sioux braves had seemed friendly enough. Joshua wanted to talk to them, but he wasn't sure how to go about it. If he was going to try to talk to them, he had to do something and do it quickly if he wanted them to stay. They were starting to go to their horses.

In an effort to start some kind of communication with them, Joshua pointed to himself and said, "Joshua, Joshua."

The leader turned back and looked at Joshua. He began to smile.

"Joshua," the leader said as he pointed at the white man.

"Yes, Joshua," he said with a smile and nodded.

He then pointed to the leader and asked, "What is your name?"

"Spotted Horse," he replied in his own language as he pointed to himself.

Joshua didn't know the meaning of what the leader had said, but he repeated what the young brave had said as he pointed at him and smiled. It was obvious that the brave was interested in talking to Joshua, too.

It was an opportunity for Joshua to hopefully learn enough of the Indian language to be able to communicate with them. Maybe by knowing a little of their language, it might save his life someday. If nothing else, it might allow him to trade with Indians for things he might need. It certainly wouldn't hurt to know what an Indian was saying to or about him.

Spotted Horse must have thought it might be important for him to be able to talk to the white man, too. Spotted Horse turned and talked to the other braves. Joshua was not sure what they were talking about, but he got the impression Spotted Horse wanted to stay and try to talk. It seemed to Joshua that the other braves were not sure it was a good idea. The others also seemed to be in a hurry to get on their way. It wasn't long before the others went to their horses and rode off leaving Spotted Horse with Joshua. Spotted Horse turned back and looked at Joshua.

Joshua smiled at Spotted Horse, but he wasn't sure what to do. He looked around and saw a place at the river bank where there was no grass, just some sand. Joshua started to move toward the river and motioned for Spotted Horse to follow him. Spotted Horse followed Joshua to the river.

When they got to the river, Joshua knelt down in the sand along the river bank. He carefully brushed it smooth with his hands, then looked at Spotted Horse for a moment. He turned and drew the outline of a buffalo in the sand. It seemed to be a good way to start as the Indian would certainly know what a buffalo looked like. He turned and looked up at Spotted Horse to make sure he could see the drawing. He then pointed to the drawing and said, "Buffalo."

Spotted Horse smiled repeated the word Buffalo, then pointed to the drawing and said, "Tatanka."

Joshua repeated "Tatanka" as he pointed at the drawing.

Joshua and Spotted Horse smiled at each other as it was a big step toward understanding each other. To Joshua, understanding was the first step to peace and even friendship. From the look on Spotted Horse's face, it had a similar meaning to him.

They spent the rest of the morning drawing all kinds of figures in the sand and telling each other what it was called in their own language. They also pointed at objects like the river, the trees, the grass and even a little wild flower that was growing at the edge of the river. They even learned the word 'friend' in each other's language. In that way, Joshua learned the young brave's name was Spotted Horse in English, and started to call him by that name.

The two of them kept at it until it was mid-afternoon, each one learning a little from and about the other. Joshua learned a little about Spotted Horse and his tribe, and Spotted Horse learned a little about Joshua and where he had come from. During their time together, they began to forge a friendship.

* * * *

Late in the afternoon, Spotted Horse's friends returned with the results of their hunt. They had three deer across their horses. Spotted Horse invited Joshua to come with them to their camp. Joshua agreed without hesitation. Spotted Horse led his horse and walked alongside Joshua while he pulled his cart. Spotted Horse pointed at the cart, and Joshua told him what it was while they walked. The others went on ahead to their camp.

Joshua spent the rest of the day learning even more about the tribe. He ate with them and sat around the fire with a few of the elders learning more of their language and a few of their customs. He was even invited to spend the night.

When nighttime came, Joshua was shown to a tepee where he could stay the night. As he laid in the tepee and listened to the sounds of the night, he had a warm feeling about these people. He liked them, and they seemed to like him. Even though things had gone well for him, he was pretty sure that not all Indians would be friendly toward him. He knew he would have to be careful when he came upon other tribes. But for tonight, he knew he could sleep in peace.

* * * *

The next morning, Joshua ate with Spotted Horse and some of the elders. He shared a little of his food with them, and they shared some of their venison with him. As the sun rose higher in the sky, Joshua bid his new friends goodbye and started up the hill away from the river and on toward the west. Several of the young boys from the tribe who had listened to him tell the story of how he had arrived in the country while sitting around the fire last night, helped Joshua get his cart up the hill by pushing it while Joshua pulled it. Once on top of the hill, they waved goodbye as Joshua headed on across the wide open prairie. He waved back as he continued on his way westward.

CHAPTER THREE

Dangerous Encounter

After leaving Spotted Horse and his new friends at the river, Joshua continued his journey across the vast prairie as he thought about the tribe he had left. He was sure that not all the tribes on the plains would be friendly, but he had found one that was. It would be an experience he would keep in his memories for as long as he lived.

Continuing to travel west, Joshua found it to be a quiet and lonely time. For the next few days the only living things he saw were a few jackrabbits, lots of prairie dogs, several small herds of antelope and a few birds of which there were only a couple he could identify.

On the forth day after leaving his new friends, Joshua was meandering along an old buffalo trail that led toward a small grove of trees along the bank of a narrow river. It had been a long, hard, hot day and he had been thinking about trying to find a place with some shade where he could rest for the night. It was the first shade he had seen in the past three days. The small group of trees along the river looked like it would be a cool place for him to spend a quiet and restful night. He could hardly wait to get to the trees where he could get some rest, and get a bath in the river.

As Joshua moved closer to the trees along the bank of the river, he began thinking about Spotted Horse. He was wondering if he would ever see him again when his thoughts were suddenly disturbed by yelling and screaming. He looked off to his left and saw nine warriors as they came galloping down the long, gently sloping hill toward the river.

At first, Joshua just looked at them. It quickly became clear they were not looking or acting very friendly. He realized he was in trouble if he didn't get to some cover. He made a mad dash down the hill toward the trees. He pulled his two-wheeled cart as fast as he could. Since the Indians were on horses, they were gaining on him very fast. It was a race for his life.

Joshua had no more than gotten to the trees when he found himself with just enough time to grab his rifle from the cart. He grabbed his rifle then ran around behind the cart, putting the cart between himself and the charging Indians. He knew the cart would provide him with a small measure of cover while he tried to defend himself, but it was better than nothing. Joshua jerked his rifle up to his shoulder and took aim at the warrior closest to him. He fired his "Kentucky" long rifle. The ball from his rifle hit the young warrior nearest to him square in the chest. The Indian went flying off his horse, hitting the ground hard in a cloud of dust.

Joshua didn't have time to reload the rifle. He quickly dropped his rifle on the cart and drew his pistol from his belt. He fired it at another warrior who was trying to turn his horse while looking for a place to take cover. The slug from Joshua's pistol caught the second warrior in the upper left side of his chest. The warrior spun around and fell from his horse, hitting the ground only a few yards from the cart. The warrior turned over then stopped moving.

The remaining warriors quickly retreated to a shallow gully about one hundred and fifty to two hundred yards from the grove of trees. In a matter of a few seconds, Joshua had reduced their numbers from nine to seven. When he tried to run from them, they had not expected him to turn on them and kill two of them so quickly. If nothing else, he made them more cautious about attacking him again.

While the warriors tried to regroup in the gully and plan their next move, Joshua quickly reloaded both his pistol and his rifle. He readied himself for another attack which he was sure would be coming very soon. He laid out his powder and shot within easy reach so he could load his weapons fast. He was hoping that if they charged him, he could get at least two shots off with his rifle. That way he could save his pistol for when they got in close.

Once he was ready, he waited. There was no way for him to tell what they would do next. He had surprised them, and that was a good thing. Another good thing was he had his cart. He had everything in his cart he would need to put up a fight. Even so, seven against one were not the best odds.

Joshua began to look around at where he found himself. He was fairly close to the river and he had some cover from the trees in the small grove. He thought his position among the trees was good, but he could make it better if he moved his cart closer to the river where a very large cottonwood tree had fallen. If he put his cart closer to the dead tree, the tree would help protect his back. It would make it easier for him to see his enemy if they should try to circle around and attack him from the river.

He laid his rifle on the cart then pushed the cart closer to the water and nearer to the fallen tree. Once he was close enough to it, he gathered his powder and balls and set them on the log where they would be a little more accessible. He then turned the cart over on its side. He felt his position was probably as good as he could make it under the circumstances.

Joshua again looked around at his position. He was looking for ways to make it even better. He was also looking for any weaknesses in his position.

The one thing he would need that he was a little short of was water. The grass along the narrow bank of the river was fairly tall. If he was careful, he could crawl down to the river after dark and fill his canteens with water. For now there was nothing for him to do but wait to see what the warriors were going to do, and wait until dark. He was hoping they would give it up and leave, but seriously doubted that was going to happen.

As Joshua looked around, he heard something hit one of the trees about five feet away. It was quickly followed by the sound of a rifle shot. He was a little surprised because he had not noticed in his hurried run to the trees that one of the Indians had a rifle. He immediately looked for a sign indicating where the shot had come from. He could see the smoke from the gun as it slowly drifted away. It gave him a good idea where the Indian was who had fired the shot.

The Indian who had fired the shot was a good distance away. Joshua thought that the Indian was not a very good marksman, probably because he was not familiar with the rifle. That gave Joshua the advantage because he was used to shooting long distances.

Joshua was about to show the Indian that a gun was of little use if he didn't know how to use it. He laid his rifle over the top of his cart and took aim at where the Indian had shot from. He waited patiently for the Indian to show himself. When the Indian stuck his head up and tried to take careful aim at Joshua, Joshua fired. His shot hit its mark just as the Indian fired. The Indian's shot went into the dirt about twelve feet too short and to the right of Joshua, while Joshua's shot hit the Indian hard on his right shoulder. He didn't think he had killed the Indian, but he was sure he had taken him out of the fight.

After the exchange of rifle fire, it was quiet. There were no more attempts to fire the rifle by the Indians. Joshua was not sure if it was because none of the other Indians knew how to shoot it, or if they had decided the rifle was of little use to them when shooting long distances. Joshua was sure it was not the kind of rifle needed to shoot long distances. The Indian probably had a saddle rifle which was a fairly short range rifle. It was nothing like the long range rifle Joshua carried.

Time passed slowly as Joshua waited and watched to see what the Indians were going to do next. It was getting late and the sun was getting low in the west. The late evening sun shining on the tall prairie grasses made the prairie look like it was made of gold against the darkening blue sky to the east. It seemed strange that the prairie could be so beautiful and seem so peaceful when just a short time ago he had been attacked and had killed two warriors and wounded another.

Time drifted by very slowly. The warriors seemed content to wait and watch him. It was a bit unnerving for Joshua. Every once in a while he could see an Indian pop his head up and look toward him, but that was all. They were too far away to hit him with an arrow. It was one time when Joshua was glad they didn't know how to use a rifle.

As time passed, it became clear they had no intentions of leaving. They were planning something. The only question was what? As long as it was light it would be hard for them to get closer to him. He wondered if they would wait until it was dark and then move in on him.

As darkness fell upon the land, Joshua could hear the wild animal calls of the warriors. He had no one to help him keep watch so he could get a little sleep. Several times Joshua dozed off only to wake up at the sound of an animal call. It almost seemed as if they wanted to keep him awake. Maybe it was their plan, to keep him awake and tire him out so he would not have a clear head in the morning when it came time to fight back, he thought.

After it had been quiet for awhile, Joshua began to think he should sneak out in the tall grass to the river for water. It suddenly occurred to him that if he could sneak out to the river, the Indians could use the tall grass to sneak up on him.

Joshua began to think it might be better if he were to try to escape rather than stay and fight. After all, he was outnumbered. If the river was deep enough, he could swim out into the river and float downstream until he was far enough away to be out of danger. Joshua knew he would have to leave his cart and most of his supplies behind. He could pack everything he needed in his backpack so he could travel light.

Joshua began to select just those things he would need everyday to survive and put them in his backpack. He saved one tin cup, some hardtack, a little coffee, a canteen and his field glasses along with his bedroll, powder and shot. He wrapped his powder in oil cloth so it would stay dry. Since his backpack was made of hides, it would help keep things inside dry if he was not in the water too long. He kept his pistol and rifle where he could reach them.

As soon as he had everything he would need sealed in his backpack, he got down on his hands and knees and slowly began to crawl down to the river's edge dragging his backpack behind him. He moved as quietly as possible, stopping occasionally to listen for any sounds that would indicate someone else was moving in the grass. When he got to the river, he found the current was fairly slow which led him to believe it might be deep enough to swim in, or at least deep enough so he could stay almost hidden in the water.

His first thought was to move out into the river where it might be deep enough to float. Then he would simply float downstream out of harm's way. As he thought about it, it occurred to him that his enemy might be waiting for him downstream. They might be thinking he would try to escape by doing just that. The more he thought about it, the more he thought it would be harder, but safer to go upstream instead. He looked both ways before he decided to go upstream. Going upstream seemed his better choice.

Joshua crawled out into the water. He soon found it was deep enough that he could stand up with just his head and shoulders out of the water. He floated his backpack ahead of him. Joshua held his pistol and rifle tightly on top of the backpack to keep them dry.

In order to make as little noise as possible, he moved slowly and carefully. One slip and he would not only give away his escape, but he could lose his balance and dump his rifle and pistol in the river. At best, it would make them useless until he dried them out. At worst, he could lose them in the darkness. Either way, he would not have anything to fight with except his knife.

Time passed slowly as Joshua pushed his backpack upstream. He took a moment to look up at the sky. It was full of stars, but there was no moon. It made it very dark and almost impossible to see anything more than just a few feet away. He could not help but think it was a good night to make his escape. As he moved along in the river, he could hear the occasional wild animal calls of the Indians gradually fade as the distance between him and his enemy grew.

Moving against the current of the river made it tough going. Joshua was beginning to feel the cold of the water. It was making his body ache. He knew he had little choice but to keep moving if he was to survive.

Joshua had no idea how far he had gone when he began to see the eastern sky start to show signs that morning was coming. If he had not gone far enough, the morning light could make it easy for his enemies to find him. If that happened, he would be caught out in the open.

He had to find some place to hide where they could not find him. From what he could see along the bank of the river, there was little or no cover except the tall grass at the very edge of the river. If he left the river, he would not only be out in the open, but it would not be difficult for the Indians to discover where he left the river and follow him.

He kept looking around for someplace to hide as he slowly continued to move upstream. In the faint morning light, he noticed a fairly large area of cattails that looked like they went back into a narrow draw. From the looks of the contour of the land there was a creek or small stream that flowed into the river from behind the cattails. He decided the cattails would provide a good place to hide until he was sure the Indians had given up hunting for him.

Joshua worked his way toward the cattails. When the water was too shallow to continue to keep low, he stood up. He tucked his pistol in his belt, then took his rifle in one hand and his backpack in the other. Joshua waded through the shallow water and mud into the cattails.

He carefully worked his way back in among the cattails. He had to be very careful to make sure he didn't break off any of the cattails or leave any signs where he had gone. Joshua moved back in among the cattails far enough so he could not be seen from either bank of the river, or from the creek. He also made sure he could not be seen by anyone on the river as well. It was hard wading through the mud in among the cattails. It didn't help that he was already cold and tired.

As Joshua slowly moved deeper into the cattails, he discovered a large rock that would provide him with a place where he could lay his backpack, as well as a dry place where he could sit. When he was seated on the rock, the tall cattails still rose well above his head. He rested his rifle on his backpack while he took a few minutes to catch his breath.

He was wet and cold from being in the water so long. Not knowing what to expect, he checked his rifle and pistol to make sure they had remained dry. Once that was done, it was time to wait and hope the Indians would not find him and give up the search.

The sun slowly came up over the horizon and began to warm him. It felt good, but he was hungry. He had not eaten since yesterday morning. His need to travel light and to get as far away from the Indians as quickly as possible had caused him to leave most of his food behind. He had only a little coffee and a few hardtack biscuits. Joshua thought about starting a small fire on the rock to brew some coffee in the one metal cup he had kept. A cup of hot coffee would help warm him, but he knew it was too risky to build a fire, even a small one. Any smoke from a fire would certainly draw attention to where he was hiding. For now, he would have to let the sun warm him and dry his clothes. It was a time to remain quiet and to listen for any indication the Indians had come searching for him.

Time passed slowly. His clothes were slowly drying in the warm sun. He closed his eyes and wished he had a place large enough to lie down so he could get some sleep, but that was not to be. The rock was barely large enough to provide a place to set his backpack and still leave him with enough room to sit so he could be out of the water.

Suddenly Joshua's eyes flew open at the sound of horses galloping along the bank of the river. He grabbed his rifle and readied himself for whatever might be coming his way. He slowly stood up until his head was just above the cattails. He could see two Indians coming toward him. They were riding along the bank of the river looking for some sign where he might have come out of the water. He quickly ducked back down.

Since there were only two Indians, he figured some of the others had gone downstream from where he had left his cart. There might be one or two of them that he couldn't see on the other side of the river checking to see if he had crossed the river. He thought about rising up again to see if there were any Indians on the other side of the river, but he didn't dare. Those on his side of the river were too close and might see him.

Joshua kept his head down and listened for any sound that would indicate they were going to search the cattails. He could hear the sound of horses wading in the shallow water around the edge of the cattails. It was obvious they were looking for a sign that he might be hiding in among them.

He mentally prepared himself for a fight. There was no doubt in his mind that it would be a fight for his life. He held his rifle in his hands as his eyes searched for any movement among the cattails that would tell him they were close. Joshua could feel his heart pound in his chest and sweat run down his face as he waited and listened.

The Indians were so close that he could hear them talking. Joshua didn't understand very much of what they were saying, but it was clear they were not sure where he went. He quickly checked his rifle to make sure it was ready for a fight as he waited to see if they would come into the cattails looking for him.

It seemed to take forever for the Indians to make up their minds. After what seemed like an eternity, Joshua heard the sounds of horses running off. From the sounds of the horses, the Indians were headed back in the direction they had come. Joshua let out a sigh of relief and set his rifle on top of his pack. He thought they had decided he had not come that way, and were heading back to see if the others might have found him. It came to mind that there was also the possibility they had decided he was no longer worth the effort it would take to find him. Either way, they were leaving.

As soon as it was quiet, Joshua thought about getting out of the cattails, but didn't move. He was not sure if what he had heard was them leaving, or a ploy to get him to show himself. He wondered if they had actually left. He waited. He waited until the sun was almost directly overhead before he decided it was safe to move.

Convinced that the Indians had given up their search for him, he gathered his belongings and slowly started working his way out of the cattails. Since the Indians had gone back south, he decided it might be best if he continued to head north for a while longer.

Once Joshua was out of the cattails, he looked around. He was still on the east side of the river. Joshua could not see anyone in any direction. His decision to move north still seemed like a good idea. He would go north until he found a place where he could cross the river and continue on his journey west. Even though his supplies were south of him, he figured there would be very little left he could use once the raiding party had finished with it.

Joshua began moving north. At least for the next couple of miles, he would keep an eye to the south just in case the raiding party came back. While looking south, he noticed a thin column of smoke off in the distance. He moved away from the river and climbed up a hill to get a better look. When he reached the top of the hill, he could see there was something burning, and it appeared to be near the river. It was a long way away. Although he could not see what was burning, he was sure that the raiding party had taken out their frustration of not finding him by setting his cart on fire and destroying everything he had they could not use.

Joshua sat down and took a quick inventory of what he had managed to take with him in his escape. It had not been much. It would be difficult for him to survive for very long with what food he had left. He had been traveling for weeks and never seemed to get any closer to the great blue-gray mountains that he was hoping to see.

CHAPTER FOUR

The Need To Survive

Winter would be coming soon. Joshua had no idea how far it was to the great mountains, but he was sure they were still a long way away. There was little doubt in his mind that he would need a place to hole up for the winter.

He had quickly learned, while walking across the wide open prairie, there was very little material to build even a small cabin. Even if he could build a cabin, there was not enough wood to heat it during a long winter. He had heard how harsh the winters could be on the open prairie. There was also the fact that it would be hard to find a place where he could build a cabin he could defend by himself, if he were attacked again.

Joshua had a choice to make. Should he continue on west and hope he could find a place to hole up before winter set in? Or should he go back the way he had come in the hope of finding Spotted Horse and his tribe where he might find some help?

Joshua knew he would be able to move faster without the cart and its load. Traveling much lighter, he should be able to get back to where Spotted Horse's tribe was camped in a couple of days. He wondered if they would still be there. His only other option was to continue on into the unknown.

Looking around at the vast prairie and the loneliness of it, he decided there was much he needed to learn about surviving in the vast untamed land. The sooner he learned it, the better his chances of living a long life.

It was clear that the best thing for him to do would be to go back and try to join Spotted Horse and his tribe, if they would let him. Joshua could teach them a good deal about his world, but more importantly they could teach him how to survive on the open plains he knew almost nothing about. The more he thought about it, the more joining Spotted Horse seemed like the wise thing to do, and the best chance he had to survive.

Joshua took a deep breath, stood up and looked around one more time. He had made a decision. It was to go back and see if he could find Spotted Horse and his tribe.

As he lifted his backpack and put his arms threw the straps, he once again looked toward the column of smoke. He then turned and started down the side of the ridge as he headed east.

Early on the third day, after Joshua had left his cart and most of his supplies for the raiding party to plunder and destroy; he arrived on the ridge overlooking the river where Spotted Horse and his tribe had been camped. He stood on the top of the ridge looking up and down the valley in the hope of seeing Spotted Horse's encampment. He saw nothing but the river flowing slowly southward in the bottom of the valley. There were no tepees, horses, or people. His first thought was that he was in the wrong place. There was nothing moving except a small herd of antelope south of where he thought the camp had been.

Joshua walked down the hill and began looking for a clue or some sign that would tell him where Spotted Horse's tribe had camped. He discovered a lot of tracks made by unshod horses, but nothing else.

Joshua looked up and down the river. He noticed a bend in it south of where he was standing. He remembered he had gone south around a bend in the river to avoid the encampment when he first came upon the tribe. Joshua smiled to himself as he looked north. He started walking north along the west bank of the river.

He had gone less than a mile when he found the first signs of where Spotted Horse and his people had been camped. He found where their fires and tepees had been. They had been camped there, all right, but they had moved on.

Joshua once again looked around in an effort to find out where they had gone. The only consistent thing he found were the tracks of the horses and what looked like a number of long narrow depressions in the ground as if something had been dragged. There were the tracks of horses between each set of depressions, and they were all going in the same direction, north along the bank of the river.

At first, Joshua had difficulty making sense of the drag tracks he was seeing. It wasn't until he remembered the American Indian used travois´es to move their tepees and other belongings that the tracks made sense. A travois was made of two long poles with a hide stretched between them. One end of the poles was tied together over the back of a horse while the other ends dragged on the ground making long, narrow and shallow depressions in the earth. He quickly realized all he had to do was to follow the depressions left by the travois´es to find his friend and the tribe. It soon became clear to Joshua that Spotted Horse and his tribe had traveled north along the river.

Joshua immediately began to follow the tracks. It was getting close to dark when Joshua came to the place where they had stopped for the night. Since he would not be able to follow the tracks after dark, he decided to spend the night there and get a good early start in the morning.

After abandoning his cart, Joshua had been able to survive on coffee, a prairie Grouse and a couple of rabbits. However, he had nothing solid to eat tonight. He had seen fish in the river when he was there before. Since he had not seen any small animals to hunt, he decided to try his hand at fishing.

Joshua found a good place to fish. He took his fishing line out of his backpack and walked down to the river. He dug around in the damp dirt near the edge of the river with his hands until he found a worm. It took him a little while, but he finally caught a fish. Joshua had no idea what kind of fish it was, but it mattered very little. It was something to eat, and that was all that mattered at the moment.

Using his knife, he cut the fish open and cleaned it in the clear water of the river. After making a small fire, he let it burn down to coals, Joshua placed the fish on the coals, the scales against the coals. He watched it very closely to make sure he didn't burn it. When the fish was done, he removed it from the fire and began picking pieces from it to eat. Joshua found the fish to be tasty.

He had saved a small amount of his coffee from his supplies. Joshua went to the river and dipped his tin cup in the water. He brewed himself a cup of coffee in his tin cup on the embers from his fire, then let it cool enough to drink.

After he had eaten, he spread his bedroll out on the ground. He lay down and listened to the sounds of the night. After he was familiar with them, he looked up at the stars for a little while before he drifted off to sleep.

* * * *

The following morning, Joshua was up before the dawn. He caught another fish and made himself a cup of coffee for his breakfast. By then the sun had come up and was beginning to spread its warming light across the prairie. Once again he began to look for the tracks among the many left by Spotted Horse and his tribe where they had camped.

He quickly discovered they had left the river and had headed off in a westerly direction. Joshua began to wonder where they were going. Not being familiar with the country, there was no way for him to know. He would have to trust that they knew where they were going.

Joshua knew he could probably travel further in a single day than they could since there were more of them, and they

had a lot of things to move. They would have to stop earlier
than he would to set up camp and fix dinner for the whole
tribe. It would also take time for them to break camp every
morning. He was sure they would move slower with women
and children walking while leading the horses carrying their
belongings.

However, they had the advantage of having horses to
carry or pull their belongings, while he had to carry his on
his back. They would also have food and would not have to
hunt everyday just to eat.

Joshua had no idea when they had moved on, or how far
ahead of him they might be. He packed what little he had
and began to follow the trail left by Spotted Horse and his
tribe. While he walked, he kept his eyes open for a rabbit or
some other small animal that would make a good meal for
him. He managed to get a prairie grouse during the day and
hung it on his belt until he was ready to cook and eat it.

* * * *

One of the many things concerning Joshua while he
followed the tracks was the weather. If it should rain, he
might lose their tracks and never find them again. That
thought caused him to step up his pace a little. He would
push himself hard in the hope of catching up to them before
the weather changed and wiped out all signs of where they
had gone.

Joshua had been following Spotted Horse and his tribe
for four days when the weather began to change. The wind
started to blow fairly early in the morning and seemed to
pick up as the day wore on. By noon, the wind was causing
small dust devils to form and dance wildly across the open
prairie. By mid-afternoon the sky was filled with threatening
dark gray clouds rolling in the sky like water in a pot over a
hot stove. The temperature changed, too. It was getting
cooler, much cooler.

By late afternoon it had started to rain. It rained slowly
at first, hardly more than a drizzle. Within an hour it was

coming down hard enough to make the tracks Joshua was following harder to see. The rain was slowly washing away the tracks, and there was nothing Joshua could do about it.

As time passed, the rain seemed to be getting worse. Joshua continued on for as long as he could make out bits and pieces of the tracks. It wasn't long before the tracks had completely disappeared. There was nothing else for Joshua to do but to try and find shelter from the storm.

Joshua continued to walk in the general direction Spotted Horse and his tribe had been going. He had traveled for about a mile in the rain before he came upon a rock ledge that stuck out from the side of a rocky outcropping. Since he had already lost the tracks, he decided to hole up under the ledge at least until the rain stopped, or until morning if it continued to rain into the night. He wasn't sure what morning would bring, but to continue on in the rain would not change the fact that the tracks were gone.

When Joshua walked up to the ledge, he discovered a few dry tree branches under it. They looked as if they had been dragged there by someone who had been there long before him. There was a small blacken area on the ground just under the edge of the ledge where a fire had been built sometime ago. It was clear that someone else had used the place as a shelter.

Joshua used the tree branches to build a small fire to help dry his wet clothes and to brew some coffee in his metal cup. He cleaned the rabbit he had shot earlier in the day, and cooked it over the fire. When he was finished eating, he leaned back against the rock wall to relax.

His fire was going good and the warmth of it had dried his clothes and warmed him. He sat next to the fire and looked out over the prairie. Joshua watched the rain as it continued to fall. He was feeling a little depressed as he wondered how he was going to find Spotted Horse and his tribe now. The rain had washed away any signs that they had even passed by there.

Joshua watched as the rain changed from a steady down pour to a gentle rain. It was the kind of rain that soaked into the soil and brought new life to the dry brown buffalo grass. Although the rain would help the prairie become green again, it would certainly not help him in his quest to find Spotted Horse and his people.

Since it was getting dark, Joshua rolled out his bedroll, laid down and pulled the blanket over himself. He laid there for over an hour looking at the fire as it slowly burned down to embers. He spent the time thinking about what he was going to do. The only thing he could think of was to continue to move on west in the hope of finding Spotted Horse and his tribe, or tracks left by them. As the fire burned down and there were no longer any flames, he closed his eyes and fell asleep.

* * * *

When morning came, Joshua woke just as the sun was starting to come up over the horizon. He sat up and looked over the vast prairie that spread out before him. The sky was clear and a bright blue. The sun sparkled on the wet grass. It was going to be a beautiful day, but Joshua was not thinking about that. He had something else on his mind. He was wondering how he was going to find Spotted Horse now that his tracks and the tracks of his tribe had been washed away by the rain.

As he stood up and began looking around, something in the distance caught his eye. Whatever it was, it didn't look natural to the prairie. With the rain and the darkness when he settled in under the ledge, he had not noticed anything different on the horizon. In fact, when he settled in for the night, he couldn't see very far because of the rain and the increasing darkness. But with the clear sky and bright sun, he could see something off to the west that didn't look like it belonged there.

Joshua quickly grabbed his field glasses from his backpack and scrambled up on top of the rocky outcropping in the hope of finding a better vantage point. He looked toward the west. With the help of his field glasses, he could see several thin columns of smoke slowly rising up into the air. He could also make out several tepees.

Although he could not be sure, he believed he had found Spotted Horse's encampment. It was hard to tell, but he thought he could see the tepees being taken down. Joshua would have to hurry before they had time to break camp and move on. Without taking time to fix himself breakfast, he quickly packed his gear and started toward the encampment.

When he was a little less than a mile from the encampment, he could see several warriors hurrying to their horses. Joshua smiled to himself thinking that they must have seen him coming. His first thought was they were coming to greet him. But as he thought about it, he wondered how they would know it was him. He no longer had his cart, and he was too far away for them to be able to identify him. He began waving his arms to let them know he was a friend.

It wasn't until they were close enough to recognize him that they realized it was Joshua. They slowed their pace, but still rode up to him. When only a few yards away from him, Spotted Horse reined up, swung his leg over the neck of his horse and slid gracefully to the ground. He then walked up to Joshua and greeted him.

"It is good to see you again," Spotted Horse said in his native language while smiling at Joshua.

Joshua didn't know all of what he said, but he understood enough to know it was a friendly greeting. He smiled back and raised his hand as a sign of a friendly greeting.

Together, they walked back to the encampment. They sat down at a fire and Joshua ate with his friend. He was very hungry.

Spotted Horse had the women stop breaking camp. He told the members of the tribe they would be staying there for another night. He instructed several of the braves to go and hunt.

Taking his time, Joshua tried to tell Spotted Horse about the attack on him by a raiding party. He told him about his escape and how he had come to be without his cart. He wasn't sure how much of it Spotted Horse understood.

Spotted Horse had learned enough at their last meeting to get the idea of what had happened. Using a combination of English he had learned from Joshua, sign language and the Lakota language he had taught Joshua, Spotted Horse was able to make Joshua understand that he was welcome to travel with them.

While some of the other braves went hunting, Spotted Horse and Joshua sat by the fire learning more of each other's language, and to share a laugh or two. By the time nightfall had come, they had learned much about each other and their languages. Their friendship grew even stronger.

Spotted Horse told Joshua he could remain with them through the winter at their winter campsite at the Southern end of the Black Hills on the Cheyenne River, if he wished. Joshua told Spotted Horse he would like to spend the winter with them, and that he would do his part to provide for the needs of the entire tribe as long as he was with them. They shook hands in agreement.

The next morning, Spotted Horse and his tribe packed up all their belongings and once again headed west toward the Black Hills. While Spotted Horse rode with some of the men at the head of the tribe, Joshua walked along with the women and children as he had no horse to ride, and no packhorse to carry his backpack. Each evening, Spotted Horse would spend time with Joshua learning more of his language and teaching Joshua the ways of his tribe.

* * * *

After about five days of traveling with Spotted Horse and his tribe, they came upon a large herd of buffalo. The herd was grazing in a long narrow valley where the grass was green and thick. From what Joshua had learned about the tribe's way of life during his time with them, he decided it was his chance to help provide food for the tribe. It was also his chance to increase his standing among those within the tribe who did not completely trust him, yet. It was an opportunity for him to show his worth as a hunter to the rest of the tribe.

While Spotted Horse and the other braves sat down on the ground to plan their attack on the buffalo herd, Joshua left his backpack with the women. He took his rifle, powder and shot, and ran up ahead to a place where there were several large boulders, a place where he could look out over the herd. The boulders provided him not only with cover, but good support for his rifle. It was a good place to hunt buffalo with a long rifle. Being very careful not to make any more noise than necessary, he took careful aim at one of the big bulls in the herd. Cocking his "Kentucky" long rifle and taking careful aim, he pulled the trigger.

The loud bang from Joshua's rifle startled everyone. Spotted Horse and the others quickly sprung to their feet, then looked to see what had happened. They were expecting to see the buffalo running away. What they saw was a big buffalo drop to the ground, dead. What they didn't see was the other buffalo run away. The remaining buffalo milled around for a moment or two, but soon went right back to grazing.

Spotted Horse looked to see where the sound had come from and saw Joshua behind the rocks. He was reloading his rifle. Spotted Horse wasn't sure what to do. At first he was angry at Joshua for firing his gun. He thought the shot would scare off the buffalo before they had a chance to kill any of them. If that happened they would miss a very good opportunity to have fresh meat. Plus, they would be without the meat they would need to feed the tribe until they were settled in at their winter camp. They would also be without the buffalo hides that would provide warm blankets and warm clothes for them during the cold winter.

Spotted Horse stood there watching as Joshua took aim at another buffalo, slowly pulled the trigger and fired. Again, the buffalo fell right where it stood and the rest of the buffalo did not run away. It was something incredible to Spotted Horse. He had never seen a buffalo shot from a stationary position with a rifle before. He was puzzled by the buffalo's response to the loud noise.

Spotted Horse and his braves had always charged into the herd on the backs of their horses and speared the buffalo they could get close enough to, or shoot them with arrows while going at breakneck speed on their horses. It was a very dangerous way to hunt. Many a brave had been injured, crippled, or even killed while hunting buffalo, but it was all they knew. It was the way their ancestors had done it since they had horses.

The only other way Spotted Horse had seen buffalo hunted was to drive the herd over a cliff, when there was a cliff nearby to drive them over. Even that was very dangerous because they never knew if the buffalo would suddenly turn and trample someone.

Spotted Horse continued to watch as Joshua continued to shoot buffalo, one buffalo at a time. Joshua had killed ten buffalo in all, by himself, and without any danger to himself or to his friends. And he did it in a very short time. He looked over toward the tribe and saw the whole tribe watching him from the nearby hill. He wasn't sure what he should do, but he felt that ten buffalo was more than enough to keep the tribe in meat for sometime, and to provide him with the hides he would need to make his own shelter. There might even be enough hides to make himself a coat, and maybe trade for a horse or two.

Joshua turned and looked up the hill to where Spotted Horse and some of his people were standing watching him.

He motioned for Spotted Horse to join him among the boulders.

Bent over, Spotted Horse ran down the slop to where Joshua was kneeling behind the rocks. He knelt down behind one of the rocks and looked out over the herd of buffalo. He looked at the distance Joshua had been shooting from. He could hardly believe Joshua had killed so many buffalo at such a great distance.

"Enough meat for your people?" Joshua asked.

Spotted Horse first looked at Joshua, then looked out at the dead buffalo again before he replied, "Yes," in English.

"The meat of the buffalo is for everyone in the tribe," Joshua said. "I would like to make a trade."

Spotted Horse again looked at the buffalo and then toward Joshua to hear what he had to say.

"You have many horses. I would like to trade four hides for two horses. I will need a few hides to make a shelter, and for a coat for the winter, and for a blanket."

Spotted Horse thought about it for a moment. Four buffalo hides for two horses was not a very good trade as far as Spotted Horse was concerned. On the other hand, having someone like Joshua with them might prove to be very helpful in keeping the tribe supplied with food during the winter, especially if it was a long hard winter. Also the meat from the buffalo would feed all his people until they reached the winter campsite.

Spotted Horse took his time to think about the trade. He thought he would gain the meat from ten buffalo and the hides from four without any danger to him or any of the braves. When he looked at it that way, it was not such a bad trade. Since he had a few more horses than he really needed, he smiled, then nodded his head in agreement.

"Do you need more meat and hides?"

"No. This will be all we can carry."

"Can I get one of the women to help me with the hides I will keep?"

"Yes," Spotted Horse said. "All the women will help skin all the buffalo and prepare the meat for travel. My sister will help you prepare your hides as well as prepare some of the meat for you. It will take us the rest of the day and tomorrow to take care of the buffalo you have killed."

"Then we best get started. I think we should run off the rest of the buffalo," Joshua suggested.

"I agree. This will be all we can handle until we get to our winter camp."

Joshua smiled. He was not only pleased that he was able to help the tribe, but he was able to trade for a couple of horses. It meant he would not have to walk and carry his pack on his back.

Spotted Horse had a couple of braves run off the rest of the herd, and gave instructions to set up camp. As soon as the buffalo were gone, the women of the tribe ran out to where the buffalo lay and began to skin them right there. Joshua joined the women in skinning the buffalo. The men of the tribe watched as Joshua skinned one of the buffalo. They thought it was woman's work, but it didn't bother him. He was used to doing his own work.

Once the buffalo had been skinned, the women stacked all the hides Joshua was going to keep for himself in a pile, then took the others to where the tepees would be set up. They began preparing the meat for travel and staking out the hides Joshua had traded Spotted Horse for horses. They also took most of the meat from the buffalo.

* * * *

Joshua was working hard on a buffalo hide when Spotted Horse came riding up to him. There was a young woman riding one of the horses while leading a second horse. They were good strong looking horses.

Joshua stopped and looked at the young woman while she slid off the horse. She was hardly more than about sixteen. She was wearing a plain tan deerskin dress, deerskin boots, and a simple beaded belt at her waist. There was what looked like a very sharp knife in her belt. Her skin looked like it was tanned by the sun. Her black shining hair was braided into a single braid and fell down her back between her shoulders almost to her waist. He thought she was a beautiful young woman. His attention was distracted from her when Spotted Horse spoke to him.

"This is Dancing Flower. She is my sister. She will help you prepare the hides."

"Thank you," was all Joshua could say.

Dancing Flower smiled politely, then went right to work as Spotted Horse rode away. Joshua couldn't help but glance over at Dancing Flower from time to time as she worked beside him. He even caught her glancing at him. She was a hard worker, but then why wouldn't she be. Her life, and the life of the others, depended on everyone doing their share of the work.

Dancing Flower showed Joshua how to stake out the buffalo hides on the ground using pieces of the rib bones of the buffalo for stakes. She showed him how to scrape off all the meat and flesh from the inside of the hide to prevent it from smelling and rotting, thus becoming useless.

She also showed him how to prepare the meat from the buffalo for travel. Some of the meat was dried by cutting it into strips then hanging it above an open fire, not to cook but to dry. Some of the meat was boiled to make it tender and to make it last longer.

Joshua quickly discovered Dancing Flower was very good at preparing the meat and hides. They worked together the rest of the day and all the next day. The other women of the tribe joined in to prepare the meat so the entire tribe would have meat to eat on the trail.

By the third day, all the meat and hides had been prepared for travel. The first thing in the morning all the supplies were packed up and put on travois'es. Dancing Flower helped Joshua make a travois for one of his horses. She then helped him pack his supplies and hides on it.

CHAPTER FIVE

Dancing Flower And Joshua Grow Close

Spotted Horse rode up to Joshua when it was time to leave and push on toward their winter campgrounds. Joshua turned and looked up at Spotted Horse. He was ready to lead his horses along with the rest of the women who were going to lead the other horses.

"You ride with us," Spotted Horse said.

"What about my packhorse?"

"Dancing Flower will lead it for you."

Joshua looked at Dancing Flower. She smiled at him, then tipped her head down and looked at the ground. Joshua was not sure what to say. He turned and looked at Spotted Horse.

"Dancing Flower is not my woman," Joshua reminded Spotted Horse.

"She could be."

Joshua looked at Spotted Horse with a surprised look on his face. He didn't know what to say. Dancing Flower had been a great deal of help to him, and she had taught him a lot about caring for hides and preparing meat so it would not spoil too quickly. She had also shown him how to make a travois and pad it so it would not hurt the horse pulling it. She had done all those things without any indication she even liked him.

"You ride with me," Spotted Horse said again.

Not wanting to offend Spotted Horse, his friend and one of the young leaders of the tribe, he nodded that he would join Spotted Horse in leading the others to their winter camp in the Black Hills. He watched as Spotted Horse turned his horse and rode off to join the others.

Joshua turned and looked at Dancing Flower. She was looking at him. He couldn't miss the smile on her face, or the hand gesture that told him he should hurry and join the other men. Joshua mounted his horse, then after briefly looking back at Dancing Flower again, he turned and rode off to join Spotted Horse at the head of the tribe.

Over the next couple of days, Joshua rode with Spotted Horse in the lead, along with some of the other warriors. Dancing Flower led his packhorse and walked with the other women. Joshua was provided with a tepee to sleep in and was given respect by the people in the tribe. Providing the tribe with food and several extra buffalo hides had put him in good standing with them.

In the evenings, Dancing Flower would set up his camp and prepare his meals. They would eat together. After eating, she would then clean up and make ready a place for him to sleep. She seemed to be willing to do those things for him, and he appreciated it.

In exchange for the things Dancing Flower did for Joshua, he spent time with her teaching her English as well as some of the ways of the white man. She was a good student and seemed eager to learn. She also seemed happy to be around him and to please him.

* * * *

It was on a day when they were approaching the Black Hills where the tribe would spend the winter when Spotted Horse rode up close to Joshua. Joshua looked at Spotted Horse and smiled. Spotted Horse turned to Joshua and grinned at him, but didn't say anything. Joshua had a feeling that Spotted Horse wanted to say something to him, but had no idea what it might be.

"What is on your mind, Spotted Horse?" Joshua asked, curious as to what caused Spotted Horse to be grinning.

"I think Dancing Flower would like to be your woman," Spotted Horse said with a slight laugh in his voice.

His comment almost caused Joshua to fall off his horse. It wasn't that he hadn't thought about taking her to be his woman, because he had. It was the fact Spotted Horse had said it. Joshua had found Dancing Flower to be very beautiful, a hard worker, and she was very attentive to him. He had often wanted to hold her hand while they walked together, and talk to her about becoming his woman, but wasn't sure how she would feel about it.

"Has Dancing Flower said something to you?"

"No. She would never do that. It is the way she looks at you."

Joshua didn't say anything for sometime. In fact, the rest of the day they rode in silence. He was busy thinking about Dancing Flower. There was no question she was a hard worker and they worked well together. He couldn't help but think she was a pretty woman. He even had to admit to himself that he liked being around her. But Joshua needed time to think on the matter. It was not something Joshua was ready to discuss with Spotted Horse, not yet anyway. He felt he should talk to Dancing Flower to find out if she was really interested in him.

As they moved closer to the winter campsite, Joshua continued to teach Dancing Flower his language. He also continued to grow closer to her.

When Spotted Horse and his tribe had reached the winter campsite, Joshua and Dancing Flower set up the tepee she had helped him make from his buffalo hides, and the pine poles he cut from nearby trees. He set his tepee off to one side of the rest of the camp near the edge of the forest. Joshua used one buffalo hide on the ground inside the tepee so he didn't have to sleep on the cold ground. He used one for a blanket along with his bedroll and one hide he planned to make into a buffalo coat for himself.

The nights were starting to get longer and the days shorter. The days in the late fall and early winter were cool, but the nights were getting cold. Joshua spent most of his time hunting and trapping beaver. He used the deer hides he got from the deer he had killed to make pants and shirts. He also gave a few of the deer hides to Dancing Flower so she could make herself clothes and a coat. He even gave her a buffalo hide to make herself a warm winter coat.

Dancing Flower and Joshua spent a lot of time together getting to know each other. She would help him make his clothes, cook his meals and take care of the animals he killed. She prepared the beaver pelts, and tended to Joshua's horses. Joshua would teach her his language, and how to use a rifle and pistol so she could protect herself and hunt. They would also spend a lot of time just talking. They talked about everything, the future, what they liked and what they didn't like. As time went by, Dancing Flower and Joshua became very close.

* * * *

It was early December when Joshua walked with Dancing Flower to a nearby creek to get water. He had never walked with her to the creek before. She wondered why he was walking with her, but didn't ask him. She was simply glad he did.

While they were at the creek, Joshua reached out and took hold of her hand. She looked up at him and smiled, but the smile disappeared from her face when she noticed he had a serious look on his face. It worried her. Her first thought was that he didn't want her being around him any more. She wondered why he would hold her hand if he didn't want her to be with him.

"Have I done something to upset you?" she asked, needing to know what was on his mind.

"No. You have done nothing to upset me," he said with a reassuring smile.

"Why are you so serious?"

"I have something to ask you?"

"What is it?" she asked as she looked into his eyes.

"Dancing Flower, would you be my woman?" he asked shyly.

"Yes," she replied with a big smile. "I would like to be your woman, but you will have to ask Spotted Horse. He is my closest relative."

"I'm sure he will give us his blessing," he said as he grinned at her.

Dancing Flower threw her arms around his neck and kissed him. Joshua was a little surprised by her action, but certainly did not mind.

As soon as Dancing Flower stopped kissing him and got her excitement under control, they sat down on a log next to the creek. Joshua held her hand as she sat close to him.

Joshua let go of her hand and built a fire. They sat on a log next to the fire. While they sat together, Dancing Flower told Joshua he would need to present gifts to Spotted Horse before he would give his permission for them to wed. They spent most of the afternoon sitting by the fire next to the river just to be close. It was getting on toward darkness before they headed back to his tepee. Joshua spent time during the evening selecting gifts to present to Spotted Horse in the morning.

The next morning, Joshua took one elk hide, three deer hides and the six beaver pelts he planned to give Spotted Horse and carried them to his tepee. Joshua laid them down in front of Spotted Horse's tepee as Dancing Flower had told him to do.

"Spotted Horse, I would like to talk with you," he called.

Joshua waited for Spotted Horse to come out of his tepee. When he came out, he looked at the hides and pelts neatly stacked in front of his tepee. He then looked up at Joshua and smiled.

"Spotted Horse, I would like to make Dancing Flower my woman. I would like to marry her."

Spotted Horse smiled and gave his blessing. Joshua ran to his tepee where Dancing Flower had agreed to wait for him. Dancing Flower immediately knew what Spotted Horse's answer had been when she saw the look on Joshua's face, but she waited for him to tell her the news. Once he told her that Spotted Horse had given his blessing, she threw her arms around his neck and kissed him several times before she would let go of him. Joshua was in no hurry to have her let go. He liked being kissed by her, and he liked holding her in his arms.

Several days later, Dancing Flower and Joshua were married in front of the whole tribe. There was a big party with gift giving followed by dancing around a large fire to celebrate. There was also a large chunk of buffalo roasted over the fire for everyone to enjoy. Later that night, Dancing Flower and Joshua retired to his tepee. It would be their tepee from now on.

For the next few weeks, Dancing Flower and Joshua worked side by side. They hunted deer, buffalo, and elk. They worked together to skin and prepare the pelts of the beaver they trapped. They also did some fishing in the river. They cleaned and stacked their hides and pelts in a shelter to store them until they could be taken to a trading post in the spring. They would be traded for things they would need. They traded some of the hides and pelts to Spotted Horse for three more horses Joshua would need to take his pelts to market. Trapping and hunting had been very good.

As the winter progressed, Joshua turned more to trapping beaver he could take back east to trade. He knew of a place on the Missouri River where he could trade his pelts. It was Fort Pierre. In the spring he would go there and sell his beaver pelts and the hides he didn't need.

CHAPTER SIX

Joshua Fights Alongside Spotted Horse

On several occasions during the winter, Joshua would go out with one of Spotted Horse's hunting parties to hunt for food for the tribe. Late one afternoon in early February while out with a small hunting party, they came upon the tracks of a large buffalo. Joshua had learned how to track from Spotted Horse and a couple of the other members of the tribe who had become his friends. He had learned what kind of tracks each animal in the area made, and if the tracks were fresh or old. He had gotten very good at it.

They had been following the fresh tracks of the buffalo for some distance when they came across the fresh tracks of several unshod horses. The tracks came in from a draw off to their right, then turned and followed the buffalo tracks. Joshua got down off his horse and checked out the tracks, then looked up at Spotted Horse.

"Twelve, maybe fourteen horses. It looks as if they are following the buffalo north."

"A hunting party," Spotted Horse said as he looked north.

"What do you want to do?" Joshua asked.

"We go back south. We are not prepared to fight so many."

Joshua stood up and walked to his horse. Before Joshua could get back on his horse, an arrow came flying out of the trees and struck Running Deer in the side. Running Deer fell from his horse.

For the next couple of minutes there was total chaos. Everyone was trying to find cover while their enemy was shooting arrows at them from the trees.

Joshua grabbed his rifle and ducked down behind a log. As soon as he spotted one of those who were attacking them, he took aim and fired. The lead ball from his rifle hit the Indian, dropping him immediately. As he started to reload, two of their enemies came rushing out of the trees toward Joshua. They had apparently figured out that the rifle only fired once before it had to be reloaded, and it took time to reload. What they didn't seem to count on was the pistol Joshua carried in his belt, and his ability to use it.

Joshua drew his pistol from his belt, shot and killed the one closest to him. He then dropped his pistol and drew his knife. When the Indian jumped over the log to attack Joshua, Spotted Horse shot an arrow hitting the Indian in the chest. He collapsed on the ground at Joshua's feet.

When their enemies realized that they were getting the worst of the fight, they turned and ran. With two of Spotted Horse's braves injured, Spotted Horse decided not to continue the fight and let them go. He called his braves to hold their ground.

The fight was over almost as quickly as it had started. Joshua and Spotted Horse could hear their enemies riding away at a very fast pace. It was not the time to give chase with two of their own having been wounded, one of them seriously. The immediate need was to care for the injured.

Joshua quickly reloaded his rifle and pistol then turned his attention to the wounded. The arrow grazed the top of Running Deer's hip causing a deep cut and bruised the hip bone. While Joshua did what he could for Running Deer, Spotted Horse and a couple of the other warriors made a travois to carry Running Deer for the trek back to camp.

As a couple of the braves put Running Deer on the travois, Joshua dressed the wound to Fast Horse's shoulder. His wound was not serious, but it needed attention to avoid infection. The others in Spotted Horse's hunting party kept a close watch so they would not be surprised if their enemy decided to regroup and attack them again.

Once Spotted Horse and the rest of his hunting party returned to their camp, Running Deer was taken to his tepee where he was cared for by several of the women. Running Deer would survive his injuries from the skirmish, but he would be laid up for a long time. Everyone in the camp pitched in to provide what was needed for him and his family. Joshua and Dancing Flower did their part to make life easier for Running Deer's family by helping to provide food and making sure they had wood for their fire.

From that time on, everyone was on watch. Spotted Horse and the others expected the Indians who had attacked them to try to get revenge for the death of several of their warriors, but nothing ever came of it. It had become clear to them that Spotted Horse's tribe had some serious fire power, namely Joshua's rifle and pistol.

CHAPTER SEVEN

Building a Permanent Home

The winter went by slowly. There were times of heavy snow and almost blizzard conditions making it dangerous to go out of their tepees. There were also times when it was sunny and bright, giving them time to restock their wood piles and do a little hunting. There were times when it was very cold, and times when it was warm enough to melt some of the winter snow.

During the tribe's stay at their winter campgrounds at the edge of the Black Hills along the Cheyenne River, Dancing Flower and Joshua would sit by the fire in their tepee and talk about the future. Joshua had found a nice valley where there was plenty of game and a small creek running the length of it. The soil under the snow was dark and rich, and would grow good crops, better than could be grown in his native England. There were also a couple of beaver ponds where the creek ran along one side of the valley.

One end of the valley opened out onto the plains which spread for miles to the south and east. To the north and west of the valley lay the Black Hills and gently rolling hills. Most of the rolling hills were sparsely covered with trees, while the Black Hills were covered with pine trees. The Cheyenne River ran along one side of the valley.

Joshua wanted to settle there and make a permanent home for them. He would build a cabin near the northwest end of the valley closest to the forest. Dancing Flower was not sure she liked the idea of a permanent home, but agreed to think on it.

By the time spring arrived, Joshua and Dancing Flower had decided to settle in the valley. Although Dancing Flower still had some reservations about having a permanent home, she was willing to give it a try.

They decided they would keep the pelts and hides they had gathered over the winter until next year. They would wait until next spring to take them to the trading post to sell them along with any others they would get during the next winter.

They moved their tepee to the end of the valley nearest the forest. It would be their home until they built their cabin to live in. The tepee was not very far from where Spotted Horse and his tribe had their winter encampment.

Joshua and Dancing Flower immediately began working to build a cabin. It would not be a very big cabin, but it would be larger than a teepee and much more secure. They would build it so it could be added to as needed.

It would take Joshua and Dancing Flower most of the summer to build the cabin complete with a stone fireplace. It would be a strong cabin that would provide them with shelter from the weather.

Spotted Horse and the members of his tribe stopped by Joshua and Dancing Flower's tepee shortly after they moved to the valley. It was springtime, and time for Spotted Horse and his people to say goodbye. They where going out on the plains to follow the buffalo herds as their ancestors had done for hundreds of years before them.

"We wish you were coming with us," Spotted Horse said to Joshua.

"I wish to build a place here for Dancing Flower and myself. I was not born to wander over the land and follow the buffalo like you. It is your way. It is not my way."

"I understand," Spotted Horse said. "We wish you well. We will return in the fall and set up our winter camp in the same place."

"I look forward to your return. Upon your return, we will go hunting together."

"I would like that," Spotted Horse said.

After Dancing Flower said goodbye to her family and friends, she stood with her arm around Joshua as they watched them leave. It wasn't long before Spotted Horse and his tribe were out of sight.

As soon as they were gone, Joshua and Dancing Flower went back to work on the cabin. They worked side by side, cutting down trees, trimming off the branches and the bark. They used their horses to drag the logs close to where they would build the cabin. They dug down to firm ground and built a stone foundation for their cabin. They cut the logs so they would fit together tightly to make a strong home. They also took time to hunt and trap, and to cut wood for the winter. It took Joshua and Dancing Flower most of the summer to build the cabin. During that time, Dancing Flower missed her family, but she never complained.

Once the cabin was built they moved into it from the tepee, but kept the tepee for any visitors they might have as the cabin was fairly small. The cabin would be warmer in the winter than the tepee, and had more room. The cabin would allow a person to stand up straight, something that could not be done in a tepee. It even had space to store a few things.

The fire place would provide not only a place for Dancing Flower to cook their meals, but would provide warmth for the cabin during the long cold winters. It would also be much more comfortable during windstorms and heavy rains that often rolled across the open plains during the spring and summer months.

When the cabin was completed, Joshua began to lay the foundation of stone for a barn to keep the horses in during the winter and during storms. He also did some hunting and trapping between times, and made a few pieces of furniture for the cabin. He built a corral for the horses for those times when he needed to keep them close. Joshua cut and gathered the long prairie grass, and put it in piles next to the barn so he could feed the horses when the snow was too deep for the horses to get to the grass.

When fall came, Spotted Horse returned to their winter camp on the Cheyenne River. He stopped and visited with his sister and his friend, Joshua. It was a time to celebrate their safe return. There was dancing and feasting.

The summer had been good to Spotted Horse and his tribe. Hunting had been good and the weather had been fairly mild. Although there were a few minor injuries while hunting, all of Spotted Horse's tribe had returned in good health.

Again during the winter, Joshua and Dancing Flower spent a good deal of their time trapping beaver and preparing their pelts. They had worked hard in the cold to get a good stash of pelts. It would not be long before spring weather would melt the snow and the wild flowers would bloom once again.

It would be a time to pack up all the pelts and hides they had trapped over the past two winters and take them to the trading post. With the sale of their pelts and hides, they would be able to get supplies to help them get through the next winter and to help them plant a garden.

When spring finally settled in the Black Hills, the snow melted away. The ice melted off the ponds and the creeks ran full. The wild flowers began to show themselves, and the grass turned to a deep green. It was time to check the traps for the last time and pull them from the ponds. It was also time to pull the animal traps from the forest as well. Joshua and Dancing Flower gathered and stacked the pelts and hides into bundles.

Dancing Flower and Joshua bundled up the beaver pelts and the few hides from wolves and coyotes they had taken over the past two years. They piled the bundles in front of their cabin. They were getting them ready to be taken to the trading post at Fort Pierre. It was a trading post that Joshua had seen when he started his journey to the blue-gray mountains. He heard from a mountain man who passed through the area that the trading post was still in operation. The Fort Pierre trading post would be closer than taking his pelts all the way to Omaha to trade.

"I want you to stay here while I am gone," Joshua said to Dancing Flower. "I have talked to Spotted Horse. He is going to stay here in the Black Hills this summer and will be close by. He and his people will hunt in and around the Black Hills during the summer. He will look in on you from time to time. You will have much to do with the garden."

"My brother has told me he will give me hides from his hunts if he does not need them. If hunting is good, he should have several for me. I will make some more clothes while you are gone."

"That will be good. I will take his pelts and hides with me to trade for sugar and coffee for him."

"That is good. How long will you be gone?"

"About three months if the weather is good, maybe a little longer."

"That is a long time to be away from you," she said sadly.

"I know, but I need you here," Joshua said. "Spotted Horse has agreed to provide for you if you should need anything."

"I will not need anything. You have taught me to shoot so I can hunt. I will have the garden to tend and many other things to do to keep me busy, but I will still miss you."

"I know you will. I will miss you, too," Joshua said.

"I will think of you often and worry about you," Dancing Flower said.

It was at that moment that Spotted Horse came around the corner of the cabin. He came with two bundles of pelts on a horse.

"Are you sure you have room for these?" he asked as he pointed at the bundles stacked in front of the cabin.

"I am sure. I will do my best to trade well."

"I'm sure you will."

Nothing more was said for sometime. They were busy taking the bundles of pelts and hides and tying them on the backs of the horses Joshua was using for packhorses. Once it was done, Joshua tied the lead of one horse to the next so the horses could walk in single file along the narrow trails he would have to travel on his way to the Missouri River.

CHAPTER EIGHT

Joshua Travels To Fort Pierre

After giving Dancing Flower several kisses and saying goodbye to Spotted Horse, Joshua took the reins of the lead horse, swung onto its back and started down the trail. He looked back and waved several times at Dancing Flower before she was out of sight.

It was going to be a long journey to the trading post. Joshua would leave the Black Hills and follow the trails leading to the Cheyenne River. From there he would follow the Cheyenne River downstream to where it flowed into the Missouri River.

He had been told by some mountain men heading west that the Fort Pierre Trading Post was not very far south of the juncture of the two rivers. Since he had not come to the Black Hills following the rivers, he wasn't sure if the information he had was correct. Even if it wasn't, it didn't matter. He would just continue to follow the Missouri River down stream until he found it.

Travel was slow, but the weather had been fairly comfortable. His travel time was shortened on some days due to heavy afternoon and evening thunderstorms. Other days he could travel until it was almost dark.

The days soon turned into weeks. The horses fed on the grasses along the river bank. Joshua would stop regularly so the horses could drink from the river. He would camp under the large cottonwood trees along the river's edge. The large cottonwood trees would provide him with branches to hang his shelter on when the weather was not good. They would also provide him with firewood for cooking.

As the summer grew hot, Joshua came to where the Cheyenne River flowed into the Missouri River. Staying on the west bank of the Missouri, he headed south toward the place where the trading post was located. He was not sure how far it was, but it didn't really matter. He had pelts and hides to trade. He had to go to wherever he could trade them.

Joshua had not traveled very far along the Missouri River when he came upon a place where four men were sitting around a campfire. Joshua stopped suddenly and looked over the men. There was something about these men that caused Joshua to become vigilant and cautious. It was probably the fact they were sitting around a fire in the middle of the day that caused Joshua to become cautious. It was reason enough for Joshua to be suspicious of them. Any man sitting around in the middle of the day was either sick, lazy or up to no good, at least to Joshua's way of thinking. None of the men looked sick or injured. He thought about going a different way, but it was too late. He had already been seen.

One of the men saw Joshua and smiled. He leaned over and said something to the man next to him. They looked back at Joshua and smiled.

"Come in," the man said pleasantly. "Sit down and have a cup of coffee."

Joshua was hesitant, but what choice did he have? They were on the only trail in the area, and it was too difficult to go around them. There was also the fact he had been seen. Joshua cautiously moved closer to their camp, stopping just long enough to tie his horses to a nearby tree. He then took his cup from his pack and walked over to the campfire.

"Help yourself to the coffee," one of the men said.

Joshua leaned down, picked up the coffee pot from the fire and poured some into his cup. He then set the pot back on the fire, but didn't sit down.

"Sit a spell," another one said.

Joshua sat down then looked at each of the men. The one who had invited him to sit at their fire was a short, rather stocky man with broad shoulders. He had the look of a frontiersman, but Joshua thought he looked like he might be a bit on the lazy side. He might have thought that because the man was lying against a log, and he looked unkempt. The man had a rather large potbelly, his hair was uncombed and his beard was dirty with tobacco stain in it. His clothes were as dirty as the man himself. He carried a rather long sharp knife on his belt, and there was a rifle leaning against the log he was reclining against.

"Where ya headed?" the one who had told him to help himself to coffee asked.

Joshua didn't like the looks of that man any better. He was a little taller than the others, and had shifty eyes. He was also slimmer than the others and seemed a bit nervous. He had a thick mustache stained with tobacco juice. He was wearing a coonskin cap. His hair hung out from under it and looked tangled enough that he would not be able to get a comb through it. He looked as if he had not had a bath in a month, maybe more. He also had a rifle leaning against a tree about three or four feet away. What troubled Joshua the most was he kept eyeing Joshua's horses and the load of pelts they carried.

"I'm going to Fort Pierre."

"Tradin' furs, are ya?" the third man asked.

Joshua didn't really want to answer his question, but it was a little too obvious what he had on the horses. The third man was as dirty looking as the others. He was sitting on a log holding a cup of coffee in both hands. His hands looked like they hadn't done a day's work in years.

However, it was the forth man who seemed to bother Joshua the most. He hadn't said a single word. He just sat there looking at Joshua with cold dark eyes. He was a tall man with dirty blond hair. His beard was short and his teeth yellowed from tobacco and strong coffee. The way he looked at Joshua made him think it would not take much for the man to become violent. He just looked mean.

"Yeah," Joshua answered as he turned his attention to the man who had spoken to him.

"Looks like ya had a good season."

"I did okay," Joshua replied casually.

Joshua was getting a bit nervous. There were too many guns and knives very close to the men. He had a feeling these men would do him harm, and take his pelts if they thought for one minute they could get away with it without getting hurt in the process.

Joshua wanted nothing more than to get away from them. He decided it would be best if he could figure out a way to get away from them without making them suspicious, or without upsetting them which might cause them to attack him. He would try to leave in such a way as to avoid making them angry, or make them think he didn't trust them. Joshua was sure they already knew he didn't trust them.

Joshua finished his coffee and stood up. He shook the few drops of coffee left from his cup.

"Thanks for the coffee, but I have a long way to go. I think I should get a move on."

"What's your hurry? The tradin' post ain't goin' nowhere," the short stocky man said with a grin.

"I need to get back to my woman," Joshua said with a smile.

Joshua turned and walked back to his horses. He didn't like having his back to them. He felt it was more dangerous to turn his back to them than it was to turn his back to an Indian. He held his hand on the pistol in his belt while listening to make sure they didn't try to sneak up behind him or go for their guns. He heard no movement on the part of the four men. He was sure they had seen the gun he carried in his belt as well as the knife.

As he untied his lead horse, he watched the four men. They remained at the fire and watched him as he swung up onto the back of his lead horse. They watched as each of his horses walked by their camp. With the way they were looking over his horses, Joshua was sure they were appraising the value of the load each horse was carrying.

Since Joshua had not seen any horses around the camp, nor had he seen a canoe or any other kind of boat; he thought they might be on foot. If that was the case, he would move a little faster. Just because he had not seen or heard their horses, didn't mean they were on foot. He couldn't picture them walking. He thought they were too lazy to walk. He was sure they had horses somewhere close by.

As soon as he was around the next bend where they could no longer see him, he nudged his horses along a little faster than he had been traveling. He wanted to put as much distance between him and the men as he could before dark. He kept up the faster pace for several miles before he let the horses slow down to a steady walk. Joshua may have slowed his pace a bit, but he kept his horses moving.

It was getting on toward dark when he found a place where he felt he could stop for the night. It was off the trail a little ways, and it would be easy to hide his horses from anyone on the trail. After unpacking his horses and staking his bundles of furs, he hobbled them in a small clearing to eat and sleep. He set up his camp close to the edge of the woods so he could duck back into the woods if he should be attacked. He decided he would do without a fire, and eat hardtack and jerky with a little water tonight. It would be too easy for an enemy to find him if he had a fire. Even if it couldn't be seen, a fire could be smelled for some distance.

He ate his meal then leaned back against a tree where he could look out over the small clearing where his horses grazed and slept. It had been a long day and he was tired, but he sat under the tree and listened to the night. As the night went on, he found himself dozing off, then waking with a start. He couldn't seem to keep his eyes open. He finally drifted off to sleep.

* * * *

Joshua had dozed off, but woke suddenly when he felt something wrap around his chest. It pulled him hard against the tree he had been leaning against. His eyes flew open. Joshua quickly realized someone had wrapped a rope around him and was pulling him tightly against the tree. He struggled for only a moment before he realized it was of little use. He would have to wait and hope his moment would come, then he would strike back and strike back hard.

"Thought you could get rid of us, did ya?" the short stocky man said to him. "Sam, take his guns and knife."

The one who had said nothing at their camp, reached over and took Joshua's knife then looked it over. He smiled as he looked at it before holding it up for the others to see. It was obvious that Sam thought it was a good knife.

"That's a nice knife, Sam. You can keep it if'n ya want. He ain't goin' ta have no more use for it."

Sam smiled then slipped the knife in his belt. He turned around and took Joshua's rifle and pistol as well. Joshua should have kept going, even if it meant traveling all night. It was too late to worry about that now. Instead, it was time to figure out what he could do to escape, and get his pelts back.

"Hey, Jessup. You should see these," the taller of the four men said. "These here are some of the best furs I've seen in a long time."

"I had a feelin' they'd be nice, Lester."

"Billy, tie him tight. I want ta take a look at them furs."

"Okay, Jessup," Billy said.

Joshua could feel the rope being tied tighter around him, but he also noticed Billy was not paying attention to what he was doing. He seemed to be more interested in Joshua's furs than in tying a proper knot. Joshua could see that the knot Billy was tying was not a very good one. Billy apparently didn't know how to tie a knot that would hold fast. Joshua was also well aware of the fact they had failed to search him for any other weapons.

"Leave them furs bundled, Lester," Jessup said. "We'll load 'um back on his horses and take them, too."

"But won't they get us for horse stealin'?" Billy asked. "We could get hung for that."

"Look at them horses, stupid. Them's Injin ponies. Ain't nobody goin' ta think twice about 'um. Besides, by the time they find his body, ain't nobody goin' ta be able ta recognize him anyways. Now let's get outa here."

"What about him?" Lester asked as he pointed at Joshua.

"Lester, you and Billy get them horses loaded up," Jessup said. "Sam, you wait here 'til we've been gone for a little while, then you can take your time killin' him."

Sam didn't say a word. All he did was nod his head and smile, and occasionally make a grunting sound.

While three of the thieves loaded the bundles of pelts onto the horses, Sam watched impatiently. He could hardly wait to get at Joshua.

Joshua worked to loosen the rope while Sam watched and waited for the others to get the pelts loaded onto the horses. The knot Billy had tied allowed the rope to slip a little when Joshua moved against the rope. Each time it slipped, it gave Joshua a little more room to move. When he finally had enough room to move his arms, he leaned forward while watching Sam. When he was close enough, he reached inside his high-top moccasins and pulled out a small knife. He concealed the knife in his hands, then waited for his opportunity.

Once the pelts had been loaded on the horses, Jessup walked over to Joshua. He knelt down next to him with Sam standing close by watching.

"Sam can't talk none. Ya see, an Injin cut his tongue out after he screamed at the Injin for scalpin' his folks. Now he's goin' ta scalp ya, then he's goin' ta cut your throat,"

Jessup said with a grin. "By the time anybody finds ya, there won't be nothin' left of ya".

Joshua didn't say anything. Joshua wanted more than anything to kill Jessup, but if he did he would certainly be killed by the others. He could wait for a little while. He would wait until the others had gone, and he would have only Sam to deal with. Once they were out of sight, he would kill Sam.

"Got nothin' ta say?" Jessup asked, then laughed.

Again Joshua said nothing. He simply looked at Jessup. There was nothing to say. He would simply wait for his chance.

Jessup stood up, looked at Joshua for a moment and then started walking away while Sam stood by Joshua and watched them leave. Sam was too busy watching the others as they were leaving to pay any attention to Joshua.

Keeping an eye on Sam, Joshua cut the rope then held the ends together in his hands so Sam would not be able to see that the rope had been cut. Joshua then prepared himself to do what he had to do.

Sam began to smile to himself as he watched the other three thieves leave. He was sure he was going to enjoy what he had planned for Joshua.

As soon as three of the thieves had gone around the bend and were out of sight, Sam turned and looked down at Joshua. Sam held the knife up in front of Joshua's face giving him a chance to look at it. He wanted to make sure Joshua would know that he would be scalped and then killed with his own knife. Joshua waited.

When Sam knelt down beside Joshua, he reached out and took hold of Joshua's hair. Just as he started to lean forward to scalp Joshua, Joshua swung his arms free. In one swift move, he stabbed Sam just under his ribs. Sam's eyes got big with surprise and his mouth flew open as if to scream, but he only made a groaning noise. The knife fell from Sam's hand. When Sam looked down at Joshua,

Joshua stabbed him again, then rolled to the side as he pushed Sam away. Joshua quickly got out from under the rope and stood up. He looked down at Sam.

Sam was lying there on the ground with his eyes open. He was dead, but the look of terror and surprise remained on his face.

Joshua quickly grabbed up his knife and tucked it into his belt. He then took Sam's gun along with his ball and cap pouch and powder horn. They had left behind Joshua's pouch of hardtack and jerky, and his bedroll. Joshua rolled everything he could into his bedroll and put it over his shoulder like a bandoleer.

After taking back his own pistol from Sam, he started off at a run to go after the thieves and his pelts. Joshua grabbed up his rifle that was leaning against a tree on his way by it. He wasn't sure how he would get his pelts back, but he was now armed and would get them back or die trying.

Joshua suddenly stopped. He slowly turned and looked back at where he had camped. He had suddenly realized that the three thieves left riding on horses that were not his. It could only mean they had left a horse somewhere back in the woods for Sam. Without a horse, he might not be able to catch up with them before they got to a trading post and sold the pelts they had stolen from him.

Joshua began slowly walking back toward where his camp had been. He moved very quietly in the hope of hearing something that would tell him where Sam's horse was hidden. By the time he got back to where his camp had been he had heard nothing. He stood silently while looking around. Just as he was going to start his search of the area, he heard what sounded like a horse chomping on grass. He smiled to himself and started walking toward the sound. He found a horse saddled and ready to ride tied to a tree. The horse had eaten all the grass around the base of the tree.

He untied the horse, put his foot in the stirrup, swung his leg over the saddle and sat down. Joshua had never used an American saddle before, but found it very comfortable. Having been raised in England, he was only familiar with the smaller, lighter English saddle.

Joshua nudged the horse in its sides and started down the trail after the thieves. He set a gait that would allow the horse to cover a lot of ground without wearing out the horse too quickly. He was going after his pelts, and he didn't want to waste any time getting them back.

The horse Joshua was riding was a good horse. It was strong and liked to run. Joshua rode along the trail at a good pace hoping to catch up with those who had stolen his pelts well before they got to the trading post. Once his furs were sold, he would not be able to prove they had been stolen from him.

Joshua kept an eye on the trail to make sure the thieves didn't cut off the trail somewhere along the way. He also paid close attention to what was ahead of him. Joshua wanted to make sure he saw them before they saw him. He knew he was outnumbered and would need every advantage he could get, no matter how little it might be.

As Joshua rode after the thieves, he noticed the trail made a sweeping turn as it followed the bend in the river. Off in the distance, he thought he could see several horses through the trees. They were walking along the trail as if out for a stroll.

Joshua pulled up and sat on the horse as he looked through the trees. He had to make sure it was his horses he was seeing. After a moment or two he was sure. Now all he had to do was figure out how to get them back.

While trying to figure out how he was going to get his pelts and horses back, the horses stopped moving. Joshua continued to watch the thieves carefully as he wondered what they were doing. The thieves appeared to be discussing something. He wasn't sure what was going on until he saw one of the riders swing his horse around and start back up the trail at a pretty good pace.

Joshua realized they must have started to wonder what had happened to Sam. If Sam had killed Joshua like he should have, Sam would have caught up with them by now. He knew he had to do something very quickly or the rider would see him. He looked around and saw a large cottonwood tree hanging over the trail. The branches were full of leaves making it hard to see if there was anything or anybody in the tree.

Joshua jumped down off the horse and quickly tied it behind some bushes where it could not be seen from the direction the rider was coming. He then ran over to the tree and climbed up into it as fast as he could. Once in the tree, Joshua quickly moved out onto the branch that was directly above the trail. Gripping his rifle with one hand and holding on to a branch with the other, he waited.

Through the leaves, Joshua could hardly see who was riding so fast, but he was ready. Holding onto the branch tightly with one hand, he swung the rifle down as the rider passed under the branch. The rider saw the rifle coming at him a split second before it hit him. He had not been quick enough to duck the rifle as it came at him. The butt of Joshua's rifle caught the rider on the side of his head and knocked him off his horse. The horse continued to run down the trail a little ways without its rider.

Joshua scrambled out of the tree and ran toward the rider. He got to the rider just as he was trying to stand up. Joshua hit him again with the butt of his rifle, knocking him out. He turned the rider over and found it was the younger of the thieves, Billy. Since he was out cold, Joshua dragged him off the trail and down into a shallow ditch. Joshua quickly tied Billy to a tree and put a gag in his mouth to prevent him from warning the others if he should come around.

Leaving his horse tied to the tree, Joshua began to work his way along the edge of the trail toward the thieves. Keeping close to the bushes along the trail, he was able to sneak up to within less than thirty feet of the two remaining thieves without being seen. He hunkered down behind a bush and watched them as he tried to decide what to do next. He could hear Jessup and Lester talking.

"Ya don't think that trapper got loose and kilt Sam, do ya?" Lester asked.

"Na. Sam would have killed him. He was tied pretty good," Jessup said.

"Then why do ya think he's takin' so long?"

"Ya know Sam. He enjoys his work. Remember what he did ta the last trapper we took furs from?" he said as he laughed.

"Yeah. Ya could hear him scream for miles," Lester laughed.

Joshua had heard enough. He raised his rifle and pointed it at Jessup then slowly cocked it.

"Don't either of you move unless you want to die," Joshua said in a clear firm voice.

Hearing the sound of Joshua's voice confused the two men for a few seconds. Suddenly, Jessup dove into the bushes alongside the trail. Joshua had no time to shoot at him.

Lester was confused and looked around as if he didn't know what to do. He suddenly started to move around behind the horses, but he was too slow. Joshua pulled the trigger and shot at Lester. The slug from the rifle hit Lester in the leg, putting him down in the middle of the trail. Lester screamed with pain as he laid on the trail grabbing his leg. The horses shied and trotted down the trail a little ways.

Joshua quickly drew his pistol from his belt and waited. He listened to see if Jessup was going to try to fight back. Being careful to keep his pistol where he could reach it quickly, he began reloading his rifle. As soon as his rifle was ready, Joshua tucked his pistol back in his belt and called out to Jessup.

"You ready to give me back my furs?"

"I wondered if'n it was you. At first I thought it was someone else tryin' ta steal our furs," Jessup replied.

"They are not your furs."

"They is as long as I have 'um."

"Well, I guess they won't be yours much longer."

"That remains ta be seen."

Just then there was the sound of a gun being fired and a lead ball crashing through the branches of a tree just to Joshua's left.

"That was close, weren't it?" Jessup said with a laugh.

Joshua didn't say anything. He had seen were the shot had come from. It was time to move, but he had to do it very quietly.

"You'll never sneak up on me. I've got good cover here. I can wait ya out 'til Billy gets back."

"Jessup, help me," Lester called out in pain as he looked toward Jessup.

Joshua could see Lester and where he was looking. It gave him a good idea where Jessup was hiding. Slowly and carefully, Joshua pulled back away from his position behind the bushes. He worked his way back along the trail. Joshua stayed in the bushes so he could not be seen by Lester or Jessup.

When he was far enough back around the curve in the trail, he cut across the trail to the other side then ran in among the trees. Joshua quickly began working his way back to where Jessup was hiding.

It wasn't long before Joshua could see Jessup hiding behind a large rock. He was still looking toward the bushes where Joshua had been. He could see Jessup was getting a little nervous. He had not heard or seen Joshua for several minutes, although to Jessup it probably seemed more like hours.

Joshua took careful aim at Jessup. He was about to tell him to give it up when Jessup turned and spotted him. Jessup started to swing his rifle around, but he was not quick enough. Joshua pulled the trigger. His gun fired and the lead ball caught Jessup square in the chest. Jessup rose up and fell backwards over the rock.

Lester had tried to scream to warn Jessup, but he had been too late. Jessup lay in the grass behind the large rock with his eyes looking upward at the sky. The front of his shirt was covered with his blood.

Joshua reloaded his rifle before he stood up and walked to the trail. He turned and walked back along the trail to where he had left Sam's horse. He gathered up all the horses and secured them to a tree so they would not run off.

He then walked back down the trail and got Billy. Billy was awake, but had a terrible headache. He marched Billy to where Lester was lying on the trail, then tied him to a tree at the edge of the trail.

He gathered up all the weapons and added them to the packs on his horses. When he had everything secured on the packhorses, he walked back to Lester and Billy.

"Jessup and Sam are both dead," Joshua said. "The two of you are the only ones left. By all rights, I should hang both of you for stealing my horses and furs."

"Oh, God, please. Don't hang me," Billy cried.

"Why shouldn't I? You knew what you were doing."

"Please, mister," Lester pleaded as he looked up at Joshua.

Joshua looked at the wretched souls. He knew they would have taken his life in a heartbeat, and two of them had even tried. Although Joshua had no reason to show them mercy, he couldn't help but think killing them when they were so helpless was not the right thing to do. He had never killed a man for the sake of killing. He certainly had never killed anyone except to protect his life, his family or his property.

"I will spare your miserable lives on two conditions," Joshua said as he looked at them. "The first is I get to keep your horses."

"You can't leave us here without horses," Lester said.

"Since you put it that way, I'll just hang you now and take them anyway. I think I have earned them."

"No. You can have them," Billy said.

"Lester?" Joshua asked as he looked at him.

"You can take them," he said relenting, not really having a choice.

"You said two conditions." Billy said, getting a harsh look from Lester.

"The second is you leave this territory forever. If I see you again, I will shoot you on sight with no warning."

"We'll leave," Billy said then looked to Lester for his response.

"Yeah. We'll leave," Lester agreed reluctantly.

"Good. I will leave you one horse. Back along the trail is a trail that goes south. I suggest you take it. I hear Texas is nice this time of year. It's a lot nicer there than it is for you here. If you choose to follow me, I will kill you both. Do you understand?"

Billy looked at Lester, then turned and looked at Joshua. He nodded that they understood.

"What about our guns?" Billy asked. "We'll need them for protection."

"I will leave you one gun with a small amount of powder and shot around the next corner. I'll leave it with a horse. If you are smart, you will take my advice and leave this territory as quickly as possible. And Billy, clean and dress Lester's wound as soon as you can. If it gets infected, he will most likely die."

"Yes, sir."

Joshua turned and walked to where he had tied the horses. He picked out one of the horses, tied one rifle to the saddle and put a few rounds of shot and one powder horn in the saddle bags. He then walked over to the other horses. He mounted the one he had been riding, took the reins of the lead horse and headed on down the trail. When he got well around the corner, he stopped long enough to tie the horse with the rifle on its saddle to a tree, then went on his way. He had gained three horses with saddles and saddle bags, three rifles, four pistols and several knives. He considered them payment for all the trouble he had gone through to recover his furs.

Joshua rode on down the trail leaving the thieves behind to make their way as best they could. It may not have been the right thing to do, but it pretty well assured Joshua they would not be following him anytime soon. He would keep an eye out for them, just the same. He hoped they would take his advice and head south.

CHAPTER NINE

The Trading Post

It was another three days before Joshua arrived at the trading post in Fort Pierre on the Missouri River. He tied his horses to the hitching rail out in front of the trading post, then looked around before going inside.

The trading post was a fairly large log building with only two windows in the front. It had a large covered porch with a few of the items that were for sale or trade scattered around it. As Joshua stepped up on the porch, he noticed there was a single blade plow that could be drawn by a horse, or pushed by a man. There were hoes, shovels and rakes, many of the things it would take to make working in a garden a little easier. There was also a barrel containing some axes. He could see hammers and other smaller tools through the window.

Joshua walked into the trading post. The first thing he noticed was a good number of weapons on the wall behind a long counter made of rough cut boards. Standing near the end of the counter was a tall slim man with wire rim glasses hung low on his large nose. He was wearing black pants, a white shirt with the sleeves rolled up and a black vest open in front. The man had a pad of paper in one hand and a pen in the other. He was looking over the top of his glasses at Joshua.

"There somethin' I can do for you?" the man said as he looked Joshua over.

He noticed Joshua was dressed like a frontiersman and had probably been trapping furs. He took note of the rifle Joshua held in his hand and the pistol he had tucked in his belt. The man smiled mostly to himself as he thought he had a trapper in front of him who would be more interested in a jug of whiskey to get drunk on, than anything else he might have to trade.

"I have some furs I'd like to trade, if the price is right."

"Well, that's what I do," the man said with a smile. "You just go right ahead and bring 'um on in?"

"I've got a lot of them. You might want to come outside and take a look. Besides, there's better light out there."

The trader realized the man in buckskins standing in front of his counter was no ordinary backwoodsman. He spoke better English than anyone he had heard for a very long time, and he was prepared to trade. The trapper was obviously well educated and was not going to be easily taken.

"Okay," the man said as he put the pad of paper and pen down on the counter.

Joshua watched the man as he came around the end of the counter and walked toward the door. Joshua let him go out first then followed him out onto the porch. He could see the man's reaction as he looked at the horses with the packs of pelts on them. He turned and looked at Joshua. He smiled. Joshua wasn't sure if the smile was because he was surprised to see so many pelts of such good quality, or if he was thinking he was going to make a good deal of money off the trade. Either way, Joshua would make sure he got what was due him.

"You sure have a lot of furs. You must have had a good season. Where were you trappin'?"

"Out west," Joshua replied, not wanting to say too much to the trader, especially about where he had come from.

"I don't think I know you."

"You don't. I'm new to this part of the country."

Joshua watched him as he began to look over the pelts again. He watched as the trader checked them for quality. He could see the trader nod his head slightly as he looked at what Joshua had to offer for trade. He seemed to like what he was seeing. When the trader finished looking at the pelts, he glanced over at the three saddled horses. He then turned and looked at Joshua.

"If you don't mind my askin', where'd you get the saddled horses?"

"What business is that of yours? I don't plan to trade them."

"I think I know who they belong to."

"You might, but they don't have any use for them anymore," Joshua said as he looked the trader straight in the eyes.

The trader looked at Joshua for a minute. He understood what Joshua meant. He turned and looked at the other horses, then turned to look at Joshua again.

"The horses with the furs on them, they look like they might be Indian ponies. Did you get them the same way?"

Joshua had no problem understanding what he meant, either. He was getting a little impatient with the trader asking so many questions.

"You ask a lot of questions," Joshua said. "Just so we understand each other, the three saddled horses once belonged to some highwaymen. I believe you call them robbers in this country. They tried to kill me and steal my furs. I took my furs back. Two of the four who tried to steal my furs are dead. The other two are headed south toward Texas on one horse, if they know what's good for them. I figure I earned those three horses just getting my furs back from them.

"The Indian ponies, I traded fair and square for them. They are not for sale."

"You won't get no argument from me. The fellas that once owned them saddled horses have been stealin' furs from trappers for the past couple of years. They got what they deserved. I got just one more question for you. Why did you let the other two go? You coulda hung 'um and no one would care."

"One was shot up a bit. He'll be crippled for the rest of his life, but he will live if he takes care of himself. The other was a young fella. He wasn't ready to die. I left him to help the other."

"You interested in selling the Indian ponies? I'll give you a good price for them."

"No. They're darn good horses and I plan to keep them," Joshua said. "Now, are you ready to talk about trading for my furs, or do I go on to Omaha?"

The trader began to think he had better trade fair with this woodsman, or he would go downriver to trade. He wanted the pelts. It had been a long time since he had seen pelts as good as these, and he knew he could get a good price for them back east. He also knew the trapper was no fool. If he tried to skin him on the value of the pelts, the woodsman would take his business somewhere else.

"I'll trade with you, and I'll trade fair," the trader said. "I ain't seen furs like these in a long time. I'll give you a good price for them."

Joshua and the trader commenced to talk about trading. When all was said and done, Joshua traded his pelts for supplies that would help get him and Dancing Flower through the winter to come. He also got a few tools to help him build a barn and enlarge his cabin. Joshua picked out some tools to use to build fences and to work around their garden. He got several sacks of flour, coffee and sugar, and a good amount of gold, too. He picked out a bolt of calico cloth he thought Dancing Flower might like to make curtains for the cabin and maybe a table cloth. She might want to make herself a summer dress, too.

Joshua also traded for the small plow on the front porch to turn the sod so they could have a larger garden and plant an area to raise oats for the horses. He took the guns he had taken from the robbers and traded them for two breach loading rifles and a few boxes of cartridges, and a new colt pistol that could be loaded with six shots.

Once all the trading was done, Joshua loaded his supplies and tools on his packhorses. He tied the horses together, one after the other. Joshua mounted up and started back along the same trail he had used to get to the trading post. He glanced over his shoulder to make sure all was well, and that he was not being followed. He quickly noticed the trader was standing on the porch of the trading post watching him.

Joshua knew he had made a good trade with the trader, but he didn't trust him to keep quiet about it. The trader was very talkative, a little too talkative to Joshua's way of thinking. He was more than likely to brag about the fine pelts he had gotten at such a good price. Joshua especially didn't trust the trader to keep his mouth shut about the fact he had paid Joshua a good amount of gold in the deal.

CHAPTER TEN

Trouble On The Plains

As Joshua moved along the trail, he began looking for a place where he could leave the trail and head off in a different direction. After he was a couple of miles away from the trading post, and he was well out of the sight of the Fort Pierre Trading Post; he left the trail that ran along the river. He started off across country. He headed due west like he had when he first headed out to seek his fortune.

Shortly after he turned off the trail, he stopped. He swung out of the saddle and tied the lead horse to a tree. Joshua walked back to check to make sure he didn't leave any tracks for others to follow. Satisfied that he had not left a trail, he mounted up and headed straight west away from the Missouri River instead of going on north to where he would have turned west along the Cheyenne River.

As darkness started to come over the land, Joshua continued to travel under the light of an almost full moon for several hours. He traveled well into the night before he found a place where he could spend the night. He hobbled the horses, then laid out his bedroll near some trees next to a small creek where he could keep an eye on them. He sat against a tree and listened to the sounds of the night. He soon fell asleep to the sounds of the horses chomping on the lush green grass that grew at the base of the trees.

Joshua woke as the sky to the east was just starting to get light. He looked around and found all his horses still sleeping. Joshua rolled out of his bedroll and sat up. He pulled his rifle and pistol out from his bedroll where he had put them for the night. He had wrapped them in the bedroll to keep them out of the morning dew. They would also be where he could get at them in a hurry.

He stood up and leaned his rifle up against a nearby tree. While he stretched to take the stiffness out of his muscles, he heard a twig snap somewhere behind him in the trees. Joshua quickly grabbed his rifle and ducked down behind a large tree near his bedroll to wait and listen. He had not been able to tell if it was an animal or a man that had made the noise, but he was ready for either. He glanced over at the horses. Their ears were up and they were all looking toward where the sound had come from. They gave him no hint as to what was there, but they had obviously heard the twig snap, too.

Time passed slowly as he listened for any sound that shouldn't be there. In the early morning quiet, he heard a sound that was almost like someone whispering. He realized there was someone out there.

Since whoever it was had not called out and asked to come into his camp, it was clear they were there to do him harm. There was little doubt in Joshua's mind they were there to steal his horses, supplies and the gold he had been paid for his pelts.

Joshua also had a pretty good idea how they found out what he had. He didn't trust the trader he had dealt with at Fort Pierre to keep his mouth shut. It occurred to him that the trader might have hired these men to follow him and steal back all he had traded to Joshua, plus his horses. The trader had shown a good deal of interest in his horses.

Joshua listened for a moment, then slowly and quietly slipped back away from the tree into the brush. He had to make sure he was not anywhere near where they thought he would be. Since they seemed to think he was close to a big cottonwood tree, Joshua moved further away from the tree. He slowly worked his way around behind them, being very careful not to make a sound.

By the time it was light enough for them to see, Joshua had moved behind a fallen tree about fifteen feet or so behind them. Joshua could see them clearly. They were hiding behind a couple of trees and had their guns in their hands.

Joshua quietly laid his rifle over the top of the fallen tree and aimed it at one of the men. It seemed as if the two men were ready to ambush him.

"I can't see him," the younger man whispered. "Where'd he go?"

"When you stepped on that twig, he must have heard it. He probably rolled over behind that old cottonwood tree. He's probably layin' down at the base of it waiting for us to make our move," the older man said.

"Then again he might be behind you with a gun pointed right at your back," Joshua said in a calm clear voice.

The sudden sound of Joshua's voice behind them caused them to freeze. There was little doubt in their minds that with a man like Joshua behind them, they stood little to no chance of getting out of there alive. They were sure he was the kind of man who would give them the same kind of a chance they had planned to give him. But to make a move against him without knowing exactly where he was would be about the same as committing suicide.

"Very carefully, put your guns on the ground and slowly stand up. I suggest you make no sudden moves if you expect to live very long. You with the red sash first."

Joshua watched the two men very carefully for any sign they might try something foolish. The older man was the one with a red sash around his waist. The older man reached out to his side with his rifle in his hand. He very carefully set his rifle down on the ground. He then stood up and slowly turned around. He thought about drawing his pistol from his sash as he turned, but when he saw Joshua had his rifle aimed right at him, he quickly changed his mind.

"Very slowly drop the pistol on the ground. If you touch it with more than two fingers, you will be dead before it hits the ground," Joshua assured him.

Joshua could see the look on the old man's face. His eyes were squinted and Joshua could see the anger on his face. The old man was mad as hell that he had been caught so easily by a frontiersman.

The older man knew he had no choice but to do as Joshua said or he would die. He dropped the pistol on the ground then put his hands in the air.

"You're next," Joshua said to the younger man. "Drop your guns on the ground."

Still keeping his gun pointed at the older man, Joshua watched the movements of the younger man. The younger man dropped a rifle and a pistol on the ground, put his hands up, then turned around. It was clear to Joshua that the young man was in fear of losing his life. He could see the sweat run down the young man's face even though the morning air was cool.

"Now put your hands on your head and step away from your guns."

They did as they were instructed, reluctantly.

"Now, turn back around."

As soon as they had turned around, Joshua moved in behind them. He knew if he gave them even a hint of a chance to get to him, they would take it. Joshua realized if he took his eyes off them for only a second while he gathered their guns, they might turn on him. He also realized he could not handle their guns and his own without leaving himself vulnerable.

Since the older man was the one who had shown in the way he looked at Joshua to be the one most likely to cause problems, Joshua needed to put him out of action. He needed to search him for any other weapons he might have. In order for Joshua to search him and maintain control of them at the same time, he walked up behind the older man and laid the handle of his heavy knife over the back of the old man's head. The old man fell to the ground out cold. At least for the moment, the younger man was the only one Joshua would have to deal with.

Joshua set his rifle against a tree and drew his pistol from his belt. Keeping an eye on the younger man, he walked him over to his camp. He then took a rope and tied the younger man to a tree. Joshua was now free to move around without fear of them getting the best of him. Joshua searched the younger man for weapons and found a small knife in his boot. He took the knife and put it in his belt.

He went back to where the older man laid. After tying the older man's hands behind his back, Joshua searched him and found a knife in his boot and one in the red sash. He put the knives in his belt, then gathered up their guns and stacked them near his bedroll. He discovered they had newer guns that were much better than what he had. Even better than the ones he had just gotten at the trading post. He packed his horses with all his things. He took the two new rifles, the two new pistols and the knives, along with the holsters for the pistols and added them to his gear. He then walked over to the young man and stood in front of him.

"Where are your horses?"

The young man didn't say anything. It was clear he would need a little urging to get him to tell. Joshua drew his large and very sharp knife from his belt and held it in front of the young man's face.

"Now, where are your horses?"

"Back over behind those big bushes," the young man replied quickly, the fear for his life in his voice and on his face.

Joshua slipped his knife back in his belt and walked back to the bushes where he found two horses. The horses were saddled and ready to ride. He took the horses to where his horses were standing and tied them to a tree. As soon as he was ready, he walked up in front of the kid and looked him square in the eyes.

"Since it was your plan to kill me and steal my supplies and horses, I figure you owe me. In payment for sparing your miserable lives, I'm taking your horses and your guns. You have any objections?"

The kid just looked at him. He was afraid if he objected, he would be killed and Joshua would take them anyway.

"I didn't think so," Joshua said after a moment. "If you don't panic, you should be able to get lose after awhile. I suggest you don't try to follow me. If I should ever see you again, anywhere in this country, I will kill you on sight. You explain that to your friend. Is that clear?"

Yes, sir," the kid said.

"If you do get loose before some critter comes along and has you for dinner, I strongly suggest you start walking back to where you came from. I'm doing a lot more for you, than you planned to do for me. In fact, I'm leaving you alive which is more than you would have done for me. But that will change very quickly if I ever see you again. Is that clear?"

"Yes, sir."

Just then the older man came around and looked at Joshua. His face showed how angry he was. He tried to move but found his hands tied behind his back.

"I will hunt you down and kill you for this," the older man swore, his voice showing how mad he really was. "You can count on it."

Joshua looked at the man and decided he had to make a decision. He would either have to watch over his shoulder until the man found him and one of them died, or he could dish out justice right here and right now.

"You really mean that, don't you?" Joshua asked him.

"You can put money on it. I'll find you and kill you and all your family," the old man said with his jaw clinched tight with anger.

"I guess you have made it clear what I have to do," Joshua said as he let out a long breath of disappointment.

As Joshua walked over to the man's horse and took the rope off the saddle, the man kept yelling profanities and threats in defiance. Joshua tied a loop in the rope as he walked over to a large cottonwood tree and tossed the rope over a large branch. He then went to the man, grabbed him by the front of his shirt and jerked him to his feet. The man spat at Joshua.

Since the man still had his hands tied behind his back, Joshua spun him around and marched him over to his horse. He set the man in the saddle then led the horse to the tree, all the time the man was cursing him.

"You goin' to hang him?" the kid asked as Joshua put the rope around the man's neck.

"You bet. He tried to steal my horses and supplies. That is a hanging crime. I gave him the chance to live, but he decided that if I let him live he would come after me. I'm not going to be looking over my shoulder for him to try to kill me and my family."

"You can't just hang him," the kid pleaded.

"I can, and I will. I can also hang you for the same crime. You want to hang with him?" Joshua asked in anger.

"No," the kid said softly.

"When you get loose, you can bury him or not. I can assure you, I will not care."

All the time Joshua was preparing to hang the man and talking to the kid, the man continued to threaten Joshua. Joshua couldn't believe the man had so much hate in him that he would continue to curse and threaten him.

Joshua looked up at the man and said, "May God have mercy on your soul, not that you deserve any."

Joshua took the reins of the horse and walked the horse out from under the man. As the horse came out from under the man, the man's legs kicked and thrashed around for several seconds. It didn't take long before the man hung limp from the tree. As soon as Joshua was sure the man was dead, he took his knife and cut the rope. The man dropped to the ground in a heap. He then turned and looked at the kid. The kid was looking at the ground in front of him.

"It's up to you, kid. You can bury him or let the coyotes have him."

Joshua looked at the young man for a moment or two before turning around and walking over to the horses. He tied the horse to his string of horses, then mounted up. He nudged his horse forward and started off with his string of horses, while leaving the kid tied up and the man lying on the ground below the cottonwood. He never looked back.

CHAPTER ELEVEN

New Friends And A Surprise

The days had turned into weeks as Joshua moved across the prairie. It was late in the afternoon when he came upon a place that looked inviting. The water in the creek was clear as it flowed slowly by, and the grass along the edge of the creek was thick and green. Large cottonwood trees grew along its banks spreading their shade over the grass. Joshua decided it was a good place to spend the night.

After taking his supplies off the horses, he took the horses down to the creek for a well deserved drink of cool water. When they were finished, he took them back in among the trees where the grass was rich and plentiful. He hobbled the horses there, then returned to the creek to wash his face and fill his coffee pot with water.

After building a small fire, Joshua began setting up his camp while he brewed his coffee. He cooked his meal, then cleaned up after he was finished eating. He then had time to lean back against a tree and watch the sun set over a low ridge off to the west.

It was a very quiet evening with only the sounds of a couple of coyotes howling at the moon as it came up in the eastern sky. The sky was filled with tiny specks of light. There was a slight breeze coming out of the northwest. It was just enough to cause the leaves in the trees to move slowly back and forth on the branches.

It seemed so peaceful. He wished he was already home, but knew he had many more miles to travel. He was missing his wife, and longed to hold her again.

Although Joshua was thinking about his wife and their place at the edge of the Black Hills, he was well aware of his surroundings. Every sound was registering in his head where he would decide if it was something for him to worry about, or if it was just the normal sounds of the prairie at night.

Joshua slept very peacefully that night. When morning came, he rolled out of his bedroll, stood up and looked around. It was a quiet and peaceful morning. There were antelope off in the distance and birds singing in the trees. He fixed himself breakfast then packed his horses. As soon as he was ready, he put out his fire, took a look around then went on his way.

* * * *

As the days went by, Joshua kept an eye out for any danger that might come his way. He also kept an eye on the land. He wasn't looking for anything special, just getting to know the lay of the land, so to speak.

As Joshua made his way across the prairie, he came upon a herd of buffalo. He stopped and looked over the herd. He first looked at the herd of buffalo, then at his horses. He was trying to decide how many of them he could use. He wanted the hides and some of the meat, but he didn't want to waste any of them by killing more than he could use.

While looking over the herd, Joshua quickly discovered he was not the only one interested in the herd. Off on a ridge to the north of where he was, he saw a small hunting party of Indians who were looking over the buffalo. They didn't seem to know if they should try to kill some of them or not. They looked like members of the tribe that had befriended him, but he wasn't sure. Since there were only five braves, and he carried a six-shooter, he decided to take a chance and began waving until they saw him.

When they saw him waving, they rode closer. He realized he didn't know them, but they continued to come toward him. He slipped his hand over the handle of his pistol and waited for them to come closer. They stopped only a few yards in front of him, Joshua raised his hand in peace and began talking to them in their own language.

"Are you planning on hunting a few buffalo?" Joshua asked.

He knew they couldn't carry more than two or three. Joshua also knew they were not prepared for the task of hunting buffalo.

"Yes, but it is dangerous to hunt so many buffalo when we are so few," one of the older braves said.

"I can help you if you would like. I can kill them from here."

One of the younger braves laughed and pointed at Joshua. It was clear that he had never seen a rifle like the one Joshua carried, and had no idea how far it could shoot. They knew nothing of hunting buffalo from one position.

Joshua noticed there were two of the Indians who had rifles, but they were both saddle carbines. They were not made for shooting long distances.

"I will show you, if you like," Joshua said with a grin.

"Show us," the young brave said as he grinned, feeling pretty sure of himself.

Joshua walked over to a slight rise in the ground and laid down. He took careful aim and pulled the trigger. The gun fired and a buffalo went down, but the others did not run.

Joshua turned and looked over his shoulder at the young brave and smiled. The young brave could not believe his eyes. He looked from the downed buffalo to Joshua, then back at the buffalo.

"How many would you like? I can get more for you," Joshua asked the older brave.

Still very surprised at what Joshua had done, they found it hard to answer him. After a short time the oldest of the braves looked at Joshua and spoke.

"We can only handle two."

"I will kill four, two for you, if you will help me prepare the other two for me."

The braves looked at each other as if trying to decide if it was a good deal. Since there was little to no risk to them, and they didn't have to do anything but skin them and prepare the meat for travel, which they would have to do anyway if they killed any of the buffalo, they nodded that they agreed. After all, if he could kill the buffalo without them having to risk injury or death, then it was a good deal all around.

"We will help you," the older brave promised.

Joshua went to work and killed four buffalo in all, then ran off the others. The Indians kept their promise to help with the buffalo. The hunting party stayed and worked alongside Joshua for two days to prepare the buffalo hides and the meat for travel. Once the buffalo had been prepared for travel, Joshua said his goodbyes to the hunting party. He then continued on his way across the prairie while the hunting party went in a different direction.

Joshua was sure they would have a story to tell around the council fire when they got back to their camp. He smiled to himself as he wondered how many of their tribe would believe them.

* * * *

Joshua had been gone for over three months when he returned to his cabin at the edge of the Southern Black Hills. As he came into the valley where the cabin was located, he noticed there were several Indian ponies grazing in the small corral he had built before he left. There was not only the horse he had left with his wife, Dancing Flower, but one he knew belonged to Spotted Horse. He wondered who the other horses belonged to and why they were there.

Joshua rode up to the corral and swung down out of the saddle. He tied the lead horse to the top rail of the corral then turned to go inside the cabin. Just as he got to the door, Spotted Horse came out. He had a serious look on his face.

"It is good to see you, but what are you doing here?" Joshua asked Spotted Horse. "Is there something wrong?"

"Dancing Flower has not been feeling well. We have come to help her care for your place until she gets better."

"What is wrong with her," Joshua asked as a concerned look came over his face.

"She is going to have a baby. Not today, but when the heavy snows come. She had been working too hard and needed to rest. We just came to help her."

"She's going to have a baby?"

"Yes, but there is nothing to worry about," Spotted Horse assured him. "She is fine. She just worked a little too hard. You can go in and see her. We will take care of your supplies and horses."

Spotted Horse stepped aside and let Joshua pass him. When Joshua entered the cabin, he saw Spotted Horse's wife, Morning Star, sitting beside Dancing Flower on the bed. Dancing Flower was lying on the bed. Morning Star looked at Joshua and smiled as she got up and left the cabin. Dancing Flower smiled up at Joshua as he sat down on the bed next to her.

"Do not worry, my husband. I just did a little too much today. I will be fine with a little rest."

Joshua leaned down and kissed her lightly on the forehead. After a moment or two of looking at each other, Joshua began to tell her about his trip to Fort Pierre and how well he had traded his goods. She was pleased with his success. She didn't really like to hear how he came to have so many horses, but he had made it home safe, and that was all that was important.

In the following days, Joshua took over the heavy work around the cabin as well as setting the traps for beaver. He built a larger corral for the additional horses with the help of

Spotted Horse, Running Deer and several of the other Indians.

While he worked on the corral, Joshua explained to Spotted Horse how he came to have so many more horses. Spotted Horse wondered why Joshua had not killed all of those who had stolen from him.

Joshua spent a lot of his time working in the fields around the cabin cutting hay. He stacked it in piles so they would have something to feed the horses during the winter when it would be too difficult for the horses to forage for themselves.

Dancing Flower recovered quickly and once again worked alongside Joshua. As the days went by, Dancing Flower grew larger. She carried the child well, but tired easily. It became more and more difficult for her to do several of the heavier chores that needed to be done.

Although some of the chores were considered women's work by a few of the men of Spotted Horse's tribe, Joshua simply did what had to be done. He had grown up in a home where it was the job of the husband to help out even if it was considered woman's work by some.

* * * *

It was a cold evening in late November when Joshua came home after checking his trap lines. He heard what sounded like Dancing Flower scream as if in pain. Joshua dropped the line of beavers and ran toward their cabin. With his gun in his hand, he crashed through the door. Expecting the worst, he was surprised to see Dancing Flower lying on the bed. He looked around the room, but saw nothing wrong. Looking at Dancing Flower, he could see her face was covered with sweat, but she was smiling at him.

"The baby is coming," Dancing Flower said, breathing hard.

"What do I do," Joshua asked, his voice showing how nervous he was.

He had never had any experience delivering a baby. The closest he had ever come to helping in the delivery of a baby was when he helped deliver a colt in his father's barn in England. That hardly provided him with the experience he would need to deliver his own child.

"Get Morning Star. And hurry," Dancing Flower said anxiously. "And hurry."

Joshua hesitated only for a second before he turned and ran out to the corral. He quickly put a bridle on one of the horses then jumped up on its back. He raced across the field and through the woods to where Spotted Horse and the rest of the tribe had set up their winter camp.

As he rode into the camp, he began yelling for Morning Star. When he pulled up in front of Spotted Horse's tepee, Morning Star came out. She looked up at him.

"Is it time?" she asked.

"Yes. She needs help," Joshua said almost in a state of panic.

"I will go to her," she said with a smile. "Give me your horse."

Joshua jumped down from the horse and held the reins. Morning Star swung up on the back of the horse, grabbed the reins from Joshua, then quickly started out at a gallop toward Joshua's cabin.

Spotted Horse came out from behind the tepee and took Joshua by the arm. He began leading him toward the area where the tribe kept their horses. They picked out two horses then swung up on their backs and headed to Joshua's cabin together.

When Joshua and Spotted Horse arrived at the cabin, they found his horse grazing peacefully in front of the cabin. They slid down off the backs of the horses. Joshua ran to the cabin, opened the door and rushed in. He found Dancing Flower lying on the bed with a baby lying quietly on her chest. The baby was wrapped in a small piece of a buffalo hide.

Dancing Flower looked very tired, but she had a big grin on her face.

"You have a son, my husband," she said proudly.

Joshua moved over next to the bed and sat down on the edge of it. He leaned down and kissed Dancing Flower on her forehead. He then looked down at the small bundle and saw his son for the first time. He had never thought about what it would be like to be a father. It was a strange feeling for him. He was both proud and scared at the same time. What did he know about raising a child?

"He is so small," Joshua said as he looked at his son.

"He will grow up to be strong and handsome like his father," Dancing Flower said.

"What should we name him?"

"You told me that the boys in your family were often named after elders of your family."

"That is true."

"What name from the elders of your family would you like to name him?"

"What would you think of naming him, Jeremiah? It was my grandfather's name."

"Jeremiah Higgins. That is a good name," Dancing Flower said with a smile.

"We must give Dancing Flower time to rest," Morning Star said interrupting the moment. "It is time for you to take care of the horses and the beavers you left lying on the ground."

Joshua looked at Morning Star as if he didn't understand what she was talking about, but quickly remembered he had dropped the line of beavers on the ground and ran to the cabin when he had heard Dancing Flower's screams. He also realized she was trying to get him to let Dancing Flower get some rest. He again leaned over and kissed his wife on the forehead, then stood up. He took another look at his wife and son, smiled, then left the cabin.

As Joshua took care of the beaver pelts and the horses, he had a hundred thoughts go through his mind. He now had two people to provide for. Maybe it would be wise if he were to change his way of providing for his family. He didn't like the fact that hunting often took him away from their home. Farming and raising a few cattle was all he knew how to do, other than hunting and trapping. It was not the first time he had thought of changing the way he provided for Dancing Flower and himself, but now he had another to take care of and provide for.

Although the beaver had provided them with much of what they needed, it was becoming harder and harder to trap them. There seemed to be fewer of them. It was becoming clear that he would not be able to support his family by trapping for many more years. He would have to think on it. Maybe it was time to build a farm like his parents had in the old country.

Although they had built a cabin for Dancing Flower for while he was away trading his pelts, it was mostly to give her better protection from the weather and to give her more room than was found in a tepee. He couldn't help but think it would not be very difficult to make it their permanent home. The cabin had been built so it would be easy to make it bigger.

When he finished taking care of the beaver pelts, he looked over the land around him. He began thinking about making the place into a permanent home for him, Dancing Flower, and now his son, Jeremiah. It was good land. It had plenty of good grass, good soil and plenty of water.

Although he had thought about turning to a different way of making a living for his family, he had not planned on doing it so soon. Whatever he decided to do, he would have to start planning for it now. Winter was just around the corner. He would need to start by hunting and harvesting the vegetables from their garden and from the forest. He would have to work hard to get more beaver pelts. The coming winter could very well be the last winter he would be able to get enough beaver pelts to provide for his family.

CHAPTER TWELVE

The Winter Visitor

The days soon began to turn colder as time passed and winter began to spread over the southern Black Hills and the bordering rolling plains. The days grew short and ice formed on the ponds making it more difficult for Joshua to clear his traps and reset them.

It was on the day after New Years Day when a nasty storm suddenly blew in and made even going outside difficult and extremely hazardous. Dancing Flower was cooking a meal in the fireplace while Joshua was playing with his son on a rug made from the hide of a large bear Joshua had killed several months ago. Although the wind was blowing hard and the snow was blowing around the small cabin, it was warm and cozy inside.

"It will be very cold tonight," Dancing Flower said as she stirred the pot on the fire.

"Yes, it will," Joshua replied. "I will have to stoke the fire in the middle of the night tonight."

Suddenly there was a noise at the door. It was a sound they had not heard before. At first Joshua thought it was an animal trying to get in out of the wind and snow, but he wasn't sure. The more he heard the sound, the more he began to think it was not an animal.

"Take Jeremiah," Joshua said. "Wrap him up warm and take him over to the bed."

As soon as Dancing Flower took Jeremiah, Joshua got his pistol and checked it as he moved next to the door. He reached out and took hold of the latch. He then looked at Dancing Flower and saw she had Jeremiah wrapped in a buffalo robe. She was clutching him close to her as she looked at Joshua.

Joshua turned and looked at the door for a second as he mentally prepared himself for a confrontation with whatever was out there. He silently counted to three then jerked open the door. As the door flew open, an Indian wrapped in a heavy blanket staggered into the cabin. Joshua grabbed the Indian as he started to fall. He held him upright as he pulled him into the cabin then quickly kicked the door closed.

It was not hard for Joshua to see that the Indian was almost frozen to death as he lowered him to the floor. He knelt down next to the Indian and pulled the blanket away from his face. Joshua immediately recognized the young brave as one of those who had attacked Spotted Horse and his braves almost two years ago, but they had been driven off. He didn't know the Indian's name, but he remembered him as being very young to be in a raiding party.

"This young brave was in the raiding party that attacked us while we were out hunting. It was when Running Deer was wounded," he said to Dancing Flower.

"I remember. What will you do with him?"

"I should toss him back out in the cold to freeze to death," he said looking at Dancing Flower.

"But he is just a boy," Dancing Flower replied with a shocked look on her face.

"He is old enough to be a warrior now."

"He is still just a boy."

Joshua looked at the young brave, then at Dancing Flower. He thought of a time when he needed help.

"Your people took a chance on me. I will take a chance on him. He may not live, but we will try to save him," Joshua said to Dancing Flower.

"I will get a couple of buffalo robes to cover him. Move him over next to the fire so we can warm him," Dancing Flower said as she laid Jeremiah down on the bed.

After laying the young brave on a buffalo rug near the fire, Joshua moved back. He sat down on the bench next to the table where he could keep an eye on the brave. He laid his pistol on the table within easy reach. If the brave came around suddenly, he wanted to be close enough to his pistol so he could protect his family. He didn't really expect the brave to be able to cause him any problems, but he needed to be ready just in case.

Once they had done all they could for the young brave, Dancing Flower took Jeremiah and put him down for the night. She kissed Joshua before she laid down on their bed.

"If you get tired, you can wake me. I will watch over him so you can rest," Dancing Flower said.

It was well into the night and the sky was starting to get light before the young brave started to come around. He was still shivering when he opened his eyes and looked around. One of the first things he saw was Joshua sitting at the table looking at him. His eyes got big when he recognized Joshua as the man who had the long rifle that could kill at a great distance.

"Are you feeling better," Joshua said in the Lakota language.

The young brave just looked at him and didn't say anything.

"Can you speak?"

"Yes," the young brave said softly.

"If you promise to cause me and my family no trouble, I will not tie you up. We will help you until you are able to travel, then we will let you return to your family. Do you understand what I'm telling you?"

"You will not kill me?" the young brave asked, somewhat surprised at the man's trusting attitude.

"No. I will let you go as soon as you are able to travel and the weather improves. In return, you will leave me and my family alone to live in peace. All I ask is for your promise."

"You will kill me."

"If I wanted to kill you, I would have thrown you back out into the storm and let the storm kill you slowly. I would not have brought you into my cabin so you could live."

The young brave looked at Joshua and wondered what kind of a man he was. He had never seen or even heard of anyone doing anything like it before. If all he had to do was to promise not to cause any trouble, he could stay there until he was able to travel. He was not sure if he should trust the man, but to be thrown out into the cold was not a pleasant thought, either.

"I will do as you say. I will not give you any trouble."

"Good. What is your name?"

"It is Runs Fast."

"That is a good name. You are welcome in our home. Are you hungry?"

"Yes," he replied cautiously, still not sure if he should trust the white man.

Joshua had heard Dancing Flower moving around by the bed. He looked over his shoulder and saw her sitting on the edge of the bed watching them. She got up and moved over next to the fireplace. She dished up a bowl of buffalo stew for Runs Fast and gave it to him. He began to eat. When he was finished, he laid back down and rested.

Over the next few days Runs Fast improved as did the weather. He even started to follow Joshua around as he went to his traps and cared for his horses. Joshua had found Runs Fast's horse while he was out taking care of his own horses. He found the horse where it had taken shelter in a grove of trees. The horse had been eating on a stack of hay Joshua had cut to feed his horses. He had put the horse in the corral with his horses.

During his stay with Joshua and his family, Runs Fast had kept his promise. Finally the day came when it was time for Runs Fast to return to his family. The day was sunny and bright, but it was still rather cold. Joshua walked with Runs

Fast to the corral where Joshua had taken his horse. Dancing Flower had made up a bag with some food for Runs Fast.

"I must be going," Runs Fast said. "My father will be worried about me."

"Have a safe trip back to your people," Joshua told him.

"I will tell my father how you helped me. He will be pleased and will not attack you again."

"Thank you. I would like to have your father as a friend. I must tell you, if your tribe should attack my friend Spotted Horse and his tribe again, I will take the side of my friend and fight with him. I will show no mercy. You see, I'm a member of Spotted Horse's tribe. His sister is my woman."

"I understand. I will explain it to my father. I'm sure he will understand."

"Good. As long as you come in peace, you and your father will be welcome here."

Runs Fast nodded that he understood then swung himself up onto the back of his horse. He smiled at Joshua then turned his horse and headed off to the northeast.

Joshua watched Runs Fast until he was out of sight. When he was gone, Joshua returned to the cabin.

"Do you think he will keep his word?" Dancing Flower asked.

"Don't know. I hope he does."

"So do I," she said, then turned and went back into the cabin.

Joshua looked out over the fields he had claimed and wondered if he had done the right thing as far as Runs Fast was concerned. Deciding that it was too late to worry about it, he set out to check the ponds for any beaver he might have caught in his traps. Joshua knew he must keep a sharp eye out for danger. He was not sure Runs Fast would keep his word, or his father would listen to his son.

CHAPTER THIRTEEN

A Time To Plan For The Future

The days slowly passed making for a long cold winter. Joshua continued to trap and hunt, although there were days when the weather would not even let him go outside. He was rapidly finding it was getting harder and harder to trap enough beaver to make a good living. Dancing Flower and Joshua would sit up late into the night and talk about what they needed to do if they were going to continue to live there.

Joshua spent time with Dancing Flower telling her what it was like growing up in England on a small country farm. He told her about the farm his parents had, and about milking cows, raising pigs, and growing their own vegetables. And he told her about hunting different birds and small game on the land.

He told her about the few fruit trees on the farm, and of picking the apples to make apple sauce and apple pies. He had to take a moment or two to explain what apple sauce was, and how to make it. She hoped someday she could try the thing he called apple sauce. It sounded very good.

As Dancing Flower listened to stories of how Joshua had lived in England, she became more and more interested. She had spent most of her life moving with the buffalo as the large herds roamed over the vast plains. She had never lived in such a place as Joshua had described to her. It was something she would have to think about, and think about it she did.

Some of the things she thought about were the difficulties in always having to move. Taking down and putting up of the tepees, packing and unpacking the animals, and never knowing where the buffalo were going to go. There was also the problem of finding enough fuel for the fires to cook their food when out on the plains.

The weather was always a concern. Lightening storms would often start wildfires on the open plains, which could race across miles of the prairie faster than a horse could run.

Dancing Flower also thought about the comfort and the protection from the weather the cabin provided. The tepees did not provide good protection from the heavy thunderstorms and the strong winds that often occurred on the plains. There was no question life on the plains was a hard life.

One evening after Joshua had come home from a hunting trip with Spotted Horse, and after Jeremiah had been put down to sleep for the night, Dancing Flower sat down at the table with Joshua. She looked over at her son, then back at Joshua. She looked down at the table as she gathered her thoughts. She wasn't sure how to tell Joshua what she had been thinking about over the past few weeks, but she wanted him to know what was on her mind. Dancing Flower then looked up at Joshua and smiled.

"This spring you will go and sell your furs again?"

"Yes," he replied, then waited for her to continue as he wondered what was on her mind.

"You have talked to me about what you think will happen to the buffalo. You have also talked to me about how you lived in that far away land you call England. When I think about all the things we have talked about, I think it is time to talk about the changes we will need to make if we are to stay here and live here all the time."

"Okay."

"The way you talk about how you lived when you were a child, I think you would like to live that way again?"

"Yes, but not there. I do not want to go back to England to live. I would like to settle down and live here much like that, but different."

"I do not understand." She said, looking confused. "You have told me about how you lived in that far away land, and how much you liked it. How would you want it to be different?"

"We have much more land here than my parents had in England. Here I would take the money from the pelts and hides and buy a few cows and a bull or two. We would raise cattle and horses on our land. We already have a good start on raising horses.

"We would raise our own meat, but we would still do some hunting for deer, antelope, elk and a buffalo from time to time so we would have a variety of different kinds of meat.

"We would have to raise most of our own vegetables as we did this past year, but we would not have to move around as the buffalo move.

"This place would become our home all the time?"

"Yes. We would live here all year round."

"We would no longer move about on the plains?" she asked as she began to think seriously about what Joshua was suggesting.

"That is right," he said with a grin. "We could raise enough cattle to cover the land with them like the buffalo of the plains."

"We would do that from only a few cows and a bull or two?" she asked as she looked at him with surprise.

"Well, no. Not from a few cows. We could get a lot of cows and a few bulls. Then we could raise cattle for a living."

"Are you sure they would cover the land like the buffalo," Dancing Flower asked, smiling, not sure he was being totally honest with her.

"Well, maybe not that many, but there could be a lot of them."

"Would there be more than we could use?"

"Yes. Well, maybe not at first, but we could raise a lot of cattle."

"What would we do with the cattle we do not need?"

"We would sell them back east to help feed the people there. By selling some of them, we could buy other things we need like sugar and coffee."

"It would be much like we trade beaver pelts?"

"Yes. Very much like that," he said with a smile. "Except we would not have to kill and skin them first. We would drive them east and sell them there. Other people would kill and butcher them, then sell the meat to those who live in the cities. We would only kill and butcher what we need."

Dancing Flower sat and looked at Joshua while she thought about what he had said. She wasn't sure if he was being truthful, or if he was exaggerating a bit. But she did have some concerns she wanted to talk to him about.

"Most of my family would follow the buffalo herds during the summer. I would not see my family as much." She said with a concerned look on her face.

"I'm sorry, but that is probably true. We would still see them in the fall and winter when they come back to their winter camp and hunting grounds."

He thought it might not be a good time to tell her that he thought Spotted Horse's days of hunting the buffalo might be numbered. But he knew she needed to know what he thought the future might bring them.

"The day may come when Spotted Horse will not be able to follow the buffalo any more. If that day should come, he could work with us here. There would be plenty of room for all of us."

Dancing Flower looked at Joshua for several minutes as she thought about what he had said. Although she would not be following her family around the plains, she would still have them near during the winter.

She would also not have to pack up and move every few days which was a pleasant thought to her. She would have a cabin that would keep out the cold, the wind and the rain much better than the tepee. That too was a pleasant thought.

"I think maybe I would like to live like you say, too. We would have to make the cabin bigger if we are to stay here all the time."

"We can do that. We could even have a few more children," he said playfully.

"Yes. That would be nice. We will need more children if we have to watch such a large herd of cattle," she said with a serious look on her face, but with a twinkle in her eyes.

"That is true," he agreed.

"When do we start?" she asked with a smile.

"Start?" he asked looking at her. "You mean, when do we start having more children, or when do we start making the cabin bigger?"

"Both," she said with a smile. "We could start with the children now. I think it is too late in the day to start making the cabin bigger," she said with a smile and a sparkle in her eye.

Joshua smiled at her as he stood up. He led Dancing Flower to their bed. Joshua put a couple of logs on the fire to help keep the cabin warm. He then turned around, blew out the lantern and quickly joined Dancing Flower in their bed.

CHAPTER FOURTEEN

Dancing Flower Attacked

When spring started to show itself, the days began to get longer. Joshua split his time between cutting trees for logs for the addition to the cabin and trapping beaver.

Since Jeremiah was still very small, Dancing Flower would carry him around on her back while she skinned the beaver and prepared the beaver pelts for trading. Sometimes she would put him in his cradleboard and lean it against a fence post so he could see her as she worked in the garden.

The day was sunny and fairly warm. Joshua was out in the woods cutting trees for the new addition to the cabin when he heard a loud scream coming from near the cabin. He dropped his ax and grabbed up his rifle, which he always kept nearby, and ran toward the cabin. As he came rushing out of the woods, he saw three young Indians. They were grabbing at Dancing Flower while she was trying to fight them off. They were too busy fighting with Dancing Flower to see Joshua come running across the yard to rescue her from her attackers.

Joshua ran up and quickly struck one of the Indians in the head with the butt of his rifle. The blow to the young brave's head knocked the Indian to the ground with a nasty deep gapping cut.

The second Indian saw his friend go down. He let go of Dancing Flower and started to come at Joshua with a knife. It was the last thing he did. Joshua swung his rifle up and pulled the trigger. Shooting from the hip, he shot the Indian at point-blank range. The slug from Joshua's rifle hit the Indian in the chest killing him instantly.

Joshua turned and looked for Dancing Flower, but didn't see her. He did not know where she had gone. He wondered if there were others around who had taken her. He knew there was at least one brave, but didn't see him. It suddenly registered in his mind that he had not seen Jeremiah, either.

"Joshua!"

The sound of Dancing Flower's cry for help behind him caused him to swing around quickly. He saw Dancing Flower standing in front of the cabin door. Her eyes were big with fear. The third Indian had chased Dancing Flower into the cabin and now had one arm around her waist. He held a big knife at her throat.

Joshua did not have to be told what to do. He slowly and carefully laid his rifle down on the ground and stepped away from it, never taking his eyes off the Indian. He watched the Indian very carefully for some clue as to what he would do.

Joshua was a patient man. He would wait for his chance to get the upper hand. When he did, he would do whatever was necessary to free Dancing Flower from danger.

"I will kill your woman if you do not back away," the Indian said in Lakota, his native language.

It was obvious the young brave was scared and very nervous. Their effort to take Dancing Flower had not worked out anywhere near like the Indians had planned. The brave now found himself trying to figure out how to get out of the mess he found himself in with his skin still intact.

"If you harm my woman, you will never hunt the buffalo again. You will never see your family again. You will not even see the sun rise again. And you will feel pain as you have never felt it before. This I promise you," Joshua said in the young brave's language.

There was no question in the young brave's mind that Joshua meant what he said. The Indian looked around as if he was looking for a way to escape, but what he saw were his two friends lying dead on the ground.

"I have killed your friends. You cause any harm to my woman and you will join them in death, only it will be a slow death. If you let her go unharmed, I will let you go. But believe me when I say, if I see you again, I will kill you on sight."

The Indian wasn't sure if he should believe the white man. He didn't trust the white man. But as he thought about his present situation, there was little else he could do if he wanted to live.

Just as he was thinking about what he should do, he heard the sounds of several Indians as they came rushing out of the woods near the cabin. The sudden appearance of the band of Indians coming to Joshua's aid, made the lone Indian very nervous and very much afraid. He began twisting and turning in an effort to keep his eyes on all of those who had encircled him. There was little doubt in the young brave's mind they wanted to kill him. He could see the anger in their eyes.

"Spotted Horse, stop. STOP," Joshua yelled out for fear that their sudden appearance would cause the lone Indian to panic and kill Dancing Flower.

Spotted Horse called to the others to stop and stand their ground. There were eight of Spotted Horse's braves who had circled the lone Indian. He was now surrounded and growing more nervous and more terrified by the minute.

"You have my word that you will not be harmed if you let my woman go unharmed," Joshua said, trying very hard to keep his voice calm.

"What of the others?" the young brave asked. "Will they not harm me?"

"They will not harm you if you leave without harming my woman, but you must leave and never return. If you return, you will be killed. It is your only way to get out of here alive. It is your only way to ever see your family again. There is no honor in killing a defenseless woman. Even the

Great Spirit will be unhappy with you, and you will never get to the happy hunting ground," Joshua said.

Looking at Spotted Horse, it was clear to Joshua that Spotted Horse didn't like the idea of him letting the young brave just walk away. Joshua was not sure if the young brave tried to leave that Spotted Horse and his braves wouldn't kill him anyway.

The young brave looked around. It was obvious he was trying to think of some way to get away without losing his life. He had no desire to die. It was rapidly becoming clear that there was no other option for him if he wanted to live. He could only hope the white man would keep his word.

"I will do as you say," the young brave said. "I will leave your land and never return."

"That is good. You let my woman go, unharmed, and we will step aside and spare your life."

The young brave was still not sure they would let him go. He had but one choice if he was to leave there alive. The young brave slowly took his knife away from Dancing Flower's throat.

"Spotted Horse, tell your braves to step back and let him leave," Joshua said.

Reluctantly, Spotted Horse did as Joshua asked. He stepped back and told the others to do the same. He also told them to honor Joshua's promise to the young brave.

As soon as they had backed away, the young brave took his arm from around Dancing Flower's waist. She immediately ran to Joshua and stood behind him and looked at the young brave.

"You go, and don't ever come back." Joshua said.

The lone Indian looked around at the others watching him. He slowly began to walk as if he was going to leave, but stopped when Spotted Horse moved toward him. Spotted Horse stepped up close to him and looked him in the eyes.

"That was my sister you held a knife on. If I see you anywhere, I will kill you. Now go before I change my mind and kill you now."

The brave looked at Spotted Horse for only a second before he took off running. He quickly headed north. As he disappeared into the woods, Spotted Horse motioned to three of his braves to follow him and make sure he kept running north. When Joshua saw the three braves follow the lone brave, he looked at Spotted Horse.

"I promised him he could go free if he let Dancing Flower go free unharmed."

"I did not promise him anything except he would die if I ever saw him again. My braves are not going after him to kill him. They are just making sure he leaves. If he decides not to leave this place, they will kill him."

With a sigh of relief, Joshua smiled at Spotted Horse. He then turned and took Dancing Flower in his arms. It was at that moment they heard Jeremiah cry. Dancing Flower smiled up at Joshua then turned and went into the cabin.

"We will take care of the dead," Spotted Horse said. "You should spend time with Dancing Flower and your son. They need you now."

Joshua nodded then went to the cabin. Once inside he sat down on the edge of the bed with Dancing Flower. He watched her as she held their son in her arms and comforted him. Joshua wasn't sure if Dancing Flower was comforting her son, or if she was being comforted by holding him in her arms. Either way, it seemed to help them both.

Joshua spent the rest of the day close to the cabin. He didn't want Dancing Flower to be left alone at least for the rest of the day. He worked on the corral and worked to clear the area beside the corral for a shelter for the horses.

It wasn't long before three of Spotted Horse's braves came back to Joshua's cabin. Although they had followed the young brave on foot, they returned riding horses. Joshua greeted them as they rode up to him.

"Spotted Horse told us to bring you the horses of the two Indians you killed and the one you let go. He said the dead no longer have a use for them, and the one you let go owed you his horse for letting him live," Running Deer said with a grin.

"Put them in the corral, and thank Spotted Horse for me," Joshua said. "And thank you for coming when you did."

Joshua watched as Running Deer smiled then took the horses to the corral. He knew better than to refuse the horses. Joshua did not wish to offend Spotted Horse. He knew that it was the practice of Spotted Horse to take the horses of his enemy. Joshua had done the same when he was attacked while on a trip to the trading post. It was only right, in Spotted Horse's mind, that Joshua should have the horses since he had killed two of the three Indians that had come to his place and attacked him and his family.

CHAPTER FIFTEEN

A Prediction Of The Future

Time passed and another winter had gone by. The days continued to grow longer, and the wild flowers began to bloom in the fields. The footings for the addition to the cabin were finished, and the stack of logs to build it was growing smaller as they were used to build the addition. The time was once again coming when Joshua would have to take his pelts to the trading post on the Missouri River.

The thought of taking his pelts to the trading post at Fort Pierre reminded him of the problems he had had in getting them there, and in getting what he traded for back home. He did not want to go through that again, but he could see no way around it. His first thought was to find a different place to trade his goods, but the only other trading posts he knew anything about would mean a longer time away from home. He would have to go all the way to Omaha. As far as he knew, Fort Pierre was the closest trading post.

Joshua was walking out to gather his pelts when Dancing Flower called to him from the cabin. He turned and walked back to the cabin. Since he had left the cabin only a short time ago, he had no idea what it was she wanted. Joshua had talked to her of his hesitation to take his pelts to the trading post at Fort Pierre. Maybe she had come up with an idea so he didn't have to go to Fort Pierre.

"What is it?" he asked her as he approached the cabin.

"Morning Star was just here."

"I'm sorry I missed her."

"She was here to tell me of a new trading post south and a little east of here."

"Where is it? Did she tell where it is?" he asked, his excitement clearly showing in his voice.

"Yes. It is located on the Platte River. She said the trader was very honest and would trade with anyone, including Indians. Spotted Horse is going there. He hopes to get a fair trade for his furs. If you were to go there with him, you could travel together. You wouldn't have to travel alone or as far. She said it wasn't as far as the one on the Missouri River."

"It would be nice not to have to travel alone. It would be nice not to have to go to Fort Pierre again. I don't trust that trader."

"Yes, it would be nice if you didn't have to travel alone," Dancing Flower agreed. "It would be safer for both of you."

"When does he plan to leave?"

"In two days."

"That would be good. We could be ready. I will go talk to him. Maybe he would like to travel together."

Joshua kissed Dancing Flower and started off toward Spotted Horse's village. It didn't take him long to get there as it was only a short ways into the Black Hills. When he arrived, he saw several of the women preparing stacks of pelts for travel. They were tied in bundles and stacked inside a shelter Joshua had helped Spotted Horse build. It wasn't a very big shelter, but it would keep the pelts dry and up off the ground. He saw Spotted Horse coming around a tepee. Joshua called to him. They met just outside of the shelter.

"Greetings, my friend," Joshua said as he raised his hand in peace.

"Greetings, Joshua. What brings you here today?"

"Dancing Flower tells me you know of a trading post where we can trade our furs that is closer than the Fort Pierre Trading Post. I was thinking we could go together, if you would like."

"I would like that. Let us talk," Spotted Horse said as he led Joshua to his tepee.

Joshua and Spotted Horse sat down at the fire in front of Spotted Horse's tepee and smoked a peace pipe. Then they talked about where the trading post was located and about traveling together. It didn't take them long to plan their trip, and to discuss what difficulties they might encounter in getting to the trading post.

Once all was settled, they sat and told stories, which was the custom of the Indians when a friend would come to visit. It was a time to enjoy the company of a good friend.

When Joshua returned home, he sat down with Dancing Flower and told her about his visit with Spotted Horse. He also told her about the arrangements he had made to have her looked after while he would be gone and how a couple of the braves would help her with the work that needed to be done.

* * * *

The morning arrived when it was time for Spotted Horse and Joshua to leave for the trading post on the Platte River. Although Joshua had his pelts packed on the back of his horses, Spotted Horse had loaded his pelts on travois'es.

Spotted Horse came out of the woods only a short time after the sun had come up. Morning Star was leading one of the horses. When Joshua saw them, he wondered if Morning Star was planning to go with them.

"Spotted Horse, is Morning Star going with us?"

"No. She wishes to stay here with Dancing Flower while we are gone."

"That is good. Dancing Flower will have someone to talk to while we are gone."

Spotted Horse had three horses pulling travois'es. Joshua had four horses with pelts on them. Joshua tied the horses one behind the other to make travel easier if the trail should be narrow. Spotted Horse did the same with his horses.

When all was ready, Joshua took Jeremiah in his arms and kissed him on the cheek.

"You be a good boy and take care of your mother," he told the boy as if he was old enough to do anything. He kissed his son, then handed the small child to Dancing Flower who was smiling up at the two of them.

"Take good care of him and be sure to take good care of yourself. I do not wish to leave you, but I'm hoping this will be the last time I have to leave you to trade furs."

"It would be nice if you did not have to leave. There is so much to do here," Dancing Flower said.

"I know. When I return, we will start working on building up our place so we don't have to be separated every spring."

"That would be nice. I will look forward to it. Please be careful, my husband. I will miss you every minute you are gone."

"I will miss you, too," he said.

Joshua reached out and took her in his arms. He then leaned over and kissed her as he held her close. He then kissed his son again before he turned to his horses. As he mounted his horse, he looked over his shoulder and saw Spotted Horse kiss Morning Star goodbye.

Spotted Horse swung up on the back of his horse then looked over at Joshua. He smiled then turned his horse and headed out toward the prairie. Joshua waved goodbye to Dancing Flower and Jeremiah then turned his horses and followed Spotted Horse. Spotted Horse and Joshua rode east for a few miles before turning south.

* * * *

The days passed slowly as Joshua and Spotted Horse moved south across the vast prairie toward the Platte River. It would take them several weeks, maybe a little more to get to the trading post they had heard about.

As they traveled across the prairies of the Dakota Territory and the Nebraska Territory, they had seen several herds of buffalo grazing on the buffalo grass that covered the prairie for as far as the eyes could see. Spotted Horse thought of the time when Joshua had killed several buffalo for them and began to wonder why Joshua was thinking about raising the animals he called cattle. It didn't make a lot of sense to him. Why raise cattle when there were so many buffalo on the plains? Was there something different about them that made him want them?

The buffalo had provided the Indians with most of their needs for food and shelter for hundreds of years. The bones were used for such things as utensils and needles for sewing. The hides were used for robes, blankets and tepees, and the meat provided food for all in the tribe. Little of the buffalo was wasted.

Joshua was thinking about the buffalo, too. He was also thinking about how to tell Spotted Horse what was on his mind without upsetting him.

Late one evening while sitting around the fire after their evening meal, Joshua decided to talk to Spotted Horse about the buffalo, but he hesitated. Joshua wasn't sure how to bring up the subject as he wasn't sure how Spotted Horse would take what he believed needed to be said. The last thing he wanted to do was to upset his friend. But wasn't it better to upset a friend than to let him go along blindly to what might happen? A true friend would not do that. He would tell his friend what he thought and how he thought things would be.

They had seen a small herd of buffalo in the evening just before stopping for the night. It had once again brought to mind the subject of hunting them. Spotted Horse decided to talk to Joshua about his decision to raise cattle.

"Why do you wish to raise cattle, my friend, when there are so many buffalo roaming the land? You can hunt them anytime you need them." Spotted Horse asked.

"It is true that there are a lot of buffalo on the plains. But I believe it will not be so in the future," Joshua replied.

"I want to raise cattle not just for my own need for meat, but to replace hunting and trapping for furs as a way to provide for the needs of my family. We can raise enough cattle on the land we have now to help supply meat for those who live back east. There are many people back there and they need meat.

"Why do you think that way? The buffalo have been roaming the plains forever."

"Why do I think that the buffalo will not be so plentiful? I think, - - - no," Joshua said, then took a moment to think about what he was about to tell his friend. "I believe the white man will move out onto the plains of this land, and he will kill off the buffalo in very large numbers.

"I have heard there is a war brewing in the east between the white men from the north and the white men from the south. If the war comes about, it will end one day. When that day comes, when the war is over, I believe more and more white men will move west. Some will move on across the land to make new homes for themselves and their families on the other side of the great blue-gray mountains. But not all of them will go to the other side of the mountains. Some of them will settle out here on the plains. It is the ones that will settle on the plains that worry me.

"They will build roads and expand the tracks for the locomotives to travel on. That will bring even more people to settle the land. They will build towns along the roads and tracks, and people will settle in and around the towns.

"When that happens, it will not be long before the white man will come to kill the buffalo by the hundreds. They will kill the buffalo just for their hides. The buffalo hides make very warm coats. Many will be killed to feed the men that will build the roads and tracks across the plains. They will kill the buffalo by the hundreds," Joshua said again in the hope Spotted Horse would understand.

"It will not happen," Spotted Horse insisted. "There are too many buffalo for the white man to kill."

"My friend, I do not wish to upset you, but take a minute to think back to the time when we met and became friends. It was shortly after I joined up with you, and I was traveling with you to your winter camp. Do you remember the day I killed ten buffalo from a great distance?"

"Yes, I remember."

"Did I kill all ten of them without the rest of the buffalo running off?"

"Yes. You did," Spotted Horse said as he began to think about that day.

"What was there to stop me from killing almost the entire herd?"

Spotted Horse just looked at Joshua as he thought about what he had said.

"If I had had enough powder and bullets, I could have killed almost all of the buffalo in the herd without having to move from the rocks I was shooting from," Joshua said. "I could have killed buffalo all day without fear of having them stampede over me, and without any concern that they would run away."

Spotted Horse sat and looked at Joshua as he thought about what Joshua had said. He could remember the day that Joshua had killed the ten big buffalo. He remembered that he had seen nothing like it. Thinking about it made it easier for Spotted Horse to understand what Joshua was telling him, and why he might believe that way.

Spotted Horse looked out over the plain as the sun was setting in the west. He was wondering if Joshua's vision of the future would come true. The thought of it caused him to also wonder what would happen to his people if all of the buffalo were gone. It saddened Spotted Horse to think what Joshua said might come true.

The buffalo provided many of the things that his people needed just to survive. It gave Spotted Horse reason to be thinking about the future of his people, and to wonder what the future of his people might be.

For the first time in his life, Spotted Horse began to have many disturbing questions race through his mind. What would life be like without the buffalo? Would they have to turn to farming or raising cattle? Would they have to build cabins like Joshua did, and live in one place never to move about freely on the plains?

It was getting late so Joshua and Spotted Horse turned in for the night. Spotted Horse did not sleep well. His mind was filled with thoughts of what Joshua had told him.

When morning came, Joshua noticed that Spotted Horse seemed to be a bit down, and looked tired. He wasn't as talkative as he had been on previous mornings while they were getting ready to move on. Joshua was sure that Spotted Horse was afraid he might be right.

Joshua didn't know what to say to Spotted Horse to make him feel better. Maybe there was nothing he could say. He almost wished that he had not said anything about the buffalo; but he knew that he would feel badly if it all came true, and he had not at least warned Spotted Horse.

Spotted Horse was the first to break the silence.

"Joshua, I have never met a man like you before. You are a white man, yet you tell me what you think the future will be for my people."

"I believe that it was better that I say something than to keep it to myself. I am sorry if I have upset you, my friend. For now, we must get moving. We have a long way to go to get to the trading post. We can talk about it again some other time."

Spotted Horse and Joshua didn't talk any more about the future that day. They continued on to the trading post on the Platte River.

Joshua knew that he had caused his friend to worry. He was also worried about his friend and his people. He was worried about the future as much as Spotted Horse.

CHAPTER SIXTEEN

A Trading Post At A Fort

It was a beautiful early summer day when Spotted Horse and Joshua arrived at the trading post on the bank of the Platte River. As they approached the trading post, Joshua noticed there was also a military fort nearby guarded by U.S. Army soldiers. He also noticed there were four soldiers walking toward the trading post from the fort.

Joshua and Spotted Horse rode up to the hitching rail in front of the trading post just as the soldiers stepped up onto the porch. Joshua took notice of how the soldiers looked at Spotted Horse. The looks on their faces indicated they were interested in knowing what an Indian was doing there, especially with a white man. It was obvious they didn't see very many Indians at the trading post, probably because of the fort close by. Most Indians would tend to avoid a trading post that was located near a military fort because of their feeling about soldiers.

However, there was one of the soldiers that seemed to dislike the fact Spotted Horse was there. He was an older man with a long scar on his face, yet his rank was that of a private. He was a big man with broad shoulders, a barrel chest and big hands. From the looks of him, Joshua was sure he could start trouble at any moment, and he should be ready for it.

Joshua watched the soldier as the soldier watched Spotted Horse. Joshua didn't want any trouble with the soldier, or with any soldier, or with the U.S. Army for that matter. Spotted Horse and Joshua were there for only one reason. They were there to trade their pelts, then be on their way. That was all.

As the distance shortened between Spotted Horse and the big soldier, Joshua reached down and put his hand on his gun. He wasn't looking for trouble, and he was going to do everything he could to prevent it and still protect his friend.

"Where ya think you're goin', redskin?" the private asked of Spotted Horse with a harsh tone to his voice.

The private's dislike for Spotted Horse showed clearly in his voice and on his face. Spotted Horse knew enough English to understand what the soldier had asked, and to answer him.

"Into the trading post to trade my furs," Spotted Horse said in clear English.

"Not at this trading post." The soldier said as he stepped in front of Spotted Horse.

"Excuse me, private, but do you own this trading post?" Joshua asked, knowing it was very unlikely the soldier owned much of anything, let alone a trading post.

"No. Not that it's any of your business," he said as he glared at Joshua.

"That's where you are wrong. It is my business."

"How ya figure, Injun' lover?"

"This Indian is a friend of mine. He has never killed or harmed a white man. I'm sure that is more than can be said about you," Joshua said while keeping a close watch on the private.

"What's that supposed to mean?" the private asked angrily as he clenched his fists.

"It means you are the savage here, not this Indian."

"I'll rip your head off," the private said then he lunged at Joshua.

Joshua was ready for him. He quickly sidestepped the big private as he came rushing at him. Joshua quickly drew his pistol and hit the private across the back of the neck with the barrel of his gun as he went by. The private went crashing face down in the dirt.

Joshua quickly turned around. He was ready to fight with the three other soldiers who had been walking toward the trading post. The first thing he noticed was none of the other soldiers had made a move to come to the aid of the private. One of the soldiers looked at Joshua and smiled, then turned and went into the trading post without saying a word. The other two soldiers followed him into the trading post without comment. Joshua looked at Spotted Horse and together they walked into the trading post, leaving the private lying in the dirt.

"Aren't any of you going to help your friend?" Joshua asked of the soldiers.

"He ain't our friend," was all that one of the soldiers said, then turned and went about his business.

Joshua and Spotted Horse walked up to the counter while the soldiers began looking around the trading post. They talked to the owner of the trading post for several minutes before they went outside. Joshua noticed the private was no longer lying on the ground. He wondered where he might have gone, but was not all that concerned.

"I would be very careful if I were you," the trading post owner said. "That was Private O'Malley you hit on the back of the head. He's as mean as they come, and he'll want you to pay for making him look like the fool he is."

"He had it coming, but we will be watchful. Thanks for the warning," Joshua said with a slight nod of his head.

Joshua and Spotted Horse watched as the trader looked over the pelts they were offering for trade. After several minutes of bargaining back and forth, they agreed on a deal for both Joshua's and Spotted Horse's pelts. Once all the haggling was done and a settlement was agreed upon, Joshua and Spotted Horse started to go outside to load the things they had traded for on their horses.

"You be careful out there," the trader said with a smile. "I would like to see you again, maybe next year."

Joshua looked back at the trader, smiled and nodded. He then turned and started out of the trading post. Spotted Horse was right behind him.

Just as Spotted Horse stepped outside, he saw O'Malley out of the corner of his eye. The big man had a gun in his hand and he was pointing it at Joshua. Spotted Horse reacted instantly by rushing up behind Joshua and immediately pushing him off the porch of the trading post just as O'Malley pulled the trigger of his gun.

Everything happened very quickly. Joshua went stumbling off the porch and fell into the dirt. He heard a shot behind him and quickly drew his gun as he rolled over to see what was happening. He saw O'Malley with a gun in his hand. O'Malley was starting to swing his gun toward Joshua, but Joshua was quicker. Joshua shot O'Malley before he could pull the trigger. Private O'Malley fell backwards from Joshua's shot that hit him squarely in his chest. O'Malley was dead before he hit the ground.

Joshua turned and looked toward Spotted Horse to see if he was hurt. His friend was leaning against one of the posts on the porch. He had his arms wrapped around it. His face showed the pain he was feeling. It was clear he had been hit by O'Malley's shot. Joshua got up and ran to the aid of his friend. He put his arms around Spotted Horse and gently lowered him to the porch.

Two of the soldiers who had been in the trading post came out on the porch to see what was going on. When they saw Spotted Horse lying on the porch, one of them took off toward the fort. One of the other soldiers grabbed a blanket and put it under Spotted Horse's head. It was only a matter of a couple of minutes before one of the soldiers returned with a man in a long white coat. It was the post doctor.

"Move over, young man," the doctor said as he pushed his way toward the injured man.

After Joshua moved out of the way, the doctor looked down at Spotted Horse. He then looked at Private O'Malley lying on the ground in a pool of blood. It was obvious that the private was dead. He looked up at Joshua with a strange look on his face.

"This is an Indian. You want me to treat an Indian after he killed a soldier?" he asked with noticeable anger in his voice.

"He didn't kill the private," Joshua said angrily. "I killed him. He was trying to bushwhack me. Spotted Horse saved my life by pushing me off the porch. As a result, he was shot. That Indian saved my life. Now you're going to save his."

There was no doubt Joshua would backup what he said. He slipped his hand over the pistol grip of his gun as he looked at the doctor. He waited to see if the doctor was going to help Spotted Horse, or not.

"That's right, Doc," one of the soldiers who had been in the trading post said. "Private O'Malley tried to bushwhack him, but this here Indian saved his life."

"That's the way it happened," one of the other soldiers said. "As far as I'm concerned, O'Malley should have been shot a long time ago. He was no good."

The post doctor looked at the two soldiers. It was clear that none of the soldiers felt one bit sorry for O'Malley. They knew O'Malley was mean and would pick a fight with just about anyone, often for no reason at all. Everyone knew O'Malley had spent many a night in the brig for fighting with his fellow soldiers. He had lost several stripes over the years for fighting.

The post doctor didn't like O'Malley any more than the other soldiers. He had patched up a number of solders that O'Malley had picked a fight with. He looked up at Joshua, then at the soldiers standing nearby.

"You two," he said as he pointed to the soldiers. "Get him over to my office."

As the soldiers picked up Spotted Horse and started carrying him toward the fort, the doctor stood up and looked at Joshua.

"I'll do what I can for him. But you'll have to explain to the major what happened and why one of his soldiers is dead."

"Just do the best you can for him," Joshua said as he took his hand off his gun. "He has been a friend of mine for a very long time. And doc, I can assure you, he has never killed a white man, soldier or not. He wasn't even carrying a gun."

The post doctor looked at Joshua for a second, then simply nodded before he headed off toward the Post Infirmary. Joshua started to follow the doctor to the fort.

As Joshua entered the fort behind the doctor, he was met by two soldiers with rifles walking toward him. They immediately stopped him.

"Are you the man who killed Private Sean O'Malley?" one of them asked.

"Yes," Joshua replied.

"You'll have to come with us."

"I would like to see how my friend is doing first."

"The major wants to see you, now," one soldier insisted.

It was clear to Joshua that he had little or no choice in the matter. He looked toward where the doctor had gone and saw the doctor going into a log building with a sign above the door that read "Post Infirmary". He looked back at the two soldiers then looked toward the log building with a sign that read "Post Commander" above the door.

As he started toward the major's office, the two soldiers stepped in behind and followed him to the office. When he stepped onto the porch, another soldier opened the door. The two soldiers that had escorted him to the office followed him inside, then stood at attention on opposite sides of the door.

Joshua saw a man in an officer's uniform sitting at a desk. He couldn't tell how tall the man was, but he looked like he was in good physical shape. Not being familiar with U.S Army uniforms, he was not sure of the rank of the officer. Since he had been told he was to see the major, he assumed the officer in front of him was the major. Joshua waited patiently for the major to look up at him and say something.

The major turned and looked Joshua up and down for a minute before he looked at Joshua's face. He could see Joshua was a strong man with broad shoulders and narrow hips. He was dressed in buckskins and had a pistol and a long knife on his belt.

"Sergeant, take this man's weapons," the major ordered.

Reluctantly, Joshua handed over his pistol and knife to the sergeant.

"What is your name?" the major asked.

"Joshua Higgins."

"What are you doing here, Mr. Higgins?"

"I am here with my friend to trade our furs at the trading post."

"It is my understanding you killed one of my soldiers. Is that correct?"

"Yes. I did kill him, but it was not something I wanted to do, or something I came here to do," Joshua said, his voice clear and unshaken. "I never saw the man before."

"Tell me what happened," the major said as he leaned back in his chair to listen.

Joshua explained what had happened from the time he and Spotted Horse arrived at the trading post. He told the major about their encounter with Private O'Malley. It didn't take him very long to relay a detailed description of what happened.

"I see," the major said. "I will have to detain you here at the post until I have had a chance to verify your story."

"It shouldn't take you very long as several of your soldiers saw what happened. In fact, they are over at the doctor's office right now."

"At least for now, we will care for your Indian friend. But if we find you did anything illegal, we will punish both of you."

"That will be fine with us, because we did nothing but protect ourselves. I know there are many soldiers who do not trust Indians, and with good reason in some cases. There are many Indians who I do not trust. There are also a lot of Indians who don't trust the white man, either. There are many of them who also have good reason. However, Spotted Horse has saved my life several times over the years I have known him, and he did again today. As I told your doctor, Spotted Horse and his small tribe have never killed a white man."

"Sergeant, you will confine Mr. Higgins to a room in the barracks until further notice."

"Yes, Sir."

"Major, I would like to see how my friend is doing first, if you don't mind."

"Yes, of course. Sergeant, you can escort him to the infirmary so he can see his friend then take him to the barracks."

"Yes, Sir."

"Dismissed," the major said.

Joshua turned and looked at the sergeant, then started for the door. He glanced back over his shoulder and saw the major looking down at some papers on his desk. Joshua was not sure if he was looking at the papers, or if he was thinking about what he had been told. Joshua began to wonder how long it would take the major to complete his investigation.

Joshua was escorted to the infirmary by the sergeant and one other soldier. When he entered the infirmary, he saw Spotted Horse lying on a bed. He had his eyes closed, and there was a large bandage on his side. The doctor was over in the corner washing his hands. Joshua walked over to the doctor.

"How is my friend doing?"

"It's hard to tell. He has lost a lot of blood. I got the bullet out and the bleeding seems to have stopped. If all goes well, he stands a good chance."

"I want to thank you for helping him."

"You're welcome," the doctor said with a smile. "It must be nice to have such a good friend, one that would take a bullet for you."

"It is. I would take a bullet for him, if I had to. Can I talk to him?"

"Not right now. He is sleeping. It is best to let him rest."

"I understand."

"Time to go to the barracks," the sergeant said.

Joshua looked at the sergeant then looked back at his friend. He didn't want to leave his friend, but he had little choice. He turned and nodded to the sergeant. The sergeant followed him out of the infirmary, then moved up beside Joshua as they walked toward the barracks.

"I'm kind of glad it was you that shot O'Malley," the sergeant said as he walked beside Joshua.

Joshua looked at the sergeant before he asked, "Why is that?"

"If your Indian friend had shot him, he would have been shot right where he stood."

Joshua didn't say anything more. He knew how a lot of soldiers felt about Indians. Joshua walked to the barracks and went inside. The sergeant pointed to a door to a small room in the corner. Joshua entered the room.

There was a small table and a bed in the room. The sergeant indicated Joshua was to sit down on the bed and wait for the major to complete his investigation. Joshua did as he was directed while the two soldiers stood guard near the door.

Time passed slowly while Joshua waited for the major to do his investigation. The sun was starting to set when the sergeant returned. He took Joshua to the major's office.

"I have completed my investigation and have cleared you of any wrong doing. You are free to go," the major said. "Give Mr. Higgins his weapons."

The sergeant gathered Joshua's weapons and returned them to him.

"I would like to find a place to stay until my friend is able to travel. Is there any place close by?"

"I think that can be arranged. Since it was one of our soldiers that caused you to be delayed here, we will make arrangements for you to stay here. We have no quarters for visitors, but we can put you up in the barracks, if that will be satisfactory?"

"That would be fine."

"Sergeant, find him a bed in the barracks. He can also eat with the rest of the men while he is here."

"Yes, sir.

"I will need a place to put up our horses."

"Yes, of course."

"Sergeant, put up their horses in the corral and make sure they are fed."

"Yes, sir.

"Thank you, major," Joshua said. "But I will take care of our horses. I do not wish to be any more trouble for you than necessary."

"I appreciate that. I hope your friend is well soon."

"Thank you," Joshua said again, then turned and followed the sergeant out of the office.

Joshua found his time at the fort to be a time to think, and a time to plan for the future. It was also a time to wonder about the future of his friend and his tribe. It was easy to see the white man was moving west. The white man had been crossing the plains for a good number of years, but now he was starting to see white men settle on the plains. That alone was reason enough to believe the buffalo was not long for the prairie.

The white man was starting to come in too great a number for the Indians to stop. The more they came, the more resistance the Indians would put in their way. It was also clear the Indian would not be able to stop the encroachment on their land by the white man.

Days at the fort passed by slowly. It had been about ten days before Spotted Horse was able to be up and about. It was only a couple of days after that before he was ready to return home.

Spotted Horse and Joshua bid the major goodbye on a bright and sunny morning. They thanked him for all he had done for them. Although their stay at the fort had been unwanted, they had both been treated well.

The trip back home was long, but uneventful. Everyone was glad they had made it back and were well. Joshua was glad to see Dancing Flower and Jeremiah. He couldn't get over how much his son had grown.

Joshua also got a surprise when he arrived home. That very evening, Dancing Flower told Joshua they were going to have another child. Before he left, she was pretty sure she was pregnant, but didn't want to tell him until she was certain. She also told him that she didn't want him to worry about her all the time he was gone.

CHAPTER SEVENTEEN

Plans And Bears

The months passed rapidly as Joshua worked hard to build up his farm. During the winter he split his time between hunting for food and cutting timber for his barn. He worked hard to get his place ready to make it a permanent all-year-round home.

In early spring, Dancing Flower had a little girl they named Susan Flower Higgins. Joshua stayed close to the house for the first few weeks to make sure Dancing Flower didn't work too hard. He worked to plant a garden near the house.

As Dancing Flower grew stronger, she spent more time in the garden. Joshua built a tall fence around the garden so the deer and other large critters of the land could not destroy it.

It took two more years before Joshua and Dancing Flower had built up the place to make it into what was to become a ranch. It would soon be ready for them to get a few cattle and start ranching.

Very few settlers came near where Joshua and Dancing Flower had built their farm. Most of those headed for the Promised Land were traveling along the Oregon Trail many miles south of where Joshua and Dancing Flower had settled.

On occasion a Frontiersman would come by on his way east with his pelts to trade, or would be headed back toward the blue-gray mountains in the west for another year of trapping. Joshua would get information from them about the migration of families headed west to the Promised Land. It had become clear there were a lot of people crossing the plains. They would also get news of Indian attacks on the long wagon trains as they slowly moved across the plains. Occasionally they would hear of wagon trains that were almost wiped out due to illness quickly spreading through the wagon trains.

What information Joshua was able to obtain simply reinforced his belief that the white man was slowly, but surely, moving west. He felt it was only a matter of time before the white man would take over the plains as well.

* * * *

It was still dark on an early morning in mid-summer when Joshua was awakened by the sounds of a horse that seemed to be in trouble. The commotion was coming from the corral. He quickly got up, grabbed his pistol and started out the door. He looked toward the barn and saw a large grizzly bear attacking one of his horses in the corral.

The bear was on its hind legs and had the horse trapped in a corner. The horse was doing its best to defend itself, but was clearly outmatched. The bear took one swipe with his big clawed paw across the horse's throat killing the horse almost instantly.

Joshua lifted his gun and fired a shot at the bear. The bullet hit the bear just as it moved. The bullet struck the bear on his left shoulder. The bear took off running toward the woods, disappearing in seconds.

Joshua knew that a wounded bear could be very dangerous. There was little doubt the bear would be back to kill again. There was nothing else for Joshua to do, but to go after the bear and kill it before it could kill again.

Joshua returned to the cabin. Dancing Flower was lying in bed when he returned.

"What happened?"

"A grizzly bear just killed one of the horses. I'm going after it. I want you to stay in the cabin until I return."

"Can I fix you something to eat?"

"I don't have time," Joshua said as he finished dressing.

As soon as he was dressed, he grabbed a few pieces of buffalo jerky and put it in his pocket. He took his fifty caliber Spencer off the wall, then put a handful of cartridges in his pocket. Joshua strapped on his pistol, and he was ready to go.

"Stay inside."

"Should I go get Spotted Horse to help you," Dancing Flower asked.

"No. I want you to stay inside. Keep a watch out for the bear. If he comes toward the cabin, shoot him. Use a rifle and aim for his chest. I will hear the shot and come back."

Joshua leaned down and kissed Dancing Flower. He looked up at the loft and saw his son looking down at him. Joshua smiled up at him, then turned and left the cabin.

As Joshua stepped out of the cabin and pulled the door closed, he immediately began looking for the bear. When he didn't see it, he began walking toward the corral. He found the horse with its throat slashed lying in the corral. All he could think about was if the horse had not been in the corral, it could have escaped. The horse had been in the corral because it had an injured leg. It had sprained its left front leg. The injury had been healing very nicely. Joshua was sure the horse would have been well enough to ride within a couple of days.

Joshua quickly picked up the blood trail and the paw prints left by the bear. Since the bear had returned to the woods, there was nothing else he could do but follow the trail of the bear into its own territory. Hunting a bear in the woods with all the places for it to hide made it difficult and very dangerous. He knew how cunning a bear could be, and how difficult it was to kill a bear, especially a large grizzly bear.

Joshua checked the Spencer rifle to make sure it was ready to use, then moved very carefully into the woods. He followed the droplets of blood on the ground and on the leaves of bushes. Following a wounded bear was slow and tedious work, especially if he didn't want to end up facing an animal that was over eight foot tall when standing on his hind legs, and somewhere in the area of seven to eight hundred pounds or more.

As Joshua moved through the woods looking and listening for the bear, he passed by an area where there were a number of large boulders and rocky outcroppings. He kept a close watch for the bear as he continued to slowly follow the blood trail.

Suddenly, Joshua heard a noise behind him. He swung around as quickly as he could only to discover the bear had gotten behind him. It was so close he had to quickly step back away in order to keep from getting hit by the animal's big paws.

In stepping back, Joshua tripped on a branch and fell over backwards. As he fell, his rifle went flying. It went off when it fell against a rock. The loud bang of the rifle going off startled the bear, and caused the bear to look away from Joshua for just a second.

The sudden distraction gave Joshua a split second to draw his pistol. At point blank range, Joshua fired six shots, each bullet hitting the bear in the chest. The bear let out a loud growl and began to fall. Joshua quickly rolled out of the way as the bear fell to the ground, it roared once, then let out a long slow breath. The bear was dead.

Joshua laid on the ground not more than a couple of feet from the dead bear. He turned his head and looked at the bear. He could not remember ever seeing such a big bear.

It took Joshua a couple of minutes to catch his breath and stand up. He walked over and picked up his rifle. He loaded it, then reloaded his pistol.

Just as he was about to turn around and head back to the cabin, he heard the sound of a twig breaking behind him. He quickly turned in time to see another bear rise up on its hind legs and roared at him. The bear was not as big as the one he had just killed, but just as dangerous.

Joshua didn't step back this time. Instead, he pulled his rifle up and quickly shot the bear in the middle of the chest. The bear raised its head slightly, then fell over on it side. The slug from the fifty caliber Spencer had done its job well.

Joshua looked around to see if there might be a third bear close by. He didn't see any more bears. He sat down for a few minutes on a large rock and looked at the two bears he had killed, and to catch his breath. The bears would make very good bearskin rugs for the cabin, he thought as he looked at them. He took a deep breath, then started back to the cabin to get some help with the bears.

Spotted Horse had heard the shooting at Joshua's cabin and was still there when Joshua returned. Joshua told him about what happened. Spotted Horse and two of his braves went into the woods with Joshua to help him recover the bears.

Once they got the bears to the cabin, they skinned them and prepared the hides to make rugs for the cabin. Joshua also cut up the meat and shared it with Spotted Horse and his tribe. From that day on, they kept a watch for any signs of bear in the area.

CHAPTER EIGHTEEN

The Civil War Comes To Joshua's Door

On an early morning in the late spring of 1864, the sun slowly rose above the horizon and began to spread its warmth across the land. The sky was clear and the sun was bright. There was a gentle warm breeze coming out of the southwest. It looked as if it was going to be a beautiful day.

The prairie that stretched south and east from the southern Black Hills had been blessed with good rain and plenty of sunshine. The meadows were thick with a bounty of grass and spring flowers. Joshua's horses grazed peacefully on the rich grass making a magnificent picture of tranquility. However, the peace and tranquility was not to last.

Jeremiah was eight years old and was in the barn with his father. He was helping Joshua help one of the mares deliver a foal. Over the years Joshua had been able to gather a pretty good sized herd of horses. That spring alone there had been eleven new foals born to his herd. This would be the twelfth. His horses were good solid animals with the ability to run long distances. They had grown strong and healthy on the tall grass that grew at the base of the Southern Black Hills.

Dancing Flower was working in the rich dark soil of the garden. She would hoe a small part of the garden then make a row to plant corn. After making the row, she would make evenly spaced holes in the row. Once the row was ready, her daughter, Susan, sat on the ground and put kernels of corn in each hole then covered them.

Dancing Flower took a moment to stop and stretch her back, then wipe the sweat from her brow. She also took a moment to look over what she and Joshua had built over the years. She smiled to herself because she was pleased with what she saw.

As she looked off toward the southeast, she thought she saw something moving across the open prairie toward their home. With the bright morning sun, she wasn't sure what was moving closer. Dancing Flower put her hand up to shade her eyes from the morning sun in an attempt to get a better look at what was coming toward their farm. It soon became clear. She was seeing a column of horse soldiers riding toward them.

The smile quickly left her face as Dancing Flower dropped her hoe and picked up her daughter. She ran as fast as she could toward the barn.

"Joshua! Joshua!" she called out as she ran across the yard.

As she was getting close to the barn door, Joshua stepped into the doorway. He had heard Dancing Flower's call and wondered what the trouble was.

"Horse soldiers are coming," she said with a note of panic and fear in her voice.

"Get in the barn and stay out of sight. Keep Jeremiah with you. I have heard rumors of Confederate soldiers roaming around the territory looking for horses to use in the war. I will talk to them. If I wave my hand behind my back, sneak out the back of the barn and get Spotted Horse and his warriors to come in a hurry."

Joshua stepped out of the barn while Dancing Flower went into the barn and hid behind the door. When Jeremiah tried to go out of the barn to be with his father and to see what was going on, his mother stopped him and held him tightly.

Joshua walked a little ways away from the barn and stood out in the open so the soldiers could see him. He watched them as they rode in close and stopped in front of him. The one thing Joshua had noticed was they didn't ride in very close ranks. Their formation was not what he would have expected to see from Union soldiers, especially when led by an officer. They were too strung out and didn't ride in an orderly manner like he had seen before.

The fact that the soldiers were in Union uniforms that did not fit the men very well, did nothing to make Joshua believe that they were Union soldiers. He knew it was easy to obtain Union uniforms. They could have taken the uniforms from soldiers who had been killed, or from soldiers who had been taken prisoner.

"May I help you," Joshua said to the lieutenant who was leading the soldiers.

"I'm Lieutenant John T. Hamilton of the United States Army," the officer said as he sat on his horse looking down at Joshua. "I'm out rounding up horses for the United States Government for the war effort."

Joshua didn't miss the hint of a southern accent in the officer's voice. Joshua was very careful not to let on that he thought there might be anything wrong. He carefully slipped a hand behind his back and waved it slightly.

Joshua noticed several of the soldiers were looking around as if looking to see if there was anyone else nearby. Their actions made Joshua even more suspicious of them.

Dancing Flower saw Joshua's signal and quickly picked up Susan and took Jeremiah in tow. She ran out the back of the barn and into the nearby woods. She wasted no time in running to Spotted Horse's camp. Meanwhile, Joshua talked to the lieutenant in an effort to delay him as long as possible to allow Dancing Flower time to get to Spotted Horse's camp for help.

"Most of my horses are not broken, they're pretty green. They would not be suitable for military use. Most of them are wild and have never been ridden, or even had anyone attempt to ride them. They are wild in the true sense of the word."

"It doesn't matter. The army will break them to suit our use."

"I have to wonder if you have taken a close look at my horses, lieutenant. Most of them are either Indian ponies or from Indian ponies. They are not anything like the larger horses you ride now. I happen to know the government wants larger horses for the army."

"It doesn't matter. With horses so hard to come by, we take almost any healthy horse. The war has drained our supply of them back east. I've been instructed to gather any and all horses that are healthy and in good shape. The army will break and train them for whatever use they see fit to put them to. We will take all your horses. You will be paid for them with a U.S. Government voucher," the lieutenant said.

"I don't think so. I can sell you about twenty to twenty-five horses, but I will not sell you all of them. I will need breeding stock and a few to work the farm. By the way, I will not accept a voucher. You will have to pay for them in gold."

"I don't think you understand, sir," the lieutenant said. "That was not a request."

"I understand clearly."

"Are you refusing to comply with a government order?"

"No, not really," Joshua said calmly. "I don't think you have any government order, and I'm sure you don't even have a U.S. Government voucher. In fact, I don't think you are U.S Army soldiers. If I had to guess, you're not even an officer."

"And what gives you that idea?" the lieutenant asked with a slight grin.

"You may be wearing Union uniforms, but they don't fit your men like they should. You and your men don't ride like Union soldiers. And you, sir, have a slight southern accent. Everything about you says you are Confederate soldiers. We have been warned about you guys roaming the territory, stealing horses and taking them back to the south to use to fight against the Union troops."

The soldier looked around a bit then looked back at Joshua. He began to smile.

"You're a pretty smart man, but you've overlooked one very important thing."

"I don't think so," Joshua said. "But what is it you think I have overlooked?"

"You're outnumbered. There are twelve of us and one of you. I would hate to have to burn your place down because you were uncooperative," he said with a smile of confidence.

"About this outnumbered thing you mentioned, I think you should reconsider that part of your statement," Joshua said with a note of confidence in his voice. "And about this burning down of my place, I don't think that will happen, either."

Joshua watched as the soldiers began to look around to see if there were maybe more people around than they had thought were there. When they didn't see anyone, they looked back at him and wondered if he knew something they didn't, or if he was bluffing.

"I think you're bluffing," the lieutenant said with a grin.

"I'm not bluffing. So far you have not threatened me. Should you decide to change that by pointing a gun at me, the one who does will be dead before he hits the ground and the rest of you will stand little to no chance of making it to the end of the day."

"Hey, Sarge," one of the others said softly as he pointed toward the barn. "I think you best be listenin' ta him. Look."

The sergeant, who had been pretending to be a lieutenant, looked toward the barn. There were armed Indians coming out of the barn, from around behind the barn and from behind the corral. As the sergeant turned and looked toward the house, he could see more Indians pouring out of the woods and from behind the house. Every Indian had a rifle. He then looked down at Joshua and could see Joshua looking up at him.

"It's up to you, Sarge. I'm sure you've heard what Indians do to white men when they capture them," Joshua said, then gave him a moment to think about it.

The Indians, with their guns aimed at the Confederate soldiers, continued to move in closer and closer. The soldiers were outnumbered by three to one, plus the Indians had the drop on them. The closer the Indians got to the soldiers, the more nervous the soldiers got. They had no idea what would happen to them.

"Sarge, you can either surrender to me and sit out the rest of the war in a Union Prison Camp, or you can be a prisoner of Spotted Horse and his braves. I might point out that Spotted Horse doesn't have a prison to hold you in, if you get what I mean."

The sergeant looked at Joshua. He knew he had no chance at all of surviving if they chose to make a fight of it. He didn't like the idea of being a prisoner of the savages any better. He took a deep breath then turned in his saddle and looked at his men. He then turned back and looked at Joshua.

"We will surrender to you, sir," he said, then turned to look at his men.

"Very carefully, drop your weapons on the ground and dismount," he ordered. "Don't try anything stupid. Don't give them a reason to cut us down. Stand tall."

The sergeant and his men dropped their weapons, got off their horses and stood next to them. They looked to Joshua for instructions. They were afraid the Indians might torture them before killing them.

"March over to the corral," Joshua said. "Each of you will be searched for weapons then placed in the corral. You will have water and food. You will be able to move around freely inside the corral during the day and sleep in the barn at night. You will also be able to keep your personal possessions, with the exception of any weapons, as long as you cooperate. You cause me any problems, and I can assure you Spotted Horse and his braves know how to make it so you will want to cooperate. Do I need to say more?"

"No, sir," the sergeant replied. "We will not give you any trouble."

"I would like to speak to you, Sarge. Come with me."

Joshua walked over to the barn door with the sergeant following. When they got to the barn door, Joshua turned and looked at the sergeant.

"Sir?"

"What is it?" Joshua asked.

"I hope you will not hold my comment about burning your place down against my men."

"Don't worry about it. You were not going to do anything anyway," Joshua said with a grin.

"Thank you, sir."

"First of all, I don't like the situation any more than you do," Joshua said. "The Indians will be watching you and your men until we can turn you over to the Union Army. You will be fed well while you are here as long as you and your men are cooperative. Just so you know where you stand, death will come very slowly to any of you who do not cooperate with me or Spotted Horse.

"Should any of your men attack or injure any of my family or Spotted Horse's braves, they will die a slow and very painful death. There will be no give on this. Do I make myself clear?"

"Yes, sir."

"As long as we understand each other, I see no reason to cause harm to you or any of your men. I don't want to have to prove that I mean what I say, but I can assure you that I will keep my word. You and your men can survive to return home after the Civil War is over, or you can die right here.

I'm sure there are friends and family who would like to see you and your men again."

"Do you know when we might be turned over to the Union Army?" the sergeant asked.

"No, I don't. I will have to contact one of the local forts to find out. You can return to your men, but remember what I said. Make sure your men understand what will happen if they do not cooperate," Joshua said, ending their conversation.

"Yes, sir."

Joshua watched as the sergeant returned to the corral. He had no idea what might happen over the next few days. One thing was sure, he would need to keep a close eye on these men until the army could come and get them.

* * * *

Time passed by slowly for all. Word had been sent to the nearest fort, Fort Robinson in the Nebraska Territory, that Joshua was holding a dozen Confederate soldiers as prisoners. Joshua explained in a letter to the commander of the fort why and how he had come to have them as prisoners.

After about a week and a half, he received a dispatch by messenger that they did not have the manpower to hold the prisoners. The fort was apparently short of men due to the war. Joshua was advised to do with the prisoners as he saw fit, which included hanging them as horse thieves or as spies. The letter had been very clear on that point.

Joshua showed the letter to the sergeant. He said he would have to think about what to do about it. Most of the prisoners understood they could be hung for stealing horses even if they were soldiers. It didn't matter what reason anyone had for stealing the horses in the first place. In the Dakota Territory, people caught stealing horses were hung just like in most other parts of the west. Stealing was stealing, and hanging often came quickly, especially on the Frontier where laws and courts were almost nonexistent.

Most of the prisoners also knew that by posing as Union soldiers, they could be hung as spies.

The sergeant and his men also knew that they had been sent on a fool's errand. They knew stealing horses would only prolong the inevitable. The longer the war continued would only cause more ruin to the South and more hatred by the northerners for the South and southerners.

Joshua talked the situation over with Spotted Horse and Dancing Flower. From what he had heard from people passing through, the war would probably not last much longer, probably a year at the most. The South was being overrun by the North, and supplies were few and far between. It was decided that they would keep the prisoners until the war was over, then let them go home.

Joshua took the sergeant off to one side to have a talk with him. He explained the situation. After Joshua and the sergeant finished discussing their options, the sergeant talked it over with the men. They decided it was better to be held here, than to be hung as horse thieves or spies, or to be taken back east to spend the rest of the war in a Union prison camp.

Most of the prisoners knew and understood the South was losing the war. Supplies were being cut off, and the South was being ravaged by Union forces. In some cases, the ravaging of the South was being done by southerners who had already figured out the war was lost. They were trying to save what they could even if it didn't belong to them.

There was a need for almost everything in the South. Guns and ammunition were hard to come by as was food and clothing. Boots were almost impossible to get, and horses were impossible to get. Confederate money was fast becoming worthless in most places, and there was no gold to buy those things the South would need to carry on the fight.

There was no doubt in the minds of the Confederate soldiers who had come to the Dakota Territory for horses that the war was a lost cause, and the best they could hope for was an end to the war soon, and to get out of it alive. It was not hard for the sergeant and his men to understand that the best place to sit out the war was on Joshua's farm.

Joshua explained they would have to work around the farm while they were his prisoners. He began to put a few of the soldiers to work cutting hay and stacking it in large piles close to the barn to be fed to his horses during the long Dakota Territory winter. Many of the prisoners found the work helped make the days go by faster. They soon found being prisoners on Joshua's farm was not all that bad when compared with the prisoner of war camps run by the Union Army. In fact, they had it pretty good.

The U.S. Army prison camps were only slightly better than the Confederate prison camps. The prisoners had little food, little room to move around to get any kind of exercise and nothing to do to take their minds off their depressing situation. The camps were overcrowded, often muddy, and lacked anything even close to good sanitary conditions. Because of it, many of the prisoners died of disease and untreated wounds that became infected. Thousands of solders died in the prison camps on both sides.

At least being held prisoner at Joshua's farm there was fresh water, plenty to eat and the sanitary conditions were good. There were things they could do that would keep them busy and give them some exercise.

A few of the prisoners learned how to break horses the Indian way, and found it to be a great diversion from sitting around and doing nothing. Those that helped around the farm seemed to take to it very well. There were even a couple of the prisoners that talked about becoming cowboys and staying in the west to ranch or farm after the war. Some of them talked about returning home to get what they could salvage, then move out west to start a new life.

CHAPTER NINETEEN

Trouble With A Prisoner

Not all the prisoners being held at Joshua's farm accepted their situation without difficulty. There was one Confederate soldier in particular that grew angrier with his situation as the days went by. His name was Private Billy Joe Wilson.

While many of the soldiers had been forced into service to the South, they had no real animosity toward the North. However, Billy Joe's heart was full of hatred for northerners, any northerner. He spent a good deal of his time complaining about anything and everything. He really had nothing to complain about because he would not have been treated very well in a Union prison camp. His constant complaining would probably have gotten him shot by a guard who got tired of listening to him. If he had been caught by anyone else while out looking to steal horses, he would have been hung on the spot for horse stealing, or as a spy. At least on Joshua's farm, there was a good chance he would live long enough to return home.

Billy Joe tried to get one or two of the others to escape with him, but the others knew that they had been sent on a mission that would prove useless. The end result would just breed more hatred between the North and South, and accomplish nothing. It would not have changed the outcome of the war one bit. At least at Joshua's farm they could sit out the war in relative peace with a good chance of living long enough to be able to return home when it was over, but Billy Joe wanted out now.

Everything seemed to be working out as Joshua had hoped. The Confederate soldiers had settled into their routine and seemed to be doing well, except for Billy Joe. Joshua had heard about Billy Joe's discontent with the situation. So far, Billy Joe had not done anything but complain. However, that was about to change.

One morning when Joshua left the ranch house and headed out to the barn to have his usual morning talk with Sergeant Hamilton, he found the sergeant pacing back and forth in front of the barn door. It was not like the sergeant to be pacing while waiting for Joshua to give his morning work assignments. It was obvious the sergeant had something on his mind that was troubling him. It was apparent he wanted to talk to Joshua about something important as soon as possible.

"Something up, Sarge?" Joshua asked as he approached the sergeant.

"Yes, sir."

"What's on your mind?

"I know I have no right to ask anything of you as a prisoner of war. You have kept your word and have treated us fairly. You have certainly treated us better than we would have been treated if we had been turned over to Union troops and sent to a Union prison camp where most of us would have probably died. If we had been caught by civilian authorities, we'd have all been hung for horse stealing by now."

"I can see in your eyes you have something that is disturbing you. Why don't you get to the point?"

"Well, sir, I would like you to remove Private Billy Joe Wilson from the rest of the men."

"Why? What has he done?"

"Nothing, yet, but I'm afraid he's going to cause trouble. He's been trying to get a couple of the men to escape with him. So far he hasn't gotten anyone to go along with him. If he keeps talking to the men, he could get, maybe, one or two to join him. If Billy Joe tries to escape, some of Spotted Horse's braves could get hurt. I'm afraid if that happens, Spotted Horse will not only kill the ones that try to escape, but he will kill the rest of us as well. I don't want that to happen. The war is over for us. I want my men to live long enough to go home."

"How long do you think I have before he will try to escape?" Joshua asked as he thought about what Sarge had told him.

"The word is he's planning on trying to escape tonight."

"Do you think he might try to escape sooner," Joshua asked.

"He might, if he has a chance."

"I see," Joshua said as he looked down at the ground while he thought about what he was told.

Joshua was not sure what to do about it. He knew Sarge was right. If any of Spotted Horse's braves were injured or killed while any of the prisoners were trying to make an escape, Spotted Horse would take it out on all of them. If Joshua didn't do something quickly, he could have a real problem on his hands.

"Since I usually give you and your men their job assignments at this time, I'll do just that," Joshua said thoughtfully. "Return to the barn and give orders for six of your men to work on cutting grass and stacking it near the barn. But keep them away from the back of the barn for at least a couple of hours. Have another four of them work on breaking horses in the corral on the front side of the barn. Assign Private Wilson to the job of cleaning the stalls in the barn, alone. I want you to get him started then leave him to work alone."

"Yes, sir," the sergeant replied with a smile.

"I want you to oversee the breaking of the horses. That will keep you close to the barn if something should go wrong. You need to make sure none of the others go into the barn or around to the backside of the barn. And remember,

Spotted Horse's braves will still be watching everyone as they have for the past almost three months.

"You might want to remind your men of the conditions of their stay here. They can still be hung for trying to steal horses. One wrong move and it may be the last any of you make. Is that clear?"

"Yes, sir. I'll remind the men, sir," Sarge said. "Should I remind Billy Joe?"

"No. Just get him started cleaning the stalls in the barn, then go out and talk to the rest of the men and give them their assigned duties."

"Yes, sir."

Joshua watched as Sarge turned and walked back to the barn. As soon as Sarge was inside the barn, Joshua returned to the house. While he walked, he put together a plan which would not only prevent an escape attempt, but could convince the others it was useless to try to escape.

When Joshua got to the house, he stepped up on the porch where Spotted Horse was sitting. He sat down next to Spotted Horse and looked at him.

"I can see you have something on your mind, Joshua."

"Yes, I do."

"What is it that troubles you?"

"We are going to have a problem if we don't do something about it," Joshua said.

"What is the problem?"

"I'm told one of our prisoners is planning to escape tonight."

"Why not let him go? You have shown them that you are smarter, and you have beaten them. There is nothing else to prove."

"That is true. But if I let this one get away, it could cause others to escape. More importantly, there is the possibility that the one who escapes will try to steal horses from us or someone else. It could get someone hurt. He might even kill someone in order to escape. I would prefer it doesn't happen. I do not want that to happen. I want to prevent it if at all possible."

"I see your point. I take it you have a plan in mind?"

"Yes, and it requires your help," Joshua said, then he began to lay out his plan.

"My plan is to have a few of your braves sneak into the barn in a little while and remove the soldier who is planning to escape. I want it done so the others will think he escaped while everyone else was working. You and a couple of your braves will take him someplace, not too far away, and tie him up. You will then scare him half to death. A little screaming from him wouldn't hurt."

"I take it you do not want us to kill him?"

"No, but a little torture might prove to the others we mean business. It might also make him think twice before he tries to escape, again. I will arrive just in time to save him from being skinned alive," Joshua said with a smile.

"I understand. When do we do this?"

"As soon as they finish eating breakfast, and they have started working at their assigned jobs."

"I'll be ready," Spotted Horse said as he got up and walked off the porch. "How will I know which one to take?"

"He will be the only one in the barn."

Joshua sat on the porch and watched what was going on at the barn. As soon as he could see the men were working at their assigned jobs, he set his plan into motion. He found Spotted Horse behind the barn and told him to go get the prisoner from the barn. Joshua then returned to the house.

Spotted Horse and three of his braves snuck into the barn from the back. They could see Private Billy Joe Wilson leaning against one of the stalls with a pitchfork in his hand. He was mumbling something about the job he had been assigned. He had not seen or heard Spotted Horse and his braves sneak into the barn.

"I'm getting out of this damn place, Indians or no Indians," Private Wilson said aloud. "No damn Indian lover is going to keep me prisoner here."

Suddenly, Private Wilson felt a hand come over his mouth and felt the cold steel of a knife at his throat. He dropped the pitchfork and his eyes got big as the realization that he was about to die filled his mind.

Private Wilson was quickly tied, gagged and blindfolded. He was then led out the back of the barn and into the nearby woods. He was taken to a place where he was tied spread eagle between two trees. As soon as he was secured between the trees, the blindfold was removed. One of the Indians quickly stripped him of his shirt.

Spotted Horse had been standing back a few feet watching his braves. As soon as Private Wilson had had a chance to see him, Spotted Horse walked toward Private Wilson. When he was close to Private Wilson, he stopped, then slowly drew his knife from his belt. He carefully examined the edge of the blade as if to make sure it was sharp enough for the task at hand. He then looked at Private Wilson with a sinister grin. It was easy to see the fear in Private Wilson's face as Spotted Horse removed the gag.

"You should not have tried to get others to escape," Spotted Horse said while holding the knife so that Private Wilson could see it clearly.

"You skin him first, or scalp him first?" one of the braves asked Spotted Horse.

"I think I will skin him first."

"Oh, God. Please," Wilson begged as tears came to his eyes.

"You planned to escape. You were told that to escape meant you would die. You will die slowly as we promised," Spotted Horse said as he stepped up close to Billy Joe and showed him the thin shiny edge of the big knife.

Billy Joe let out a blood curdling scream as Spotted Horse put the knife against his bare chest. He slowly drew the blade diagonally across his chest, just barely cutting the skin. He only drew a little blood, but it was enough to scare the hell out of Billy Joe and cause him to scream, again.

"STOP!" Joshua yelled as he came rushing toward Spotted Horse.

Spotted Horse turned and looked at Joshua and said, "He was going to try to escape. I was doing what we told him we were going to do to any of them that tried to escape."

"I know, but he hadn't really tried to escape. He was just planning to escape."

"It's all the same," Spotted Horse said.

"I probably should let you skin him. It would probably save me a lot of headaches. But it doesn't seem right to skin him when he didn't hurt anyone, and he was just planning to escape."

"If he had, I would still skin him."

"I know. And if he had escaped I would let you," Joshua said.

"If it is your wish that I spare his miserable life, I will. But if he, or any of the others even think about escaping, I will kill them."

"That sounds fair enough."

Joshua turned and looked at Billy Joe. It was obvious that Billy Joe was waiting to see who would win the discussion on whether he would live or die. During the discussion, no one made a move to cut him loose. Finally, Joshua stepped up close to Billy Joe and looked him in the eyes.

"I should let Spotted Horse and his braves skin you alive. If you had tried to escape from a Union prison, they would have simply shot or hung you. For the life of me, I can't think of one good reason for me to do anything different. Can you?"

"Please, don't shoot me," Billy Joe said crying openly.

"Oh, I wouldn't shoot you. That never entered my mind as an option. I would let Spotted Horse carve you into little pieces and feed you to the coyotes."

"Oh, God. Please," Billy Joe begged as tears rolled down his face.

"I'm going to have them cut you down. You will return to the barn and clean up the wound on your chest. You will then return to work. You will work without any more complaining. And if you try to escape, or try to talk anyone else into escaping, I will turn you over to Spotted Horse and his braves, and let them kill you in any way they want. Do I make myself clear?"

"Yes, sir. I won't give you any more trouble, sir."

"You best not. If you even talk of escaping, I will turn you over to Spotted Horse to do with you as he pleases. Do you understand that?"

"Yes, sir."

Joshua turned and looked at Spotted Horse, then motioned for him to cut Wilson loose from the trees. As soon as Billy Joe was loose, Joshua led him back to the farm. He had Dancing Flower clean his wound and put a dressing on it so it would not get infected. He then returned Billy Joe to the barn and told him to clean every single stall like he had been instructed earlier. Billy Joe didn't even wait for Joshua to leave the barn before he was hard at work cleaning the stalls.

Joshua left the barn and went out to the corral where several of the men were standing around as if waiting for word on what happened to Billy Joe. Joshua saw a number of braves nearby watching the prisoners.

"What happened?" Sarge asked.

"It seems Billy Joe tried to escape. He didn't get very far."

"Did the Indians kill him?" one of the others asked, his eyes showing he was sure they had killed him.

"No, not this time. I got to them before they could skin him. Billy Joe is in the barn doing the work he was assigned. I suggest you do the same," Joshua said, then turned and walked toward the house.

Joshua was pretty sure they would hear about what had happened to Billy Joe. The large bandage across his chest would speak for itself.

When Joshua got to the house, Spotted Horse was waiting for him.

"Do you think our little play did any good?" Spotted Horse asked.

"Only time will tell," Joshua replied.

The days passed slowly. There were no more attempts to escape, and no more talk of escaping among the prisoners. During slow times on the farm, Joshua had the men working on building a bunkhouse where it would be more comfortable for the men to stay, especially during the winter months. It would also provide a place for cowboys to live once he turned his place into a cattle ranch.

CHAPTER TWENTY

The War Ended

Work on the farm continued until word was received that the Civil War had ended. Once the war ended, the soldiers were told they were free to leave. Each of the prisoners who wanted to leave was given a few days supply of food, a horse and the guns that had been taken from them when they became prisoners. They were then released to go wherever they wanted.

They were also warned that it might be a good idea for them to leave the Dakota Territory as quickly as possible because horse thieves were not welcomed around the area. They were also reminded that most of the people in the area, whites as well as Indians, knew they had been prisoners for attempting to steal horses. A couple of them, including Billy Joe, had been planning to return to the South where they had lived before the war. It was now time for them to leave.

Several of the soldiers knew what Joshua had planned for his farm. Several of them asked Joshua if they could stay on and help him turn his place into a cattle ranch. Since Joshua was going to have to find some cattle and drive them to the ranch, he would need good ranch hands. What better men to hire than those who had helped him build up the place?

Joshua agreed to hire five of the men and Sarge to help him. The one thing Joshua knew about the men who decided to stay was they were good horsemen. They may not know much about herding cattle, but they could learn.

Those who decided to stay continued to help Joshua build his place up to where it was finally ready to become a working cattle ranch. All that was needed to make it a fully operational ranch were cattle.

* * * *

By the spring of 1866, the time had come for Joshua to find the cattle he needed to make his place into a fully operational cattle ranch. He, his family, and those who had chosen to stay had lived off the land since the end of the war. They hunted and raised crops over the past year while they made the place ready to be a ranch.

They had also raised enough horses so Joshua had been able to sell a number of the horses to the U.S Army to pay for whatever else they needed. With the money from the horses he sold, and from the gold he had saved from the sale of his pelts at the trading posts along the Platte and Missouri Rivers, he had enough money saved up to buy enough cattle to get a good start at establishing a cattle ranch.

The time had come for Joshua to leave his ranch at the southern end of the Black Hills and head out to find some cows and a few good breeding bulls. He had heard about the cattle ranches in Texas, and of one place in southwest Texas where there were a lot of cattle he might be able to purchase at a good price.

It was a long way to go to get cattle, but that was the way it was in that part of the country. It was a long way to go to get anything you couldn't find where you lived, or make yourself. The country had not had a lot of settlers move in to stake a claim on the vast open prairie land. Now that the Civil War was over, more and more people were starting to move west to begin a new life.

A few of Spotted Horse's braves worked on the ranch from time to time. However, most of Joshua's crew was made up of ex-Confederate soldiers that stayed on to work for him.

Since John Hamilton had asked Joshua if he could stay on and work for him, Joshua asked him to be his foreman. He quickly agreed. Who better to be the foreman than the man who had been their leader for the past few years? There was no doubt that John knew the men better than anyone.

One of the men who had decided to stay on was a pretty good cook. He had cooked for the men while they were prisoners. After the war, he continued to cook for the men who stayed on to work for Joshua. Since it was time for them to take the trip south to get cattle, Joshua made Chester Gerrine the cookie. He would cook for the men on the trip south to Texas and on the anticipated cattle drive back to the ranch.

As the time approached for them to search for cattle for the ranch, the men began gathering the supplies they would need. Some of the men worked to outfit a wagon so it could be used as a chuck wagon.

A string of horses for herding the cattle was prepared for the trip as well. It would take a lot of horses to herd the cattle back. When all was ready, they gathered in front of Joshua's house on the morning they planned to leave for Texas.

Jeremiah was now ten years old and would soon be eleven. His little sister was seven. Jeremiah was a smart boy. He understood his father was planning to leave to get some cattle. He didn't like the idea of his father leaving, but he understood that it was necessary for his father to leave for awhile. That did not make Joshua's leaving any easier for Jeremiah, or his sister and Dancing Flower.

"How long will you be gone, Father?" Jeremiah asked.

"I'm not real sure, son. It could be for most of the summer."

"Do you have to be gone so long?"

"I hope not, but it may take a long time to find just the right cattle for our ranch. After we have the cattle, we have to get them back here. That will take time, too."

"Oh," Jeremiah said as he thought about what his father had told him.

Joshua smiled at his son, then knelt down in front of him.

"You need to stay here and take care of your mother and sister. They will need your help. You will be the man of the ranch while I am gone. Can you do that, and help your mother?"

"Sure. I can help Mama."

"Me, too," Susan said as she looked at her father.

Joshua smiled at his children. He then kissed his daughter on the cheek. He stood up and shook his son's hand rather than embarrass him by kissing him in front of everybody.

Joshua turned to see Dancing Flower smiling at him. Joshua reached out a hand to her and she stepped up close to him. Joshua put his arms around her as he looked into her eyes.

"I will miss you," Dancing Flower said.

"I will miss you, too. We will return as soon as we can."

"I know you will. Please be careful."

"I will," Joshua said as he leaned toward her and kissed her.

Reluctantly, Joshua let go of her then turned to his horse. He put his foot in the stirrup, swung up into the saddle and looked down at his family. He knew it was going to be one of the hardest trips he would have to take. He never liked leaving his family, but their future largely depended on the success of the trip.

Joshua blew each of them a kiss from the back of his horse, then turned his horse. As he started to ride south from the ranch house, his men and the wagon fell in behind him. He turned in his saddle and looked over his shoulder as he rode away. He waved to them one last time before he could no longer see them.

* * * *

Once he and his men were out of sight, he turned around in his saddle and looked south. He was not sure what the trip to Texas would be like, but he had good men with him. If trouble should come their way, he had men who were seasoned fighters. They would do whatever it took to protect their interests.

Joshua had never traveled with a chuck wagon before. He was sure he would be able to make better time if they didn't have the wagon. But he also knew hard working men needed good food and plenty of it. The wagon would be indispensable if they found the cattle Joshua hoped to buy. Driving cattle across the country was hard work with no time off to do anything else.

Days turned into weeks as Joshua and his men continued to move south toward Texas. Once they were riding in the open country of west Texas, Joshua soon had a good idea of how hardy the cattle in that part of the country had to be just to survive. From the looks of the land, the cattle would have to do a lot of walking just to find enough to eat.

Most of the cattle he had seen were longhorns, probably originally from Mexico. They were a sturdy breed of cattle that had learned to survive on what little the land had to offer them. Although he was thinking about getting longhorns, he hoped he didn't have to go as far as Mexico to get them.

Joshua had heard about the longhorn cattle. He knew they were tough and could fend for themselves very well, often in the harshest of conditions. He also knew they did well in rough areas of the country.

The most important thing he had heard about them was they were often hard to handle. That was important to know for the safety of himself and his men. It would make his cowhands cautious when working with them.

Longhorns were a large animal, and when left to themselves without much contact with humans could become very wild. That made rounding them up difficult as well as dangerous for cowboys and their horses. Many a cowboy had been injured, crippled or killed by those long sharp horns. Many a horse had been killed by their horns as well.

Joshua had no illusions about the longhorn cattle. It could prove difficult to get longhorns back to the Dakota Territory. Driving cattle was a difficult and dangerous business. The longhorn was a skittish animal. They could take off in a stampede because of a loud sound such as thunder, or even just an unfamiliar sound. All it took sometimes was one scared cow to start a stampede. Once they started to run, it was almost impossible to stop them. They would often run for a couple of miles before they would stop, and they would run over anything and everything in their path.

Joshua knew it was not going to be easy to get the cattle back to his ranch. It would be a long hard trip, but he knew he had good men to help him.

CHAPTER TWENTY-ONE

Cactus Flats And The Trap

Joshua and his ranch hands had been gone from the ranch the better part of a month when they came to a town just a little south of the Texas panhandle. They stopped on a ridge overlooking the small town. They took a few minutes to look over the town and the surrounding area.

The town was nothing special. Crossing the vast prairie, they had seen several towns just like it. They were small towns that had sprung up along the trails or roads that wound their way across the country. In looking over the town, there appeared to be only about five businesses built along both sides of the narrow dirt road.

Joshua hoped he might be able to find a rancher in the area who would be willing to sell him some cattle so he could get his ranch started. The town was in the area he had heard about where there might be the kind of cattle he was looking for, in the numbers he was hoping to purchase. The one thing he knew was he needed cattle that could survive the harsh winters in the Dakota Territory, and the longhorns were as tough as they came. It was longhorns they had seen from time to time, but not in the numbers they would need.

Joshua's thoughts were disturbed by John Hamilton as he rode up beside him.

"Well, boss. What do you think?"

"I'm not sure. I guess the only way we are going to find out if anyone in the area has any cattle to sell is to go into town and start asking around."

"You want us all to go into town?"

"Sure. Why do you ask?"

"I was thinking with so many of us, they might think we're here to cause trouble."

Joshua thought about what John had said. He could understand what John was thinking. There was really nothing to separate them from those raiding the small towns. A good size number of men traveling across the country would certainly alert the town folks of possible danger.

Joshua was aware of the fact there were some die-hard rebels from the South still raiding small towns. Although they were mostly raiding places in the North, some were robbing banks in the South. Sometimes they would rob stagecoaches, or an occasional freight wagon. They had become a thorn in the side of almost any bank in a small town. Joshua had a hard time thinking of them as southerners. He thought of them as just criminals, plan and simple.

"I think we can all go into town," Joshua said after giving John's question a moment of thought. "But stay out of trouble. We don't know how they will take to strangers, especially so many of us. And I'll do the talking," Joshua added.

"You heard him," John said looking over his shoulder at the men. "We don't want any trouble, but keep your eyes open and stay together. Don't anyone wander off. Stay close to the wagon."

Taking a deep breath, Joshua nudged his horse down the long dusty road toward the town. John rode next to Joshua while the rest of the men followed along behind with Chester pulling up the rear with the wagon and the string of extra horses.

As they rode into town and looked around, they noticed a small sign that gave the name of the town. It was Cactus Flats. The name seemed to fit the town well, at least the "Cactus" part. The "Flats" part of the name didn't seem to fit very well since the country around the town was anything but flat. It was crisscrossed with gullies and ravines. Off in the distance there were several large buttes.

In the town there was a general store and a bank on one side of the road. On the other side of the road were a boarding house, a livery stable and blacksmith shop, and a saloon. There were only a few houses anywhere near the businesses indicating there were only a few people who actually lived in the town.

Joshua noticed he and his men were being watched by a few of the town folks as they rode along the road. He was sure they had not seen many men ride into their town all at once for sometime, if at all.

The owner of the general store stopped sweeping his porch to watch the strangers. The blacksmith across the road straightened up from his work to watch them as they slowly moved by his stable. There was someone standing inside the saloon watching them through the front window.

Joshua stopped in front of the general store and looked around. He then turned and looked at the storekeeper.

"Excuse me. Are you the owner of this general store?" Joshua asked.

"Yeah," the man on the boardwalk replied as he leaned against his broom.

"We'll be needing some supplies."

"I'm sure I will have about everything you would need," the storekeeper said with a smile.

Joshua smiled back and nodded, then turned and looked back at the wagon.

"Chester, you and Frank go in the general store and order what supplies you need. I'll meet you back here in a little while to pay for it."

"Okay. Frank, you heard him," Chester said.

Frank Sanders had worked in supply when he was a soldier. Before that, he worked in his father's general store in Willow Creek, North Carolina. He knew what supplies were needed and what supplies a small town general store was likely to have on hand.

Chester tied the reins to the brake handle and got down off the wagon. He then tied the lead horses to the hitching rail. Frank got off his horse and tied his horse to the hitching rail as well. They followed the storekeeper into the general store while Joshua and the rest of the men moved on down the street a little ways.

Joshua and the others tied their horses in front of the bank. Joshua looked around, then looked at his men.

"Stan, I want you to have a talk with the blacksmith. See if he knows of any ranchers in the area that might have some good hardy cattle for sale. Take Marcus with you."

"Right, boss."

Stan Wilcox had worked in a blacksmiths shop and was a wheelwright by trade. Marcus Powell had worked on a plantation taking care of the animals which included shoeing and training the horses. He had been a great help to Joshua in training his horses and teaching the others how to break horses for different uses.

As Stan and Marcus headed across the street to the blacksmith's shop. Joshua, John, Bobby Hanson and Will Sutton headed for the bank. Before the war, Bobby had worked at a cotton mill; Will had been a school teacher in North Carolina.

Bobby and Will followed Joshua and John into the bank. Joshua and John walked up to the teller's window. Bobby and Will waited close to the door. The teller looked a little nervous. Joshua was sure it was because he and his men were strangers and they were well armed. He was sure it didn't help that two of his men held back and stood close to the door.

"You've got nothing to worry about from us," Joshua said with a smile. "I would like to talk to the headman."

"That would be Mr. K. R. Waterman. He's the president and owner of the bank," the teller said nervously. "He's also the mayor of Cactus Flats."

"Well, I would like to talk to Mr. Waterman, please."

"I'll get him for you," the teller said as he quickly closed the window to the bank cage.

Joshua waited for a couple of minutes before a rather large man came out of an office to greet him. He was followed by the teller who still looked a bit nervous.

The large man wore a brown suit with a matching vest. He had a gold chain across his more than ample belly. His beard was well trimmed and he wore glasses down low on his nose. Joshua immediately noticed he carried a small pistol on his left side under his coat.

"I'm K. R. Waterman. How can I help you?" he asked in a deep booming voice.

"I'm Joshua Higgins from up north. I'm interested in finding someone who might have some cattle to sell. Do you happen to know of anyone in the area who might be willing to sell some cattle?"

"I might know someone like that," he said as he looked Joshua over.

"I don't want just any old cows, mind you. I'm looking for good breeding stock. I'd like about two hundred cows and several bulls, maybe a few more if I can get them."

"I see," he said with a slight grin. "I might just know of someone who could supply you with what you want."

"Would you be willing to tell me who this someone might be, and where I might find him?" Joshua asked as he wondered if he was going to have to drag the information out of the banker. "I would be most interested in seeing what he has to offer. And the sooner, the better. If I buy his cattle, I'll need to drive them back north. What is the rancher's name?"

"Of course. Jessup Jeffrey of the J bar J Ranch might have some cattle to sell. He lives about three or four miles southwest of here. It's a little hard to find, but I could probably find someone to guide you out to his place."

"If he's a rancher with enough cattle to fill my needs, I'm sure he has a large spread. I would think I could find his ranch if you were to give me directions."

"No disrespect, but you might want a guide. Someone Jessup would know if you're goin' out to his place."

"Why's that?"

"He's a mite nervous about strangers on his land, you might say," Waterman said with a grin.

"Has he had some trouble?" Joshua asked looking suspiciously at Waterman.

"You might say that."

"What kind of trouble, if you don't mind my asking?"

"Jessup runs a good number of cattle over a wide range of land. He's had some trouble with rustlers lately, at least according to him. I think it's probably Indians stealing a few of his cattle," Waterman said as he continued to grin.

Joshua noticed that Waterman appeared to think it was funny. It wasn't that he laughed out loud. It was more the way he said it, and how he looked that gave Joshua that impression.

"I take it you don't believe him," Joshua said.

"Let's just say I have my doubts. We haven't had any trouble with rustlers around here for sometime. But Indians, that's a different matter. You know Indians. You can't trust them."

Joshua looked at the big man as he thought about what he had said. There was something about Waterman that didn't set well with Joshua. It might have been his comment about not being able to trust Indians. Joshua knew there were Indians that couldn't be trusted. Joshua also knew that there were white men that couldn't be trusted, either. He had a feeling Waterman might just be one of them.

One thing that passed through Joshua's mind was that Waterman might know more than he was saying when it came to rustlers. He wondered if Waterman could be trusted. That thought caused Joshua to decide that trusting Waterman could prove to be a mistake. Joshua decided it might be best to change the subject, and be leery of anything Waterman said.

"What kind of cattle does Jeffrey have on his place?"

"Same as most of the folks around here, longhorns. I'll say this much, he runs some of the best longhorns in this part of Texas. They would make very good breeding stock if you need hardy stock, and you're willing to pay good money for them."

Joshua didn't comment on Waterman's statement. He guessed Waterman was fishing for information on how much money Joshua might have with him, but Joshua was not about to offer that kind of information to a total stranger. Especially to someone he didn't trust.

"You said I would need a guide. Would you be so kind as to find me someone who knows the way out to Mr. Jeffrey's ranch? I'd be willing to pay him for his time."

"Sure. Why don't you and your men go over to the saloon and have a drink on me. I'll get someone to take you out there and send him over to the saloon. It shouldn't take me long."

"Thank you, Mr. Waterman. That's very kind of you," Joshua said as he reached out his hand.

Joshua shook the big man's hand, then turned and left the bank with his men following him. Once they were outside and away from where anyone could hear him, Joshua turned and looked at John.

"What do you think, John?"

"I think I don't trust that guy. He strikes me as someone not to be trusted."

"I agree. I don't trust him, either," Joshua said as he looked up and down the street.

"Will, I want you to find the others. Tell them to make sure their guns are ready to use. Be sure to tell them they are to keep their eyes open. Don't let anyone hear what you tell them. No telling who we can trust in this town, or who might be eavesdropping on us."

"You think we're in for some trouble?"

"I don't know, but we might be. I just want to be prepared for anything."

"I'll get right on it," Will said."

Joshua watched as Will headed across the street to the blacksmith's shop. Joshua stepped off the boardwalk in front of the bank and stepped out into the street. He then turned and started down the street. John moved up beside him, but didn't say a word. He could tell Joshua was thinking pretty hard about something.

"John, when we start out of town to the J bar J Ranch, I want you to stay very close to our guide. You keep a good eye on him."

"Yes, sir. He won't be able to breathe without me knowing every breath he takes," John said.

"I'm going down to the general store and pay for our supplies. You get the men together and bring them down to the general store. We'll wait there for you. Bobby, you come with me."

"Yes, sir. We ain't meetin' the guide at the saloon?" Bobby asked.

"No. I don't want any of us to be boxed inside a building in case it is a trap."

"Right," Bobby said as he walked beside Joshua on their way to the general store.

As Joshua started down the street toward the general store, he kept his eyes moving. The last thing he wanted was to be surprised.

When Joshua and Bobby got to the general store, they found Frank sitting on a barrel out in front of the store. He didn't see Chester anywhere around.

"Where's Chester?" he asked as he approached Frank.

"He's inside with the storekeeper. The storekeeper won't let us load the supplies until you pay him for them," Frank said as he stood up.

Joshua nodded, then went into the general store. Frank followed him inside. Joshua saw the storekeeper standing behind the counter. Chester was standing in front of it. Chester looked over toward Joshua as he came inside. He waited for Joshua to come closer before saying anything.

"The storekeeper won't let us load up until you pay for the supplies. He don't seem very trusting of us."

"It's all right. I'll pay him while you load up."

Chester nodded, but didn't move until Joshua paid for the supplies. Joshua joined Chester, Bobby and Frank in helping them load the wagon. While they were loading the supplies, Joshua told them to keep their eyes open and to be ready for anything. It wasn't long before the others joined them in front of the general store. They all gathered next to the wagon and waited for Joshua to give them their instructions. Chester was the first one to speak.

"What's goin' on, boss?"

"I talked to the local banker. He told me where we might find some good breeding stock, but I don't entirely trust him. He's supposed to be getting us a guide to the J bar J Ranch because the owner doesn't like or trust strangers."

"You thinkin' we're bein' set up?" Chester asked.

"I don't know, but we need to be ready."

"Say, boss. What do you think might be causin' that dust cloud over that way?" Marcus asked. "There ain't no wind taday."

Joshua looked at Marcus, then looked in the direction that Marcus was looking. He could see a thin cloud of dust being kicked up by something moving fast across the open prairie well behind the town's buildings. If Joshua had to guess, it was kicked up by several horses running across the prairie in a southwestern direction.

"That might answer our question. If I'm right, there should be a guide coming along soon."

"What question is that?" Stan asked wondering what Joshua was talking about.

"I think Waterman has sent out a welcoming committee for us. He knows that if we are here to buy cattle, we must have money. I doubt he plans on letting us spend it on cattle."

"What do you want us to do?" John asked.

"That depends on you, all of you."

"What do you mean by that?" John asked.

"If we go along with Waterman and the guide he provides us, we could end up in a trap we have to fight our way out of."

"You've got to remember we were all soldiers, Mr. Higgins," Frank said with a grin. "Fighting is what we were trained to do."

"Yeah," Stan agreed. "We need cattle for the ranch. I say we find this J bar J Ranch and see what he has for cattle he's willin' ta sell. There won't be no trap if we are ready for one."

Joshua took a minute to look at each of his men. They all seemed willing and able to take on any threat to their mission of getting a herd of cattle to take back north.

"Okay. Get yourselves ready. We may have a fight on our hands. The guide should be here at any minute. And John, remember what I told you about keeping a close eye on the guide. If he makes a sudden break to get away from us, shoot him."

"Yes, sir," John said with a grin. "If it is a trap, he will be the first one to die in it."

"Speak of the devil," Marcus said. "I think he's comin' now."

Joshua and his men turned and looked up the street. They could see a man walking toward them. He was dressed like most of the cowboys in western Texas, but carried his gun low and tied to his leg like he might think of himself as a gunfighter. He had a cigarette hanging from the corner of his mouth with the smoke swirling around his head. He squinted as the smoke got into his eyes. His dark hair flowed out from under his cowboy hat onto his shoulders, and his long sideburns came down almost to his chin. He was leading a chestnut colored horse with a heavy western saddle. As he walked up to Joshua, he sort of looked him over as if sizing him up.

"You the fella lookin' fur the J bar J Ranch?" he asked without taking the cigarette out of his mouth.

"Yeah," Joshua replied.

"I was told ta meet ya at the saloon."

"I didn't want to go to the saloon," Joshua said, hoping the man would understand things would be done his way or not at all.

"Well, it don't matter none ta me. We best get along. It ain't no easy ride," he said as he turned, put his foot in the stirrup then swung into the saddle.

Joshua nodded and put his foot in the stirrup. He swung his leg over the saddle and sat down. The rest of his men mounted up except Chester. He untied the string of horses from the hitching rail, then tied them to the back of the wagon. After untying the team of horses from the hitching rail, he got up on the wagon seat. As soon as he was seated, he picked up the reins and kicked the brake handle loose. He was ready to go.

The guide looked back over his shoulder at the wagon, then looked at Joshua.

"You takin' that wagon and all them horses all the way out ta the J bar J?"

"Sure. You didn't expect me to leave it here, did you? The cattle are out there, not here," Joshua said as he pointed off toward the distant hills.

"Well, no never mind ta me, but it ain't no easy ride."

"So you said. But it hasn't been an easy ride getting here," Joshua said. "We are not a bunch of greenhorns."

The guide looked at Joshua as if he was trying to figure out what Joshua meant by his last comment. The guide shook his head, then looked toward the edge of town.

When the guide looked back at Joshua, he motioned for the guide to lead the way. The guide shrugged his shoulders, then nudged his horse and started toward the edge of town.

Joshua rode a little behind John while John rode up close to the guide. John was riding just a little behind the guide and to his left. He rode with his right hand resting easy on his gun, just in case the guide had something stupid in mind.

As they rode along, the guide kept looking off to the left, but only glanced off to the right occasionally. Joshua wondered what was so interesting off to the left. In watching the guide, Joshua got the idea that if trouble was going to come to them, it would come from their left, but there was not much to see off in that direction except for cactus, a lot of open land and several ravines. He wondered if there was trouble hiding in one of the ravines.

Joshua kept a close watch on the guide. He noticed the guide seemed to be growing just a little more edgy as they came closer and closer to the top of the hill. He kept shifting his weight in the saddle as if the saddle was uncomfortable. Joshua didn't believe that for a minute. The guide's saddle looked to be well worn. A well-worn saddle isn't an uncomfortable saddle. With as much time as a cowboy spends in a saddle, he would not use an uncomfortable saddle, unless he had no choice.

As they came closer to the top of the hill, Joshua could see in all directions except over the hill. He had no idea what was on the other side of the hill, but he had a feeling it was not good. He decided it was time to find out what it was that made the guide so nervous.

Joshua rode up close to John. John knew Joshua was now beside him, but didn't take his eyes off the guide.

"Take him," Joshua whispered to John.

John immediately kicked his horse in its sides. The horse lunged forward putting him right alongside the guide very quickly. John reached out and grabbed the guide's shirt at his shoulder, then jerked the guide toward him as he quickly turned his horse away from the guide's horse. The quickness of John's move caught the guide and his horse off balance. It was a maneuver John had used many times during the war to unseat an enemy from his horse.

The maneuver had been done so quickly the guide never saw it coming. He tried to prevent himself from falling from his horse, but was unable to stay in the saddle. He slid out of the saddle and fell to the ground with a bone jarring thud.

Before the guide could get to his feet and grab his gun, John had swung his horse around. He was now sitting on his horse with his gun pointed down at the guide. Joshua had reined up beside the guide. He also had his gun in his hand and it was pointed down at the guide.

"What the hell ya think you're doin'," the guide yelled.

Looking up at the two guns pointed at him, he quickly realized that to reach for his gun would mean certain death. He didn't even make an effort to stand up. He stayed on the ground looking up at Joshua. His eyes showed the fear he was feeling. He was sure they had figured out what he was doing.

"I think we've caught us a Judas goat. What do you think, John?" Joshua said looking down at the guide.

"I think you're right." John replied with a grin.

"What the hell's a Judas goat?" the guide asked.

"It's a goat used to lead sheep to slaughter. We are not sheep. We do not go to slaughter easily."

"What the hell ya talkin' about? I was just takin' ya ta the J bar J Ranch."

"John, I think this guy might need a little help remembering what his instructions were before he joined us."

"Yes sir," John said, then stepped out of his saddle.

He walked over to the guide who was still kneeling on the ground. John quickly relieved the guide of his gun and the knife he had in his belt, then pushed him over so he was lying on his back on the ground.

The guide looked scared, and he had every reason to be. With the exception of Chester, all Joshua's men were sitting on their horses in a circle looking down at the guide. They all had their guns pointed at him. He knew these men had seen right through Waterman's plan. He watched as John stood looking down at him. John slowly pointed his gun at the guide's knee, then waited for instructions from Joshua.

"Now that I have your undivided attention, I want to know just what plans you and your friends have for us."

"I don't know what the hell you're talkin' 'bout," the guide said defiantly, but there was no doubt in his mind he might be shot if he didn't answer their question.

"I want you to take a good look at the man standing over you. He doesn't have a lot of patience when it comes to getting information out of someone. He has lived with Indians for the past couple of years. He learned a lot from them about how to make a man talk. I can assure you it isn't pretty, but it is painful and very effective. I've never seen it fail to work. But we don't have a lot of time to spend with you. That being the case, we are going to do it the old fashion way. You might even say the cowboy way. I'm going to ask you just one more time. If you do not answer my question to my satisfaction, John will simply shoot you in your left knee. If you still don't answer me, then he will shoot you in your right knee. Is that clear?"

The guide didn't answer. He looked at John and nodded his head.

"Again, what plans does Waterman have for us?"

He didn't respond for several seconds, but quickly changed his mind when Joshua spoke again.

"Shoot him," Joshua said with a clear, commanding voice.

John grinned, then slowly pulled back the hammer on his pistol and put the end of the barrel against the guide's knee.

"I'll tell you," he almost screamed.

"Well?" Joshua asked impatiently.

"I was ta lead ya toward the J bar J Ranch. Just over the hill there's a place where the road turns and runs down through a narrow draw. As soon as all of ya was in the draw, the others was goin' ta ambush ya from above."

"Why?"

The guide glanced over at John before he answered. He could see John was ready to shoot him if he didn't answer.

"Waterman said that he'd bet that ya had a lota gold on ya if ya was plannin' on buyin' a lota cattle."

"Does Mr. Jeffrey have cattle to sell?"

"Yeah, I guess so. He sells cattle sometimes. He's got some good longhorns. Waterman weren't lyin' none 'bout that."

"I take it you would like to live and still be able to walk."

"Yes, sir," he replied weakly as he looked up at Joshua with pleading eyes.

"See, that wasn't so bad," Joshua said.

John looked up a Joshua and asked, "What do we do with him now?"

"Hogtie and gag him, then put him in the back of the wagon. Cover him up so no one can see him."

Joshua sat on his horse while John tied the guide up and put a gag over his mouth. As soon as he was in the wagon and covered by a heavy tarp, Joshua turned and looked at his men.

"Since they don't know how many of us are going out to talk to Mr. Jeffrey, I think we can split up. John, take Frank, Bobby and Stan, and ride around on top of the ridge. Get in behind those ready to ambush us. We'll give you a few minutes head start. We will go on down the road while you move in behind them, so don't waste any time. We are counting on you."

"Yes, sir," John said.

Joshua watched as John and the other three men rode off. As soon as they were out of sight, Joshua turned to the rest of the men.

"Chester, put your gun where you can get at it quickly. Marcus, take the guide's hat and put it on. You're about his size. Tie your horse with the rest of them and ride his horse. Keep your gun ready."

"Right," Marcus said as he rode around to the back of the wagon.

As soon as Marcus had tied his horse to the back of the wagon and got on the guide's horse, Joshua gave the order to move out. When they cleared the top of the hill, Joshua could see why they had planned to bushwhack them there. The road narrowed and went down through a long narrow draw. They started through the narrow draw moving along slowly. They knew full well they were sitting ducks if John didn't get to their attackers in time.

Suddenly, all hell broke loose. There was shooting coming from above the road. It wasn't long and two men had quickly slid over the edge to take cover from the attack by John and the others. What they didn't instantly realize was they had their backs exposed to Joshua and the men on the road below them. Joshua, Marcus and Chester opened fire on the two they could see. Within seconds the two men rolled down the steep embankment and fell dead on the road. The shooting almost immediately stopped.

Keeping an eye on the ridge above them, Joshua, Chester and Marcus remained ready while they watched to see if anyone else might be coming over the edge. They waited cautiously, hoping it was over and John and the men with him had succeeded in getting the rest of the ambushers. It was only moments before John stepped into view on the top of the draw. He had a big grin on his face.

"Its all clear up here," John said. "I see you got the other two."

"Yeah," Joshua said with a sigh of relief. "Anyone hurt?"

"None of us, but we got three dead and one gut shot up here."

"Come on back around."

"What about the guy that's gut shot?" John asked.

"What's his condition?"

"He's not going to live long." John said. "He's shot up pretty bad."

"Leave him. He chose his way of life, he can die with it."

John waved and moved away from the edge of the drop off and disappeared. It wasn't long before John and the others joined Joshua next to the wagon. The trap had failed to work. It was time to find out if the J bar J Ranch was a real ranch.

"What now?" John asked.

"Our guide is going to tell us how to get to the J bar J Ranch," Joshua said. "Get him out of the wagon."

John and Stan uncovered the guide and pulled him out of the wagon. They dropped him on the ground. John reached down and took the gag off him. The look on his face was one that showed his captors he was in fear of losing his life.

"Where is the J bar J Ranch?" John asked.

"It's just down the road a piece," he said as he nodded in the direction that they had been going. "You'll find the gate ta the ranch on your right 'bout two, maybe three miles down the road. It's another two miles or so back in ta the ranch house."

John looked up at Joshua and smiled. Joshua smiled and nodded his head.

"What do you want to do with him?" John asked. "If we were still soldiers, we'd kill him for trying to lead our men into a trap. The same as we would a spy."

"I'm sure you would, and it's not a bad idea. But I think I've got a better idea. Let's take him with us to the ranch. If we don't find the ranch where he said it is, then we'll kill him. If the ranch is where he says it is, I think that Mr. Jeffrey would like to have a little talk with him."

"Please, mister, don't take me ta Jeffrey's place."

"Now, why wouldn't you want to go there? You do something to Jeffrey that might make him angry with you?"

The guide looked at John, then at Joshua. He wasn't sure he wanted to tell them why he didn't want to go to the J bar J ranch. He also knew if he didn't tell them, he would probably be shot.

"Yeah," he said reluctantly.

"What did you do to him?"

The guide hesitated for a moment before he said, "I helped steal a few of his cattle," the guide admitted. "Waterman had us steal them."

Joshua thought for a minute, then looked at John. He smiled then looked back at the guide.

"You know, I think Mr. Jeffrey would like to find out who was behind the cattle rustling. Maybe, just maybe, if you were to tell him who was behind it, he might let you live, provided you leave the country and never come back."

"John, put him back in the wagon and let's get moving."

"Yes, sir."

As soon as the guide had been put back in the wagon, they moved on down the road. John gave instructions to Marcus to ride on ahead a little ways to make sure there were no more surprises.

CHAPTER TWENTY-TWO

J Bar J Ranch

It wasn't long before Joshua and his men came to a gate with a sign over it. It read "J bar J Ranch." There was another sign next to the gate that read, "Enter at your own risk".

"Well, it looks like we found it," Joshua said.

"Yeah. That sign don't seem none too welcomin'," Chester said.

"No, it doesn't. But maybe he has good reason. I don't think we have too much to worry about as long as we stay on the road and move toward the ranch house."

"What about this guy? If they see him they might think we are here to cause trouble," John said.

"You might be right. Put a gag on him and cover him up."

As soon as the guide was gagged and covered up in the back of the wagon, they began to move along the road toward the ranch house of the J bar J Ranch. The small band of riders led the wagon along the narrow dusty road. They hadn't gone very far, maybe a half a mile or so, when they saw several men come riding over a hill in the distance. The men were riding directly toward them. As they drew closer, Joshua could see the men were well armed and were carrying their rifles in their hands.

"Pull up," Joshua said to Chester.

Chester pulled back on the reins of the horses while he pushed on the brake arm with his foot. The rest of Joshua's men moved in close to the wagon, but stayed on their horses.

"We don't want any trouble," Joshua reminded his men. "Keep your hands away from your guns, but be ready for anything."

Joshua and his men watched as the men from the J bar J Ranch rode closer. They were a tough looking bunch of men. They all had rifles in their hands and side arms on their hips. The look on their faces showed Joshua they meant business.

The J bar J ranch hands pulled up in a line and looked at Joshua and his men. After a moment or two of just looking at each other, one of the J bar J ranch hands slowly moved closer while the rest of the hands remained in a line and watched. They never took their eyes off Joshua's men.

"Do you know you're on private land, mister?" the man asked.

"Yes. My name is Joshua Higgins. I'm here to see Mr. Jeffrey.

"Does he know you were comin'?"

"No. I was told he might have some cattle to sell."

"Who sent you here?"

"It's a long story, but simply put we found out in the town of Cactus Flats that you have good cattle. We were attacked on our way here, but they found out we don't scare easily. We have one of them tied and gagged in the back of the wagon. I think your boss would like to have a little talk with him."

"About what?"

"About who has been stealing his cattle."

"What did you say your name was?"

"Joshua Higgins. What's your name?"

"Bill Shaffer. I'm the foreman on this spread."

"You wouldn't happen to be Major Bill Shaffer of the thirty-second North Carolina Cavalry, would you?" John asked with a smile.

Bill looked at John. At first he didn't recognize him, but a smile started to come over his face.

"Sergeant John Hamilton?" he asked as he looked him over.

"Sure is, Major."

"Well, I'll be damned. I thought you were dead."

"Not yet."

"Is this your boss now?"

"Yeah. He's a good man. What he said is why we're here. We came down lookin' for good breedin' stock."

"In that case, I'll take you up to the house, Mr. Higgins. John, you and I can catch up on the past few years while they talk business.

Bill Shaffer swung his horse around and rode back to his men. He gave them instructions, then rejoined Joshua and his men. After briefly explaining why they were so careful about strangers on the property, he led Joshua and his men to the ranch house. All the way to the ranch house, Bill and John rode side by side and talked about what had happened to them since the end of the Civil War.

It didn't take long before they arrived at the ranch house. As they rode into the ranch yard, Joshua saw a man who looked to be in his sixties step out of the house. He also noticed the man had a side arm on his hip while holding a rifle in his hands. He looked first at Joshua's men, then at his foreman.

"Who are these men?" he asked Bill.

"This here is Joshua Higgins. He's come down here from the Dakota Territory looking for breedin' stock."

"You sure?"

"Yes, sir. Mr. Higgins's foreman is an old friend of mine. We fought in the Civil War together. He's a good man."

"Okay," Mr. Jeffrey said as he stepped off the porch and walked toward the riders.

"Mr. Higgins, welcome to the J bar J Ranch. You can get down."

"Thank you. It's been a hard day. Would it be okay with you if my men get down and get some water for themselves and the horses?"

"Sure," he said as the turned to Bill. "Bill, see to the men and their horses. If they're here to find breeding stock, they will be here for a while. See to it they are made welcome. They can bunk in the bunkhouse with the other men."

"Yes, sir."

"Mr. Higgins, - - -"

"Please, call me Joshua."

"Okay," he said with a smile. "You can call me, Jess. How about a drink?"

"That would be nice. My throat is a little dry," Joshua said with a smile.

"Follow me."

"Jess, before we have that drink, I have something that might be of interest to you. Sort of a gift, you might say," Joshua said with a smile.

"Oh?" Jess replied wondering what kind of "gift" this stranger could have for him.

"Yeah," Joshua said then turned to John. "You want to get our gift for Mr. Jeffrey out of the wagon."

"Sure thing."

With the help of Chester, they uncovered the guide and pulled him out of the wagon. Jess was a bit surprised they had a man hogtied and gagged. Jess looked at the man, but didn't recognize him. The look on Jess's face told Joshua he didn't understand what was going on.

"This man was to guide us to your place, but he was really sent to guide us into a trap. The rest of his friends are dead. As you can see by the fact we are here, the trap didn't work.

"To make a long story short, he is one of the men who has been rustling some of your cattle. I thought you might like to have a little talk with him about who put him and the others up to it. By the way, he will talk to you with a little convincing."

"I think this is one of the nicest gifts I've gotten in a long time," Jess said with a grin.

"Bill, see to it our gift is well taken care of. I'll want to talk to him later."

"Yes, sir. With pleasure."

Jess and Joshua went into the ranch house while John and Bill took the prisoner to the barn and secured him in a stall so he could not escape. Bill then took the rest of Joshua's men to the bunkhouse so they could get settled in before dinner.

As Joshua entered the living room of the ranch house, he looked around. It was a comfortable looking place. There was a fire in the large stone fireplace. Above the mantel there was a gun rack with several guns. On the mantel were several pictures.

"Sit down and take a load off," Jess said as he walked over to a small cabinet.

Joshua sat down and watched as Jess opened the cabinet. Jess took out a bottle of whisky and poured about three fingers of the golden brown liquid into glasses. He turned around and held one of the glasses out to Joshua. Joshua reached out and took the glass.

"Here's to a pleasant working relationship," Jess said then touched his glass to Joshua's glass.

Joshua took a sip of the liquor and smiled.

"Very good. Very good, indeed."

"It should be. It's good old Kentucky whiskey. It's about eight years old."

"It has been a long time since I've had a shot of whiskey, let alone one as good at this."

"It's one of the few pleasures I have out here. Now tell me, what are you doing so far south?"

"I heard there were very good longhorn cattle down this way."

"You don't have good cattle up north?"

"Not yet. I plan to be one of the first," Joshua said.

"How many are you looking for?"

"Oh, I was thinking about four hundred and fifty to five hundred or so, and a couple of good bulls. Maybe a few more."

"That's a good number. I take it you're just getting started in the cattle business?"

"Yes. You probably noticed the men riding with me. They are all ex-Confederate soldiers. In fact, they were prisoners of mine for almost a year before the war ended."

"As you know, I have a few ex-Confederate soldiers working for me."

"They're good men."

"Sure are. How is it they were your prisoners?" Jess asked.

"They tried to steal my horses while dressed as Union soldiers. A good friend of mine, who is an Indian, helped me hold them. It seems the Union Army couldn't spare the men to take them to a fort to be held there. Rather than hang them as horse thieves, we held them prisoners. They worked hard to help me build up my place. When the war ended, I turned them loose. The ones with me decided they had nothing to return to and stayed on as ranch hands."

"Interesting. You must have treated them pretty good to get them to stay."

"We took care of them while they were with us."

"Well, it's a little late to go out and look over my cattle today. We can go out first thing in the morning and see if I have anything that interests you. In the meantime, I want you to make yourself at home. You will stay here in the house with me. I have a spare room down the hall you can use while you are here. You will eat with me. Your men can eat with the hands in the bunkhouse kitchen."

"That sounds good."

"There's a wash bowl on the back porch. You'll probably want to clean up before dinner. Help yourself. I'll let the cook know I'll be having a guest for dinner."

With that said, Jess drank down the rest of his liquor then stood up. Joshua did the same. Joshua went out back and washed up for dinner. After washing up, he returned to the living room where Jess was waiting for him. They went into the dining room and sat down to a very good dinner.

After dinner, Jess invited Joshua's foreman and his foreman to join them in the living room. They spent a good part of the evening talking about cattle and planning for the next day. Their day would start early as it usually did on a ranch.

"I guess that about covers things for tonight," Jess said. "A good night's sleep seems to be in order since we will have a long day tomorrow."

As the two foremen started for the door, Joshua interrupted their leaving.

"There is one small item I think we should discuss."

"What is that?" Jess asked with a confused look on his face.

"The gift I brought you. Namely the guide who admitted to being hired to steal your cattle."

"Oh, him," Jess said, then looked over at his foreman, Bill.

"Bill, is he secure where he is?"

"Yes, sir."

"Has he been fed?"

"Yes, sir."

"In that case, I think he can wait until tomorrow. Make sure that you post a guard on him. I don't want anything happening to him before I get a chance to talk to him."

"Yes, sir," Bill said before he turned to leave the ranch house.

With that taken care of, the four men turned in for the night.

CHAPTER TWENTY-THREE

Getting Cattle For The Ranch

Morning came early as it always does on a ranch. The sun was just breaking over the hills to the east. It looked like it was going to be a sunny day with only a few clouds drifting across the otherwise clear blue sky. The ranch hands had already had their breakfast and were ready to ride. Joshua's men and several of Jess's men rode up to the ranch house just as Joshua and Jess came out onto the porch. Bill had brought a horse up to the house for his boss, and John led a horse for Joshua.

"Gentlemen, we are going out to look at cattle Mr. Higgins might be interested in buying. As I'm sure you have figured out, his men will be going with us. I want you to work with them. If Mr. Higgins finds some cattle he wishes to buy, you will help his men pick them out and keep them together until we can take them back to the holding pens. Since we have had a bit of trouble around here, I want all of you to keep your eyes open."

When Jess had finished giving instructions to his men, he looked at Joshua to see if he had anything to add.

"What Mr. Jeffrey said goes for my hands as well. I would like to see you all working together. If trouble should start, you will fight alongside Mr. Jeffrey's hands. Now let's get out there and get some work done."

Joshua and Jess stepped off the porch and went to their horses. As soon as they were mounted, Jess signaled for Bill to lead the way. Bill turned his horse and started out of the ranch yard and headed out toward the open prairie.

It didn't take but an hour or so before they came upon a fairly small group of longhorns down in a shallow valley. The longhorns were enjoying the thick green grass that grew along the edge of a narrow creek that ran along the bottom of the valley. Bill raised his hand and everyone stopped. Joshua and Jess rode up beside Bill.

"Well, what do you think?" Jess said as he looked over at Joshua.

Joshua was looking over the herd of longhorns. He began to grin as he nodded his head in approval. What he saw were good healthy looking longhorns. There was little doubt in Joshua's mind these were just the kind of cattle he was looking for.

"They look good to me. They seem strong and healthy."

"Are you interested in them?" Jess asked.

"I sure am," Joshua said with a smile as he looked over at Jess.

"Well, let's round them up. There's about fifty of them. We'll get them rounded up and have a few of the men drive them back to the holding pens," Jess said, then turned to Bill.

"Bill, get them rounded up.

"John, go with them and get a good look at them," Joshua said. "If they look as good up close as they do from here, we'll want them. And pay attention to Jess's men. We can learn a lot from them."

"Yes, sir," John said as he looked to Bill for directions.

Bill gave instructions on what he wanted the men to do. Joshua and Jess sat on their horses overlooking the small valley and watched as several of Jess's ranch hands along with three of Joshua's ranch hands moved slowly into the valley. The men slowly worked their way around the small herd of longhorns in an effort not to spook them. The cattle slowly began to move in the direction the ranch hands wanted them to go.

Jess looked over at Joshua. He saw Joshua watching what was going on in the valley with a great deal of interest.

"One thing about longhorns, you don't want to spook them if you can help it. They are much easier to handle if you just slowly ride into them and gently pick out the ones you want. Longhorns don't take to sudden movements, or loud yelling, or almost any unfamiliar noise, for that matter. They're much easier to handle if you just sort of coax them along. Once you have them moving, they will move along pretty well. After a couple of days on the trail they become trail broke. In other words, they get used to what is expected of them and usually go along with it. Usually," Jess said with a grin.

"I had heard they are hard to handle."

"Only if you try to ride roughshod over them or scare them. Treat them gently and they'll cooperate pretty well. Most of the time," Jess added, still grinning.

Joshua watched the men work. Since his men had little experience at handling cattle, he was very much interested in how they did. It looked as if his ranch hands were paying close attention to what Jess's ranch hands did and followed instructions from them. They seemed to catch on quickly. It pleased him to see his men were quick learners.

"Looks like you have some good men there. They'll make good cowboys," Jess said.

"You think they will be able to handle a herd the size I want all the way back to the Dakota Territory?"

"I won't say you won't have problems, but I think you have good men. They will learn quickly. By the time we have rounded up enough cattle to fit your needs they will have learned how to handle them. They'll do fine," Jess assured him.

Joshua was glad he had treated his men well while they were his prisoners. They had shown they were loyal and would do what it took to have a good working ranch. They seemed ready, willing and able to take on the task before them.

Just then, they saw Bill ride on ahead of the small herd. He rode up beside Jess.

"John and I counted the cattle and agree. We have fifty-five head. There are a couple of good breeding bulls in that bunch, too," Bill reported.

"Have a few of the men take them back to the holding pens. When they get them in the pens, come back out and find us. We'll be riding west a little more to see if there are more cattle out that way. There's another little valley out there where they like to gather. There's plenty of water and grass in the valley," Jess said for Joshua's benefit.

"Meet us there," he said to Bill. "Take a couple of Joshua's men with you so they can learn how to handle the cattle and get them into a pen."

"Yes, sir," Bill said then swung his horse around and headed back to the herd.

"Thanks for helping to teach my men how to handle the cattle."

"No problem. I had to teach some of my ranch hands when I first came out here. Consider it pay back for the fine gift you brought me."

"You never told me how you came to have ex-Confederate soldiers for ranch hands," Joshua said.

"Bill and several of the men had escaped from a Yankee prison camp near the end of the war. It was obvious the war was lost to the South, and the South was being pretty much destroyed by the North.

"Bill, and those who escaped with him, headed west with the idea of starting a new life. A couple of my men found them huddled in a ravine trying to keep warm. It had been an unusually cold night. They had nothing to eat and had little to keep them warm.

"We brought them to the ranch, fed them, gave them warm clothes and a place to bed down. As soon as they were well enough to leave, they asked to stay on. I put them to work and they learned fast. Now I have some of the best ranch hands in Texas."

Joshua was thinking Jess was not so different. He helped others when he could and those he helped, helped him in return.

"We best catch up to the others," Jess said.

Jess and Joshua rode off to join the others. They started riding toward another valley where there was fresh water and plenty of green grass. It was a pretty good bet that some of the cattle might have gathered there.

The two groups of men worked together to gather the cattle that Joshua would buy. By the end of the day, they had found and gathered a total of ninety-six head of cattle. In among them were five very nice bulls that would make good breeding bulls.

It took the better part of a week to gather the cattle Joshua wanted. They had gathered a total of five hundred and seventy-five head plus twenty good breeding bulls and a few bull calves that would make good breeding bulls in the future.

Joshua's men had learned a lot about handling the cattle and were getting much more confident in working with them. He was also getting more confident in his men's ability to get the cattle back to his ranch.

It was the last evening Joshua and his men would spend at the J bar J Ranch before heading back home. Joshua and Jess were sitting at the table after a very good dinner. They were enjoying a cigar and a glass of Kentucky whiskey after dinner.

"It looks like we have the cattle I came to get for my ranch. I guess it's time to settle up so we can head back home."

"I guess so. I will miss having you and your men here. I don't get much company out this way. Do you think you will ever be back this way?"

"Ya never know," Joshua said with a smile.

"Shall we," Jess said.

"Anytime you're ready."

Jess nodded he was ready for them to settle up for the cattle. Joshua got up from the table and went out to the wagon. He retrieved a small box from under the seat of the wagon and brought it into the house. He set it down on the table. As soon as they were both seated, Joshua got his gold out of the box and counted out enough to pay for the cattle. As soon as the gold had been counted and both of the men agreed it was the amount they had decided on, Jess wrote out a bill of sale for the cattle. When the deal was done, they stood and shook hands.

"I think this calls for another drink," Jess said as he walked over to the cabinet and got his bottle of Kentucky whiskey.

Jess poured each of them another drink, set the bottle on the table, and raised his glass in a toast.

"To good friends. May we always remain friends."

Joshua smiled and said, "To friends."

They drank a bit of the whiskey and sat back down at the table.

"I suspect you will be changing the brand on your critters?"

"I guess I hadn't thought much about that. I haven't even thought of a brand."

"In that case, may I suggest one for you?"

"Certainly."

Jess took out a piece of paper and drew his brand on it. The brand was two Js with a single bar in between them which was his brand. Joshua watched him as he drew a circle around his brand and added a second bar between the Js.

"I know it is kind of simple, but it might work for you. You could call it the Circle Double J Bar Ranch, unless you have a better idea."

"No. I like it. Since my son's name is Jeremiah, I think I'll just call it the Circle Double J Ranch for now," Joshua said as he looked at it. "What do you think?"

"Sounds good to me."

Joshua took the paper, folded it and put it in his pocket after Jess wrote the name Joshua wanted to call his ranch on the paper. He then stood up. As soon as Jess stood up, Joshua reached across the table and shook Jess's hand, again.

"I want to thank you for all you have done for me and my men. I hope we will see each other again someday. You will always be welcome at my place."

"It was a pleasure to have your company these past few days, and to do business with you. I hope you have a safe trip home. If you ever need more cattle, you're welcome to come and take a look at mine."

"Thank you. I'll do that. We will be leaving first thing in the morning."

"I've told my foreman to take a few hands and help you get the herd started. They will travel with you for a couple of days. I would like you to have a couple of extra hands to ride with you and your men until the cattle are trail broken."

"Thank you. I appreciate that."

"By the way, I don't think it would be a good idea to go back the way you came. Bill will show you an easy way to get the cattle past Cactus Flats. I don't expect trouble after the whipping you gave them on your way out here, but it's better to be safe than sorry."

"Thanks for the advice. I guess I should get a good night's sleep. It may be the last one I get until I get home," Joshua said with a smile.

"You're probably right about that. By the way, tomorrow two of my men are going to take your gift to the territorial capital for trial."

"Did he tell you who put him up to stealing your cattle?"

"Yeah, but I already had a pretty good idea it was Waterman, I just couldn't prove it until now. He said

Waterman was the one who had them steal the cattle. Now I have something that should help the territorial marshal when he gets here."

"Good. It is good to see there is some law coming to the Frontier."

"Me, too, but it's still a little hard to find sometimes," Jess said with a grin. "I'll see you off in the morning."

There was nothing else to say so the two men turned in for the night.

* * * *

The sun had not yet come up over the horizon when Joshua and Jess's men sat down for breakfast in the ranch hands' dining room. They sat down at the long table and began to eat. John and Bill sat together and talked about the times they had riding together during the Civil War. Before long, Bill stopped talking about their days as soldiers, and began to ask John about how he liked living in the Dakota Territory.

"It's a lot different from what it was like in South Carolina, and certainly a lot different than it is here. There are very few settlers so far, but the land is wide open. The plains don't have a lot of trees, but there is a lot of grassland. More than there is in this part of Texas. Now the Black Hills have a lot trees, mostly pine trees. The hills are very pretty and are full of game."

"What about Indians?"

"We have some that live near the ranch, and there are a lot of Indians that roam the Dakota Territory. Joshua is married to an Indian and has a son and a daughter by her. She is very nice. Her tribe spends a lot of time in and around the southern Black Hills. In fact, they helped guard us while we were prisoners at Joshua's place. They were good to us. As long as we didn't give them any trouble, they treated us fairly."

"What made you want to stay there after being held prisoner, especially going to work for the same people that held you prisoner? I don't think I could have done that."

"I don't know. I think it was probably the way I was treated, and the way the others were treated by Joshua, his family and his friends. We were given plenty of food and water. They even provided us with warm blankets and a place to get out of the weather as well as clothes. We built a bunkhouse for him and when it was finished, we used it instead of the barn to live in.

"He had us do things to help build up his place. It gave us something to do. It made the time go by faster. If we had been captured by almost anyone else, we would most likely have been hung as horse thieves or spies.

"There was no doubt he treated us better than we would have been treated in a Yankee prisoner of war camp. In a Yankee prisoner of war camp, most of us might not have lived to see the end of the war. We had it pretty good compared to those in prison camps."

"What about the country?"

"Like I said, there's a lot more grass there than there is here. There are areas where it is pretty dry and not much grass, but the area where Joshua has his ranch has got pretty good grass and good water. The cattle we're taking up there should get a lot fatter than they do here. They certainly won't have to walk as far to get enough to eat," John said with a slight laugh. "It's not very rocky except in the Black Hills, and there isn't as much cactus there.

"That's not to say it's perfect. The winters can be pretty harsh. It gets darn right cold there, and there is often a lot of snow during the long winters. I would say that the winters are often more severe than they are here, but we don't get as many ice storms. Sometimes we get some real nasty blizzards out on the plains. It also gets down right hot in the summer, but it doesn't usually last very long. We have some of the same kinds of storms you have here."

Bill turned and looked off into space as he thought about what he had been told. He was wondering if maybe he would like it there. Jess had been good to him, but he had been thinking for sometime he would like a change of scenery. He didn't like the barren country of southwestern Texas. Most of the area where Jess's ranch was located was rocky, and grass and water were not very plentiful. The grass in the pastures was often dry and scarce in the hot summers. It took a lot of land to raise cattle in that part of Texas. It was also very hot in the summer, and there were long stretches of hot weather. However, the winters were usually fairly short and fairly mild.

It was still dark outside when the men had finished eating. They all went out and saddled up their horses. The wagon to be used as a chuck wagon had been stocked with food and supplies the night before so all that had to be done was to hitch up the team. Chester and Marcus were doing that when Jess and Joshua came out of the house. John had already saddled up a horse for Joshua and tied it to the hitching rail in front of the ranch house.

"Well, I guess it's time for us to get this herd moving. I want to thank you for all you have done."

"I enjoyed the company. A few of my men will accompany you for a couple of days to help you get the cattle trail broke. They can be a little hard to handle at first. After that you'll be on your own. I wish you well."

"Again, thanks," Joshua said as he shook Jess's hand.

Joshua turned and untied his horse from the hitching rail. He then put his foot in the stirrup and swung into the saddle. He turned his horse and started out of the ranch yard toward the holding pens. His men followed along with six of Jess's ranch hands.

CHAPTER TWENTY-FOUR

The Cattle Drive

Bill and John slowly moved into the holding pens and began to gently push the cattle out of the pens. With the help of Jess's ranch hands, the cattle were started north. Joshua took the point with Bill while the others took their places around the herd. Marcus and John rode the flank positions, one on each side of the herd. Stan and Will took positions as swing riders, again one on each side of the herd. Frank and Bobby took positions as drag riders, pulling up the rear and keeping the lazy cattle from becoming stragglers. Jess's men rode with the others and helped them learn what their duties were in each of the positions around the herd. Chester headed out with the wagon and the string of extra horses.

The cattle moved out slowly. There were a few of the cows that didn't seem to want to go with the rest. A couple of Jess's ranch hands would ride after them and move them back in with the others. By midday, the cattle seemed to figure out what was expected of them.

The cattle moved along at a slow pace, but it allowed time for Joshua's ranch hands to learn what they had to do. By nightfall, the herd had made only about ten miles, but the cattle had done well for the first day. It was now time to give them a rest.

Each man took his turn as a night rider. They would circle around the cattle as they talked softly or sang to the cattle to keep them calm. One of Jess's men would ride with one of Joshua's hands during the night. He would teach the new cowboys what to do and what to watch for in order to avoid problems.

Bill and John had spent a lot of time together during the day. They mostly talked about the Dakota Territory and what it was like to live there. John didn't try to talk Bill into coming to the Dakota Territory, but got the feeling Bill was thinking about giving up his job at the J bar J Ranch and hiring on with Joshua, if Joshua would have him. There was no question he would be a great asset to the ranch. He knew a lot about herding and handling cattle, especially longhorns.

When morning of the second day came, the men had a quick breakfast then went to work. They slowly started the cattle moving north again. Bill rode alongside John, but didn't say anything for the longest time.

"John?" he finally said. "Do you think your boss would let me join up with him?"

"Are you sure you want to join us?"

"Yeah. I've been thinkin' about leavin' Texas for a while now."

"Why would you want to give up your job as foreman? It's a good job, you're good at it and it pays well."

"Don't misunderstand me. I'm not tryin' to take your job. I would be just another hired hand."

"I'm not worried about that. I just don't understand why you would want to give up a good paying job and move to someplace you know nothing about."

"I'm tired of this country," Bill said as he waved his arm to indicate the vast open land of west Texas. "There's nothin' out there. It's very lonely."

"It's kind of lonely in the Dakota Territory, too."

"I'm sure it is, but I would like to find out what it's like for myself. I've never been any further north than Oklahoma, that is west of the Mississippi River. Would you talk to Mr. Higgins about takin' me on as a ranch hand?"

John looked at him for a moment or two before he answered him.

"Sure. I'll ask him tonight if you're sure that's what you want."

"It's what I want. I'm sure."

"Okay."

"Great," Bill replied with a grin.

"But right now I think we should go after that cow that has decided she doesn't want to go with the rest of them."

"I'll get her," Bill said.

Bill kicked his horse in the ribs. The horse took off after the cow. It wasn't long before Bill had caught up with the cow and started driving her back to the rest of the herd. As soon as the cow was back with the rest of the herd, Bill again joined John and rode beside him. They didn't talk much for the rest of the day. They just did their job of keeping the cattle together and keeping them moving north.

When it came time to stop for the night, John went over to the wagon where Joshua was getting a cup of coffee. He walked up beside Joshua, but didn't say anything.

"Something on your mind, John?" Joshua asked.

"Yes, sir."

"What is it?"

"Bill Shaffer asked me to talk to you."

"What about?"

"About him staying on with us."

Joshua looked at John for a second before saying anything.

"Did he say why?"

John said he did, then went on to tell Joshua about what Bill and he had talked about earlier in the day. After hearing what John had to say, Joshua sipped his coffee as he thought about it for a minute.

"Does he understand he will be a regular ranch hand? I will not make him foreman just because he was a foreman at the J bar J Ranch, or because he was a major during the war."

"He understands that."

"Okay. If that is what he wants. You make sure he understands he will be just like any other ranch hand. You might make it clear that he will be taking orders from you."

"Yes, sir. I'll go tell him what you said."

"Okay. Let me know what he says."

"I will," John said then turned and walked away.

John walked over to where the rest of the men who were not on watch were eating their evening meal. He got a plate full of food then walked over to Bill and sat down. John told Bill that if he really wanted to join up with them, it was okay with Joshua. He also told him what Joshua had said. Bill smiled and thanked John.

"I'm really glad I'm not a foreman any more. Don't get me wrong, it's a good job, but I'd like sometime off once in awhile. Don't get much time off as a foreman."

"You won't get any time off, and very little sleep until we get these cattle back to Joshua's ranch," John said with a grin.

"You're right about that," Bill agreed.

After everyone had finished eating, those assigned to watch the herd went out to spend their time watching over the cattle while those who had been watching the cattle came into camp to eat and rest. Those who had finished eating laid down on their bedrolls to try to get as much sleep as they could.

It was Chester's job to made sure there was coffee on the fire all night so there would be some when those on watch came in after being relieved. Chester did a good job of feeding the men. He always had something for them to eat and always made sure the coffee pot was on every time they stopped.

* * * *

It was the third night out on the trail. The cattle were slowly settling into the routine of the day. Joshua and his men had taken the cattle around Cactus Flats and were well north of it. The night was quiet except for the snoring men sleeping near the wagon. There was no wind to rustle the leaves in the trees along the creek, and the temperature was cool, but not cold. The sky was full of stars, and an almost full moon was slowly coming up in the east. It would soon cast faint dark shadows over the land.

Bobby was riding night watch over the herd with Joseph Powell, one of Jess's ranch hands. Jess's men were due to start back to the J bar J Ranch first thing in the morning. The only sounds that could be heard around the cattle were the sounds of a few cattle moving around and munching on grass, the sound of an owl off to the west near a lone tree, and of course, the sound of Bobby singing softly to the cattle. Bobby's voice had a mellow and soothing quality to it. He was singing a lullaby his mother had taught him when he was a child.

It was well past midnight when the quiet of the night was suddenly shattered by the sound of gunfire. The loud bang of gunfire startled the cattle at first. The cattle began to mill around as if confused by the sudden noise. The first shot was followed by a couple more just moments after the first. The shooting had scared the already nervous cattle. The frightened cattle began to stir and bump into each other. It wasn't long, only a matter of seconds, before the cattle began to run wildly across the open plains.

Bobby quickly realized what was happening. Although he had never seen a stampede, he was aware of what it could do. He kicked his horse in the ribs and started after the herd in an effort to catch up with the cattle in the lead. It was his hope he would be able to get to the front of the stampeding cattle so he could turn them back against themselves. In that way, he hoped to get them to stop running.

Joseph saw what Bobby was trying to do and took off after the cattle. It was his plan to do what he could to catch up to Bobby and help him turn the cattle.

The sounds of the gunshots also woke the rest of the men. For several seconds, there was a lot of confusion. It

didn't take but a few seconds for the men to understand what
was happening. They got to their feet and ran to the horses.
The men saddled their horses as fast as they could then
headed out to help catch the herd. They knew when cattle
stampeded they could run for several miles before they
would stop on their own. They also knew the cattle would
run over anything and everything that got in their way,
including cowboys and their horses.

No one knew where the shots had come from, but
everyone was sure it was someone trying to steal the herd. It
was everyone's responsibility to stop the cattle and protect
them from being stolen.

Bobby was slowly gaining on the herd as he rode at full
gallop across the prairie in the dark. Suddenly, he felt a
sharp pain in his side causing him to drop the reins. He
never heard the shot that hit him because of the noise made
by the stampeding cattle. Bobby tried to stay in the saddle
by holding on to his saddle horn, but the pain and the shock
of being shot made it impossible. He knew he had been shot,
but no matter how hard he tried he couldn't stop himself
from falling out of the saddle. Falling from his horse meant
certain death. The cattle would run over him and trample
him to death. Unable to hang on any longer, he fell from the
saddle onto the ground and was immediately trampled to
death by the onrush of frightened cattle.

John and the others finally chased down the cattle and
got them turned. Shortly after the cattle were turned back
into themselves, they stopped running. The men surrounded
the herd and rode slowly around them to help calm them.
They watched the cattle until they were sure they had settled
down.

Once the cattle had stopped and were calm again, Joshua
started to slowly ride around the herd looking for John. It
was hard to tell who was who if they were more than ten or
twelve feet away in the dark. As he rode around the herd, he
came upon Bill first.

"Bill, any idea what happened?"

"No, sir. I heard what sounded like gunshots. There were at least two or three shots, maybe more. It startled the cattle and they stampeded."

"Any idea what damn fool fired the shots?"

"No, sir, but I doubt it was any of our men."

"Have you seen John?"

"No, sir. The last time I saw him he was ridin' hell bent for leather on the other side of the herd. He should be over that way somewhere," he said as he pointed toward the other side of the herd.

"Work your way around that way," Joshua said as he pointed up along the herd and I'll go around the other way. See if everyone is accounted for. If you find John, tell him where I am, and that I want to see him."

"Yes, sir," Bill replied then started moving around the outside of the herd in the direction Joshua had told him to go.

Joshua started in the opposite direction around the herd from Bill, all the time hoping all the men had survived the stampede. As he came to each rider, he mentally made a note of them. He knew a stampede could take the life of a cowboy if his horse fell, or he fell from his horse, or the herd turned on him. Since cattle in a stampede can often run for miles, it was hard to tell where someone might be if he had been trampled to death by the wild-eyed cattle. A head count of the men would tell Joshua if anyone might have become a victim of the stampede.

By the time Joshua got to John, he had at least half of the men accounted for. He was talking to John when Bill came up and told them who he had seen. Joshua went over in his head the men he had seen and the ones he had been told about by Bill. It quickly became clear Bobby was the only one that appeared to be missing. He was the youngest of the men working for him.

"Has anyone seen Bobby?" Joshua asked.

"I saw everyone on the other side of the herd, but I didn't see Bobby," Bill said. "He's the young fella who likes to ride that brown and white paint?"

"Yes."

"I didn't see him or his horse."

Just then Frank Sanders came riding up leading the brown and white paint Bobby had been riding.

"I found Bobby's horse, but I didn't find Bobby," Frank said as he reined up next to Joshua. "I think you should take a look at his saddle, Mr. Higgins."

Joshua moved over next to the paint and looked at the saddle. There was a large dark spot on the saddle. Even in the dark, he had a pretty good idea what it was. Joshua reached out and touched the spot with the tips of his fingers. It was still damp. He looked at the ends of his finger and rubbed them together. It was sticky on his fingers. He was quickly reassured that the dark spot was blood. Joshua looked at the others.

"It's blood, ain't it?" Frank asked.

"Yes," Joshua said. "It looks like someone may have shot him."

"We best start lookin' for him," Frank said.

"No. John, you and Bill work your way back to camp. I want you to follow the tracks left by the cattle. I want you to look for Bobby, but don't take too much time at it.

"The rest of you keep the herd here and keep them calm. I know everyone would like to spread out and look for Bobby, but we can't afford to leave the herd unattended. It is still too dark to see anything. We have no idea who might still be out there. If someone shot Bobby and started the stampede, they might do it again if we don't keep the cattle calm and our eyes open."

"Yes, sir," Frank said, but was reluctant to agree.

Frank knew the cattle had to be watched, even though he wanted to start looking for Bobby. He also knew it would be hard to find him in the dark, especially if he had been trampled.

"And, John, have Chester bring the wagon up here. We'll spend the rest of the night here. If you don't find Bobby on your way back to camp, we'll take time to look for him after the sun comes up."

"Yes, sir," John said.

Joshua watched as the men returned to their duties of watching the herd while John and Bill left to get Chester. The men were quiet and knew there was little hope of finding Bobby alive. Joshua also knew the men wanted to make someone pay for what had happened. He could certainly understand that, he felt the same way. The only thing they didn't know was did someone shoot Bobby because of some grudge, or was he shot accidentally while the shooter was attempting to stampede the herd. He couldn't think of anyone who might have a grudge against Bobby since he had been at his ranch for the past two years.

There was also the possibility he was shot to keep him from identifying the person who started the stampede. No matter what the reason, there wasn't a man among them who didn't want to get the person who had caused Bobby's death.

Joshua watched Frank as he sat on his horse just looking out across the prairie in the darkness. He knew Frank and Bobby had partnered up whenever they could. They had been very good friends. Since Frank was much older than Bobby, Frank was like an older brother to him. Frank had always looked out for him.

"Frank, are you okay?" Joshua asked.

Frank turned in the saddle and looked at Joshua. He wanted to say "Hell no, I'm not okay", but knew it wouldn't make any difference.

"I'm okay, Mr. Higgins," Frank replied, not believing a word of it.

"I'll take care of Bobby's horse for now, if you don't mind," Joshua said.

"I know it's really your horse, Mr. Higgins, but Bobby liked to ride it. He more or less considered it his horse. He called it his Indian pony. The rest of us let him think it was his horse. He took real good care of it."

"I know he did. And to tell you the truth, I thought of it as his horse, too," Joshua said.

Frank looked at the horse then looked back at Joshua.

"I'll leave him with you," Frank said as he held out the reins to Joshua. "I should be out there helping to keep watch over the herd."

Joshua simply nodded as he took hold of the reins. He watched as Frank swung his horse around and rode off into the darkness. As soon as he was out of sight, Joshua looked at the horse. The longer he looked at the horse, the more he wanted to find out who had caused the stampede. He made a silent vow to find Bobby before they left the area.

No one slept that night. Everyone was on watch except for Chester. He had moved the wagon closer to where the herd had been stopped, then built a fire and put the coffee pot on. He spent the rest of the night making sure there was something for the riders to eat, and there was plenty of strong hot coffee. The riders would swing by the wagon and grab a bite to eat and drink some coffee from time to time during the night, then return to watch over the herd.

CHAPTER TWENTY-FIVE

The Search For Bobby And Justice

As the sun came up, several of the riders rode over to the wagon where Joshua was leaning against it. He was looking out over the prairie while sipping on a cup of coffee. Joshua turned and looked at the men. He knew the men wanted the same thing he did. They wanted to start the search for Bobby. They wanted to find Bobby and bury him properly.

Joshua split his men up into pairs. He asked the men who worked for Jess if they would stay on to keep an eye on the herd, even though they were to head back that morning. They quickly agreed to stay on and would watch the herd while the others looked for their friend. They all knew what it was like to lose a friend in a stampede. An extra day didn't mean that much to Jess's ranch hands. This time of year, things were pretty quiet at the ranch, at least they would be for the next couple of weeks.

Joshua then gave his men instructions on where they were to search. They spread out in a long line the width of the trampled ground where the cattle had stampeded during the night. If Bobby was found, one of the men was to report to Joshua. Joshua would then gather the men around so they could bury Bobby.

It didn't take very long before they found Bobby. He had been trampled by most of the herd. He was almost unrecognizable. He was covered with blood and mud, and almost every bone in his body had been crushed under the hooves of the stampeding cattle.

Joshua had Bobby's bedroll brought to where his body had been found. He and Frank carefully rolled Bobby's body onto the bedroll. Chester brought a shovel to where they had found Bobby and began digging a grave. He hadn't dug very much of the grave when Frank took the shovel from Chester and finished it.

A couple of the men took hold of Bobby's bedroll and gently lowered him into the grave. Frank, who was a Bible reading man, read a piece from the Good Book he always carried. He then took a handful of dirt and gently pitched it into the grave.

"From dust we come, and to dust we will return," Frank said. "Lord, he was a good cowboy. He never hurt no one, and he never asked for much. Take good care of him."

When Frank finished speaking, he turned and walked to his horse. He swung up into the saddle and rode off toward the herd. The others at the grave waited until Frank had ridden away before they began filling the grave with dirt. Once it was covered, each of them paid their last respects and said their goodbyes. When all was done, Joshua was the last one to leave the grave.

When Joshua got back to the wagon, he found Frank and Stan standing there. They were waiting for him. He knew they wanted to talk to him.

"Mr. Higgins, Frank and I would like ta go after the man who shot Bobby," Stan said.

"Let me ask you this. Do you know who shot him?"

"No, sir." Stan admitted reluctantly while looking down at the ground in front of him.

"Then how do you know who to go after?"

"I guess we don't. But Bobby said he thought he saw a man on a horse some distance away yesterday. He couldn't identify the man, but he said the horse was black and the rider was wearin' a black hat and shirt."

"Why didn't he tell me about it?"

"He didn't think too much of it since it was just one rider and he was a ways off. He said the rider was alone and just seemed ta be going in the same general direction we was. He didn't have no reason ta think one rider was there ta cause us trouble."

Joshua didn't want to let any of the men go off hunting for a man wearing a black hat and riding a black horse. He took a moment to think about it. While he was thinking, he sent the men back to work.

After a little while, Joshua began to think about Cactus Flats. He wondered if Waterman might have had something to do with the stampede as a way of getting even with Joshua. He remembered seeing a black horse in Cactus Flats. It had been tied in front of the saloon while they went into the bank to talk to Waterman about the cattle. It was the only black horse Joshua could remember seeing on the entire trip. There were very few black horses in that part of the country. Black horses were not used very much by the average cowboys. They tended to get too hot in the summer, and they required more grooming than most other horses to keep them looking good, something cowboys don't want to spend a lot of time doing.

When he put together the black horse and the trouble they had had from Waterman's men, it all seemed to make sense. Waterman was probably the one responsible. He probably sent out one of his men to stampede the cattle as revenge for Joshua and his men killing some of Waterman's men.

Joshua looked around. He could see Stan and Frank next to the wagon getting a cup of coffee.

"Stan, go find John and Bill," Joshua said.

Stan nodded then immediately turned and went to his horse. He swung into the saddle and rode off looking for John and Bill. It didn't take him long before he returned with them. Bill remained in the saddle while John stepped out of the saddle and walked up to Joshua.

"You want to see us, boss?" John asked.

"Yes. Do you think Jess's men would mind staying on for a couple more days?"

222

"I don't think so."

"I'm sure they will stay on if it means getting the guy who caused Bobby's death," Bill said looking down from the back of his horse. "They liked Bobby."

"Good, because that is what we are going to do. John, I'll need you to take charge of the herd and get the herd moving north. Don't push them too hard today. They have already run partway to where we were planning on stopping for the night.

"I'm taking Bill, Frank and Stan with me. Bill knows the terrain around Cactus Flats. It may take us a couple of days to catch up with you, but you keep moving north. Your job is to get these cattle to the ranch."

"Yes, sir," John said.

"We're going to take care of a little unfinished business, namely finding the man who started the stampede."

* * * *

Joshua and three of his men, Bill, Frank and Stan, packed up a small amount of grub and their bedrolls. As soon as they were ready, they headed back south toward the little town of Cactus Flats. Bill rode alongside Joshua and filled him in on the town, and how things were there. He also filled him in on the people who could be the biggest problem for them.

"The banker, Waterman, is the one who runs everything in the town. Most, if not all, of the people who have businesses in the town hate his guts."

"Why don't they run him out of town and take control of the town?" Joshua asked.

"The town's people are afraid of him. They can't seem to do anything without Waterman knowing about it. It seems Waterman has eyes and ears everywhere.

"About a year ago several of the town's people were planning on running Waterman out of town. Some of the town's businessmen held a secret meeting to talk about how they were going to do it. The man who got the town's businessmen together turned up dead the day after the meeting. His body was found in a gully behind the saloon. He had been beaten to death and left in the gully for the buzzards. The word got around very quickly that he was killed because he was trying to get the others to run Waterman out of town," Bill said.

"It sounds to me like they had a snitch in the group."

"They did, but no one has ever been able to find out who it was. Without knowing who the snitch was, the businessmen never tried it again. Shortly after that, Waterman got himself a couple of gunslingers to help him keep the citizens in line, and to make certain they never tried it again."

"What about the gunslingers? Do you know who they are?" Joshua asked.

"Yeah. There are two men who work for Waterman that you should be careful of," Bill said. "They are very dangerous men. One is Vasquez, Juan Vasquez, and the other is a guy by the name of Truman.

"Vasquez is easy to spot. He dresses like a Mexican vaquero and looks like one, but the word is he is only half Mexican. He has a long mustache that hangs down from the corners of his mouth. His hair is dark brown and fairly long. His eyes are almost black and cold looking. But most important is the fact he is very good with a gun. By the way, he's also very good with the big knife he carries in his belt. Never underestimate his slow and easygoing way. He can turn on you as fast as a rattlesnake. Whatever you do, don't give him a chance to draw. He's fast, and he's accurate.

"Harold Truman, better known as Lefty, is the other one to watch. He is a tall man with dark brown hair and sleepy looking eyes. He has a long scar that runs from the corner of his mouth almost to his ear. It is said he killed the Indian who gave him the scar by shooting the Indians eyes out while he was looking at him.

"He carries two guns. He carries them low and tied down. He's very fast with them, but not very accurate. He doesn't hit his target very well unless he is close. I don't think he can see very well at a distance. If you have to draw against him, try to be at least thirty feet from him, more if you can," Bill said.

"That's good to know," Joshua said. "Why is he called lefty?"

"He always draws his left gun first. I think he is left handed."

"That's good to know, too," Joshua said as he thought for a minute.

"I saw a black horse in front of the saloon when we passed through there. Do you have any idea how we can find the guy who rides that black horse?"

"Yeah, that's easy. That horse belongs to Waterman's kid, Kyle. He considers himself something of a gunfighter. I've never seen him in a gunfight, but he could be good. I know he's fast getting his gun out of the holster, but whether he can hit anything becomes another matter. I've heard he has never killed anyone in a face to face fair fight, but that doesn't mean he's not good with a gun. He just prefers to shoot people when they aren't looking at him, or can't shoot back.

"Kyle hangs around the saloon a lot. He's kind of lazy. He never pays for anything in town because his father holds a tight grip on the town's people."

"Would he be likely to start a stampede?" Joshua asked.

"I think he would. His old man lost a lot of money by not getting you when you came out to the ranch. I wouldn't put it past him to seek a little revenge. Kyle would never attack you head-on, not after what you and the guys did to his father's men. Something like the stampede, I think, would be just his style. He wouldn't do anything that would get him hurt in any way."

Joshua thought about what Bill had told him as the four men rode toward the small town of Cactus Flats. Joshua also thought about what they were riding into. He had no doubt the men with him would take on a fight. All of them had been in the army and had fought in some major battles during the Civil War. There was no doubt they knew how to fight and they had the courage to fight. However, it might be different because they would be going up against professional gunfighters.

CHAPTER TWENTY-SIX

Justice Is Found

Once Joshua and his men arrived on the ridge overlooking Cactus Flats, Joshua reined up and looked down at the small town. He took a deep breath as he looked over the town. Joshua was not sure what he was looking for, but the idea that he and his men were going into battle was certainly on his mind.

After looking over the town, Joshua began to look at the terrain around it. He saw a narrow gully off to the left that wound its way down the hill toward the town. It straightened out at the edge of town then turned and ran behind the saloon and on out the other end of town. The gully was deep enough it would conceal their approach toward the town if they didn't try to take their horses, and they kept low. Seeing it gave Joshua an idea.

"I think if we leave our horses here, we can use the gully to get into town without being seen. What do you think, Bill?"

"It looks good to me," he said after looking around for a moment. "That gully will take us right behind the saloon. We're most likely to find who we're lookin' for there."

Joshua looked around behind them. Just off to the back and below the top of the ridge were a couple of small trees. There was grass around the base of them. The trees would provide some shade while the grass would provide something for the horses to eat if it took them very long. Since the town was on the other side of the ridge from where the horses would be, no one would be able to see the horses from the town.

"Let's tie our horses over there. We'll go in on foot," Joshua said as he turned and rode his horse over to the trees.

Joshua and his men tied their horses to the trees, then took their rifles from their saddle scabbards. As soon as they were ready, they started over the ridge to the gully. From the beginning of the gully, it was well over a hundred yards to the edge of town, and another twenty to thirty feet to the back of the saloon.

Keeping crouched down low, they moved closer and closer to the saloon. Suddenly, Joshua stopped and didn't move. Bill was right behind him and was the only one who could see the reason Joshua had stopped so quickly.

Only a couple of feet in front of Joshua was a large western diamondback rattlesnake. The snake was coiled and ready to strike.

"Don't anyone make a move or a sound," Joshua whispered as he looked at the snake.

Joshua didn't want to have to leave the protection of the gully in order to go around the snake. Instead, he slowly reached out toward the snake with the barrel of his rifle. The snake struck at the barrel. When the rifle barrel didn't retreat, it struck a second time. The snake apparently didn't like banging its fangs against the hard steel rifle barrel. The snake decided they were not going to go away, so he moved off into a smaller gully then slithered away.

As soon as the snake had moved away, Joshua and his men continued on down the larger gully toward the saloon. Each one of them looked down the smaller gully to make sure the snake didn't change his mind and come back toward them. It wasn't long before they had worked their way to a position directly behind the saloon. Joshua gathered the men in close to him.

"Bill, you and Stan work your way up alongside the saloon and watch to see if anyone comes toward the saloon. Frank, you and I will go in the backdoor and try to get whoever is in there covered. If Waterman's kid is in there, I'll want to deal with him."

"What if there's shooting in the saloon," Stan asked. "What do you want us to do?"

"You make sure no one comes across the street to help."

"Okay," Stan said, nodding his head.

"Let's get on with it," Joshua said.

Bill and Stan climbed out of the gully and ran up alongside the saloon. Joshua and Frank climbed out of the gully and ran up to the backdoor of the saloon.

Joshua and Frank looked at each other to make sure they were ready. Just as Joshua was reaching for the door, it swung open and the barkeep stepped out. Joshua immediately grabbed the barkeep and jerked him away from the door. He stuck his gun in the barkeeps face while Frank quickly and quietly shut the door.

"You want to live to see the sunset, you will be quiet," Joshua said.

The barkeep nodded he understood and made no move to do anything that might get him shot.

"Who's in the bar right now?"

"Just Juan and Kyle."

"Juan Vasquez?"

"Yeah."

"Kyle Waterman?"

"Yeah. The banker's kid."

Joshua looked over at Frank before speaking again to the barkeep.

"Where's Truman?"

"I don't know. I haven't seen him today."

"Frank, tie him up and gag him."

Joshua held his gun on the barkeep while Frank tied him with one of the piggin' strings he always carried on his belt. He then used the barkeeps bar towel to gag him. The barkeep did not resist even a little. Once Frank had the barkeep secured, he looked up at Joshua and nodded he was ready.

Joshua reached up and opened the backdoor. He leaned over and looked in. The door opened into a backroom. Joshua went inside and Frank followed.

Once inside, Joshua moved up to the door leading into the barroom. He opened the door a crack and peeked in. He could see one man in the barroom with a beer setting on the bar in front of him. He looked like a Mexican. He fit the description of Vasquez.

Joshua could only see the back of another man sitting at a table. He was wearing a black hat pushed back on his head. The hat had a silver hat band. He was dressed all in black. Joshua was sure it was Waterman's kid, Kyle. He didn't see anyone else in the barroom.

"Looks like we have two of them in the barroom, Vasquez and the kid," Joshua whispered. "I'll take Vasquez, you take the kid."

Frank nodded he understood and left his rifle next to the door. Frank drew his pistol then moved up close to the door. He nodded again to let Joshua know he was ready.

Joshua leaned his rifle against the wall and drew his pistol. He moved to the door then jerked it open. Joshua stepped into the barroom and quickly moved to one side making room for Frank to get by him. Frank swiftly stepped up behind Kyle while Joshua kept his gun pointed at the Mexican.

The Mexican turned away from the bar and saw what was happening before Kyle had a chance to be aware of what was going on. The Mexican started to reach for his gun, but he wasn't fast enough. Joshua pulled the trigger of his gun and shot the Mexican square in the chest. The Mexican didn't even live long enough to know what was happening. Joshua's bullet pushed him back against the bar, then he fell face down on the barroom floor, dead.

Kyle went for his gun. Before he could get it out of his holster, he felt the cold steel of Frank's gun barrel pressed against the side of his head.

"Go ahead. Give me a reason to blow your head off," Frank said pressing the barrel of his gun hard against the side of Kyle's head.

The kid took his hand away from his gun, then slowly turned his head. He looked up at Frank with hate in his eyes. Frank smacked him alongside the head, then quickly relieved him of his guns before he could react.

"One move and you will be dead before you hit the floor," Frank said, ready to kill him if he decided to do something really stupid, which was about anything as far as Frank was concerned.

Suddenly there was the sound of several shots coming from outside the saloon. It sounded as if they had come from the side of the saloon and from across the street. It was clear in Joshua's mind that Bill and Stan were doing their job of keeping everyone else out of the saloon. It was only a matter of moments before the shooting stopped. Joshua wanted to call out in order to find out if Bill and Stan were okay and still in control of the main street, but decided against it.

"Frank, cover the backdoor. I'll watch the kid."

Reluctantly, Frank took his gun away from Kyle's head. He wanted nothing more than to kill the kid for what he believed he had done to cause the death of his friend, Bobby. Instead, he did as his boss had told him and hurried to the backdoor of the saloon. He positioned himself so he would have the first shot if anyone tried to come in from the back.

With his gun pointed at the kid's face, Joshua asked him one question.

"Did you cause my cattle to stampede last night?"

"You ain't getting' out of here alive if you do anythin' ta me," Kyle said defiantly.

"You won't live long enough to know if we did or not. Now answer my question." Joshua demanded.

"Go ta hell," the kid responded still believing his father could get him out of any jam he might get in, including this one.

Joshua let out a sigh of frustration just before he grabbed the kid by the wrist. In one swift motion, he pushed Kyle's hand down on the table with his fingers on the edge of the table. He then slammed the barrel of his gun down across the kid's fingers. Kyle let out a scream as the bones in the fingers in his right hand broke under the force of the gun barrel hitting them.

"Now answer me or I'll shoot you in the knee." Joshua said angrily.

The kid was in a great deal of pain. He didn't answer until Joshua pressed the barrel of his gun against the kid's knee and pulled back the hammer.

"Yes. Yes. I fired the shots that stampeded the herd," Kyle screamed, obviously in pain.

"That stampede killed one of my men. You are going to pay for it."

Joshua looked over at Frank. They knew there were men gathering outside who would try to prevent Joshua and the others from leaving. Joshua called Frank over to tie Kyle's hands behind his back.

Frank tied Kyle's hands tightly with a piggin' string. He had no more than got him tied when suddenly there were several shots fired from across the street into the saloon. The bullets hit high on the back wall of the saloon. It was clear they were meant to do nothing more than get the attention of those inside.

"This is Waterman. You have my son in there. You let him go and I'll spare your lives."

Joshua knew it was an attempt to get them to drop their guard. The minute they let Kyle go, they would be killed. They had the kid, but the biggest problem for Joshua and his men was how to get out of there alive with the kid so he could be turned over to the law.

"The only way you are going to get him back alive is for you to gather your men in the middle of the street in front of the General Store without their guns. If there is so much as one of your men who is not there, or even one of them has a gun, I will shoot you and then your son. Do you understand that?"

"I understand, but you will never get out of town alive."

"Then there's no sense wasting my time. I guess your kid dies now. And since you feel that way, you might as well see him die," Joshua said.

Joshua grabbed Kyle by the scruff of his neck and pushed him over to the window. Placing the kid where he could be seen from the buildings across the street, Joshua put the barrel of his gun against the side of Kyle's head. The kid was sure he was about to die. He began to cry and beg for his life.

"Oh, God. Please don't kill me. Please."

"Frank, get a rifle and see if you can get a good shot at Waterman. If you can, we'll kill him first.

Just then Stan came in the back of the saloon. He had his gun in his hand and seemed to be rather excited. Joshua glanced at him and wondered why he had come inside.

"Mr. Higgins," he said breathlessly. "Bill snuck back into the gully. He said he was going ta get back ta our horses, then cut across country ta get Jess and some of his men. He wants the three of us ta hold them off 'til he gets back."

"Bill is our best chance to get out alive," Joshua said. "We'll try to hold them off until he gets back with help."

"Boss, I've got an idea that might help," Frank said. "In the backroom I saw a rope. I've been lookin' around. Look up above the door."

Joshua looked but didn't see anything but rafters and beams that held up the roof. He looked back at Frank as if he didn't understand what he was getting at.

"We could toss a rope over that beam right in front of the door. Wrap it around the kid's neck and put him standing on a chair. It would let them know if they attack us or shoot at us again, the kid would hang before they could get to him. What do you think?"

"No. Please, don't hang me," Kyle cried pleading for his life.

"Good idea. Get the rope."

"Oh, God," Kyle said as he started to cry again.

Frank and Stan got the rope and made a hangman's knot in it while Joshua held the kid at the window with his gun against the side of Kyle's head. Very carefully, Frank pushed a chair over in front of the saloon's swinging doors. Frank grabbed Kyle and put the rope over his head. Using the kid as a shield, Frank stood him up on the chair, then tossed the rope over the beam. After securing the rope to another beam so the kid had to almost stand on his tiptoes, Frank tied another rope to one of the chair's legs. When they were ready, Stan broke the swinging door off one side while Joshua broke off the one on the other side. Now the kid's father could see his son with the rope around his neck ready to be hung. The kid could also see his father looking at him.

"I take it you can see your son," Joshua called out.

"Yeah. I can see him. If you harm him, I will cut you to pieces and feed you to the buzzards," Waterman said angrily.

"If you or any of your men try to make a move against us in anyway, or even fire a shot into the saloon, we will pull the chair out from under him. He will die before you can get to him. Do you understand?" Joshua said.

"I understand, but I don't think you have the guts to do it," Waterman said.

"Your son shot one of my men for no reason. It wasn't even a fair fight. In the process, it caused my herd to stampede. That stampede killed one of my men who was only a little older than your son. That makes him a murderer. Murderers are hung, even in this part of the country. I can assure you that I will have no problem pulling the chair out from under him," Joshua said with a heavy note of anger in his voice.

"You will never get out of here alive. We will just wait you out," Waterman said.

"If you say so," Joshua said.

Joshua was hoping they would want to play a waiting game. It would give Bill time to get to the J bar J Ranch and return with help.

* * * *

Time passed slowly as everyone sat on pins and needles wondering who would make the first move. Joshua kept an eye on the kid while Frank watched the backdoor and Stan watched the front.

Kyle seemed to settle down a little even with the rope around his neck. He was nervous about what was going to happen to him, but at least for now he just had to keep his balance and not move too much. The chair was not very stable.

As the time passed, Kyle got more and more uncomfortable. His hand had swollen as a result of his broken fingers. The swelling was making the piggin' string get tighter around his wrists, cutting off the circulation to his hand. Also, he was not used to standing for long periods of time in cowboy boots on the uneven surface of the chair seat, or standing in the same position for very long.

Kyle had been standing on the chair for more than three hours when there were a couple of shots fired. Joshua quickly tightened the rope on the chair. He was ready to pull the chair out from under the kid when Frank yelled at him.

"No. Don't. It's Bill."

Joshua saw Bill come rushing in the backdoor. They turned to look out the front window in time to see Jess and several of his men leading Waterman, and several other men, out of the General Store with their hands up. The general store owner was one of the men holding a gun on Waterman and the others.

"Looks like you're ready to carry out a little Frontier justice here," Bill said as he looked up at Kyle still standing on the chair with the rope around his neck.

"Yeah. You came just in time. Thanks for getting help."

Just then, Jess came into the saloon and walked around behind the bar. While Bill and Frank took Kyle down, Jess took a bottle from under the bar and poured whiskey into two glasses. He held one out to Joshua.

"You probably need this. It ain't as good as you'd get at the ranch, but it will have to do," Jess said with a smile. "By the way, where's the barkeep?"

"Hogtied out back."

"I think we can let him go. He's one of the good guys. He's the one person in town who has kept me informed on what old man Waterman was up to. We'll keep Waterman, his kid and the others locked up until the territorial marshal gets here."

Joshua motioned for Frank to untie the barkeep. Frank went out the backdoor as Joshua turned and looked at Jess.

"Any idea when the territorial marshal will get here?"

"In a couple of days, probably. I sent for him about two weeks ago."

"It's good to hear there is some justice around here," Joshua said.

"It's a little hard to find sometimes, but we do have some justice."

"What about this guy, Truman. Have you seen him?"

"Yeah. The shooting you heard just before we started leading Waterman and his crew out of the general store were from a couple of my men. They shot and killed him when he tried to draw on us."

"Thanks for coming to our rescue. I don't know how much longer we could have held out."

"No problem. I'd hate to see a good man killed," Jess said with a grin.

"I'm glad of that," Joshua said with a smile.

"By the way, what's this about you stealin' my foreman?"

"I didn't steal him. He asked to go with me," Joshua said, a little afraid he probably should have talked to Jess before he agreed to hire Bill.

"It's okay. He's been thinking about going somewhere else for sometime. I was just glad to have him for as long as I did. He's a good man."

"I know. As much as I would like to stay here and spend time drinking your good Kentucky whiskey, I think I'd better go catch up with my cattle. I'm sure you would like the rest of your ranch hands back."

"I understand. Here's hopin' the rest of your cattle drive is a safe one," Jess said as he raised his glass.

Joshua raised his glass, then took a drink. He set the glass on the bar and looked at Jess.

"If you ever need anything, you just let me know," Joshua said as he shook hands with Jess.

"I will. You take care."

"I will. I'll send your men back as soon as I catch up with my herd."

"You do that," Jess replied with a grin.

Joshua smiled at Jess, then turned and started out the front door of the saloon. When he looked down the street, he could see a couple of the businessmen and a few of Jess's men leading Waterman, his son and several of Waterman's hired gunmen down the street to a small stone building. He was sure it was where they would keep them until the territorial marshal or a circuit judge showed up.

Joshua and his men returned to where they had hidden their horses. They mounted up and headed north to join up with the men who were driving his cattle north to the Dakota Territory.

CHAPTER TWENTY-SEVEN

Driving The Cattle Home

It only took Joshua and the others two days to catch up with the herd. When they did, the ranch hands who had been with Joshua went right back to work driving the cattle. In the evening around the campfire, their story was told to the rest. They missed Bobby and his smooth voice as he sang to the cattle, but they also knew it was the life of a cowboy. Driving cattle hundreds of miles was hard work. It was also dangerous work. Many a cowboy had lost his life on a trail drive.

The morning after Joshua and the others returned from Cactus Flats, Jess's men said goodbye to Joshua and headed back to the J bar J Ranch. After they left, Joshua and his men started pushing the cattle toward home.

The rest of the cattle drive went fairly smoothly with a minimum of injuries. Stan injured his ankle while trying to rope an uncontrollable and obstinate bull that got it in his head he didn't want to cross a shallow river. Stan had chased the young bull into some bushes. He had to get off his horse in order to get a rope around the bull's head. While he was tugging on the rope to get the animal out of the brush, he stepped on a loose rock that rolled out from under his foot. It caused him to lose his balance and twist his ankle. After he fell, the young bull simply walked out of the brush and rejoined the herd. Needless to say, Stan had a few colorful words to say to the bull.

Frank almost lost a finger when he dallied his rope on the saddle horn after roping a steer that was running off in the wrong direction. He caught his finger between the rope and saddle horn. He was fortunate not to lose his finger. All he got was a rather painful rope burn and a nasty cut on his finger. It was pretty common to see a cowboy with a missing finger because he caught it between the saddle horn and the rope while roping a steer.

The cattle drive turned out to be not the best of times for Marcus, either. He roped a steer that was headed in the wrong direction while crossing a river. It seemed the steer didn't like the rope very much and quickly turned and pulled Marcus off his horse into the river before he could dally the rope on his saddle horn. Marcus was not a very good swimmer and Frank had to rope Marcus and drag him to the river bank. It was rather embarrassing for Marcus, but he decided right then and there he was going to learn to swim at the first opportunity.

A couple of days later while camped for the night, Marcus came in off his night watch for a cup of coffee. After getting the cup of coffee, he walked over to sit down on the ground while he drank his coffee. He was so tired that he wasn't paying attention to where he was sitting. He accidentally sat down on a small prickly pear cactus. It was more embarrassing than it was painful, especially since he had to have one of the guys pull the thorns out of his behind. It was also a little uncomfortable riding herd for a couple of days.

The cattle drive back to Joshua's ranch took a little longer than it had taken them to find the cattle, but that had been expected. Longhorns are not known for being the most cooperative animals to drive. Driving them day after day for several hundred miles didn't help their disposition any, either.

* * * *

Days turned into weeks before Joshua and his men reached the ranch with the cattle. It was late in the afternoon when they arrived at the ranch. They were all tired, but there was still work to be done before anyone was going to get any rest.

The first thing they had to do was to get the cattle settled in their new surroundings. That meant moving them into a large area that had been fenced off behind the barn. It was to be used as the winter pasture as well as a place to get the cattle accustomed to their new home.

Joshua and his men started moving the cattle into the winter pasture they had built before they left for Texas. The cattle would remain in the pasture for a couple of days before they would be turned out to feed on the thick buffalo grass that covered the vast prairies of the Dakota Territory.

Once the cattle were secure in the pasture behind the barn, Joshua rode over to the ranch house. Dancing Flower, Susan and Jeremiah were very excited to see Joshua as he rode toward the house. They ran out to greet him. Joshua jumped off his horse and took Dancing Flower in his arms and swung her around. He kissed her and held her tight as Jeremiah and Susan joined in by hugging their father.

"Wow. You sure have grown. You must be a foot taller than when I left," Joshua said as he reached out and rubbed his son's head. Jeremiah looked up at his father and grinned. Joshua picked up his daughter and hugged her.

"I've been helping mom," Jeremiah said with a big grin. "Uncle Spotted Horse came by to help, too."

Joshua looked at Dancing Flower. She smiled at him.

"You didn't have your uncle doing your chores, did you?" Joshua asked the boy.

"No. He made me do my own chores. He only helped when it was something I couldn't do by myself."

Joshua laughed. He knew Spotted Horse would not let Jeremiah push his chores off on him. Spotted Horse would teach Jeremiah that he was responsible for doing his own work.

"I helped mommy, too," Susan said with excitement.

"I'm sure you did," Joshua said as he gave her another hug and squeezed her.

Susan giggled and wrapped her arms around his neck. She kissed him on the cheek.

Just then John rode up to the house. He smiled down at them from the back of his horse as he watched the greeting Joshua was getting from his family. John would have gone back to North Carolina after the war if there had been anyone waiting for him. He knew there was nothing left that meant anything to him there.

"Excuse me," John said as he remained in the saddle.

"What is it, John?" Joshua said as he turned and looked up at him.

"I was wondering if you would need us for awhile."

"If the cattle are secure in the pasture, you and the men can go ahead and get cleaned up and get some well earned rest. You can decide how you want to work out a watch schedule. You might want to keep the watch times fairly short for awhile so everyone can get some rest."

"I will. Thank you."

"I would like you to tell the men that tomorrow we will be having a little celebration here," Dancing Flower said. "We would like all of them to be here. We are going to have a feast to celebrate your safe return."

"We will also be celebrating this place becoming a real cattle ranch," Joshua said with a big grin. "It will also be a big thank you party for all the help you men have been in getting it started."

"The men will like that," John said.

"Tell them to come hungry. I'm sure Spotted Horse and his people will be joining us. I will send word to them," Dancing Flower said.

"That would be nice," John said as he looked at Dancing Flower.

"I think there are a couple of young women in Spotted Horse's tribe that have been waiting for the return of a couple of the men," Dancing Flower added with a grin.

"I'm sure you're right. I've seen a couple of the girls making eyes at a couple of the hands before we left," Joshua said. "There wouldn't be one of them that is of interest to you, would there, John?"

"There might be," John answered with a sheepish grin.

John reached up and touched the brim of his hat to Dancing Flower, then swung his horse around and rode off toward the pasture.

CHAPTER TWENTY-EIGHT

A Welcome Home Party

When the sun came up in the morning, Joshua and Dancing Flower were tending a fire they had started well before dawn. There was the hindquarter of a buffalo already on the spit, and the smell of it roasting was beginning to fill the air.

Joshua was slowly turning the roast over the fire when Spotted Horse and his tribe arrived. Morning Star and several of the women of the tribe had prepared vegetables, nuts, and herb salads from the forest. It was going to be a meal fit for a king. Several buffalo hides and blankets had been laid out on the ground for everyone to sit on while they ate.

When it was almost noon, the ranch hands started to drift over toward the house. They had worked hard to finish their chores so they could enjoy the feast.

As soon as all was ready, everyone got in line. The ranch hands talked with the Indians while they waited in line to get a good sized portion of meat. Even though the ranch hands had been held prisoner by the Indians, there didn't seem to be any hard feelings toward them. It was probably due to the treatment they received from them. They had been treated well and in many cases they had worked side by side, each doing his share of the work.

Dancing Flower even noticed Stan was being very polite and speaking very softly to Little Dove, a young Indian woman. Little Dove seemed to be listening to Stan's every word. It was easy to see why Stan would like her. She was a pretty girl, friendly and attentive. Dancing Flower nudged Joshua and pointed to them. She smiled at Joshua.

"It looks like love is in the air," Joshua said with a grin.

"Yes. You might want to have a talk with Stan."

"About what? It seems to me they are getting along just fine."

"You should talk to him about who and how he should ask for Little Dove to be his woman."

"Oh. Do you think it has gone that far?"

"Look at them. They were making eyes at each other long before you went to get cattle."

"I'll have a talk with him," he replied.

"You might want to talk to John as well."

Joshua looked over at John and saw him sitting on a blanket. He was talking with Yellow Bird, another young Indian woman. They seemed to be getting along pretty well. They were talking and laughing together.

The festivities continued for several hours. During the singing and dancing, Joshua noticed not only were Stan and John spending a lot of time with Indian women, but Frank seemed to show an interest in one of the Indian women, too. The young woman was Swift Doe, the niece of Spotted Horse.

Joshua decided it would be a good idea if he had a talk with all the men about courting an Indian woman. It wasn't because he didn't think they should have an interest in the women, but rather to explain how to court the women if their interest was in taking one of them for a bride. He also felt it might be a good idea to find out what their intentions really were.

Joshua expected his men to act as gentlemen and know enough of the Indian ways as possible to avoid any problems with their Indian neighbors. The last thing Joshua wanted was to have difficulties that could hurt the relationship between the ranch hands and the Indians, and between Spotted Horse and himself. By talking to his men about the

Indian ways of courting now, might save some problems later.

After the party broke up and Spotted Horse and his people were leaving, Joshua went to find Stan, Frank and John. He found Stan and Frank near the barn. They were getting ready to saddle up a couple of horses and ride out to check on the cattle. He looked around, but John was nowhere in sight. He decided to talk to John later.

"Stan, Frank, I'd like to talk to you for a minute."

"Yes, sir," Frank said, as he turned and looked at Joshua.

"We do somethin' wrong, boss?" Stan asked with a worried look on his face.

"No. You didn't do anything wrong. I just wanted to talk to you about the girls I saw you talking to at the festivities.

"We didn't do nothin', boss," Stan said. "We was only talkin' to 'um."

"That's right. We didn't do anything to them."

"It's okay," Joshua said with a grin. "I just want to know if you have, shall we say, a romantic interest in those girls."

Stan and Frank looked at each other, then looked at the ground. Joshua waited patiently for an answer.

"Well - - -, I guess you could say I really like Little Dove," Stan said. "I think she likes me, too."

"That's fine. I'm not one to tell you who you should like or shouldn't like. I just want you to know their customs are a little different from ours. If you want to court one of the Indian girls, you have to have the permission of the elder male of the girl's family. You need to get permission to go for walks with her, to visit her, that sort of thing."

"You mean we shouldn't have been talking to the girls without permission?" Frank asked.

"It was fine at the gathering of the tribe and us. That is, as long as you didn't go wandering off by yourself with one of them."

"Do you have any problem with me getting permission to court Little Dove?" Stan asked.

"No. Not at all. But you need to talk to Running Elk. You need his permission to court her. If you would like, I will have Dancing Flower talk to him about it for you," Joshua said.

"I would like that. Little Dove is beautiful. I think she likes me. I would like ta get ta know her better," Stan said rather shyly.

"I will ask Dancing Flower to talk to Running Elk on your behalf. What about you, Frank?"

"I don't know. Don't get me wrong. Swift Doe is nice, and I like to talk to her. It is good to hear a woman's voice, and she does speak English pretty good. We seem to get along, but I'm a bit older than she is. Maybe a little too much older, if you know what I mean.

"It's okay. If you want Dancing Flower to speak to Spotted Horse for you, she will. I have seen you talking to Spotted Horse. You seem to get along. If you wish to talk to him about courting Swift Doe yourself, feel free to do so. But do you and me a favor, treat the girls with respect and respect their customs. Okay?"

"Sure, boss," Stan said.

"Yeah," Frank said.

"If I have any questions 'bout what is right and what is wrong in courtin' Little Dove, would it by okay if I talk ta you 'bout it," Stan asked shyly.

"Certainly, you can talk to me. You can also talk to Dancing Flower if you would like. She would be glad to answer any of your questions."

"Thanks."

"Okay. Go ahead with your work. And thanks for understanding where I'm coming from."

"No problem, boss," Stan said.

Frank didn't say anything. He just nodded his head in agreement.

Joshua nodded, then turned toward the house where Dancing Flower was waiting for him. He told her about his conversation with Stan and Frank. She smiled and agreed to talk to Running Elk about Stan courting Little Dove.

"What about John?"

"I didn't see him around. I'll have a talk with him in the morning."

Dancing Flower smiled, then turned to go into the house. Joshua followed her.

The next morning Joshua had a talk with John. John understood and asked if Dancing Flower would have a talk with Running Elk about Yellow Bird. Joshua said that he would talk to Dancing Flower about it.

CHAPTER TWENTY-NINE

Life On A Cattle Ranch

During the next few days the men watered and fed the cattle in their temporary pasture. As soon as the cattle seemed to be comfortable with their surroundings, Joshua gave the order to open the gate of the winter pasture and let the cattle leave the pasture for the open prairie as they wished. Gradually, the longhorns drifted out onto the open prairie. They began grazing on the rich buffalo grass, and walked down to the creek for water. A few of the cattle seemed content to stay in their temporary pasture and had to be gently herded out.

Once all of the cattle were out of the winter pasture, John closed the gate to keep them out so the grass could grow and become thick again. It soon became clear that the longhorns were pretty content with where they were and had no desire to wonder off very far.

Each day a different ranch hand was assigned to check on the cattle which usually took all day. His job was to make sure the cattle were doing well, and had not wondered off too far. It was also to make sure there were no strangers hanging around the area and watching the cattle. When the men were not assigned to checking on the cattle, they took care of the daily chores around the ranch yard and the barn.

The cattle had plenty of water and plenty of rich grass. As a result they grew big and fat as the summer turned into fall. From the looks of most of the cows, there would be a lot of new calves in the spring. The bulls had done their job, and had done it well.

* * * *

The spring was always a busy time on the ranch. All the new calves had to be rounded up and branded. It was dirty hard work, and everyone did their part. Some of Spotted Horse's people came to help. The Indians would work alongside the ranch hands while the women prepared meals and kept the coffee pot hot.

During the summer and early fall, the ranch hands spent a good deal of their time building fences to enlarge the area that would be used as a winter pasture. They also repaired any buildings that had been damaged during bad weather, or simply needed upkeep. When they were not working at fixing or repairing things, they were taking turns watching over the cattle to protect them from predators and the occasional rustler.

The practice of bringing the cattle closer to the barn during the winter was not a wide spread practice where there were large areas of open rangeland for them to graze. Most ranchers who had large ranches let the cattle fend for themselves during the winter in the hope they would survive with a good crop of calves in the spring.

Some of the larger ranches had ranch hands that stayed in line cabins at the far corners of the ranch during the winter so they could be closer to some of the cattle. It was the line rider's job to protect the cattle from coyotes, other vermin and rustlers. They were also there to help the cattle that got into trouble, like getting hung up in thick brush or stuck in a ravine or gully.

Joshua, however, had a different idea. He had been raised on a farm in England. The English farms were not very large. It was the practice in England, and in the eastern states where the farms were much smaller than the western ranches, to keep the cows close to the barn during the winter. It made it much easier to feed them and care for them if the weather got bad. On the farms it was also necessary to keep the cows close because they had to be milked twice a day.

Joshua believed that by keeping the cattle close to the barn, it would be easier to feed them during the often harsh winters. It made it easier to find and take care of cows and their calves if the weather turned bad. He believed that it would improve the survival rate of not only the cows, but of their calves as well.

* * * *

As the days passed, the nights had started to turn cold. The weather was starting to change, and winter would soon be there. Joshua was ready to roundup the cattle and move them into the large winter pasture behind the barn. He had had his men stack large piles of hay near the barn. It would be easier for his men to feed the cattle after a heavy snow if they were near the barn and close to the feed.

Stepping out onto the porch of his ranch house, Joshua looked up at the sky. It was gray and cloudy, and had the look of snow in it. There was little doubt winter was coming fast. There was a cold damp breeze coming in from the northwest, too. He just hoped he had not waited too long to roundup the cattle and move them to the winter pasture.

Joshua walked across the yard toward the bunkhouse. Just as he stepped up onto the porch, the bunkhouse door opened and John stepped out to greet him.

"Mornin' Joshua."

"Good morning, John.

"Looks like it might snow," John said as he looked up at the sky.

"I was thinking the same thing. If we have an early snow, we could have problems getting feed to the cattle if they can't get to the grass under the snow. We need to get them moved into the winter pasture."

"I'll get the men together and start rounding them up. We'll get them into the winter pasture as quickly as we can."

"I'll help. Do you know where most of the cattle can be found?" Joshua asked.

"Most of the cattle have been hanging around the creek over in the east meadow. The grass is thick and good there. I'll have Bill get the men started out that way to bring them back here. I'll go out and see if I can find any more out south of here," John said. "Frank said there was a bunch of them out that way. I'll take Stan with me. We'll see if we can find them. If we can, we'll start them back this way."

"Sounds good. I'll make a swing around to the northwest and see if I find any hanging around near the river. We've got a few that seem to like it there. If I find any, I'll start them back this way. If you get back before I do, come my way. If I get back before you, I'll come help you. Otherwise, we'll meet back here."

"Okay," John said, then turned and went back into the bunkhouse to give instructions to the other ranch hands.

Meanwhile Joshua went to the barn and saddled a horse. After the horse was saddled, he led the horse over to the ranch house where he tied it to the hitching rail. Joshua went inside and packed some food in case he had to stay out overnight for some reason. With the look of the sky, it could start snowing at almost anytime.

After saying goodbye to Dancing Flower, Susan and Jeremiah, he tied a bedroll to his saddle along with the saddlebags. He then swung up into the saddle and started heading northwest toward the Cheyenne River. When he got to the river, he began riding along the river toward the Black Hills. With the weather changing, he was sure if the cattle were smart they would seek shelter in the trees out of the wind and snow. He had been riding along the tree line for well over an hour when he came upon about twenty of his longhorns. They had moved away from the open grass and the river. They were gathered close together in among the trees just a little ways from the river. It was good that they had huddled up together. It made it easier for Joshua.

Joshua had no more than found the cattle when it began to snow. Since it was an early snow, the snow flakes were large and wet. Joshua stepped out of the saddle and got his slicker from his bedroll. It would help keep him warm as well as dry.

Once he had it on, he got back in the saddle and began moving in among the trees. He slowly began to start the cattle moving toward the winter pasture. They were a little reluctant to leave the shelter of the trees, but as long as Joshua kept them close to the trees they didn't resist too much.

The snow had started with just a few flakes, but quickly turned into a heavy snowstorm that made it impossible to see for more than about twenty to thirty feet. Joshua continued to push the cattle on toward the winter pasture.

Not far from where the cattle had gathered there was a cliff of red rocks. Joshua had explored the area sometime ago and remembered there was a cave near the base of the rocky cliffs. It wasn't a very big cave, but it would provide shelter for the small herd, his horse and himself, if he could find it.

Joshua rode very slowly around the small herd of cattle so as not to cause the longhorns to run. He began moving the cattle toward where he thought the cave was located. The longhorns were reluctant to leave the cover of the trees, but with a lot of coaxing they began to move away and walked along the rocky outcropping.

When Joshua finally found the cave, he turned the longhorns and started them into the cave. A couple of the longhorns didn't seem to want to go into the cave very badly. They made it a little difficult for Joshua, but once he got a few of the longhorns to go into the cave, the rest seemed to follow and the remaining reluctant ones were less trouble. It seemed that even the cattle realized it would be a good place to get out of the wind and snow, and wait for the storm to pass. Once in the cave and out of the weather, they settled down fairly quickly.

Joshua quickly got off his horse and ran his rope between several trees that were close to the entrance of the cave. He made sort of a gate across the entrance. He thought his makeshift gate would keep the cattle in the cave if the snowstorm didn't last too long.

Joshua sat down on a rock close to the entrance of the cave and watched the snow fall. He sang softly a song to the cattle he had learned from his mother as a small child. It seemed to settle the cattle down. He thought about how pretty it was to see the snow gather on the branches of the dark green pine trees and on top of the grass. But no matter how pretty it was, it could also be dangerous if it continued for a long time.

If it continued to snow all night like it was, it could make it very difficult to get the cattle back to the fenced-in winter pasture behind the barn. At least for now, his horse and the cattle would be safe from the weather. As long as it continued to snow and the wind continued to blow, the cattle would be reluctant to leave the cave.

Time passed slowly as he watched the cattle. Some of the cows were lying down while others were standing. They seemed to know they were safe inside the cave and made no effort to leave. As far as Joshua was concerned, he was glad. If the cattle got restless, it could be a problem for him in such a small space.

As the light of day seemed to be going away, Joshua took his rifle from his saddle and laid it across his lap. He had no idea if the cave was home to some wild critter such as a bear or mountain lion. It would be best if he kept a watch. His horse, and probably the cattle, would let him know if some critter came too close to the cave.

Joshua thought about making some coffee, but didn't want to build a fire, even a small one, in the cave. Even a small fire, with the smoke it would make, might upset the cattle and make them hard to handle. It could even scare them enough for them to break out of the cave. He knew his rope gate would not keep them in the cave if they were frightened. He also knew that if they scattered, he would have a difficult time gathering them back together.

Joshua got some hardtack and jerky out of his saddle bags to eat. He also got his canteen of water off his saddle to drink. After he had eaten, he unrolled his bedroll. He wrapped his blanket around his shoulders under his slicker, then sat down near the entrance to the cave and leaned back against the wall.

With his rifle laid across his lap, he took a look around. The cattle and his horse seemed to be at ease. Joshua closed his eyes and relaxed. Even though he slept, he knew the slightest noise would wake him. His time alone on the prairie had made him attune to his surroundings even when he was asleep. Joshua slipped off into a light sleep.

* * * *

Suddenly, Joshua was awake. He wasn't sure what it was that woke him, but something had. He first looked toward the entrance of the cave for anything that might cause him harm, but he saw nothing. He then looked at his horse. The horse stood looking out the entrance of the cave. The horse had his head up and his ears pointed in the direction it was looking.

Joshua moved back away from the entrance of the cave and levered a cartridge into the chamber of his rifle as he looked out of the cave. The first thing he noticed was it had stopped snowing. The sun had not come up yet, but the sky was starting to get lighter. It would not be long before the sun would come up over the horizon. Joshua just waited and watched for something to move, something to happen that would tell him what it was that made his horse become alert.

It was slowly getting lighter outside the cave. It was just before the sun broke over the horizon when Joshua got a glimpse of an Indian pony moving slowly around behind some large bushes in among the trees. He wasn't sure if there was an Indian on the back of the pony or not. He also wasn't sure if there were any other Indians around. He drew back into the darkness of the cave to wait and watch. He readied himself for anything that might come his way.

While watching for whoever was out there, Joshua took a quick look at the cattle. He was hoping he didn't have to fire his rifle to protect himself. If he fired a shot in the cave, his cattle would want to get out of the cave as quickly as possible. With no place to go, he could get trampled.

Spotted Horse had been looking for tracks in the snow or on the ground where the wind had blown the snow away from the ground. He had not found any tracks as he slowly moved around some bushes. He was also looking for the cave. It had been sometime since he had been in the small valley and along the red rock cliffs. Since the bushes and trees had grown up, he was not sure if he was even in the right area.

As Spotted Horse pulled up to look around, he heard a horse blow. His horse's head turned and looked toward the cliff. Spotted Horse quickly turned his head and looked in the direction the sound had come from, the same direction his horse was looking. He listened very carefully in the hope of hearing it again. It seemed like it had taken forever, but he heard the sound again.

"Joshua! Joshua," he called out, but only after he was ready in case it was someone else's horse he had heard.

"Is that you, Spotted Horse?"

"It is. Where are you?"

"Right here," Joshua said as he stepped out of the cave and around the end of a large bush.

"We were worried about you. Dancing Flower asked me to find you. She said you left yesterday to look for cattle, but you didn't return."

"I found the cattle, but it started to snow hard. I held up in a cave back here."

"Do you still have the cattle with you?"

"Yes, I have them in the cave. Would you mind helping me get them back to the winter pasture?"

"I will help."

Together, Spotted Horse and Joshua moved the cattle out of the cave. They started the cattle back toward the winter pasture where they could get food and water. It was slow going as there were several places where the snow had piled up and was too deep for the cattle to get through. They had to get the cattle to go around the snow drifts, and keep them out of the snow-filled ravines. A couple of times they came upon a ravine full of snow to the point a cow was unable to tell the ravine was there. Twice a cow had stepped into a snow filled ravine and couldn't get out. When that happened, Joshua would throw a rope around the cow's neck and pull it out. It was hard work getting a cow out of a snow packed ravine.

It wasn't very far from the barn to where Joshua had held the cattle in the cave, but it took them the better part of the day to get them back to the fenced-in pasture. Once they had them in the winter pasture, Joshua took a look at the cattle that were already there. It looked like his men had found almost all of the cattle. It made Joshua feel a little better knowing that most of his cattle had been found and rounded up. After Joshua and Spotted Horse had taken care of their horses, they went up to the house where they received a warm welcome home and a good hot meal.

* * * *

The short days and long nights of winter passed slowly. The ranch hands were glad Joshua had decided to round up the cattle and keep them in the fenced pasture behind the barn. Even though it was a large pasture, it kept the cattle closer to the hay stacks, and made caring for them easier.

Winter on the ranch was not only the time of caring for the animals. It was a time to repair things. When the ranch hands were not looking out for the cattle and had some time on their hands, they would repair their saddles and tack, patch clothes and make a few things they needed. Most of the time not much happened during the winter months on the ranch. However, like most things, something will happen when it is least expected, and at the most inconvenient time.

It was the job of the ranch hand assigned to check on the cattle to make sure the cattle had plenty of water and feed. Sometimes it required the ranch hand to break the ice off the small ponds along the creek that ran through the winter pasture so the cattle could get to the water. Part of the job was to make sure the cattle could get to food. If the snow was too deep for the cattle to get to the grass below the snow, or the grass was in short supply, the ranch hand had to make sure hay was hauled out to them. Care of all the animals on the ranch was the job of every ranch hand.

While making rounds to make sure the cattle were okay, it was also time to make sure the fence around the large winter pasture was in good condition so the cattle couldn't wonder off. If any of the cattle wandered off when there was a lot of snow on the ground, they could end up falling into or getting stuck in a ravine or gully that was full of snow. That was sure death for the animal. It was also the job of the ranch hand to be on the lookout for predators, both the four legged and two legged kind.

CHAPTER THIRTY

Stolen Cattle

It was a cold day in late January. There was little snow on the ground. It was Frank's turn to make the rounds and check on the cattle and the condition of the pasture. Frank had already checked the ponds for ice and saw to it the cattle had plenty to eat. With that done, it was time for him to ride around the outside of the pasture to make sure the fence was still in good repair. It usually took about three hours, more if the weather was not good or there was a lot of snow on the ground. It also gave him the chance to make sure the cattle were doing okay.

Fortunately, there was only a light dusting of snow on the ground even though the temperature was cold. Frank started working his way around the pasture to check the condition of the fence and some of the cattle that were not hanging around near the ponds. When Frank got to the farthest part of the fence from the barn and ranch house, about a mile, he discovered there was an opening in the fence. A quick look around showed him there were no cattle anywhere near the opening in the fence.

Frank got off his horse to inspect the opening. He quickly discovered tracks in the light covering of snow from at least ten of Joshua's cattle. They had gone out through the opening. But more importantly were the tracks from five horses.

A quick inspection of the fence made it clear whoever had been there was there to steal cattle. The fence had not been pushed over by cattle that wanted out. It had been pulled down. The tracks from the horses showed they had been used to pull the fence down. The thieves had put ropes over a couple of the fence posts and pulled them down.

The tracks of the horses also showed where they went into the winter pasture then came back out. The tracks made by the horses were over top of the tracks of the cattle on the way out of the pasture. That meant the horses followed the cattle out the opening in the fence. The only way that could have happened was if the cattle had been driven out of the pasture.

Frank looked around to see if he could figure out where the rustlers might have taken the cattle, or more accurately, where they had driven the cattle once they got them out of the pasture. The cattle had been pushed off to the north along the edge of the woods.

Frank began following the tracks left by the cattle and horses. The horses were not those of Indian ponies because they had steel horseshoes. It was Frank's intention to follow the cattle in the hope of finding out who might be behind the theft of the cattle.

However, even the best of plans don't always work out as expected. Frank was moving slowly along the edge of the forest. He figured if he didn't get a chance to see who had stolen the cattle, at least he might be able to find out where they were headed.

Frank had followed the tracks for a couple of miles. He was just about ready to turn around and head back to the ranch to get help when a shot rang out from behind a large boulder. He felt a sudden, sharp, burning pain in his side. It caused him to slump over his horse's neck. He grabbed hold of the saddle horn and hung on as he swung his horse around and kicked the horse in the ribs. The horse took off at a run. There were two more shots, but they missed him.

As his horse ran, Frank tried to hang on. He grew weaker, and the pain grew more severe as his horse ran across the prairie bouncing him in the saddle. When the horse dropped down into a shallow gully, Frank lost his grip on the saddle horn. As the horse jumped out of the gully on the other side, Frank fell off the horse and landed with a bone jarring thud in the gully. The fall had knocked the wind out of him, and he lay unconscious in the bottom of the gully.

* * * *

John stood on the porch of the bunkhouse smoking a thin cigar. He was looking off toward the winter pasture. He was getting a little worried because Frank had not returned from his rounds. It was not like Frank to be so late. He was worried that Frank might have run into trouble, or was having difficulty with something.

John turned around as Stan came out of the bunkhouse and walked up next to him. Stan stood next to John looking out over the ranch yard toward the barn. He had a worried look on his face, too.

"You gettin' worried 'bout Frank?" Stan asked as he turned and looked at John.

"Yeah. It ain't like him to be so late."

"You think maybe he's run inta trouble?"

"Could be. There's a lot can happen to a guy out there," John said.

"What ya say ta Bill and I goin' 'round the east side of the pasture while you and one of the others go 'round the west side?"

"Yeah. I think that's a good idea. Have Marcus and Bill get saddled up. Marcus and I will follow his tracks. You and Bill go around the other way and keep a watch for him. Be sure you keep an eye out for any trouble, and check the fence while you're at it. Tell Chester to get dressed and go over to the ranch house and tell Mr. Higgins what's up."

"Okay," Stan said, then turned and went back into the bunkhouse.

John headed for the barn to saddle up a horse. He was soon joined by the others. It wasn't long before the four riders were ready to go looking for Frank.

As John rode out of the barn with Marcus, he saw Chester hightailing it toward the ranch house. John did not wait for instructions. He knew every minute counted in finding Frank if he had been injured. Any delay could mean the difference between life or death for Frank. He also knew Joshua would do the same thing.

John and Marcus galloped along the fence following the tracks left by Frank as he made his rounds of the pasture. They didn't push their horses too hard, but they moved along at a good pace. There was no sense pushing the horses so hard there would be nothing left in them if they really needed it.

It was already starting to get dark when John and Marcus came upon the hole in the fence. It wasn't hard to pick out the tracks left by Frank's horse among the tracks left by the cattle and the other horses. Frank had been smart enough to ride alongside the tracks left by the thieves in case someone might come along behind him.

"Looks like Frank followed whoever stole the cattle," John said as he looked in the direction the tracks went.

"We following them, or waitin' for Bill and Stan?" Marcus asked.

"Bill and Stan shouldn't be too far from here. We'll go on. They'll follow along."

John nudged his horse in the ribs and started following the trail left by Frank. Marcus rode alongside John, but didn't say anything. They hadn't gone very far when John reached down and slipped his rifle out of the scabbard. He levered a cartridge into the chamber then rested the butt of the rifle in the crook of his leg while they continued on. Marcus had seen what John had done and did the same. They rode along keeping an eye out for any danger while following Frank's tracks. They hadn't ridden very much further when Marcus saw the horse that Frank had been riding.

"John, over there," Marcus said as he pointed toward the horse.

John looked in the direction Marcus was pointing. He saw Frank's horse standing down in the bottom of a shallow gully with his head down eating grass along the bottom of the gully. John and Marcus immediately turned and rode toward the horse.

The horse's head came up and looked toward them, but it didn't run off. The horse obviously recognized the horses and riders.

Marcus slowed his horse as he rode up beside Frank's horse. He reached out and took hold of the reins. He looked over the horse and saddle.

"John, there's blood on the saddle."

"We best back track Frank's horse," John said as he swung his horse around and started following the tracks left by Frank's horse.

Marcus followed John while leading Frank's horse. It wasn't long before they came upon the gully where Frank had lost his hold on the saddle horn and fell. As they rode up to the edge of it, John spotted Frank lying in the bottom of the gully. He quickly swung out of the saddle and jumped down into the shallow gully. He knelt down next to Frank and checked to see if he was still alive. He was unconscious, but he was breathing. He was in pretty bad shape.

John rolled Frank over on his back and saw the large bloody area on Frank's coat. He opened Frank's coat and found he had been shot in the side. John took Frank's bandana from his neck and pressed it against Frank's wound in an effort to stop the bleeding.

"He's hurt bad," John said as he looked up at Marcus. "We need to get him back to the house. He won't be able to ride. You'll have to ride double so you can hold onto him."

Marcus simply nodded and swung out of the saddle. As soon as he got down in the gully, he helped pick up Frank. Together they carried him out of the gully and up to the horses. Marcus and John lifted Frank up and sat him in the saddle. John held onto him while Marcus got up on the horse behind Frank. Marcus put an arm around each side of Frank to hold him in the saddle and took up the reins.

"Take him back to the ranch house. I'll wait here for Stan and Bill. If you see them, be sure to tell them to get here as quickly as they can."

"You going after those that did this to Frank?" Marcus asked.

"Yes. We can't let them get away with it. When you get back to the ranch, tell Mr. Higgins what happened. And take Frank's horse with you."

"Okay," Marcus said as he wrapped the reins around his saddle horn.

"Take it easy with him. I don't know how much bouncing around he can stand," John said.

"I'll be careful. You best do the same," Marcus said, then turned his horse and headed back to the ranch.

As soon as Marcus was out of sight, John climbed out of the gully and looked at the tracks Frank's horse had made. The tracks showed that the horse had been running just before it had gone down into the gully.

John had no idea how long it would take for the others to catch up with him. He walked over to his horse and swung up into the saddle and rode back along the tracks made by Frank's horse. It wasn't long before he came to the place where Frank's horse had wheeled around sharply and started to run.

John swung down out of the saddle and began looking around. He found a few spots of blood in the snow. The blood and the tracks showed that Frank's horse had wheeled around hard. John had found the place where Frank had been shot.

John looked off in the direction the cattle and rustlers had gone. He began slowly walking alongside the tracks. He kept an eye out for anyone who didn't belong in the area as well as watching for Bill and Stan. John didn't want to get so far ahead of the others that he would be out there all alone for very long. He had no idea what he might find up ahead. It could be just the five riders, or there could be more.

It wasn't long before Stan and Bill came into sight. John put his foot in the stirrup and swung into the saddle. Sitting on his horse, he waved his hat in the air to get their attention. He could see one of them pointing in his direction then turn their horses as they headed toward him.

Since Bill and Stan had seen him, John once again followed the tracks left by the cattle and the rustlers. It wasn't long before Bill and Stan caught up with him. They rode up beside John.

"We saw Marcus with Frank," Bill said. "Frank was hanging in there, but he looked like he was in pretty bad shape."

"Yeah. From the looks of these tracks, I don't think the rustlers are very far ahead. Be ready for anything," John said.

It was getting dark when they came to a place where there was a hill off to the left of the tracks. The tracks were hard to see in the fading light, but they looked like they were fresh. That would mean that they were closing in on the rustlers.

The tracks seemed to go around the base of the hill. John reined up and looked around. He again looked at the tracks. They looked very fresh. If whoever had stolen the cattle was just around on the other side of the hill, they might be riding into a trap. He was not about to take that chance. John looked at Stan and remembered that he had been a pretty good scout during the war. He motioned for Stan to ride up on top of the hill and take a look around.

Stan nodded then spurred his horse on up the hill. When he got close to the top, he slowed down and stopped. He swung out of the saddle, and walked his horse toward the very top. He approached the top of the hill carefully with his rifle in his hand. Stan didn't want anyone on the other side to see him before he saw them, but he needed to be ready in case he was seen.

Stan stopped short of the top when he got to a place where he could see several men herding some longhorns toward a small wagon train. He watched them for a few minutes before he turned and headed back down the hill to where Bill and John were waiting.

"Our cattle are on the other side of the hill. It looks like five men are driving them toward a small group of wagons that are kinda strung out in sort of a line. Looks like they're taking them to the far side of the wagons."

"Any idea what's going on," John asked.

"Not for sure. If I had to guess, it looks to me like some settlers might have gotten caught in that snow we had the other day. They might have stolen them cattle for something to eat. What do you think we should do?"

"I think we should ride on in there, get our cattle back and find out what's going on," Bill suggested.

"It don't look like they're going anywhere soon. The wagons look as if they might be bogged down a mite in the snow. They must have been stopped when it snowed and it drifted in 'round them. The wagons look as if they're pretty darn heavy. All I seen was horses to pull them. Them greenhorns shoulda had oxen to pull them heavy wagons," Stan said.

"We're going to wait a little while before we go charging in there," John said. "If they get to thinking no one is coming after them, they might let down their guard a little. Stan, can you see them from those rocks up close to the top?"

"Sure can."

"Get up there and watch them. See if they put out guards, and if they do, where."

Stan nodded that he understood, then stepped down from his horse and handed the reins to John. He took his rifle from his saddle scabbard and walked up the hill to a cluster of rocks. He laid his rifle on top of a rock then settled in to watch. It had turned dark, but he could see what was going on in the camp below him because they had a large fire on his side of the wagons. Stan was thinking they were pretty dumb to build such a large fire.

Time passed slowly as darkness spread over the hill. As Stan watched, he noticed they had posted a guard looking in the direction they had brought the cattle. Stan couldn't help but think they were greenhorns because they didn't guard the other side of their camp.

When things had settled down in the camp and it looked quiet, Stan slipped away and went down the hill to where Bill and John were waiting. He was smiling when he approached them.

"What's going on," John asked.

"Them greenhorns put a guard on this side of their camp, but not on the other side. And there's only one guard. If we were to circle 'round behind them, we could be in their camp before they knew we were there."

"Good work. Have you got a good place to shoot from on the hill?" John asked.

"Sure do. I could pick off the guard. Hell, he's standing so the fire shows him as if he was standing in broad daylight."

"Okay. You give Bill and me a few minutes to circle around. Keep an eye on that guard. If he heads back toward the other side of the wagons, you stop him."

"Do I kill him?"

"Not unless you have to."

"What are you going to do?"

"We're going to take us some prisoners just like when we were soldiers," John said.

Stan smiled, then turned and headed back up the hill to the rocks. He got himself ready by laying his rifle over the rocks then took careful aim at the guard.

While Stan settled in to watch the guard and the wagons, John and Bill worked their way around to the backside of the camp on foot. As soon as they were ready, they moved in on the camp. John left his rifle with Bill, then worked his way up to one of the wagons while Bill stood back to make sure that if anyone woke up they wouldn't cause any trouble.

When John was ready, he ducked under the wagon next to one of the sleeping men. John stuck his pistol barrel in the man's face at the same time as he put his other hand over the man's mouth. The man woke up very quickly. The guy opened his eyes and saw the gun pointed at him. Fear quickly showed over the man's face and he froze in place.

"Any noise and you won't live to find out what happened," John said in a whisper. "Get up real slow and don't wake anyone. You do and you will be the first to die."

As the man silently and carefully rolled out of his bedroll, John stayed very close to him. Once he was out from under the wagon, he walked him over to Bill. Bill turned him around and tied him up, then put a gag in his mouth.

John and Bill repeated the move until they had three of the men from the group. With the three men tied together, John and Bill moved back into the darkness. It was time to let the rest of the people with the wagons know they were there.

"Everyone listen up," John called out. "Don't anyone get brave and do anything stupid. We have three of your men tied and ready to be shot if anyone tries anything. And to let you know that we are not alone and we mean business, I suggest that your guard stand very, very still, unless he wants to die."

Their presence had come as a surprise to everyone. Without knowing how many were there, they complied with John's instructions.

"One of you on the hill," John called out. "Let them know we mean business."

All of a sudden, there was a single rifle shot from the top of the hill. The bullet struck the ground right between the guard's feet causing him to jump back so quickly that he fell to the ground.

After that, everyone crawled out from under the wagons and gathered near the fire. The women and children were taken off to one side, while the men were disarmed and tied together. Bill tied the men to one of the wagons where they could be seen by Stan on top of the hill.

"We want all the weapons you have. If anyone tries to stop us from getting them, the men tied to the wagon will be shot first by our men on the hill."

Bill moved out where he could keep an eye on their prisoners while staying out of Stan's line of fire. John searched the prisoners and then their wagons for any weapons. He stacked all the weapons in the back of one of the wagons.

"Who is your leader," John asked.

No one said anything.

"Okay, if you don't want to tell us who your leader is, we will take the five men who stole our cattle and hang them one at a time until someone speaks up. Bill, take that one," John said as he pointed to one of the men. "I know he was one of them. We'll hang him first for rustling cattle."

"NO!" one of the women yelled out.

"We can hang all five of the men for cattle rustling."

"They only took them because we are hungry," the woman said as she pleaded for mercy for her husband.

"One steer would have fed everyone here for a week. Taking ten is just plan cattle rustling, especially since you stole breeding stock. Nine cows and a bull is enough for you to start a little ranch in some small valley back in the hills."

"If we give them back, will you let us go? We promise never to come back here again," she pleaded.

"We'll still hang the five who stole the cattle if the man they shot dies."

The woman turned suddenly and looked at her husband. She had a shocked look on her face.

"Charles, you shot a man?" she asked with a surprised look on her face.

"I didn't shoot him, but I did help steal the cattle. I'm so sorry, Mary."

John looked at the woman. She knew it didn't matter if her husband had fired the shot that hit Frank or not. He was with those who stole the cattle and that made him as guilty as the one who did shoot Frank.

"I still want the leader of this bunch," John said, demanding a response.

"I'm the leader," one of the men said reluctantly.

John looked at the man. John had never seen him before. The man was tall with a lean frame. He had a full beard and dark brown eyes. He looked to be one of the elders in the group.

John couldn't help but think he didn't look much like a leader. His voice was soft and he didn't speak with the authority of a leader. John walked over and stood in front of the man.

"We are going to hold you and your people here until our boss gets here," John said.

"Then what will you do to us?" the leader asked.

"That will depend on the boss. He has every right to hang the men who stole his cattle, and the man who shot one of his ranch hands. What he does will be his choice, not yours."

"We have broken the law of the land. We will pay the price for that," the man said.

Nothing more was said. Everyone settled in for a long wait.

* * * *

The sun was just starting to come up over the eastern hills when John heard the sound of horses. He turned and looked in time to see Joshua and four other ranch hands come around the base of the hill.

Joshua reined his horse to a stop and took a minute to look around. He saw the men tied to the wagon, and the women and children huddled close together in blankets near the fire. A couple of the women looked as if they were praying.

"I see you found our cattle. You want to tell me what happened here?" he asked John.

John took a few minutes to explain what had happened and why they had taken the men as prisoners. While John explained, Joshua looked over the men and women. He was trying to decide what to do with them. He knew he had every right to hang the men who had shot his ranch hand and taken his cattle. John pointed out the one who had said he was the leader of the small group of travelers.

When John was finished, Joshua pointed to the one who said he was the leader and said, "You. Come over here."

Bill walked over to the man and untied him. The man walked over to Joshua.

"Yes sir?"

"What is your name?"

"Samuel Wilson, sir."

"Well, Mr. Wilson, what do you think I should do to the men who stole my cattle and shot my ranch hand?"

"I know what we did was wrong. There is no doubt about that, sir. But we did it out of hunger for our little ones. We meant no harm to anyone."

Joshua looked at the women and children. The looks on their faces showed they were afraid of what he might do to them, but they didn't look like they were starving.

"You expect me to believe that when you tore down my fence, stole cattle that would make good breeding stock and shot one of my men?"

"It was not the intention to steal good breeding stock, nor was it our intention to shoot one of your hands. But we needed food."

"You know, I don't believe a word you say," Joshua said looking him right in the eyes. "If you needed meat, you could have gone hunting for it. There is a lot of game around here including deer, antelope, elk and a lot of smaller animals. We even have some buffalo in the area. Your men didn't have to pull down my fence. They could have come up to the house and asked for food. They didn't have to take more than one steer to feed everyone here for several days. And they certainly didn't have to shoot one of my men in an attempt to get away with it."

"That is true, sir. I guess they were not thinking of those things. They were thinking of their children."

"I doubt that. If you were thinking of the children, what would their children think when their fathers are hung for shooting a man and rustling cattle?"

Mr. Wilson didn't bother to answer Joshua's question. There was no need to answer as both men knew the answer and didn't like it.

"I'll tell you what I'm going to do. I'm going to send you on your way. Only you will not be going the way you are now. You are going to head straight south for the next eight days. That should put you at the Platte River. You will cross the river, which will put you on the Oregon Trail. You will have to hunt for food because I'm going to take my cattle back to the pasture you took them from," Joshua said.

"But sir, that is not where we intended to go."

"I don't care where you intended to go. It is the way you will go, or I will hang the thieves right here, and send you south to the Platte River anyway."

"I understand," the leader said softly.

"Now don't get the idea I'm doing you any favor. You will be followed every inch of the way to the Platte River by some Indian friends of mine who don't like it when you trespass on their land. Do you understand?"

"Yes, sir."

"I don't recommend you ever return to this area. The Black Hills and the surrounding area are off limits to you and your people. If you do return, you will be shot on sight."

"I understand."

"See that you do."

"Sir, how is it that you are allowed to remain on their land? You are obviously a white man."

"I became their friend and helped them many years ago, and I married the chief's sister a long time ago, before he was chief."

"I see."

"Actually, you don't see anything. I would not hesitate one second to hang all five of those who were involved in the shooting of my ranch hand if I was pretty sure that the man you shot would die. But just in case you think you are home free, think again. If he should die from his gunshot wounds, I'll track you down and hang every one of them involved myself," Joshua said.

"John, gather up our stock and head them home," Joshua said without giving the leader a chance to say anything. "Gather up their guns except for two so they can hunt for what food they need."

"Yes, sir," John said.

"You are taking our guns? You can't do that."

"I can and I will. In fact, I can still hang the five who stole my cattle right now. Would you prefer I do that?"

"No, sir."

"Then you will do as I say. I'm leaving you enough guns to hunt with. I'm not leaving you with guns so that you can shoot at us."

Joshua got on his horse and watched the men who had stolen his cattle while John and Bill rounded up the cattle and started driving them back to the pasture. As soon as they were out of sight of the wagon, Joshua got their attention.

"Look up there," Joshua said as he pointed to the top of the hill. "Those Indians are watching you and will watch you until you get to the Platte River. If you change direction even the slightest, it will be the end of your travels. They will kill all of you and leave your bodies for the buzzards, and I mean all of you."

With that said, Joshua swung his horse around and headed back toward the ranch.

A dozen of Spotted Horse's braves sat on their ponies and watched the travelers while the men hooked up their teams to the wagons and the women fixed them breakfast. It was a nervous time for all them as they ate their breakfast. Most of them spent their time trying to eat while looking toward the top of the hill in an effort to see who might be watching them. The thing was, they had no idea how many Indians were on the other side of the hill.

As soon as breakfast was over, they turned their wagons and headed south. Every so often, Spotted Horse would allow the travelers a chance to see a few of his braves watching them from the top of a hill, or from the edge of a distant forest. The travelers did a little hunting to get food for the group, but stayed as close to the wagons as possible.

When they got to the Platte River, Spotted Horse waited until they were all across the river. He let them know they were still there to make sure they didn't return. Two days after the travelers headed west along the Oregon Trail, Spotted Horse and his braves returned to the ranch. He reported to Joshua that they had moved on.

"The travelers have crossed the Platte River and were headed west. I still think you should have hung the five who stole your cattle," Spotted Horse said.

"Maybe you're right, but maybe they have learned a lesson. Either way, I would hate to see those children grow up without fathers. Frank is doing well. He has had good care from Swift Doe. He will be up and around soon."

"What would you have done if Frank had not survived his injuries?"

"I would have hunted down the travelers and hung the five who stole my cattle. They were the ones responsible for Frank being shot."

Spotted Horse just nodded his approval, then returned to his camp in the hills.

CHAPTER THIRTY-ONE

Changing Times

Over the next couple of years the ranch grew in size, and a few things changed. One of the men who had been there from the beginning of Joshua's ranch, left to start his own ranch. Marcus moved on west and began ranching in Wyoming. He bought a few of Joshua's cattle to help him get started.

Three of the ranch hands married into the tribe. John married Yellow Bird, Stan married Little Dove and Frank finally married Swift Doe. They all stayed on at the ranch and had a big part in helping the ranch continue to grow.

Chester, on the other hand, felt it was time for him to move on and do something different. He liked to cook and began to realize how good a cook he really was. He moved to Cheyenne and opened a café. It had been something he was going to do when the war started, but he got dragged into it. He felt that now was his chance to make his dream come true.

Shortly after Marcus left, a man by the name of James Baker stopped by the ranch. He was looking for work on a ranch. Joshua gave him a chance and he ended up staying on. He turned out to be a first rate ranch hand.

* * * *

As more settlers began to move onto the plains and settle there, more attacks were made by the Indians against the white settlers. The soldiers tried their best to protect the people on the wagon trains; but with so much territory to cover and so few soldiers, it was difficult to protect them all.

There were not many attacks against Joshua and his ranch. Of those that did occur, most of them were minor incidents. There were two reasons for the small number of attacks on Joshua's ranch. The first was the ranch was located over a hundred miles from most of the well traveled trails used by those seeking a new life on the Frontier or in the Promised Land. The second was that Joshua had lived in peace with Spotted Horse and his tribe, and had married a woman from the tribe. He had also been fair with the other tribes that lived and hunted in the area.

From time to time a steer would be stolen from the ranch by Indians to help feed their families when hunting was difficult. Joshua didn't get too upset over it. He knew Indians living in the area were having a hard time of it with most of the buffalo having been killed by buffalo hunters. He looked at it as an obligation to help the Indians that lived close to his ranch. A steer now and then was not a bad price to pay to raise his cattle on their land and maintain a degree of peace.

However, Joshua often ran into trouble with the Army for interfering with the Indian agents who would try to force the Indians onto reservations, especially those who lived on or around his ranch. He knew many of the Indian agents were appointed by politicians back east who had no knowledge of the Indian's culture or needs. And more often than not, the appointee didn't know anything at all about Indians. Many of them were crooked and diverted food to other places at a profit to themselves, especially cattle, while other agents never got the supplies for the Indians they had been promised by the government.

As time went by, Spotted Horse found that what Joshua had told him about the loss of the buffalo had come true. The buffalo had become hard to find. Unlike some tribes, Spotted Horse and his people had learned to raise cattle from Joshua. Trouble only came when Spotted Horse and his people tried to sell part of his herd of cattle to the army.

CHAPTER THIRTY-TWO

Trouble With An Indian Agent

Joshua often sold cattle to the army for the army's use and for distribution to the Indians on the reservations in the area. However, the first time Spotted Horse and his people tried to sell their cattle to the army, the army took the cattle from them because they thought the Indians had stolen them. They didn't believe the Indians were raising cattle. Spotted Horse and some of his people were arrested for stealing cattle.

One of the young braves had been away from the herd when the soldiers arrested Spotted Horse. He was on his way back to join the cattle drive when he saw Spotted Horse and some of the others in irons. They were being led away by the soldiers. He followed the soldiers at a distance to find out where they were taking Spotted Horse, his braves, and the cattle. The soldiers had marched them off to Fort Thompson where they were held pending trial on charges of cattle rustling.

Once the young brave knew where Spotted Horse and the others had been taken, he rode his horse as fast as he could back to the ranch. On arriving at the ranch, he found Joshua and told him what had happened. Joshua set out that very day with two of his men for Fort Thompson with the intention of getting Spotted Horse and the others released. It took Joshua and his ranch hands three days of hard riding to get to the fort.

When Joshua, John and Stan arrived at Fort Thompson on the Missouri River, they saw the gallows had already been constructed off to the side of the parade grounds near the center of the fort. It did not give them much hope they would be able to save their friends. Gallows were rarely built before a trial was completed, and those charged with a crime had been found guilty. Joshua knew they had already been tried and convicted.

There were several Indian women near the fort's brig chanting prayers when they rode into the fort. Joshua immediately realized one of women praying was Morning Star. The women were surrounded by guards. The guards were doing nothing but watching the women carefully, probably wondering if they were going to try to help their men escape.

It didn't take Joshua but a couple of seconds to figure out that the army was about to hang some Indians, and one of them was likely to be his friend, Spotted Horse, the leader of the tribe.

Joshua went to see Morning Star. When she saw him, she started to run to him, but a guard stopped her. Joshua walked to her.

"They are going to hang my husband for stealing your cattle," she said in her native language.

"I will talk to the officer in charge and clear things up," Joshua said then turned and started across the parade grounds toward the commanding officer's office.

Joshua was not sure if he could change the commanding officer's mind. He knew many officers and enlisted men hated the so-called 'redskin' because of what Sitting Bull and Crazy Horse had done to Custer and his troops at the Battle of the Little Big Horn only a year or so earlier.

As Joshua stepped up on the porch, a guard standing next to the door stepped in front of him. He held his rifle firmly across his chest and looked Joshua in the eyes. The look on his face was less than friendly, but Joshua didn't care. He was there to get his friends out of jail before they had a chance to hang them. And he was determined to get Spotted Horse out of there even if he had to break him out.

He had no idea how he would do it with only himself and two of his ranch hands, but he would try if the commanding officer would not listen to him.

"Please step aside. I want to talk to the officer in charge," Joshua said to the soldier standing guard. "The Indians he is planning on hanging for stealing cattle are not guilty."

"They were caught red-handed with stolen cattle," the guard said. "The Indian agent informed the major that he knew who the brand belonged to, and it wasn't the Indians."

"Did the Indian agent see the bill of sale Spotted Horse had?"

"Yes. The Indian Agent said it was a forgery."

"I can assure you it was not. I want to see the major, and I want to see him now."

"You'll just have to wait until he's ready to see you," the corporal said.

"I said now, Corporal," Joshua yelled at him as he slipped his hand over his pistol grip.

The corporal stood his ground, although it was easy to see he was a bit nervous. The man in front of the corporal was determined to see the officer in charge. The fact that there were two other men with guns behind Joshua contributed to the corporal's nervousness.

Just then the door to the commanding officer's quarters flew open and a man in an officer's uniform stepped out onto the porch. He looked at the three men standing on the porch.

"What the hell is going on out here, Corporal?" the officer demanded without taking his eyes off Joshua.

"You are about to hang several Indians for stealing cattle," Joshua said before the corporal could respond. "They didn't steal them. They got them from me."

"And just who are you?" the major asked sharply.

"I'm Joshua Higgins."

"What is your interest in this?"

"My interest is to see that my friends are not hung for something they didn't do. Namely steal cattle."

"The Indians we caught had branded cattle. Cattle that could only have belonged to a white man. I know for a fact that Indians don't raise cattle."

"That's where you're wrong. These Indians do. They are friends of mine, and I raise cattle with their help. The cattle they tried to sell to you were cattle I gave them in payment for work they did for me on my ranch," Joshua said.

"And where do you have your ranch?" the officer asked, the expression on his face showing he might have made a big mistake by listening to the Indian agent stationed at the fort.

"It's at the southern end of the Black Hills along the Cheyenne River."

"That's where they said they got the cattle," the officer said as he thought about it.

"Corporal, go get Wilbur Johnson. Now!"

"Yes, Sir."

The corporal immediately left the porch and ran across the yard toward a small building on the other side of the fort.

Joshua looked at the major before he spoke. Joshua had a confused look on his face.

"Who is Wilbur Johnson?"

"He's the local Indian agent."

"What kind of a man is he?"

"He's smart enough, but he doesn't know anything about Indians. He's from New York City. He's another government appointee," the major said with a hint of disgust.

The major was beginning to see that he might have made a mistake by listening to the Indian agent, but he wasn't ready to admit it just yet. He didn't like the Indian agent, but he wanted proof that Spotted Horse and the others had not stolen the cattle.

"Didn't Spotted Horse show you a bill of sale for the cattle?" Joshua asked.

"Yes, he did. I showed it to the Indian agent. The agent said it had probably been stolen or forged. He thought they probably stole the cattle from someone who had bought them, and took the bill of sale so they could sell them to the army for distribution to the Indians through the Indian agent."

"Think about what you just said," Joshua said as he looked at the major. "Why would they steal cattle, sell them to the army who would give them to the Indian agent who would probably sell them to someone else and keep the money?

"With all the Indians on reservations starving because of crooked Indian agents who often sell the cattle to someone else, why would they try to sell the cattle? Wouldn't it make more sense to take them to the reservation to feed the Indians there? The Indians could kill and skin the cattle before you or anyone else had any idea they had been stolen."

Joshua could see by the look on the major's face that he was thinking about what Joshua had said.

"You said you saw the bill of sale. Is that correct?"

"Yes."

"Did the bill of sale you saw have a circle with two J's and two bars between the J's inside the circle?" Joshua asked.

"Yes, it did."

"That, sir, is my brand. Spotted Horse owned those cattle free and clear."

The officer looked at Joshua as he thought about what he should do. The fact was he didn't want to look bad in front of his men. But on the other hand, how could he hang innocent men, even if they were Indians.

"I want to talk to the Indian agent about that. Here he comes," the major said looking over Joshua's shoulder.

Joshua turned and looked at the little man with a pot belly coming toward them. He was wearing a vest over a dingy white shirt. His pants looked like they could use a good cleaning, too.

"What's going on? Your corporal wouldn't tell me anything," Johnson said angrily.

"This is Mr. Joshua Higgins. He is the owner of the Circle Double J Ranch in the Dakota Territory. His brand is two Js with two bars between them inside a circle. Does that mean anything to you, Mr. Johnson?" the major asked with a stern tone in his voice.

"Not a thing," Johnson said as he looked at Joshua through squinted eyes.

"Well, maybe it should. You see, Mr. Higgins is here because you told us the Indians stole the cattle they brought here for you to buy. You swore, in court, there was no ranch with that brand, and there was certainly no cattle ranch at the southern end of the Black Hills."

"That's right," Mr. Johnson said.

"Well, Mr. Higgins seems to differ with you on that. He says there is and that is his brand."

"We have had no report of a cattle ranch where he claims to have one."

"Have you tried to find out if there is a ranch where Spotted Horse said there was?" Joshua asked.

"No. There was no need to find out. They stole the cattle. That ends it."

"Maybe not. It appears there was a need to find out," the major said.

"Well, mister, you should have taken the time to find out. My ranch has been located at the edge of the southern Black Hills since before the Civil War. Some, if not most, of the Indians you have accused of stealing my cattle have worked on my ranch. The bill of sale and the cattle were given to them in payment for all the work they did on my ranch."

Mr. Johnson was trying very hard to come up with an explanation, but there was none. Johnson seemed to be very angry that some one wearing a buckskin shirt could cause him so much trouble. He wasn't going to let him get away with it.

"Well, apparently I might have made a slight mistake," Johnson said. "Major, I think it would be a good idea if you would release the Indians immediately to return to where they came from."

"I think that is a wise choice," the major said.

"I will, however, keep the cattle," Mr. Johnson added with a grin.

"Like hell you will," Joshua said. "The only way you will keep those cattle is if you pay for them, now. Otherwise, they go back with Spotted Horse."

"They are on government land. Therefore, they are government property," Johnson insisted.

"Major, I will have my friends out of jail and those cattle returned to them, or I will simply shoot this man for stealing cattle and take the cattle back."

"You can't do that," the little man said, but the fear that Joshua or one of his men might shoot him could be seen in his eyes.

"I think he just might do that," the major said. "And under the circumstances, I might let him. If the Indians didn't steal the cattle, then they still belong to the Indians. I will return the cattle to Spotted Horse and his people."

"You can't do that."

"Yes, I can," the major said flatly.

"I'll have your head for this," Johnson yelled at the major.

The major smiled then turned to the corporal standing beside him, and said, "Corporal, if Mr. Johnson doesn't return the cattle to the Indians within the next fifteen minutes, you are ordered to shoot him for stealing cattle from the Indians. Then you are to drag his body out of the fort and leave it for the coyotes to chew on."

"Yes, sir," the corporal said with a grin.

"I'll report you to Washington for this," Mr. Johnson said angrily.

"That won't be necessary. I will be reporting you immediately. In the meantime, you are confined to your quarters until arrangements can be made to send you back east."

"You can't confine me to quarters, and you can't give them back the cattle. The cattle are government property," Johnson insisted, not sure he was on very solid ground at the moment.

"I can and I will," the major said, then looked at the corporal again. "Corporal, see to it that there is a guard posted at Mr. Johnson quarters. He is to remain in his quarters until he is shipped out of here on the next available wagon headed east. You will instruct the guard that if he should so much as step one foot out of his quarters, he is to be shot for attempting to escape. Is that clear?"

"Yes, sir," the corporal said.

With his rifle in both hands, the corporal pushed Johnson toward his quarters. Joshua watched as the corporal took Johnson back across the yard to his quarters. Johnson was yelling his objections to the way he was treated the entire time.

"I will release your friend and his people immediately," the officer said.

"Thank you," Joshua said then he turned around to leave to go to his friends in the jail.

As Joshua stepped off the porch, he could hear the major give another soldier orders to release Spotted Horse and his people at once. The one thing he did not hear was the order to release Spotted Horse's cattle back to Spotted Horse. Joshua stopped and turned to the major.

"Sir, I didn't hear the order to return Spotted Horse's cattle to him."

"I will not be releasing Spotted Horse's cattle. Instead, I will be buying them for the army. He will not have to take the herd back. I can assure you that he will get a fair price for them, and I will see to it they get to the Indians on the reservation."

"Thank you, sir," Joshua said with a smile.

"As soon as Spotted Horse is released, bring him to my office and I will pay him for the cattle. I will also give him my deepest apology."

"Thank you, sir," Joshua said, then turned to find Morning Star.

Joshua followed the soldier to the jail and found Morning Star nearby. The soldier told the jailer what the major had said. The jailer then turned and told the guards to release Spotted Horse and his men.

Joshua was waiting outside the jail with Morning Star when his old friend, Spotted Horse, was released. They greeted each other, then Joshua told him the army would buy his cattle and take them to the Indians on the reservation.

After all was settled with the army and Spotted Horse had collected his payment for his cattle, they all headed back to the ranch. From that day on, Spotted Horse and Joshua made it a point to sell their cattle together under Joshua's brand and with Joshua present.

As time went by, things slowly began to settle down on the Plains. Many of the Indians had been rounded up and relocated to reservations at various locations. Some of the Indians ran away while others still fought to the bitter end. Some went further west into the mountains while many of them went north into Canada. Spotted Horse and a few of his people remained on the land Joshua claimed for his ranch. They worked side-by-side with Joshua and his ranch hands. A couple of ranch hands married into the tribe. Over time, Joshua hired a few more ranch hands. Some of the young Indians of the tribe hired on, while a few of the braves moved away to seek their fortune somewhere else.

CHAPTER THIRTY-THREE

Running Away For Love

A young couple that had been traveling for some time across the plains stumbled onto the Circle Double J Ranch. Frank caught them near the eastern boarder of the ranch skinning one of Joshua's cows. He took them to the ranch house.

When Frank rode up to the ranch house alongside a wagon with a rifle on the man walking alongside it, Joshua wondered what was going on. He met them at the front porch of the ranch house.

"What do you have here?" Joshua asked Frank.

"I caught them skinning one of your cows over east."

"Oh," Joshua said as he looked at the young couple.

Joshua couldn't help but look them over. They looked very poor. Their clothes were well worn, and they looked like they hadn't had a decent meal for a long time.

"You want to tell me why you killed one of my cows," Joshua asked, guessing from the look of them, they had probably killed the cow for something to eat.

"We are sorry about killing one of your cows, but we haven't had anything to eat for two days. We don't have any money, but I'll be glad to work to pay you for your cow, sir."

"How is it you have come, - - - Joshua started to ask before he was interrupted by Dancing Flower.

"Joshua, I think we should get them something to eat first," Dancing Flower said. "There will be plenty of time to talk later."

"That's a good idea. Young lady, would you like to get down off that wagon?"

"Yes, sir," she said politely, then got down off the wagon.

"Frank, take their wagon over by the barn and make sure their animals get fed, watered and rubbed down."

"Yes, sir."

"Are you going to keep our horses and wagon," the young man asked, afraid of what they might do.

"No, but your animals look as hungry as the two of you do. We're just going to take care of them for you. You can have them back later."

Dancing Flower took the young couple into the ranch house and put food on the table for them. From the way they ate, it was clear they had not had anything to eat for sometime.

When Frank returned to the house after feeding the horses, he walked up to Joshua and asked him to come outside. Joshua followed Frank outside.

"I got a look in their wagon when I took the team over to the barn. They don't have anything but a few clothes. There's no furniture and no food. There was a pistol and a rifle in the wagon. The rifle was empty and the pistol only had two bullets left in it."

"Anything else?" Joshua asked.

"No, sir. I don't know how they made it this far."

"Did they complain or give you any argument?"

"No. They seemed to know what they had done was wrong, and they made no excuses for it," Frank said. "The only thing they asked was what kind of a man was my boss."

"Why do you think they asked that?"

"I think they were worried about what might happen to them," Frank said. "I think they've been traveling a long ways. I can't help but think they are running away from something or someone. They certainly don't look like they were prepared for this trip."

"I think I'll have a talk with them after they've had a chance to eat."

"If you don't mind my saying so, you might want to have that talk while Dancing Flower is there. She might make it easier for the woman to tell you what is going on."

"That's a good idea. I'll talk to you later," Joshua said.

Joshua turned and went back inside the ranch house. The young couple was still sitting at the table eating. Joshua just sat down at the table and had a cup of coffee while he waited for them to finish their meal. He had already eaten. Once the young couple had eaten, Joshua looked at them for a moment or two before he talked to them.

"First of all, what are your names?"

He looked at the woman, who couldn't have been more than seventeen years old, then looked at the young man.

"Okay. Since you don't want to tell me who you are, I don't see how I can help you. You killed one of my cows. I have no choice but to turn you over to the law."

"Joshua!" Dancing Flower said with a sharp note of surprise that he would say such a thing.

"I'm Walter Fisher," the young man said.

"Well, Walter, do you want to tell me why you killed my cow?"

"We were very hungry," the young man said. "I don't have any money to pay you for the cow, but I will gladly work off whatever you think the cow is worth, if you will allow it."

"My ranch hand seems to think you are running away from someone or something. Is that what you are doing?"

Walter looked at the young woman, but she didn't say anything. He turned and looked down at the floor for a moment. Joshua waited for him to decide if he was going to talk. Finally, the young man looked up at Joshua.

"Mary and I ran away from her father. He refused to let us get married."

"Does that mean you are not married now," Dancing Flower asked.

"Yes, Ma'am," Walter said. "We are planning on getting married the first chance we get."

"My father threatened to kill Walter if I ever saw him again. I love Walter and he loves me. My father has been very unreasonable. He doesn't like Walter because his family doesn't have much. His father is a blacksmith, and Walter wants to be a blacksmith, too. It's good honest work." Mary said as if she was pleading their case.

"I take it you know how to shoe a horse and make horse shoes?"

"Yes, sir.

"Can you make all kinds of metal things like hinges, nails, and hasps?" Joshua asked.

Walter looked at Mary before he answered.

"Yes, sir," Walter said as he wondered why Joshua wanted to know that.

"You, young lady, can you cook?"

"Yes, sir," Mary said.

Joshua looked over at Dancing Flower. Dancing Flower was smiling at him. He knew she would want him to help them.

"Okay. I need two things on this ranch. I need a ranch hand who can also be a blacksmith. I also need someone to help with the cooking to feed the ranch hands and occasionally some of the Indians that work here. I will hire both of you if you are willing to do that work. What do you say?"

Mary looked at Walter, then smiled. Walter nodded his head, and Mary replied by nodding her head.

"Thank you. We accept your offer," Walter said.

"Since I lost my cook," Joshua said to Mary. "You will help Swift Doe and Yellow Bird cook for the men. Dancing Flower will introduce you to them. Do you have any problem working alongside Indians?"

"No, sir. Thank you," Mary said, the expression on her face showing how pleased it made her.

"As for you, Walter, you will report to John Hamilton. He is my foreman. He will be your boss. You explain to him that you are to be used as a blacksmith first and a ranch hand when you are available. I'm sure you will get along fine. Do you have any problem working with Indians?"

"I've never even met an Indian before. I wouldn't think it should be a problem," Walter said. "Why do you ask?"

"Because we have a number of them working on this ranch. By the way, you have met an Indian. My wife is an Indian."

"I have a question. Where do we sleep?" Mary asked.

"You can sleep in your wagon for now. We'll move it up close to the house. We don't have sleeping places for women."

"You, Walter, will sleep in the bunkhouse with the other men, until you are married."

* * * *

Several weeks passed and Mary and Walter had proven themselves to be good workers, Dancing Flower and Joshua called them to come over to the ranch house after dinner one evening. All they knew was Joshua and Dancing Flower wanted to talk to them. It worried them when they were called to the ranch house.

"Dancing Flower and I have been talking about you. We think you are in love with each other. Since we are going to Cheyenne next week, we would like to know if you would like to come along. There's a preacher there. You can get married there. What do you think?"

"That would be great," Walter said, his excitement showing on his face.

Mary looked at Walter and smiled at him. She was as excited as Walter.

The following week the four of them took a wagon into Cheyenne where Joshua and Dancing Flower picked up some supplies and then stood up for Mary and Walter at their wedding.

On the very day they returned from Cheyenne, they found six men sitting under a tree. Their horses were tied to the top rail of the corral. Joshua noticed Mary took hold of Walter's arm and squeezed it.

"Are they someone you know?" Joshua asked.

"Yes. It is my father and some of his men. They have come to take me back home."

"They will not be taking you home if you don't want to go. Around here, we look out for all of the people who work on this ranch."

Joshua watched as the men stood up and looked at the wagon as he drove the wagon on over to the barn. John was standing at the barn door. He had been watching the six men. He reached up and took hold of the reins of the lead horse and held it while Joshua got down.

"How long have they been here?" Joshua asked.

"About two hours. I told them they could wait until dinner time, and if you were not back by then, they would have to leave because you wouldn't be back until tomorrow."

"What did they say to that?"

"He said they would stay here as long as it took. I told him that at dinner time, he and his men had better be leaving, or I would see that they did. I also reminded him that he was outnumbered, and I would not hesitate to use force."

"I'll bet that didn't set well with him," Joshua said with a slight grin.

"It didn't, but when he saw Frank show up with twenty armed Indians, he got the message."

"Okay. I want you to get a couple of the men and have them armed. Don't do anything but make a show of force."

John nodded then walked over to the bunkhouse. Joshua and Dancing Flower walked toward the men. Mary and Walter followed along behind. Mary was hanging onto Walter. It was clear to Joshua that she was afraid of her father.

When Joshua got close to the house, he directed
Dancing Flower to the ranch house while he walked over to
Mary's father.

"I'm Joshua Higgins and I own the land you are on. I
don't take kindly to some stranger coming on my ranch and
giving my foreman a hard time. What is it you want?"

"I'm Albert Nickerson. I have come to get my daughter
and take her back home where she belongs."

"We have no women or girls here by the name of
Nickerson. That being the case, it is time for you to leave."

"The young girl standing behind you is Mary
Nickerson."

"I'm sorry to inform you, but that the young woman is
Mrs. Walter Fisher. Mary and Walter work for me."

"She just told you that so you would protect her."

"No. I know for a fact that she is Mrs. Walter Fisher.
My wife and I witnessed their marriage in Cheyenne two
days ago."

Mr. Nickerson looked at Mary as if he couldn't believe
it. It slowly began to sink in that his little girl was a married
woman.

"Mr. Nickerson," Walter said. "Mary and I don't want
to hold anything against you. All we wanted was to be
happy. We are happy here. You and Mrs. Nickerson will be
welcome to visit us anytime you want, but we are going to
lead our own lives."

Mr. Nickerson looked at Walter for a minute or two. He
was wondering if they were really going to be happy, but
there was no way of knowing what the future held for them.

"I hope that you can forgive me some day. I really hope
you are happy and you have a good life," Mr. Nickerson
said. "I best be going."

Mary let go of Walter's arm and walked up to her father.
She reached out and put her arms around him.

"I am happy, Daddy."

Mary and Walter bid Mr. Nickerson goodbye, then stood there watching him leave with this men.

CHAPTER THIRTY-FOUR

Cattle Rustlers

The sun was bright in the mid-morning sky. There was a slight breeze out of the southwest. The cattle were grazing peacefully on the thick green grass along the Cheyenne River. Birds were singing and the flowers of the prairie were in full bloom.

Stan and Running Elk were sitting on their horses watching from a hill overlooking a large herd of cattle. They were talking about their families while they watched the cattle graze peacefully.

Off in the distance, Frank and Small Eagle were watching another herd off toward the east. The herd had gathered in a shallow draw with a creek that ran casually east and southward in the bottom of the draw. It was not the kind of day that one would expect trouble, but trouble was coming and it was coming fast.

Without any warning, eight or nine men on horseback came charging up the hill behind Stan and Running Elk. As they got closer, they began shooting and yelling as they rode.

Stan and Running Elk swung their horses around as they drew their weapons. Running Elk no more than pulled his rifle up when a bullet ripped through his shoulder before he had a chance to fire a shot. The bullet caused him to drop his rifle and fall from his horse.

Stan had gotten off a couple of shots at the charging men before a bullet hit his horse. The horse reared up and fell over to one side taking Stan with it. The horse landed hard on the ground pinning Stan under it. Stan had hit the ground so hard that it had knocked the wind out of him.

The rustlers rode on by Running Elk and Stan at a run. One of the men took a shot at Stan while he laid out cold on the ground. The one who had shot at Stan had missed him only by an inch or so.

The rustlers continued on down the hill toward the herd, yelling and shooting into the air. The load noise of gunfire startled the longhorn cattle and they started to run. The cattle ran as the rustlers began pushing them on toward where Frank and Small Eagle were watching the cattle in a small valley.

Frank and Small Eagle had heard the shooting and looked in the direction the shots had come from. They could see the cattle were headed right at them with the rustlers pushing them hard. Frank thought about putting up a fight, but with so many cattle headed right for them, he decided it was best to break away and get some help. With all the cattle running and the rustlers behind them, there was little for him to shoot at. It would be almost impossible to hit any of the rustlers. Frank had been in a stampede before and knew how dangerous stampeding cattle can be. He could also see that they were greatly outnumbered.

"Come on!" Frank yelled at Small Eagle, then he swung his horse around and took off at a run toward the ranch house.

Small Eagle and Frank ran their horses at full clip toward the ranch house. The rustlers fired a few shots at them while they continued to push the cattle east, but did not send anyone after Frank and Small Eagle. As the stampeding cattle ran, the small herd that Frank and Small Eagle had been watching started to run and soon became part of the larger herd.

Frank and Small Eagle raced for the ranch house to get help. As they entered the ranch yard, they could see that the ranch hands and Indians were saddling up and getting ready to ride. Joshua and Spotted Horse had heard the shots and

were ready to mount up when they saw Frank and Small
Eagle ride into the ranch yard.

"What happened out there? We heard gunfire," Joshua
asked.

"About eight or nine riders stampeded the cattle.
They're headed off toward the east. I saw Stan go down
with his horse, but don't know what happened to Running
Elk. I didn't see him," Frank said.

"Frank, get a fresh horse and come with us. Small
Eagle, get a fresh horse and take a couple of the women with
you. See if you can find Running Elk and Stan. They may
need help if they're hurt. We're going after the cattle
rustlers."

Frank rode over to the corral. He led his horse into the
corral then quickly took his saddle and bridle off the horse.
He roped another horse, put the bridle on it then saddled it.
He was ready to mount up just as Morning Star came up to
the corral.

"I will take care of the horse," she said.

"Thank you," Frank said as he put his foot in the stirrup
and swung into the saddle.

Frank then kicked his horse in the sides and rode out to
catch up with Joshua and the others.

* * * *

As soon as Little Dove and Dancing Flower had
gathered what they thought they might need to care for
anyone that might be injured, they joined Small Eagle to go
search for Stan and Running Elk. It didn't take them long to
find both of the men.

Running Elk had a serious gunshot wound to his left
shoulder. He had lost a lot of blood. Little Dove had found
him lying among some low bushes. Little Dove and Dancing
Flower rushed to his side and immediately began caring for
his wounds.

It took Small Eagle only a few more minutes to find
Stan. He was breathing, but he was trapped under his fallen

horse. Small Eagle called to Little Dove to come and help him. Together they were able to get enough of the dead horse's weight off Stan and pull him out from under it. It was then they discovered that Stan had a broken leg.

Small Eagle rode back to the ranch where he hitched up a wagon while the women did what they could for Running Elk and Stan. Small Eagle returned with the wagon to carry the injured back to the ranch house.

Once they had Stan and Running Elk in the wagon, they took them back to the ranch house where Morning Star had prepared a place to take care of the injured. She would be ready to help Dancing Flower take care of their injuries. Little Dove stayed with her husband, Stan, while the other women cared for Running Elk's wound. Running Elk's injuries were more serious then Stan's. Both men would not be able to work for sometime. After everything was done for Running Elk and he was resting quietly, Morning Star and Dancing Flower set Stan's leg. They made the men as comfortable as possible, then watched over them.

* * * *

Meanwhile, Joshua, Spotted Horse and the others followed the stampeded herd. As they rode, Joshua began to think about where they might be going. He also thought about what might happen if they continued to follow the rustlers.

It would be easy for the rustlers to have a few of their men hold back a little and wait for them to ride into an ambush. It was clear that the rustlers were headed for Pine Ridge, a long ridge that rose up above the surrounding plains. The lower parts of the ridge were covered with brush and scrub pine trees that cut across a long section of open country. The ridge had lots of small ravines and draws that had been cut in the land by years of spring rains, melting of winter snow and by the winds that blew across the plains. Some of the ravines and draws had formed small box canyons.   The upper part of the ridge was thick with ponderosa pines.

Joshua began to slow the pace.   He could tell by the tracks that the rustlers had managed to get the herd to slow down into a steady walk. He knew that once the rustlers got into the ridge county, it would be harder to follow them. There would be many places where they could hold up. It would also be easier for the rustlers to ambush them there. That gave Joshua an idea. He called for Spotted Horse to join him.

"Spotted Horse, I want you to send a couple of your braves up on the ridge. I want them to see if they can find our herd. When they find the herd, have one of them find us while the other one continues to watch and follow them. Tell them to be very careful not to be seen."

Spotted Horse nodded that he understood then turned his horse and rode off. He rode up to a couple of his braves who had been tracking the herd. When he got up beside them, he gave them instructions on what they were to do. He then swung his horse back around while the two braves rode up into the hills toward the top of the ridge.

Joshua and Spotted Horse had slowed the pace of the men. They didn't want to ride into a trap, but all were ready for a fight. If Spotted Horse's braves spotted the herd, they might be able to set a trap for the rustlers.

* * * *

The day passed on toward night with no sight of the herd or the rustlers. All they had were the tracks from their cattle to follow. By the looks of the tracks left by the cattle they were not very far ahead of them. Joshua was beginning to think that it might be best if they pulled off into a grove of trees along a creek and set up camp for the night.

It would have to be a dry camp, one without a fire, as they had no idea where the rustlers might be. Anyone who had spent anytime on the prairie knew that a fire could be seen for miles on the open prairie, and especially from the nearby ridge.

Joshua motioned for everyone to turn and go over to the grove of trees. When they got to the trees, he gave instructions to the men. Some of the men were to sleep while others stood guard.

Most of the men had settled in when one of the braves that Spotted Horse had sent out to find the herd returned.

"The herd is about two miles up ahead," the young brave explained. "They have settled down for the night in a narrow box canyon, and have posted guards."

"How many guards?" Joshua asked.

"At least four, maybe more. We were able to count at least twelve rustlers in all."

"Twelve? Are you sure" Frank asked as he looked at the brave.

"Yes. There are probably more," the brave replied as he looked at Frank.

Joshua wondered what had caused Frank to question the number of guards.

Frank turned to Joshua and said, "Boss, there were only eight, no more than nine when they attacked us."

"There must have been others waiting in case we were on them too quickly," Joshua said.

"How does it look for an attack on them tonight?" Joshua asked the brave.

"They have the cattle hidden back in a narrow canyon. There is only one way out of it. It looks like they had planned to hold up there all along. There is a new fence across the mouth of the canyon to keep the cattle in. It is a strong log fence. We saw only four guards and four horses, all of them near the fence. The horses were tied to the fence. A couple of the guards were sitting on the fence talking softly to the cattle to keep them calm.

"We worked our way around their camp. There are another eight, maybe more, behind a small rise in the ground out in front of the canyon. It looks like the only way in is from directly in front of them. I think they expected us to come riding right into them," the young brave explained.

"Can we get in behind them?"

"Yes, but it will not be easy. We found a place where we can slip into the canyon without being seen. It would put us behind the guards at the fence. It is close to the back of the canyon."

"Spotted Horse, take a few of your braves and circle around behind them. Take out those guarding the herd, but do it quietly. When you have control of the herd, knock down the fence and run the herd out of the canyon."

Spotted Horse smiled to show Joshua that he agreed with the plan. He nodded his head to show that he understood what he and his braves were to do. Spotted Horse had a pretty good idea what Joshua was planning. He was planning to use the cattle to attack those in front of the canyon from behind, while Joshua and his men attacked them from the front.

"John, you take Frank, Joe and Bill and see if you can find a place where you can out flank those watching for us. Take the left flank. They are probably very close to where the cattle were driven into the canyon, so be careful. I'll take James, Thomas and Walter with me. We'll take the right flank. Be careful out there," Joshua said.

"What's to keep them from escaping by running back the way they went into the canyon? Frank asked.

"The cattle will be running right up their backs," Walter said with a smile. "It seems like a bit of justice to me. They would get run over by the very cattle they stole."

"I'm counting on them not being able to get to their horses. If any of them get to a horse, it will be our job to stop them. We will put our plan into action just before the sky gets light. Spotted Horse, can you get your braves in position before dawn?"

"Yes," he said.

"Good. We'll do the same. When you think it is light enough that we can see who we are shooting at, run the cattle out. We'll be ready."

Spotted Horse nodded his approval then stood up. He gathered his braves together and started off toward the ridge. Spotted Horse and his braves slowly walked their horses up and over the nearby ridge. Once they were behind the box canyon, they tied their horses to trees. Spotted Horse left one brave to watch the horses and to bring them closer when the fight started. The rest of Spotted Horse's braves worked their way down into the canyon. It was slow going getting into the canyon in the dark and still keep quiet.

Once in the bottom of the canyon, they moved slowly among the cattle without making a sound. Since the cattle were used to the smell of those moving among them, they remained calm.

Spotted Horse and his braves carefully scouted out the positions of all the men guarding the cattle. As soon as they were in position among the cattle and close to the fence, they waited for the sky to lighten up the area enough to be able to see where the guards were stationed.

Meanwhile, Joshua and his men moved in as close as they dared to the low ridge in front of the canyon that was the major defensive position for the rustlers. By flanking the rustlers that were standing guard at the low ridge, they had made a narrow opening that the cattle would have to take. It would also have them running in the general direction of home.

* * * *

Time passed slowly as Spotted Horse and his braves waited. Before it was light enough to identify anyone, he began the attack. Each of the guards was attacked from behind by a brave. It only took them a couple of seconds to silently send the four guards to a permanent sleep.

As soon as the guards were eliminated, Spotted Horse and his braves quietly took down the fence. They then quickly moved to the back of the herd. When all the braves were in position and the light in the sky was enough so Spotted Horse could identify his braves, he gave the signal to stampede the cattle. His braves began shooting in the air and yelling. The startled cattle began to move. They were confused at first and started to move in all directions, but the narrow canyon forced the cattle to move in the only direction they could go to get away from all the noise. As they pushed against each other, they began to run. Once they got going, there was no stopping them until they got tired of running.

Spotted Horse and his braves ran behind the cattle until they got to where the fence was down. They then ran back into the canyon. The brave who had been holding their horses had moved the horses down into the canyon as soon as the cattle started to leave. Spotted Horse and the others quickly mounted up and followed the cattle as they ran wildly out onto the open plain.

The sound of gunfire from inside the box canyon was Joshua's signal that the fight was on. Joshua and his men started shooting at the rustlers that were hidden behind the low ridge.

A few of the rustlers that had been up with the light had not realized anything was wrong until the shooting started. But when the shooting and yelling began, even those sleeping were quick to jump up and grab their weapons.

The camp was filled with confusion and chaos. There were men trying to get nervous horses saddled while others were trying to get their boots on. There were even a couple of the rustlers that had been wakened from a deep sleep who were still trying to figure out what was going on.

Suddenly, there was the sound of cattle running, and it was getting louder. It didn't take long for the rustlers to realize that the cattle had been stampeded toward their camp. As the cattle came into view, the rustlers in the camp started scrambling for a safe place. Some of the rustlers simply ran for their lives, while others were able to find a tree to climb up in. One of the rustlers ran for shelter in a chuck wagon, but it didn't do him any good. The cattle, in their state of panic, tipped over the wagon and then ran over it.

Those in the camp could not even hear the sounds of gunfire that was coming from where the cattle were headed. The rustlers who were guarding the front of the draw quickly realized that the stampeding cattle were coming their way. They began running every which way, but soon found themselves running into the guns of Joshua's men. Several of them tried to fight their way to safety, but were cut down by Joshua's men. A few of them tossed their guns down and throw up their hands in surrender knowing it was better to be captured than to be run over by a bunch of wild-eyed cattle. The whole thing was over in a matter of minutes.

The cattle had run on by and left a path of destruction in their wake. When a tally was taken, Spotted Horse and his braves had killed the four men guarding the cattle. Joshua and his men captured four of the rustlers and killed three others. The stampeding cattle had trampled five of the rustlers to death. Spotted Horse had also captured three men who had sought safety by climbing into trees to keep from being trampled to death.

Once all the live rustlers had been rounded up and tied, Joshua placed guards to watch them. When Spotted Horse and his braves joined up with Joshua, they were assigned to watch the rustlers while Joshua and his men went after the herd.

The herd had run almost four miles before they got them stopped. As soon as the cattle had settled down and were peacefully eating and resting from the long run yesterday and the one today, Joshua returned to where the cattle had been held, and where Spotted Horse was holding some of the rustlers.

"Spotted Horse, are all your braves accounted for?" Joshua asked.

"Yes. All are here and none of them are hurt. What about your men?"

"James took a bullet in the shoulder, but it's not too bad. Walter injured his hand when he punched out a rustler, but he'll be fine."

"How many rustlers survived the fight?" Spotted Horse asked.

"I'm not sure. We have captured seven in all, so far. I don't know if any of the others are alive or not. We best take a look around and see if there are any wounded.

"We captured three of them in the trees," Spotted Horse said with a grin."

Joshua and Spotted Horse walked over the battlefield looking for anyone that was wounded. They found five that had been trampled to death by the charging cattle. They also found the one who had tried to hide in the chuck wagon. He was in pretty bad shape. Both of his legs were broken and his chest had been caved in. He was still alive, but it didn't look like he would live very long. Joshua and Spotted Horse tried to make the man as comfortable as possible. Joshua called Walter over and told him to sit with the man until he died. He was instructed to tell them when the man was dead.

Joshua got the rustlers that were capable of working. Under the supervision of a few braves, he had them dig the graves for their fellow rustlers. The braves kept a watch on them to make sure none of them escaped while Joshua and Spotted Horse looked around to make sure that all the rustlers had been found, and all the weapons had been found and stacked in one place. They also gathered the rustlers' horses.

"I think that as soon as we have the dead buried, we will be done here," Joshua said.

"One more thing," Spotted Horse said. "What do we do with the rustlers we caught?"

"I guess we need to talk about that since part of the cattle they stole were yours."

"What is the white man's penalty for stealing cattle?"

"Hanging, if they are found guilty."

"There is no question they are guilty. We caught them with our cattle."

"That is true. What do you think we should do with them?" Joshua asked.

"What do you mean by "found guilty"?" Spotted Horse asked, wondering what Joshua was thinking when he used the phrase "if they are found guilty".

"They need to be tried and found guilty in a court of law."

"Where do we find this 'court of law'?" Spotted Horse asked.

"I think we have to take them to Fort Pierre. I have heard there is a court there."

"It is too far."

"We need laws if our land is to have real justice. We can take them to Fort Pierre and have them tried there."

"I do not agree with you. I think we should hang them here and now. But if you think we should take them to the fort for trial, then I will go with you. I would like to see if white man's justice is any good."

The man that had been trampled died before the prisoners had finished burying the others. When they had finished taking care of all the dead, Joshua, Spotted Horse and his braves led the prisoners to where the cattle had been grazing. They set up camp in order to give the cattle a chance to rest.

* * * *

The next morning, everyone was ready to head for home. Joshua had a wagon brought out to carry all the guns, the rustlers, and the supplies that the rustlers had. The cattle, along with all the horses of the rustlers were driven back to the ranch. It was a slow trip back to the ranch. The cattle were left to graze where they had been grazing in peace before the rustlers had stolen them. The rustlers' horses were taken to the corral where they were fed.

* * * *

Joshua had time to think about taking the rustlers to Fort Pierre. He decided to keep the rustlers at the ranch until he could send a messenger to Fort Pierre. He would request a judge to come to the ranch and hold the trial there. As soon as Joshua and his men arrived at the ranch with the cattle, Joshua sent a message to Fort Pierre.

The message explained that they had captured several men who had stolen their cattle. Since Walter had only a minor injury to his hand and would not be able to do much around the ranch until his hand healed, he was given the job of taking the message to Fort Pierre. Walter left the next day for Fort Pierre.

In the meantime, the prisoners were held in a small building that had only a couple of small windows. The windows were too small for the prisoners to use to escape. They were fed and given water, but that was all. They were guarded day and night. It took eight days before Walter returned to the ranch with an officer and four soldiers from the fort.

* * * *

On the day that Walter returned with an officer, four soldiers and a prison wagon, Joshua's prisoners were being well guarded by four of Spotted Horse's braves and three of Joshua's men. Each of them had a rifle, plus a side arm. Joshua had allowed the men out of the small building where they were being held. He had them escorted to a corral for a little sun and fresh air, their first in eight days.

The prisoners watched as the soldiers and the prison wagon came into the ranch yard. They knew it didn't look good for them. They had chosen their way of life and knew what the consequences would be if they got caught. The soldiers rode up to the ranch house where the officer stepped down out of the saddle.

"I'm Joshua Higgins. Welcome to my ranch," he said as he stuck out his hand.

"Lieutenant Mansfield. I understand you have a few prisoners for me," the lieutenant said as he shook Joshua's hand.

"Yes. They are the ones that survived," he said as he pointed toward the corral.

"I understand that they stole some of your cattle."

"Yes. We tracked them down and took our cattle back. Several of the rustlers did not survive the fight it took to get my cattle back. Four of my men were injured, three of them are still laid up.

"Your man explained what happened. It is getting rather late in the day. Would you mind if we stayed the night on your property? We would leave for the fort in the morning."

"Not at all. In fact, your men are welcome to stay in the bunkhouse with my men. There is plenty of room. And you, sir, are welcome to stay in my house. We have an extra room. Your men can eat with my men, and you can eat with my wife and me."

"Thank you. That is very nice of you."

"Please come inside where we can sit and talk."

"I would like a minute to give my sergeant instructions."

"Of course."

With that, Lieutenant Mansfield tipped his hat to Dancing Flower who was standing on the porch watching them. He then turned and walked back to his men. He explained what was going on and what arrangements he had made. The soldiers then rode over to the corral as the lieutenant walked back to the ranch house.

Once inside the house, the officer looked around. He noticed that there was a teenage boy and a young girl sitting at the table. It looked like they were doing homework from school.

"I see that you are educating your children. They look as if they are part Indian?"

"Yes, they are. They are my children. I hope that one day my son will take over the operation of the ranch."

"I noticed that there are a number of Indians on your ranch. Is that normal?"

"Yes."

"Do they work for you?"

"In a way. Actually, Spotted Horse owns a number of the cattle on the ranch. We really ranch together."

"Well, I'll be darned," he said with a slight laugh. "Now I've seen everything. Indians ranching."

"I guess that's not something you would see everyday. I think you will see a lot more of it in the future. You see, Spotted Horse is my brother-in-law. Dancing Flower is his sister and my wife. Spotted Horse is also my friend. We run our cattle together. He, and some of his tribe, work very hard here."

"What do your neighbors think about you having Indians working for you?"

"I don't really know since we don't have any close neighbors."

The lieutenant and Joshua talked for a long time about his ranch and how it came to be. Joshua took time to write out a full report of what had happened and gave it to the lieutenant. The lieutenant thought his statement would be enough to find the rustlers guilty.

After they finished dinner, they went out on the porch for a smoke and to talk some more. When it was getting late, Dancing Flower came out on the porch and suggested they turn in for the night. The lieutenant agreed as he had a long trip back to the fort with the prisoners.

As they went inside, Dancing Flower told the lieutenant that they would have breakfast for them before they left. The lieutenant thanked her then turned in for the night.

When morning came, Joshua and Dancing Flower made sure that the soldiers had a good breakfast. After breakfast was over, Joshua and the lieutenant started across the yard toward the barn.

"Are you going to put all the men in the prison wagon?"

"Yes. It will be much easier to control them."

"I'll have my men saddle their horses. I don't think you will have room for the men and their saddles in that wagon."

"We won't be taking their horses and saddles. You might as well keep them and the rest of their gear. They will not have any use for it where they are going," Lieutenant Mansfield said.

"Are you sure?" Joshua asked.

"For one thing, I don't have the room or the manpower to take care of it. Call it restitution for the trouble they caused."

"Thank you."

Joshua and Frank waited outside the small building as the lieutenant and his soldiers went inside and put the men in irons. Once in irons, they were led out and put into the prison wagon.

It wasn't long before Joshua and Dancing Flower watched as the lieutenant and his soldiers headed out with the prisoners. It would take them several days to get back to the fort, but Joshua didn't care. He and his men had a lot to do on the ranch.

* * * *

Several weeks later, Joshua received notice of the trial date for the rustlers. Spotted Horse and Joshua went to Fort Pierre to see the trial and to be witnesses against the rustlers. All of the rustlers were found guilty and were sentenced to death by hanging. Spotted Horse seemed pleased with the white man's justice.

They didn't stay to see the rustlers hung. Instead they returned to the ranch where they had much to do.

CHAPTER THIRTY-FIVE

Big Cat Injures Joshua

Days passed, then weeks, and then years. The ranch had its problems over the years, but nothing that was very serious. The chores at the ranch seemed to become routine. Fences had to be repaired, calves had to be branded, hay had to be cut and stacked for the winter, and horses had to be shod and taken care of. There was always something that had to be done. Life was never easy on a ranch.

One early morning in late fall, Joshua and Jeremiah were awakened by the sound of a horse that seemed to be in distress. Joshua was the first one out the door with a gun. Jeremiah was right behind him with his rifle. It was still pretty dark, but they could hear a ruckus coming from the barn.

When they got to the door, Jeremiah got ready to open it. He looked at his father. When Joshua nodded, Jeremiah jerked open the door and Joshua stepped into the door with his gun ready. Suddenly a mountain lion jumped at Joshua, knocking him down, then quickly ran out into the darkness. Jeremiah didn't have a chance to even shoot at the lion without possibly hitting his father.

Joshua got up and looked at his arm. The lion had ripped his shirt and left a rather deep gash in Joshua's arm with his claws. It was not a serious wound, but it needed attention.

"See what you can do for the horse. I'm going to get my arm taken care of before we go after that lion."

"You need any help?" Jeremiah asked.

"No. I'll be fine."

Joshua headed back to the ranch house. When he got close to the door, he could see Dancing Flower waiting for him. She could see that he was holding his arm."

"Are you hurt?"

"Yes. There was a mountain lion in the barn attacking one of our horses. It clawed me when it was trying to escape. It's nothing serious."

"Where is Jeremiah?"

"He's taking care of the horse. From what little I saw of the horse, it will probably have to be put down," Joshua said as he sat down at the table.

Suddenly, there was a loud bang that came from the barn. Joshua just looked up at Dancing Flower. They knew what the gunshot was about. Jeremiah must have realized that the horse was too far gone to save.

There was the sudden clamor of running boots on the hard ground. It was obvious that the ranch hands had heard the shot. Joshua got up and went to the door.

"It's okay," Joshua called out. "A mountain lion attacked one of our horses. He had to be put down."

"We going after the lion?" John asked.

"Yeah. Would a couple of you help Jeremiah take care of the horse?"

"Sure," John said.

After the dead horse had been pulled out of the barn and had been taken care of, John and Walter came up to the house with Jeremiah. They stopped on the porch.

"I would like the two of you to go with me to get the lion," Jeremiah said.

"Sure," Walter said, then looked to John.

John smiled and nodded his approval.

Jeremiah went into the house and told his father what he was going to do and who he was taking with him. Joshua was sure that Jeremiah was capable of hunting the mountain lion. Dancing Flower simply put her hand on Joshua's shoulder and smiled at him.

"Okay, son. I'm afraid I won't be much good, anyway. You be careful."

"I will, dad. We'll get the lion," Jeremiah said with a note of confidence.

Joshua and Dancing Flower watched as Jeremiah left with John and Walter.

It was only a few hours later when they returned. Jeremiah had the lion draped over a horse. It turned out to be a big male lion, and Jeremiah's first lion kill. He was proud of the fact he was able to get the lion that had killed one of their horses and injured his father.

CHAPTER THIRTY-SIX

Joshua's Son Meets The Love Of His Life

As time went by, Jeremiah grew into a strong hard working young man. By the time he was twenty-two he had not only been on several cattle drives to take the cattle to market, but he had led two of the drives himself.

As Joshua grew older, he began turning over more and more of the responsibilities of the ranch to Jeremiah. The years of hard work that Joshua had put into making a good life for himself and his family had taken its toll on him. He had developed arthritis in his hands and knees. It was getting harder and harder for him to ride a horse for hours at a time as he had once done. And it had become very hard for Joshua to swing a rope, and wrestling a steer was out of the question.

Joshua and Dancing Flower had watched their children grow up and were proud of them. It was time to take it easy and let Jeremiah take care of the everyday things that had to be done to keep the ranch running smoothly. Joshua turned the ranch over to Jeremiah, but continued to do what he could to help out around the place.

* * * *

Jeremiah had led a long trail drive to take cattle to Omaha for shipping to points east. He had been gone for a long time. When he returned to the ranch, he was all excited. He had met a young woman in Omaha and began writing to her.

After several months of writing back and forth to the young woman, he got a very important letter from her. He kept the letter to himself until he could think of how he was going to break the news to his parents.

After finishing his work one day, he came in from the barn for dinner after taking care of his horse. He wanted very much to have a talk with his father and mother.

"Mom, Dad, I need to talk to you."

"Certainly. What's on your mind, son?" Joshua asked.

"Well - - as you know, I met a girl on my last trip to Omaha. We have been writing to each other ever since," he said as he looked a little worried about how they might take the news.

"That's great," Joshua said with a big grin.

"What's she like," Dancing Flower asked.

"I'll bet she's pretty," Susan said with a giggle.

"Yes, she is. She's the most beautiful girl I have ever seen. I'm sure that you would like her. She has blond hair and blue eyes. She has a wonderful smile. And she is easy to talk to."

"Where did you meet her, son? You never told us about how you met," Joshua asked.

"I met her as I walked by a church in Omaha. She was coming out of the church and she smiled at me, and - -well - - that was it," he said with a silly grin. "I knew I had to meet her.

"I walked up to her and asked her if I could talk to her. She smiled and said yes, but that her father would have to be close by. She said that he would not allow her to meet with a boy alone, especially a boy he didn't know.

"I had never heard of such a thing, but I agreed. We went to a little park across the street from the church and talked while her father and mother sat on a park bench a little ways away from us."

Joshua started to laugh.

"Joshua, it is not funny," Dancing Flower said.

"I was thinking that things are not so much different than when we started courting. I had to ask Spotted Horse for permission."

"You had to ask him if we could marry. As I recall, my brother asked me to help you skin a buffalo. I might add that he asked me to look out for you and teach you the things you would need to know to survive in the wilderness."

"You're right," Joshua said with a grin. "You did a lot of work with me, and taught me how to skin and preserve the hide and prepare the meat of a buffalo so it would not spoil. You taught me a lot more, too."

"Wow. I'll bet that was something to see," Susan said with a big grin.

"I'm sure it was. It was not a very long time after that when I asked Spotted Horse for your mother to be my woman," Joshua said with a smile as he thought back to his first few months with the tribe.

"What is the girl's name?" Dancing Flower asked wanting to hear more about the girl that had stolen her son's heart.

"Her name is Lucy McDermitt."

"It sounds like a good name," Joshua said.

"I have been writing to her. I told her that I would like to come to Omaha and talk to her father about us. I just got a letter from her. In it she said she would like that."

"So, I take it you will be going to Omaha to see her?" Joshua asked.

"Yes," he said sort of sheepishly. "You don't mind, do you?"

"We don't mind at all," Dancing Flower said as she looked at her son with the eyes of a proud mother.

"I have just one question, well, maybe two," Joshua said. "The first is does she know what you do for a living?"

"Yes, of course. I have told her that we have a large ranch in the Dakota Territory. I told her all about it, even how it was started. I also told her that my mother is an Indian, and that I am half Indian."

"Did she have a problem with that?" Joshua asked.

"No. Not at all."

"What about her parents? Did they have a problem with it?"

"No. Well, maybe at first. In her letter she asked if it would be all right if her parents came to visit you, after we are married."

"What did you tell her?" Dancing Flower asked.

"I told her that they would be welcome. She did ask if we could be married in Omaha, and if you would be able to be there. She even said you could stay with her folks while you are in Omaha."

"What do you think?" Joshua asked Dancing Flower. "Would you like to go to Omaha for our son's wedding?"

"Can I go?" Susan asked.

"I would like you to be there, sis."

"I'd like to go. I've never been to Omaha," Dancing Flower said with a grin.

"We will need to build a house for you and Lucy," Joshua said.

The very next day, they started work on the house for Jeremiah and Lucy. The ranch hands and some of the Indians pitched in and helped Jeremiah build a house. It was not finished when it was time for them to leave for Omaha, but several of the ranch hands assured him that they would get it ready to live in by the time Jeremiah returned with his bride.

When it came time for Joshua, Dancing Flower, Jeremiah and Susan to go to Omaha, they packed up a wagon and drove to Omaha to meet the young woman and her family, and to see their son get married. A couple of days after the wedding, Lucy, Jeremiah, Dancing Flower, Joshua and, of course, Susan, returned to the ranch. Lucy's parents said that they would come out the next summer for a visit.

EPILOGUE

Jeremiah did a good job of running the ranch. Lucy took to the life of a rancher's wife very quickly. The summer after they were married, Lucy's parents visited for a month before they returned to Omaha. It was a very pleasant visit.

Jeremiah and Lucy had four children, two boys and two girls. The four children were raised on the same ranch that their father had been raised on.

Susan met a young man by the name of James Hawthorn and married him. They had three children, two boys and a girl. James was an officer in the U.S. Army. He was stationed at Fort Pierre when Susan met him. Shortly after they were married, he was transferred to a new duty station at Leavenworth, Kansas. It was difficult at times for Joshua and Dancing Flower to visit them, but Susan and James did manage to visit the ranch from time to time.

Joshua and Dancing Flower lived out the rest of their lives on the ranch doing what they could to help out. Sometimes it was just watching over their grandchildren. They had had a good life together and lived long enough to see their grandchildren grow to young adults. They also lived long enough to see the land their ranch was on become part of a state, South Dakota.

Joshua and Dancing Flower spent a good deal of the time they had left sitting on the porch or in front of the fireplace with their grandchildren. They told stories about their life on the plains, passing along the history of their families.

Joshua and Dancing Flower died only a year and a half apart, Joshua dying first. They were buried side-by-side on a small hill only a few hundred yards from where their log ranch house stood.

Joshua never got to see the blue-gray mountains called the Rockies. However, he did live the adventure of a lifetime with a lifetime of adventure.

Made in the USA
Columbia, SC
08 January 2018